THE
QUEEN
JADE

THE QUEEN JADE

A NOVEL

YXTA MAYA MURRAY

An Imprint of *HarperCollins*Publishers

HarperCollins books may be purchased for educational, business, or sales promotional use. For information, please write: Special Markets Department, HarperCollins Publishers Inc., 10 East 53rd Street, New York, NY 10022.

Grateful acknowledgment is made to Hippocrene Books for permission to reprint the hieroglyphs from John Montgomery's *Dictionary of Maya Hieroglyphs*.

FIRST EDITION

Designed by Chris Welch

Library of Congress Cataloging-in-Publication Data
Murray, Yxta Maya.
    The queen jade : a novel / Yxta Maya Murray.—1st ed.
        p.   cm.
    ISBN 0-06-058264-2 (acid-free paper)
        1. Americans—Guatemala—Fiction.   2. Mayas—Antiquities—Fiction.
    3. Archaeologists—Fiction.   4. Guatemala—Fiction.   I. Title.
    PS3563.U832Q44   2005
    813'.54—dc22   2004051241

05   06   07   08   09   DIX/RRD   10   9   8   7   6   5   4   3   2   1

TO SARAH PREISLER

Where did the artisans of the Olmec empire obtain their fabulous trove of translucent blue jade? Scientific expeditions and treasure hunters, known informally among themselves as jadeistas or jade-raiders, have scoured Guatemala, Honduras, Mexico and Costa Rica searching for the source of the rare stone. . . . [In the aftermath of Hurricane Mitch] a U.S. team says that it has now found the fabled jade supply in a Rhode Island–sized area of central Guatemala centered on the Motagua River.

—"Scientists Discover the Long-Lost Source
of Mayan Jade Artifacts in Guatemala,"
Los Angeles Times, May 27, 2002

THE
QUEEN
JADE

CHAPTER 1

The serenity of the empty bookstore was rattled by my mother's entrance.

"Creature?" she called out, banging the front door, its brass chimes clattering. "Are you here? Awful Thing?"

"Ye-es," I called out from the shop's back room.

"Lola, where are you?"

"Here in the office, Mom. Hold on."

"Well, don't keep me waiting. Did you get my message about those copies I wanted? Are they ready? The cab's waiting at the curb."

Juana Sanchez stood in the middle of the store, her long silver hair glinting in the brandy-colored shadows, a duffel bag slung on one arm, her tweed cape flicking behind her meaty shoulders. She began impatiently humming an off-key tune while I put a third edition of Jules Verne's *Mysterious Island* down onto my desk. Being slim-boned and curly-haired, I don't favor my mother much, except in my taste for unusual clothing. I gathered up my western-style petticoat, and with my old red Patsy Cline boots came stamping out from behind a stack of books and onto the main floor of The Red Lion, the shop I owned in Long Beach.

She stopped humming when she saw me. "There you are. What are you doing in the dark?"

I walked over to her, and she began to push down my springing black bangs with quick bats of her hand.

"Just wrapping a few things up," I said.

"Has the store been busy?" She brushed imaginary dust off my shoulders and began to smooth the wrinkles on my collar with hard jabs of her thumbs, and then she finally planted a beaky kiss on my cheek.

I laughed. "What do you think?"

"Don't be negative. Things will pick up. Though the less time you have for work, the more time you have for *me*. Or did you forget that I'm leaving tonight? I'll just bet you did. That's what comes from sitting inside this shop all day and night reading these bloody books, instead of every once in a while coming out with me to the bush! I've told you this before. A couple of days in the jungle—that'll put your feet on the ground, Creature. *That'll* grow some hair on your chest. And maybe then you'll remember when your own mother is going to leave the country."

"I did remember. I was just about to start up with your Xeroxing."

She thinned her eyes at me. "Likely story."

"And I didn't think I was invited on this trip."

"Actually, you're not this time." She crush-hugged me around the waist. "Little vacation of my own that I've whipped up. Going to traipse around the haunts of old de la Cueva—that route she took, when she was looking for the Jade. Just for fun. I need some time away." My mother cleared her throat. "But don't confuse the issue. I was speaking generally."

"That's what you were saying last night—you're going to follow Beatriz de la Cueva's trail. And de la Rosa's, too, I guess. Right?"

"I suppose. But let's not talk about Tomas. It's too sad—how he died."

"Pneumonia."

"So they say. Though no one seems to know where he's buried, do they?"

"Not that I've heard."

She turned away from me and studied some of the books on the walls. "I think your father is grieving a little, strange as that sounds. And it's got to be rough on Yolanda. She'll be missing her dad."

"I feel bad about it. I haven't talked with Yolanda in years—"

"Yes. But we decided that it was better that way."

"I know."

"Though we all *were* friends, once."

I touched her shoulder. "I'm sorry, Mom."

"Let's just stick to de la Cueva," she said, in a firm voice.

"Fine by me. So. Old Governor Beatriz—"

"She was the first European to go looking for the Stone, you know."

"I *do* know," I said. "I practically know the story better than you. I'm thinking about translating it into English."

"You are?" The corners of her mouth tugged up approvingly.

"I could desktop publish it, then sell it here, in the store."

"It's an amusing idea—but I still doubt you know the story as well as I do."

"Good Lord, there was the legend of the magic queen of all Jades, which could give you absolute power if you got your hands on it—"

"But it also wound up destroying its possessors," she interrupted. "Any person who saw or touched the Jade grew obsessed with it. At least two of its owners came to gruesome ends, and then it was hidden, and *cursed* by a witch. As the story goes, if anyone tried to steal it, the world would be destroyed by water and flame—"

"No one was deterred by that threat, though," I said. "Especially the Europeans. In the Renaissance, there was a trip to the jungle, and a search for the Stone. Except it didn't go very well. There was the Maze of Deceit and the Maze of Virtue . . . a lying slave . . . some seriously naive Spaniards—"

My mother raised her eyebrows. "All of which is why the work qualifies—if I'm not mistaken—as an Adventure. And so you should have it in stock, and be able to make me a copy of it."

"I do have it around here somewhere," I said. "It'll just take me a minute to Xerox it for you."

"And her *Letters*."

"I already copied the letters," I said, running off to get the book.

I found my clothbound edition of Beatriz de la Cueva's 1541 *Leg
ende of the Queen Jade* on the highest rung of my "Great Colonial Villains in History" shelf, which is filled with some of the most flaming
thrillers in my store. I should know, since I'm a connoisseur of hair-
raisers, and my Red Lion is devoted to Adventure and Fantasy books.
Since its grand opening in 1993, I'd taken care to ensure that the store
encouraged my customers to wallow in the genre's glorious hyperbole
by buying up all the best personal libraries I could. I'd also furnished it
with graciously carved walnut shelves, and soft leather chairs that were
often inhabited by readers dressed up like myopic versions of Luke
Skywalker or Allan Quatermain, or I might find sleeping there a *Dune*
enthusiast who looked as if he'd partaken of a bit too much Spice. I
held world-class Dungeons and Dragons marathons there as well, and
during our annual *Lord of the Rings* reenactment festival you might
find me wielding a sword and answering to no other name than Ga-
ladriel. I didn't care if these readerly indulgences were bankrupting
me, as the source of my passion for Adventures was not very hard to
discern: my mother was a living Odysseus, being a UCLA archaeologist and jade specialist who for the past thirty years had made regular
escapades to the jaguar-and-relic-filled jungles of Guatemala. Almost
as proof that she remained as reckless as the tiger tamers and globe-
trotters of Jules Verne's or H. Rider Haggard's ilk, she was heading back
down to Guatemala tonight, October 22, 1998, which is why she had
come into the Lion: she'd wanted me to make some reproductions of
maps, letters, and an ancient legend for her, so that she could use them
as references on her trip.

Mom gripped my legs as I stood on a ladder propped up against the
bookshelf. "Watch it," she said. "Whenever you get on this thing, I
think you're going to break your neck."

"And you want me to go play with scorpions and snakes in the
jungle?"

"It's safe in the jungle. But look at this place, books everywhere. It's
a death pit."

"Just don't let me slip." I reached my arm up to the top shelf. "I've almost got it."

I clung onto the lodged book with one hand like a ballast as the ladder swayed and my mother barked, but when the *Legende* popped out, I tumbled into Mom's waiting arms. We took *The Queen Jade* to the back room, where I kept my Xerox.

"A lot of people died because they read this book," I said, spreading the first page of the *Legende* on the copier's glass surface. The leaves that I copied were dry with age, and filled with notes that readers had left in the margins.

"Well, de la Cueva is pretty convincing about the Jade," my mother said.

" 'The blue rock glowed as fair as a goddess, stood as tall as an Amazon, and ruled over men's greed with its terrible glory,' " I read aloud. "She believed in the story herself. Why else would she go running through the jungle while everyone around her was dying of dysentery and exhaustion?"

"Because of her slave, for one thing."

"You mean, her lover," I corrected.

"The one who took her up there."

I nodded. "He's the one who betrayed her."

We began to remind each other of the details of the famous fraud that led to the publication of the *Legende:* in 1540–41, Guatemalan governor Beatriz de la Cueva fell prey to the seductions of her paramour, a Maya servant named Balaj K'waill, who helped her translate an ancient Indian fairy tale about a magical Jade stone hidden in two jungle mazes, which he claimed she might find on the other side of the river Sacluc in the country's unmapped Peten forest. The risk would be worth it, he promised. This gem was no mere bauble, but a fantastic, glittering weapon that would allow any ruler to crush her enemies merely by wishing them dead. The power-starved de la Cueva could not resist such a temptation, even though the legend also told of the Jade's grisly side effects. The weak-brained who laid eyes on it went mad, supposedly. The soft of heart were transfixed by the memory of its gleam, its shine. It was the pre-Christian idée fixe. Laughing off any peril to her own state of mind, the governor embarked with her slave on the quest, and after six months' travel she claimed to have discovered the deadly Labyrinth of Deceit, a colossal, winding edifice composed of cobalt jade whose color matched the legendary stone's. Some scholars posit that perhaps she *did* find some structure in the jungle, a palace of curious design, say, or some ancient tomb—though none has ever been found by modern men. De la Cueva eventually realized, however, that the Jade her lover promised was nothing more than a lie, upon which point she expressed her disappointment by executing Balaj K'waill as a traitor. Yet she wouldn't be the Stone's only fool. Despite all the tragedy the legend continued to intrigue adventurers through the centuries, and many others would take up the dangerous and futile quest.

"The blue Jade stone," my mother murmured, looking at the book with me. "No wonder so many lunatics went looking for it. Blue's the rarest color of jadeite there is. Burmese green can't top it, Chinese serpentine's common in comparison. The Queen of all blue jades—that would be the rarest of the rare, my girl, if the thing ever really existed. We don't even know where the blue stuff comes from. Big enigma, where the mine might have been located. As it is, only a few worked pieces of it have ever been uncovered."

"Well, you've found a few pieces—that jaguar mask, a few bowls and pots."

"And there was the Stelae, of course," she said. "Found in 'twenty-four by Tapia."

"And those blue ax heads Erik Gomara dug up."

"You mean the ones he beat me to."

"Where was that? The Peten?"

"God, don't ruin my mood by talking about Gomara."

"Yes, all right," I said, sorry that I'd brought up the name of my mother's academic rival. "Don't get grumpy."

"Too late," she said. "Forget Gomara. Though about Tomas—he came across a few pieces while he was looking for the Queen, the old crackpot. He thought it might really be out there."

My mother paused and tweaked my ear.

"I didn't want to talk about him either, did I?" she went on. "But Tomas took Beatriz's same route through the jungle. Scampering after that fairy story. The same as that old German, Alexander Von Humboldt." She sighed, and she looked so wistful all at once that I didn't bother asking her about the arcane reference to a European explorer. "So. There'll be a lot of ghosts on the path I'm taking. But at least I'm *going*. I'm not just sitting around studying it on my duff."

She trained her glinting eyes on me.

"What?"

"Am I ever going to get you out of this bookstore?" she growled.

"Mom."

"Lola. You're thirty-one. When I was your age, I was running away from tigers, I was getting buried in landslides. I was having fun. Your idea of having an adventure is reading an etymological dictionary."

"I know, isn't it great?" I waved my arms, exasperated. "And you're forgetting that you've been hitting the books for the last few months, yourself."

"What do you mean?"

"You've been working hard, lately. I thought you were busy writing a paper, though now you're just dashing off."

She wrinkled her nose. "What gave you the idea that I was doing an article?"

"You've been buried in your office with maps and charts and papers. And . . . it's been a little while since I've seen you like that, all secretive and crazy. Since either of us have—I talked to Dad about it last night on the phone. We can't figure out why you're going."

"Now *you* sound like an old badgery mother. That's my job. And I've explained this to you already. I'm only going on a vacation."

"But you've never taken a vacation before."

"Then I'm probably overdue for one, don't you think? I've certainly done my fair share of work."

"More than your fair share!" I grabbed her by the shoulders. "*You* solved the Flores Stelae. First, that is—"

"A thousand years ago I deciphered some meaningless stones, and blah, blah blah, *blah*." She pursed her lips. "Look, don't worry. I'm only going down there, visit your father for a while, which obviously Manuel will *love*. And then I'll trudge around de la Cueva's old routes for a few weeks. Let the younger generation take over the school while I meander about among the monkeys."

"But you can't stand the younger generation, Mom."

"That's very true," she said, butting me lightly with her head, like a goat. "Present company excepted, of course."

"Of course."

"Though, now that I think of it, I suppose it bears mentioning that Gomara—"

"Erik—"

"Right. The disgusting womanizer—he's done some work around this area." She pointed back to the *Legende.* "He did some scribbling on Von Humboldt's journals, which refer to de la Cueva's mazes. You might want to pick up the old German's diary, especially if you're thinking of translating de la Cueva's legend. *The Personal Narrative of a Journey to the Equinoctial Regions of the New Continent* is what it's called."

"*The Personal Narrative?*" I asked, writing down the title on a scrap of paper.

"Von Humboldt ran around Guatemala in the 1800s, looking for the Maya king's Jade. Poor thing took de la Cueva's same path. He said he found some labyrinths, a buried kingdom, then was nearly killed by Indians. Nothing was ever substantiated, but his writings are a decent contribution. He was one of the first to do any kind of analysis of de la Cueva's work. The university has a nice edition of his book. You should look it up. I'd like to get your reading of it."

"It sounds fantastic."

"I thought you'd like it. If nothing else, at least I know my daughter." She flicked her fingers at me, and I could feel her getting pricklier and pricklier. That's how she usually became right before we were about to part, and when she showed her tenderest and stickiest feelings. "But don't let me get sentimental. You still have copying to do."

I finished the job, picked up the sheaf from the copier, and handed it to her; she crouched down and zipped open her duffel bag, a buff-colored vinyl Hartmann. Inside were some clothes, and books, and one of her small salmon-colored diaries.

I picked the last item up, and she deftly reached her arm above her head while still looking down at her duffel and extracted the journal from my hand.

"Thank you, Monster," she said. "You know you'll get spanked if you snoop."

"Just doing my best to detain you," I replied.

She stood back up and frowned at me.

"Yes. So. I guess that's it." Her mouth wobbled a little in her face.

"Yes, I guess so," I said. "Will you say hi to Dad for me?"

"Certainly."

"Are you going to—drop in on Yolanda? Give your regrets?"

"It would be awkward, I think. . . ."

I tilted my head. "I'm going to miss you, Mom."

"You'd better." Her mouth quavered some more. "Whom am I going to yell at? And who's going to listen to all my complaining?"

"I'm sure you'll find somebody. You always do. And you'll only be gone, what—"

"Two weeks. If the weather holds out. Not very long at all."

"Two weeks is really nothing," I answered, in the same stout way.

She looked at me. "Awful Thing—"

And then, as the two of us are both absolutely emotional ladies, our eyes began to turn pink and squint, and our noses twitched.

"Oh, agh!" we both said, and mashed the tears from our faces.

She stood up and wrapped her arms around me again so that I emitted a quick, sharp noise. Her shining pale hair swept around my face. She wore no scent and smelled absolutely clean, like pure soap, combined with the warm mustiness of her tweed.

"You are my darling sweet Creature," she whispered. "And I'll see you soon. We'll catch up more then." Here she gave me one last squeeze and kissed me, but when she brought her face back up, I could swear I saw that old Machiavellian glint in her eyes. She began moving toward the front door, and I thought that in her mind she was probably already in Guatemala, heading toward the jungle, where she would dig inside that soft galling mud that she loved.

Outside, the cabman groaned and muttered as he dragged the luggage to the car. She stood in the doorway of The Red Lion with her silver hair flying about in bunches, her cape sweeping around her shoulders, her busy hands pointing as she shouted her many organizational orders at the driver.

" 'Bye, my beautiful Beast!" she called out to me as she left.

And I felt no chill, no shudder, when she got into the taxi and slammed the door.

I should have, but I did not feel anything odd or ominous as I watched my mother wave at me through the cab's window, turn the corner, and disappear.

CHAPTER 2

Four days after my mother left on her holiday, my Pinto fainted on the freeway, and I found myself traveling by bus from Long Beach to UCLA to meet with an English professor who was selling some rare books. After paging through my *Los Angeles Times*, paying special attention to an article titled "Heavy Rainy Season Offers Relief to Parched and War-Torn Central America," I got off at my stop and lugged my laptop computer to the office of the prof, who had indicated an interest in unloading his complete library of Jules Verne classics. Unfortunately, the meeting lasted only five minutes, as I'd been beaten in time and price by a millionaire Verne fanatic from Wales.

I assuaged my disappointment by gawking at the school's assortment of twenty-year-old football players for a quarter of an hour, then went to look up the book my mother had mentioned—Alexander Von Humboldt's journal—in UCLA's University Research Library. In contrast to the old brick and tracery that characterized the school's great hall and undergraduate library, this beige box was strictly modern 1960s simplicity.

The second floor contained works of archaeology. A quick search revealed that Alexander Von Humboldt's 1834 *Personal Narrative of a Journey to the Equinoctial Regions of the New Continent* had been checked out, though I did find my parents' first, slightly tattered masterpiece, *The Translation of the Flores Stelae: A Background for the Study*

of the Meaningless Maya Text (first edition, 1970), alongside Tomas de
la Rosa's spanking *Meaninglessness in Maya Iconography: The Flores
Stelae Resolved* (Oxford University Press, twentieth edition, 1998).
Both of the books analyzed certain famous Central American relics,
which are a succession of four blue Jade stones covered with hundreds
of Maya hieroglyphs.

Opening the cover of my parents' *Translation,* I turned to a photo of
the Stelae's carvings:

My parents deciphered these symbols as Princeton graduate stu-
dents in the 1960s, using the few Spanish colonial texts that contained
clues about the as-yet-uncracked Maya code (a lost language that was
only fully deciphered in the 1980s). After two years spent in pains-
taking translation, however, they were crushed to discover that this
text—such as it was—amounted to nothing but gibberish, and when
translated literally read:

> *The of story the Jade once was I king Jade*
> *You without lost I'm too lost I'm too lost*
> *Fierce king true a jade under born noble and jade*

What could such babble mean? they'd wondered. What could the
Maya have been trying to say with this weird jumble of words? When
another year had passed, and they'd checked and rechecked their
translation, my mother sank into a terrible gloom. She'd filled notebook after notebook with this jabberwocky, but it was no use; she
began to see all her academic efforts as the squanderings of a fool.

But it was in the pit of this terrible despair that she struck on her brilliant hypothesis: *That the Stelae could not be read—nor were they ever intended to be any kind of coherent text.* The Stelae were only a sort of ancient wallpaper, a meaningless and confused ornament akin to the abstract patterns one might find today in a Tiffany window or a Laura Ashley print. With great excitement, she and my father wrote an article arguing that the text was senseless from a reader's point of view, a thesis that they hoped would make them the acknowledged world experts on the Flores Stelae.

They would fail miserably in their ambition. On the eve of their paper's publication, they were preempted at a 1967 El Salvador symposium on the hieroglyphs by a Marxist radical, antimilitary insurgent, and genius Guatemalan archaeologist named Dr. Tomas de la Rosa. After his blockbuster talk, *Meaninglessness in Maya Iconography,* he had become the equivalent of a rock star in the world of archaeology.

My parents didn't hold a grudge, though. The three scientists even surprised themselves by becoming friends, despite Dr. de la Rosa's increasingly dangerous involvement in the bloody thirty-plus-year Guatemalan civil war.

For decades, their fellowship survived his waxing eccentricities. Beginning in the late 1970s, de la Rosa risked his titanic academic reputation by searching the Guatemalan forest for Beatriz de la Cueva's Queen Jade. My mother also took in his very difficult daughter Yolanda to live with us for five years after de la Rosa was suspected of bombing an army colonel's home, in the process killing a young accountant as well as severely scarring a lieutenant guard. Yet the families' differences remained too marked. The archaeologist's extreme nationalism could make him a difficult companion, and his alliance with my parents would not end well.

In 1977 guerrillas killed two of de la Rosa's conservative university friends in retaliation for the army's genocidal crimes against Marxists and farmers, and afterward de la Rosa seemed to suffer a nervous breakdown. He removed himself from the rebellion and dove back into his scientific efforts with double zeal, expressing his patriotic views by objecting to the number of "foreign" archaeologists shipping off his jungle's treasures to non-Guatemalan museums (including Princeton's, where my Mexican parents worked).

De la Rosa's most brazen protests were his sabotage of foreign excavations, which he achieved by posing as a guide and leading visiting professors into the trackless and dangerous forest before abandoning them. His high jinks culminated in 1982, with a nasty little incident involving my father's near-drowning in a quicksand pit, which imbued my dad with such a galloping jungle phobia that he'd feel faint if he so much as watched an episode of *Tarzan*.

My parents had been sworn foes of de la Rosa ever since.

The first sign that their hatred had cooled occurred only two weeks ago, when we received the news that the great man had died of pneumonia in the jungle. Judging from their awkward silence, I could swear they felt some grief.

In the shadows of the library's stacks, I saw "De la Rosa" spelled out in gilt lettering on the spine of his book. I read it with a shiver. It reminded me of meeting the very contrary Yolanda de la Rosa when I was a young girl.

Yolanda de la Rosa was the best enemy I ever had. And I had not seen her in eighteen years.

I closed my eyes and imagined how all around me, the books dreamed their dark dreams on their shelves. I found the idea comforting.

My parents' *Translation* was still in my hands. The gold lettering on the black binding had begun to fade, which made me smile. I like rare old books to look their age.

I restored it to its shelf and went in search of a librarian who might help me find a copy of Von Humboldt's journal.

CHAPTER 3

I found a woman on the first floor of the library. Stationed behind an information desk, the librarian had a long blond braid, no glasses, blue eyes, and wore a wool turtleneck that fluffed up to her chin.

"As you noticed," she said, "we do have a few books dealing with Von Humboldt—the work on Aimé Bonpland is particularly good, I think—but as for the Von Humboldt *Narrative*, that won't be back for . . . I simply can't tell you. It's possible it will be months."

"Months?" I asked. "Could you tell me who checked it out? Maybe they can let me borrow it for a couple of hours."

"That, unfortunately, is totally prohibited by our confidentiality rules." Her eyes darted back and forth across the computer screen, and then narrowed suddenly. "But then again, don't you think that confidentiality rules only apply if the person in question is *deserving* of some confidence?"

"Excuse me?"

"Deserving of some confidence," she repeated. "Should we really be so scrupulous about the unscrupulous?"

"I'm sorry, I'm still not getting you."

The librarian tapped out something obscurely condemnatory onto the computer's keyboard, then leaned over her desk and whispered to me in conspiratorial tones. "I think I actually *will* give you the name of the person who has simply stolen the Von Humboldt. I've so had it up to here." She drew her finger across her turtleneck. "I really just don't even care anymore. If he wants to act as if this is his own personal collection without giving any consideration to the feelings of those who happen to work in this library, well then, too bad for him if I let his name slip, don't you think?"

I looked at her without blinking. "Yes, I guess I do."

"I mean, there are limits, aren't there? He's had that book for a year and a half now, even though I've sent him message upon message upon message upon message . . . and he hasn't returned even one of them. I haven't heard one word from that man. It's simply too much."

I nodded. "Absolutely."

"Very well, then—it's *Gomara*," she said, curling her lips around the three unsavory syllables.

"Erik Gomara?" I blinked, as I'd heard that name too many times already. "The archaeology professor?"

The poor girl edged back from me and tucked her chin even deeper into her turtleneck. "You're acquainted with him?"

"Not at all. That is, I've seen him around, at parties and things—my mother's in his department. She's told me plenty about his reputation."

She relaxed and half-smiled.

"Oh, yes," she said with some satisfaction. "So you do know."

She gave me directions to the apparent lothario's office, and I'll admit I entertained tantalizing fantasies of some fabulous dark Casanova as I wandered over there.

But as soon as I saw him, the fantasy faded. My erotic enthusiasms tend toward firefighters and policemen, and are utterly withered by chattering scholars. I like my men brooding, hyperactively muscular, and nearly mute.

Eric Gomara missed on all three counts.

Hello, Professor Gomara?" I'd caught him as he was walking out of his office in one of the stucco square boxes that made up the Humanities Department. I had no trouble recognizing him from some of those decidedly unstimulating department soirées my mother had dragged me to in the past few years.

"Yes?" Gomara was in his mid-thirties, and of a towering height and stocky build that he dressed up in elegant woolen slacks and a crisp white shirt. He also had quick-moving wide hands and large, dark, very intense eyes probably fairly capable of hypnotizing ingenues, though right now they were extruding impatiently as they stared into mine. "And don't call me that. Makes me sound too old. Known to everyone around here as Erik."

"Hi, Erik, I'm looking for a book—I was told to ask you about it? You've kept it past its due date, I believe. Von Humboldt's *Narrative*?"

"Ah, I see you've been talking to Gloria."

"Gloria?"

"One of the disgruntled employees of the university? Wants to shoot me? The librarian."

I laughed. "That's right, I have. I hope you don't—"

I was going to say, "I hope you don't mind," here, but Erik was already brushing past me, saying, "Sorry, but my research assistant is currently working with that book—I've written a paper on it, you know—and so I won't be able to return it for at least a month or so. Good-bye."

"But, Professor."

"Must leave."

"*Professor,* I'm still talking to you."

At this, he did turn around, with a little more interest than before. "Ye-es?"

"My mother told me I should look it up. I'm planning on translating some of Beatriz de la Cueva's writings, and I think Von Humboldt's work might be relevant. In fact, you know her."

"Who? De la Cueva? The Spaniard? I haven't studied her in a long time, but I do know that she influenced Humboldt, the poor bastard."

"Um—no. You know my mother. Juana Sanchez."

A pause here, then he said: "Oh, yes. You must be that daughter of hers. The . . . bookstore owner."

"Yes."

"Haven't I seen you lurking around faculty parties?"

"I wouldn't call it lurking," I said.

"My God, that's all we ever do at those fiestas. They're too abysmally boring to do anything else."

"When might you let me see that book?"

"As I said—Ms.—Ms.—well, Sanchez, obviously."

"Lola Sanchez."

"Lo-la," he said. "So. Your mother's interested in Von Humboldt?"

I explained again that I was the one interested in Von Humboldt, and that my mother had left for Guatemala.

"Oh—I knew that. In fact, I asked to go south with her. I mean, I'm from Guatemala. Lived there until I went to graduate school. But she said no, *absolutely not.* Not too encouraging. I guess you know that she sometimes likes to pretend she's not the biggest fan of mine." He paused, looking at me. "But it's possible I could help you. What's seven years of insults between friends?" He smiled with half his mouth, then hesitated again.

"Professor?"

"Sorry. Just thinking. Right now, I'm going to the Huntington Library, where I'm a reader."

"A what?"

"A reader. I have reading privileges? And they have a great eighteenth-century collection of de la Cueva's works, if I remember correctly—the *Letters* and so on."

"I'd love to see those. I've read the letters, but not in so early an edition."

"They also have a nice edition of Von Humboldt's *Narrative.* If you're interested. You could follow me in your car, and I'd get you into the Reading Room. You could take a look at the books there."

I told Erik my Pinto was malingering in the garage, and I'd come by bus.

"In that case . . . why not?" he said. "I'll give you a ride."

"I can just wait until tomorrow," I said.

"You can wait? If you're not in such a hurry, then why are we having this conversation at all?"

"I never said I was in a hurry. I just want that book."

"And I explained, I don't have it. So do you want to go, or not?" He looked at his watch. "God."

"Fine—I'll go."

"Good."

Five minutes later, he strode down the palmy quad toward his car, passing smiling throngs of midriffed undergraduates who seemed to have hulaed out of the hedges like fairies. I followed along, or rather, pressed my way through the girls, grasping my laptop as if it were a safe-conduct.

CHAPTER 4

Inside Erik Gomara's elderly Jaguar, with its clattering bucket seats, we hurtled toward the Huntington Library in Pasadena.

"Sorry about the jalopy," he said near the end of the trip, popping into his mouth a chocolate peppermint that he had extracted from his jacket pocket. "It's an indulgence I can't quite seem to do without. Would you like a mint?"

"There's a car right there, in front of you," I responded. He didn't subscribe to the theory of personal vehicular space, repeatedly almost kissing bumpers with the car ahead of us.

"What is she doing in Guatemala again? Weren't they having some sort of bad weather?"

"What?"

"*Bad weather?*"

"Oh. Some rainstorms, yes. But she just went up there for a vacation."

"A what?"

"Vacation."

"But that doesn't seem right. I didn't think Sanchez took vacations."

"Well—she went up there to see my father, too. Manuel Alvarez."

"Alvarez? The curator at the museum? *De Arqueología y Etnología.*"

"Right."

He stuck out his chin. "He's your father?"

"Yes."

"That means he and your mother . . . But he's so little and shy—how did he survive?"

"What?"

"How—did—he—stay—alive?"

"She doesn't bite the heads off her mates. Just you."

"Ouch. Suppose I deserve that. Though they don't live together—no? Divorced?"

"They were never married. My mother doesn't believe in it. She thinks marriage is just ownership, and it's more enlightened to love somebody without a contract. It's kind of romantic, actually, I think."

"Does your poor father think it's romantic?"

"Aaaah—no. He'd like to see her in a wedding dress, but he's used to her by now. He knows she's crazy about him. And he visits us all the time."

"He sounds nice."

"He is. My dad, he's—" I flicked my eyes over to him. "I'm not sure my mother would be entirely happy about my telling you our family history."

"Oh, come *on*. Don't be a bore. Your father . . ."

"All right, all right. So, my dad—he's kind of this magic person. He's like an old nervous knight, he's so courtly. He's afraid of everything except for my mother, and she's—"

"*Terrifying.*"

"Anyway, he's just great."

He turned his head and stared at me. "Is he the one who helped her out with the thesis? Her work on the Flores Stelae—how the Maya carvings are meaningless?"

"Yes—yes—that's him. They knew each other as kids in Mexico, and then they went to Princeton together. He helped her write the article—"

"But then de la Rosa trumped them with his own paper, right?"

"You know what? I'd rather talk about the fact that you're driving with your knees."

He was silent for a second, swerving on the highway. Then he said,

"Sorry—all right, I won't press. Though going back to the other question for a second—"

"About my dad?"

"No—about her being on vacation. I don't buy it. I'll bet she's looking for something. A holiday's just not like her." He winked at me. "You wouldn't happen to be—I don't know—not telling the complete truth? Just to keep me off the scent?"

"I'm serious. She's taking time off."

"Just wanted to make sure she wasn't trying to get one up on me."

"Like that time you beat her to those ax heads in the jungle?"

"Oh, those jade pieces, yes. Those were *great*. Best finds of my life—nothing's compared since then. But still, listen here: I told her I'd share credit—I was the one who did all the work! But no, she wouldn't have anything to do with me. And *then,* when I came back to her office to see if we could patch things up, and was very nice and confiding and told her that not only was she a real inspiration, but I'd already begun to regard her as a sort of role model of my own, not quite maternal—paternal, you know, as she isn't so feminine—"

"You said what?"

"I thought she was going to use one of those ax heads on *me.*"

"It sounds like she really restrained herself."

"Yes, okay. I know what she thinks—that I'm just a big, overly intelligent sexist who eats all the food at the faculty meetings, as well as most of the school's funding—which I'll admit that I *am*. But it's much better to be like me than the timid pink-eyed bunnies who pee with submission every time she stalks past their office. And I'd say that she has too much fun yelling at me. 'Professor Gomara, you are nothing but a large and ponderous ass!' 'Professor Gomara, you have all the ethics of a roundworm.' And so on. And I say, 'Yes, Professor Sanchez, I am a large and ponderous ass with the ethics of a roundworm, but isn't it fantastic how I won that medal from the Archaeological Society?' And she seethes and seethes. But all the while, in her eyes, I can see she likes it." He sniffed. "That is, I think."

A few silent seconds passed.

"I wonder if I should go down there?" he said next. "See what she's digging up, see if I might pick up a specimen or two. Watch her hair stand on end when she sees me."

"It sounds like you miss her."

"I do. Kind of. And I'd like to find out what she's up to."

"I'd advise against it."

"I suppose you're right. It's probably not worth it." He thumped the steering wheel with his hands. "I hope she's having fun, anyway. But— yes, it's too much effort, for probably a whole lot of splintered bones and smashed pots. And if I did go down there, the dowager queen would really make me pay for it."

"Dowager queen?"

Erik began to slow the car down at last. We were in the green and stately paradise of Pasadena at this point, just a few blocks away from the library. "Oh, don't mind that. Only a pet name."

I grinned at him. "That's all right. She's got a few for you too."

At this, he let out a dark and silky chuckle. "I'll bet she has."

He pulled his creaking antique up to the parking lot of the inordinately well funded library. Past the lot, with its population of late- and mid-model cars, stood the Huntington like a gorgeous anachronism. Its white Georgian facade glittered in the sunlight, as did the lush and manicured trees, the bright banners advertising its shows: WILLIAM MORRIS AND THE ART OF THE BOOK, and IMAGES OF THE MODERN WEST. Within this refurbished nineteenth-century estate exists one of the world's most expensive collection of octavos and folios, in addition to a teashop, a *Charing Cross Road*–like bookshop, and Japanese, Shakespeare, herb, and rose gardens. I climbed out of the car's low seat and found Erik holding open my door. After yanking myself out of the close confines of the Jaguar and being relieved of my laptop computer by the professor, I pursued him across the asphalt, and we entered the building's posh book-lined haunts together.

CHAPTER 5

I sat at one of the Huntington Reading Room's leather-topped tables, where Erik examined the drawings in the nineteenth-century book *Incidents of Travel in Central America,* which he had called ahead to have placed on hold. Sitting in such close proximity, I could detect just a hint of his wood-scented cologne, and though I didn't think he could yet be thirty-seven, I noticed he already had brisk brushings of white on his temples and throughout his bangs. His paisley tie had loosened, and his shirt buttons strained slightly around his stomach.

I glanced back down at the book in front of him. On each leaf of the folio were delicate etchings of Late Classic Maya picture writing. Page 261 showed a prince wearing an elaborate headdress, his mouth slightly open, his robes hanging about him in folds. He stood amid a crowd of intricately cross-hatched vipers, soldiers, plumed birds, and fanged monsters, the effect being something like a hieroglyphic version of Rodin's *Gates of Hell.* I found these drawings so beautiful that I hovered at Erik's elbow, waiting for him to turn to the next image.

He never did. I have said that Erik examined *Incidents of Travel,* yet though his thumbs rested upon the drawings, they did not flip the pages. Instead, the eyes that should have been fixed on the Maya drawings seemed more focused on other lovely things, such as one lady graduate student sitting across from us, as well as the second librarian, and another archivist who suddenly slinked toward us like a drugged cat. Erik hovered above the picture of the great prince and lobbed little soft-spoken but hot-blooded observations to the three women. "I like the way you're wearing your hair these days, Sasha." "Are you reading Casanova's *Memoirs* again?" "I swear my concentration was perfect until I felt you walk into the room."

The effects of all these bon mots on me were initially on the order of the gastric, yet a genial impulse mixed with my indigestion. According to my mother, I have a very bad habit of liking people—and though it would have given her the hives, I found that I was beginning to see some decent qualities in the immoral, ambitious, chauvinistic, orgiastically offensive Professor Gomara. Although his sexual politics were so neolithic that his knuckles dragged on the floor, I could tell from the way he burbled solicitations and chewed on his froth of mints that he had a happiness inside him, a quality I've always enjoyed in a person.

So I just rolled my eyes at him and affably whispered that he was disgusting, until the second librarian interrupted his fleshly efforts with the sound of her high heels.

"Miss? Here you go," she said, and deposited a heap of books into my waiting hands.

The volumes had pages the color of saffron and wax, which were beautifully hand-stamped with type. I stacked them in front of me. The librarian had given me Von Humboldt's *Narrative,* resplendent in green calf, as well as de la Cueva's *Letters,* in a far more splendid burgundy binding than the foxed cloth 1966 edition I had at The Red Lion.

I had come here to read the Von Humboldt, but I became so giddy at this glorious copy of de la Cueva's correspondence that I turned to these first. I had recently mimeographed these letters for my mother, yet I had not read them closely in several years.

Opposite the *Letters* colophon, an illustration was protected by a thin sheet of tissue paper. I folded back this veil. Underneath was a posthumous portrait of Beatriz de la Cueva, who in 1539 assumed the governorship of Guatemala after the death of her predecessor and husband, the conquistador Pedro de Alvarado. Though she made her reputation as a European despot in the New World, de la Cueva is just as famous for conducting that blundering quest for the Jade. Her over-reaching ambition was captured by the portrait's painter, Bronzino. The woman's sea-green eyes stared out at the observer with a challenging glare, and her ample lips neither smirked nor frowned but pouted, giving some hint of stubbornness as well as of her notorious sensuality. She wore a simple gossamer veil, a white ruffed collar, and a black velvet dress with puffed sleeves. The painter surrounded her with books, roses, a lump of blue jade, and the traditional *vanitas* symbol, the sign of earthly arrogance, a grinning skull that rested by her elbow.

I read through a decade of the correspondence. Among other missives to Philip I and Charles V, I also examined de la Cueva's famous letter to her sister, in which she describes her lessons in the Maya hieroglyphs, her quest for the Jade, and her claimed discovery of the Maze of Deceit.

December 1, 1540

Dearest Agata,

Sister—I take great delight in scandalizing you with this letter! Know that at this moment I am lolling about in the sultry jungle, and as I put my pen to this page I am utterly nude, and having my feet rubbed by a very handsome man as he tutors me in the mysterious picture language of the Savages. Are you shocked? It gives me no end of delight to know that you ARE.

See here, Agata, one particular cipher, which my lover taught me to read during today's voluptuous lesson.

"This is the word-sign for *jade,* my governor," Balaj K'waill informed me (for that is his name), as he took my fingers and with them traced this queer mark.

"A jade is a bad word for a woman," I teased him.

"Then all the better, my dear love—for truly you are the worst of women. You should take this as your crest." And upon saying this he began kissing me in many strange places, and I en-

joyed it so much I did have to agree with him that I am a won-
derfully wicked lady.

When I returned to my senses and our lesson recommenced,
it struck me that this symbol for the jade stone *is* most curious &
beautiful. And I thought then that perhaps Balaj K'waill is right,
and I should adopt this herald as my own. I believe, indeed, that
it may be the mark of my future.

Let me explain why.

I have told you of the country's great Story that my boy is helping me translate—the one that tells of a King who lived within a
city made of blue jade, and the one perfect and giant Gem of
heavenly power that made its owner invincible. No man alive has
claimed it. The Talisman has for centuries been hidden by the old
King somewhere in the Jungle, within a pair of Labyrinths—one
known as the Maze of Deceit, the other as the Maze of Virtue. At
the time I thought this rumor nothing more than a fairy tale, and
I set out to explore this jungle purely on a lark. . . .

But I know now that the Queen of Jades truly exists, and so
the King was real, too, and the beautiful duplicitous Witch once
also lived—for yesterday our camp reached the door of this first
Maze! The Maze of Deceit is a Colossus made of a clear blue
stone, and proves a veritable wonder, like the Coliseum or the
mysterious Sphinx. The architecture is most complex, with
many kinked passages and dreadful dead ends. I will admit that
I find this curious Maze a difficult bugger to scan. Yet my friend
assures me I will succeed in conquering it.

And then, who knows what might happen? Who knows what
kind of Sovereign I might become? And with what sort of king
at my side?

Do not think me mad. You know I have always hungered to
learn the great dark secrets of history. And look here. Look at the
journey I have taken already! We have traveled from the Old
City of Guatemala, up through the ruins, North, to the ancient
forest, which is cut through by a little river, the Sacluc.

The Sacluc is a very refreshing and lovely creek, which I un-

derstand is changeable, but today runs as the thinnest line of
crystal water. The Maze of Deceit sits at its very mouth.

Here is the map of our first leg:

Is it not thrilling? Are you not excited for me?

I will write you everything when I return. If my luck holds,
and I crack both this puzzle as well as the Virtuous Labyrinth, I
will be able to shower you with such riches & baubles and perhaps also lovely brown men like my Balaj K'waill—as you deserve, as you are my one true darling, Agata.

And as I am too your loving sister

Beatriz

After finishing the letter, I began to trace some of its more curious
sentences with my finger.

How would one translate de la Cueva? I thought that she might have a more subtle temperament than initially appeared. It would take a feat of moral acrobatics to fall in love with one of your slaves and not set him free, for instance.

The same shrewd style proved true of her writing. It seemed lucid, but I thought I discerned some secret, capricious, and private meanings.

In the spotless and expensive library, my already piqued interest in de la Cueva was beginning to sharpen.

CHAPTER 6

D
o you have any dictionaries?" I asked the librarian, after rereading the letter several times. I wanted to research a linguistic riddle that I'd found in it.

"We have an entire collection, ma'am."

In her missive to Agata, de la Cueva writes of the labyrinth, "The architecture is most complex, with many kinked passages and dreadful dead ends. I will admit that I find this curious Maze a difficult bugger to scan."

I found de la Cueva's idiosyncratic use of the term *escanear*, or "scan," intriguing; I thought I remembered that the word had more than one meaning. I asked the librarian for a stack of Spanish grammars and etymological glossaries, and just for fun a very nice copy of Samuel Johnson's *Dictionary*. This last book explained that "scan" means not only to read, or "examine nicely," but comes from the Latin *scandere*, "to climb."

I leaned back from my desk and entertained an image of de la Cueva clambering through the jungles of Guatemala as she tried to reach a jade inside a deadly maze. Was that the image that she tried to convey? Or was she writing in metaphor? I toyed with my pen on my pad, trying to think of a lucid way that all of this could be translated without requiring a battery of footnotes. After a very happy hour of scribbling, I had run out of theories and boxed myself into an etymological corner. I exhaled and looked up.

While I was reading, another woman had sat down two chairs from mine, and busied herself with a book of Rafael's rose-colored sketches. And three chairs away, it appeared as if Erik had begun behaving himself. He had his head bent, his elbows propped. His hand cupped his cheek as he examined his volume of Maya picture writing with renewed attention. I should get something done too, I thought. Through the windows lining the Reading Room, the early afternoon was quickly darkening, and I decided to e-mail my language questions to my computer at The Red Lion before the library closed. When I plugged in my laptop and opened my screen, though, I saw that my mother had sent me an e-mail—over three days ago. Her letter read:

Hello Terrible Creature,

You will be happy for your old mother that this trip is not, as is usual, turning out to be a total failure.

When we landed in Guatemala City, I went straight to the Museo de Arqueología y Etnología. Your pops and I had a very fine reunion, with a picnic in the museum's Jade Room, raising our glasses at least three times to toast our Flores Stelae. Now that my head is clear again, I am preparing to leave for the jungle. But I must tell you something before I depart.

You *were right*, my sweet Awful Thing. I did *not* come here for a vacation. I came to Guatemala because I think I have solved a mystery.

I think I have tripped across an old clue, to an old story.

There's that legend I asked you to copy; and the correspondence. I asked you to do that, but I didn't say why. The day after tomorrow, I am going to the far north of the country, out into the Peten forest, which fills the upper region of the country. There, I think I might find the location of the Mazes of Deceit and Virtue, as well as the Jade de la Cueva describes in her tale.

This may sound crazy, but I don't believe any longer that the fable is a work of fiction.

I haven't told anyone else—not even your father. *And you must not either.*

Tonight I'm leaving Guatemala City, and will travel down to
Antigua to spend one quiet night by myself. From there I'll make
my way up to Flores, then I'll drive and hike to the Peten, to a
part of the forest cut through by the river Sacluc. After that, I'll
stake my way farther up, and see if I might be able to excavate
anything.

It shouldn't take me too long. Two, three weeks, like I said
before.

And then I'll come back home to you, my Lola.

Maybe I'll even return with something really remarkable.
Proof of ruins of the Maze of Deceit? A fragment of a lost blue
city? A jade, perhaps?

Don't think that the old Moms has gone bananas, dear; all us
archaeologists have these fantasies—where would we be now if
nutty old Sir Arthur Evans hadn't dug around Greece?

As I write this (I'm at your father's, e-mailing you on his
computer), the rain really is slashing down the windows, and
there are some light squalls, and everyone outside is running
about like decapitated fowl. Manuel and I heard a rumor that
blue jade stones were discovered in a landslide around the
central mountains. Whether it's true or not, I don't know yet.
It only spurs me on. I can't worry about getting wet and muddy,
especially when I consider what could be waiting for me out
there.

I'll call you in a few days. Do you have your dad's number
handy? 502-255-5544 is his cell.

I love you,

Mom

"She didn't tell me the truth," I whispered out loud.

"What?" Erik asked. When I looked up, I saw he was standing above
me and packing his bag.

A gong from an unseen grandfather clock in the Huntington rang
through the building. Five P.M. The librarians floated through the
Reading Room, murmuring that closing time was not far away.

"Nothing. Gabbling to myself." I lowered the lid of my computer.

"A little schizophrenia never hurt anyone, but it's time to go, Sybil. Come on, I'll drive you home."

"No, thanks. Just—there's a bus stop by the university, you can drop me off there."

"I'm not going to have you bus all the way back to Long Beach. And if I'm driving you, I will need some dinner. So I think you're committed."

I still had my hands over my computer and its bothersome e-mail.

"Well," I said, unsure.

"Yes?"

I glanced up and saw the hair fanning out in awkward little kinks on one side of his head, and realized that my decision regarding dinner had nothing to do with my mother's confounding letter—which I still had no idea how to respond to. I shrugged and said, "Look, I didn't read even one page from Von Humboldt this afternoon. If you drive me home and tell me a little more about his connection with de la Cueva, I'll feed you something. How's coffee and snacks? That's all I have back home, I think."

Erik looked at me for a second, then smiled cheerily.

"Is this a proposition?"

"No. Seriously. So very much, no."

"Oh. How unambiguous." He looked down at my lace-trimmed skirt and my boots. "But you know what?" He pointed at me. "That's okay. I don't really think—the two of us? Would get along in that particular—"

I shook my head. "I agree. The truth is, I only like firefighters and lovely policemen."

"Firefighters?" he asked me.

"Yes. Firefighters with very large muscles. Who don't talk a lot."

Erik, with his belly and hair and pocket of mints, was so very much not conforming to my type at the moment.

Not that he seemed very sorry about it.

"I have to say I'm making some very unpleasant Freudian connections with that"—he did something bizarre with his fingers here, indicating a firehose. Then he reached down and picked up the strap of my computer, and I very nearly thought of asking him to give it back. He picked up his own bag in his other hand.

"Still," he went on, "now that we have all that cleared up, I also have to tell you that I've never been able to refuse offers of food or an audience. Even when there's no chance of sex."

And with that, off we went.

CHAPTER 7

Erik sat at my kitchen table under the light of a chandelier, and as soon as I began to rummage around the kitchen to see what I might be able to whip up for a snack, he dug through his briefcase and pulled out a long, spicy-scented cylinder wrapped in butchers' paper.

"No need to fix anything," he said. "Brought along my own. And you'll have to taste some of it, too. It's incredible."

I looked at him. "You just happen to have a giant sandwich stuffed in your briefcase?"

"I like to cook. And I like to eat. And I always like to be prepared for anything. So make us that coffee, get a knife, and sit down."

He began to unwrap what he said was a rebellious Latino version of the proper Englishman's "shooter's sandwich." He'd fashioned it out of a soft hollowed loaf filled with meats and pâtés and little marinated tomatoes, and studded it with pickled habañero chiles and splashes of mole.

He sniffed it. "Doesn't it smell delicious? I'm a great advocate of all sorts of tasty miscegenations, culinary and otherwise."

"What?"

"Never mind."

I made a pot of coffee on the stove, and also brought down from the cupboard a small bottle of brandy that my mother liked to tipple from on Sundays. For dessert, I snagged a half bar of dark chocolate that Erik dunked whole into his coffee after he devoured the rest. While we ate (and indeed, the sandwich was delectable), he sprawled low in his seat, describing in encyclopedic terms the nineteenth-century scientific explorations of the "dark continents." He spoke of how rhapsodic Darwinism replaced the more dour and doubly calamitous evangelism of the cinquecento conquerors, who invaded the Americas with an eye for stealing slaves and jade and gold to fill European coffers. The scientific Victorians had certainly been interested in discovering precious metals, if any were to be had, but their real passions were for the secrets of the jungle, whose bizarre flora and bright beasts they might inspect, label, analyze, and dissect.

Along with Von Humboldt, there had also been the antiquarian and cryptographer Oscar Angel Tapia, who discovered the Flores Stelae in 1924, and explorers like Lewis and Clark, who'd mapped the Columbia River. There was the intrepid German Johann David Schöpf, too, who scoured the Americas in search of medicinal plant specimens he might include in his *Materia Medica Americana.*

"But there was no one like Von Humboldt," Erik went on. He'd lightly dusted his shirt with bread crumbs and a smudge of pâté. "He was a friend of Goethe, a fan of Rousseau. He observed things, not like we do now. It was all wide open for him then—obviously we can't perceive Mexico or Guatemala today without his influence. Without his eye. He thought it could all be understood! With scientific explanations! Linnaeus's methods, the categories of kingdom, phylum, species. He read everything—Pliny, Copernicus, Herodotus, de la Cueva. And he made his studies of waterways, of natural wells, plant life."

But my mind wasn't on waterways or plant life.

"Didn't he write about Beatriz de la Cueva's trail?" I asked. "And didn't he record something about a jade or . . . a maze?"

"Yes, he followed her route after reading that fable of hers . . . whatever it's called."

"*The Legende of the Queen Jade.*"

"That's it. He thought the Jade was a magnet. He was an expert in the field. Magnetism, I mean. He had this idea that the Queen—you know, the Jade—could be this very large lodestone. He actually did make some discoveries of serpentine and blue jade relics, and he tried to find the source for the blue stone, the actual mine, but couldn't. He wrote about some sort of maze, too, some kind of architectural ruin. A labyrinth. Hard to believe—most people think he was a liar, or maybe that he was hallucinating. He said he'd just stumbled across it in the jungle. In my book, I made out the case that he probably *did* find something of importance. It's one of my claims that's drawn the most fire—spurred on lots of angry criticism and yelling at conferences and things like that. But his other discoveries have been verified—rare types of plants, geological specimens. And it's not as if mazes haven't been found before."

"There's the mention of those mazes in Herodotus," I said.

"Right—right. And also, there are theories about the Glastonbury tor—there's an old ruined castle in England, associated with Arthurian myth, with a kind of circular pattern in the foundation. And then there are the turf mazes in the countryside of England, too."

I played with the lace on my skirt. "And there's Knossos."

"And Knossos, exactly. The Greek labyrinth, home of the Minotaur. In legend at least. So—nothing like proof positive, and there's no other record of mazes in pre-Columbian America. But it's not impossible either."

Erik's hands gestured rapidly in the air. He knew so much about all this, I almost wanted to tell him about my mother's letter. Except that she would kill me.

"And so you wrote a book about him," I said. "Von Humboldt."

"A small monograph. Like I told you, I ran into a little hard luck on my digs—I could have spent years hacking around the area where I'd found the ax heads, but I just didn't see anything to indicate further relics. So I guess I got discouraged. I did a paper on Oscar Tapia, on his discovery of the Stelae—he was this eccentric who wrote his journal in a kind of cipher, something like Leonardo da Vinci. Which is why I became drawn to him in the first place. I have a hobbyist's interest in codes and things—"

"And Von Humboldt?" I said, getting him back on subject.

"Yes—well, Tapia's the one who led me to him. That's how I became interested in these colonial scientists. So I wrote a few chapters in a book about the German. Then I started my own, examining his Jade trek—which your mother helped edit, I'll have you know. The manuscript would come back to me bleeding with red ink exclamation marks and occasionally profane observations on my writing style, particularly where I claimed that Von Humboldt might actually have found the Maze of Deceit. . . . Anyway, he's an important figure. He was one of the first Europeans to condemn slavery. He was sort of a harbinger of Thoreau. And he tracked a lot of Guatemala with his companion Aimé Bonpland—whom he was probably in love with. If you have a map, I can show you the places they studied. Some day I'll have the whole route memorized, I've studied him so much. He interests me."

"Because of the Jade?"

"Not initially." Erik shifted uncomfortably in his seat. "I thought he was a person I would have liked to know."

"Why?"

"I just identify with him a little. Or—I don't know. Maybe I'd just like to. He was a serious sort of man. He was a committed scientist. And friend."

"A committed friend," I said. I thought again about Yolanda de la Rosa. "That's a hard thing to be, sometimes."

"You're right. It is."

We paused.

"That's what I want to be," I eventually said. "When it comes down to it."

It surprised me, actually, that I was telling him this.

He looked at me and lowered his eyebrows. For a moment, he wasn't so rambunctious or playful; he seemed different all at once. I could tell that he might be revising his opinion of this evening. Or even of me.

"Me too," he said. "Though I worry it'll take a little bit of work on my part."

I smiled at him. "Are you talking about Gloria the librarian?"

"Something like that," he laughed, though still fixing his eyes on mine. "And I'll admit I don't often find myself confessing these kinds of things to people I've just met." He was silent for another few seconds; I could have sworn that he almost looked bashful. "*Well*—before I start gasping at you about my childhood—let's get back to Von Humboldt."

"Yes. Back to Von Humboldt."

"You were going to get me an atlas? I'll show you his route."

I stood up. "You go to the living room and wait there while I go and get it. There's a television—black and white, nothing special. But you might check on the weather, if that's okay. My mother wrote something to me about the rainstorm down south. I'd like to make sure it's let up. And then we can look at the route."

"No problem."

I showed him the way down the hall and walked back to my room, where I hunted through my shelves. Under my editions of Haggard, Conan Doyle, Verne, Melville, and Burroughs, I found a decent plot of Guatemala: an 1882 *Encyclopaedia Britannica* illustration, reproduced in a little nineteenth-century travel book on the region called *The Intriguing People and Places of Central America*, which I'd bought in a church book sale eight years ago from a coven of charming old ladies.

From the living room, I could hear the purring sound a television makes when it's first turned on, and then the racket of reporters' voices. I turned the pages of my book as I moved from my bedroom into the hall. The map of Guatemala, between pages twelve and thirteen, was tinted in sepia and mauve. It showed the heart-shaped country's rivers, mountains, jungles, and cities, marked by the cartographer in lacy black calligraphy. Difficult names like *Totonleapan* and *Tasisco* were tamed in Victorian italics; the artist indicated craggy mounts with delicate wavering strokes of ink. Mauve, blue, pink, and yellow tints designated the divisions between the departments. The word *Guatemala* was branded, bold, in the center of the country.

I walked out into the living room, which is decorated with Edwardian furniture and Turkish rugs and an illuminated fish tank, and

hosts my one small TV. Erik sat beside the fish tank. He watched the
television with his hands over his face. And on the screen I saw a picture of Guatemala that bore no resemblance to the neat markings on
the map I carried. A dark and violent wind blew palm trees so that they
bent nearly horizontal to the ground. I saw footage of shacks heaved by
the blasts, their roofs splintered by the storm, large chunks of wood
and rushes spinning wildly into the air. Frothing water flooded the
streets and whipped up against storefronts, smashing windows,
drowning dogs, washing away cars and tree trunks and scattered clothing. The news station also showed some quick images of the dead. The
bodies looked wet and huddled and motionless against mud banks.
Under these pictures flashed harsh yellow letters: GUATEMALA CITY,
COPAN, ANTIGUA. And there was also an aerial shot of the rain forests,
which appeared ripped and glistening, as if they had been torn
through by giant claws.

"Lola," Erik said. "It's a hurricane."

"Oh, my God."

"Don't panic. The news is selective. Apparently most haven't died in
Guatemala. The worst of it was in Honduras. It was terrible in Honduras. But I'm sure your mother's fine."

"Look at those *bodies*."

"The people who didn't make it couldn't find shelter. But wasn't she
still in the city?"

I gripped the book and continued watching the blue-black sky and
the shaking palms and the smashed houses on the television. I stared at
pictures of the gnarled and stripped rain forests. *I'll make my way up to
Flores,* she'd written me, nearly four days ago. *Then I'll drive and hike to
the Peten, to a part of the forest cut through by the river Sacluc. After that,
I'll stake my way farther up, and see if I might be able to excavate anything.*

"I don't think she was in the city," I answered. "She wrote me an e-
mail and said she was heading north—"

"I'm sure she's fine."

"Oh, Mom," I said, snapping my head away from the television.

CHAPTER 8

Ten minutes later, I tried the phones.

"Your father will know where she is," Erik said. "He wouldn't let her get too far away in that weather. I'll bet right now they're in the basement of the museum, drinking whiskey and happily arguing over the provenance of some stela or potsherd."

"I hope so." I picked up the receiver of our phone. I dialed the number I had retrieved from my mother's e-mail and waited.

Erik sat stiffly on the sofa, glancing at the fish.

"Is there anything?"

The ring sounded over and over, like an alarm.

I let out a breath. "No, not yet. But I'm worried that she's not with him. Her e-mail was days old."

"Where else would she be? The television said the roads were washed out today. She couldn't have gotten very far one way or the other. And most of the damage was in the east, with some in the north. The forest, which she probably didn't reach. You said she was going on vacation. I'm sure she turned around once it started raining hard."

I hesitated. "No, you were right before."

"What do you mean?"

"She didn't go for a vacation."

Erik opened his mouth, then closed it; he didn't say anything.

"In the e-mail she sent me," I went on, "she said that—that she hadn't told me the complete truth about her trip. She said she thought she could find the Maze of Deceit."

He looked at me in a very steady and concentrated way. "What do you mean?"

"She wasn't that clear, but she said that she figured something out about it. She said she thought she knew where it was."

"The Maze of Deceit. The ruin that Von Humboldt writes about."

"If it's the same one that de la Cueva writes about, yes."

"No . . . I don't believe it."

"You just said it was possible—that Von Humboldt found a ruin, or something."

"What did *she* find?"

"She didn't say. She hasn't even told my father any of this. And all she wrote me was that she was heading up to Flores, and into the jungle. Past the—a river, the Sacluc—"

"Yes, the Sacluc. I know it. That is, I know about it. But she wouldn't go alone. Excavating in the Peten—that's a huge job."

I shook my head. "I have no idea what she's doing—but she'd asked me to make a copy of the *Legende* before she left. And I Xeroxed de la Cueva's letters for her, too. Do you know them?"

"No, not really. I'm more of a Von Humboldt man. I haven't looked at de la Cueva's materials in years."

"You said Von Humboldt and de la Cueva took the same route."

"As far as we know, yes."

"And *she* was going up there too. She mentioned the rain, like I said, and I don't think she went with anyone else—they were probably put off by the weather."

"But she was not."

"No," I managed to say.

He grimaced. "And is there anyone there?"

I had the receiver pressed to my ear. But there was still just the monotonous, maddening ringing of an unanswered phone.

CHAPTER 9

Five hours later, at two in the morning, I got through.

"Hello?" came my father's voice. There was a beeping, and a skipping connection between us. Occasional static, fits of silence. I looked up at Erik, who still sat across from me at the table, holding on to his tea mug. He had been there half the night, and showed absolutely no signs of impatience, or of leaving.

"Hello? Dad?"

"Lola?"

Then, simultaneously, and in Spanish:

"Did you get through to Mom—"

"Did your mother call you?"

"Dad, where is she?"

I heard a fumbling sound, and then a few blank seconds of nothing.

". . . problems with the line, darling," he said. "Tried to reach you for days, but I couldn't. Things are a mess here."

I gripped onto the receiver with both of my hands. My mother, ever the dinosaur, carried no cell phone with her, no pager, not even a portable computer. These niceties had always been transported for her by her graduate student minions, of which none could be depended on now, as she had gone out to the rain forest alone.

My father went on. "I didn't go out with her because—my stress condition. My—I'm afraid of going out there, and *this is why.* I thought she was in Antigua."

"That's what she wrote me. She was going there, and then north."

"But it seems she left Antigua a few days ago. I couldn't find her. I looked. I think she might have traveled to the forest before the storm." He had a gravelly, rasping voice; he was obviously exhausted. The phone clicked and blanked again. Then his voice returned to the line. "The police are saying she's disappeared, dear."

A blinding, painful panic brightened my mind.

"Dad, it's all right. I'm sure they're wrong—Mom doesn't disappear."

". . . not all right."

"She's probably off somewhere digging things up. Too absorbed in her work to call us."

"It sounds good when *you* say it." He made a strained sound. "Maybe that's all it is."

I made the decision in the next second, without really thinking about it.

"I'm coming out there," I went on. "I'm flying out there—"

"Yes, all right. I don't think that's a bad idea."

"I'm flying out tonight. Tomorrow—depending on the planes. I'm going up there."

"Up where?"

"Just around Antigua. Look around. Maybe Flores. Maybe farther north. If she doesn't turn up first. If I can. *Are* there planes?"

"I don't know," he said. "The roads are destroyed—the army's busy with the relocations—whole villages have been washed out. I'm not going to be of much use. And everyone's left for the mountains—all the guides—they're finding something up there. We're going to have to get someone to go with you."

"You mean—"

"Yolanda? Perhaps. I think she's still in the city. But there must be better people to ask. She hasn't been feeling very . . . well."

"We can talk about guides later. I'll get her, or someone else—" I glanced over at Erik, who listened very carefully to my side of the conversation. "To help me out."

"All right, Lola."

"All right."

"I love you, sweetheart."

"I love you too, Dad."

I said good-bye and put the phone back into its cradle. I felt Erik's leg bouncing beneath the table.

"Yes," he said, before I even asked.

"What?"

He had pushed his bangs up from his head. His eyes were large and shining.

"Yes, I'll go with you to look for your mother," he said.

"You'd do that?" I asked. "Why?"

"Why not? I know Guatemala well enough. And . . ." He looked uncomfortable. "It's the least I can do for the old Dowager. To help you look."

"Are you sure it's not that you want to find a maze?"

"Hey. I'm trying to—help you out." He appeared extremely tense, as if even he weren't sure what he was saying. "It's not an offer I make to everyone." He glanced away. "And, fine—I've told you I had a run of dry luck. So what if I'm interested in looking for some ruins while we're there?"

I placed my hands flat on the kitchen table, and tried to speak calmly, slowly. "How well do you know Guatemala?"

"I was born there."

"I might have to go up to the jungle, though"—the words sounded exotic and improbable—"how well do you know *it?*"

"Not as well as the cities. But I've been up there before, excavating."

I shook my head.

"I'll get someone to cover my classes," he went on. "I'm ready to fly out there with you. I heard what you said to your father—you need a guide. Who else have you got?"

"I might be able to ask a friend of mine who's a tracker in the area—"

"But—"

"She kind of hates me."

"Ah. Who is it?"

"Yolanda de la Rosa. Dr. De la Rosa's daughter."

"*What?* The nutbag's kid?"

"She lived with us here. For five years—until 1980. Though I haven't seen her since."

"That's right—your parents knew de la Rosa. He's dead now, of meningitis—"

"I heard pneumonia—"

"Anyway, I thought I'd heard some nasty stories about your father and de la Rosa and something about a quicksand pit."

"They weren't friends for the past few years, it's true," I said.

"He wasn't friends with anyone. He was . . . obsessed. He set traps and things for other archaeologists. Foreigners, I mean. Acted very freaked out. He was a hero of sorts, sure. During the war. And a great theoretician. But afterward, he wouldn't want the likes of you or even me looking around 'his' jungle. The whole U.S. issue. It's the same with the daughter—you definitely wouldn't want to bring her along, from what I understand. He was a loon—not only because of the booby-trapping business, but because he kept on looking for the stone, the Jade. I find it bizarre that your mother would have come around to his way of thinking." He yanked on his bangs. "But all the same, it's clear enough you don't have anyone else to help you."

"Looks that way, Erik," I admitted.

He adjusted his tie. "So. Do you want to have the alarmingly impressive Dr. Gomara to help you out? Or do you just want to flail around the jungle by yourself?"

I looked at his wild hair, his nice tie, his stocky frame; I remembered his reputation. Then I thought of my mother. I had a sudden horrid image of her alone and cold in that rain.

"All right."

"Then it's settled," he said, and smiled, his bangs gently fluttering back onto his forehead.

CHAPTER 10

The next day, Erik and I arrived in the rush and chaos of a partially flooded Guatemala City. I grabbed my copies of the *Rough Guide* and *Lonely Planet* guidebooks as we exited customs, then the airport. Along with our fellow travelers, dressed up in their sunglasses and high-tech walking shoes, we moved into the crowd of merchants outside the terminal, which included black-eyed ladies with textiles balanced carefully on their heads. Men in neat slacks and plain cotton shirts sold bits of green jade—necklaces; bracelets; little replica idols carved into the shapes of feathered serpents or dragons. Men and boys carried bags of macadamia nuts and cashews packed in plastic bags, CDs in shiny jewel cases, and cigarettes. Some folks simply stood out on the curb, offering taxi rides. And zipping up and down the street was an assortment of white and yellow cabs.

"Let's go," Erik said.

I perched on the curb along with the taxi men, and while they asked me questions about my destination, I paged through my guidebooks. Looking up from the graphs in these guides, I saw a kinetic and roving place full of obscure codes that had no clear connection to the orderly world of "good" and "bad" zones and "cheap" vs. "expensive" lodgings set forth in the *Lonely Planet*. I had somehow believed that being a multilingual Mexican-American who had traveled to Guatemala a few times as a young girl might prove of some use on this journey, but that little fantasy was quickly crushed to pieces.

"Get in, get in," Erik said, opening the door of a white cab he'd flagged down.

We sped through the watery streets of Guatemala City and toward the Museo de Arqueología y Etnología, where my father waited for us. Down we rushed in a tense silence through La Reforma, one of the largest streets in the city, which cleaves through the city's twenty-one different zones. New billboards flashed by, with their images of soap-pale models, and next to us motored brightly painted school buses, the so-called chicken buses, painted like rainbows and glittering with chrome details like glued-on Mercedes emblems and decals of Jesus Christ, and the silver silhouettes of nipple-proud girls usually found on the mud flaps of eighteen-wheelers. During the hurricane a number of trees lining the avenue had crashed into the middle of the road, causing commuters to experiment with lethal driving tactics. A wave of water hit the windshield and utterly obscured our vision. Through the wipered window, a flatbed appeared, carrying a bulk of jerking acacias that threatened to leap at any moment from the van and welcome us to Guatemala in their grassy embrace. Army soldiers stood outside stores holding shiny short rifles in their hands, which did not seem an enticement to shop.

"Are you all right?" Erik asked, frowning into my face.

"Yes," I said after a few moments. I was lying.

"Maybe so, but you're looking a little bit like Charles Manson right now."

"What?"

"We'd better perk up that complexion. I think that what you need is some more sausage and chocolate."

"You stuffed me on the plane already. I can't eat another bite."

"Hush up. Food's the best cure for hysteria. Breakfast will be just the thing." He dug into his pack and brought up the little baked breads and Saran-wrapped roasted meats, assorted murky cheeses, and foil-enfolded slices of chocolate cake that he had been feeding me on the flight.

"No, no, no," I said.

"Oh, *yes*," he said, putting a chocolate cupcake to my lips.

I ate it. Then he pinched my ear and picked up the cell phone to call my father, while I ate some of the nuts he shoved into my hand.

"No word?" he said into the receiver. "I was hoping she might have called by now."

"Mom?" I asked.

He nodded. "*She's* fine. She appears to be taking it all in at the moment. . . . The streets are completely flooded. I know it's worse in the north. We'll be there in maybe an hour, Señor Alvarez. Depending on this traffic—what do you mean?" Erik paused, and widened his eyes. "What did they find up there? It's only a rumor? But you think—"

"Who found what?" I asked.

Erik finished the conversation and hung up the phone.

"Who found what?" I asked again. "What's going on?"

"Apparently a great deal of blue jade has been discovered in the mountains," he said, blinking rapidly.

"My mother mentioned something about that—which mountains?"

"The Sierra de las Minas."

"Yes—right."

"Your father says nothing's really clear yet—and it may not be for a long time. There was some sort of landslide, it all came tumbling out. It's possible that there's a mine up there, he says. There's already a team or two racing up to the area. They're going to have to dig—and if they find something, it might be huge."

"It sounds like it." I looked out the window.

He rubbed his face with excitement, so his eyebrows sprang out from his face. "It would raise all sorts of interesting possibilities."

"Like the source of the wealth of the ancient Maya, for one," I said.

"Uh-huh. Where they got the stone for the idols and the masks and the Stelae. And it might tell why they disappeared."

"It would give us a source for the stories, too."

"The fairy stories about the Jade. And the mazes."

"Exactly."

"If we really did find them, it would be like—I don't know—sort of like when Charles Maclaren found the ruins of Troy. . . . He was this amateur archaeologist—"

"I've heard of him."

"It'd be like that, wouldn't it?"

I peered out the window again to see the thin lake that was the highway, and several macadamia sellers getting very wet. In my mind, I mapped out the country. Guatemala is composed of the highlands in the south, and the lowland Peten rain forest, or jungle, in the north; the extensive mountain range known as the Sierra de las Minas extends east-west through the mideastern quadrant of the country. But an east-west direction was very much off track from Antigua, which sits directly south of highland Guatemala City—and also came nowhere near the northward city of Flores and the Peten jungle.

"I'm not going to the Sierra," I said. "My mother wasn't headed in that direction."

"I'm not saying *I'm* going," Erik said. He was bouncing his knee with an alarming force. "I—I—well, the mountains are already crawling with Harvard diggers. But we're the only ones besides your mother who'll be going to the rain forest now. We'll be the ones to scout out the topography and get together our own team. And if she was right that the first maze is out there . . ."

"All that can happen once we find her," I said.

He began to examine the lint on his slacks with great concentration. "That's what I meant."

Outside, the air was a thin and watery gray. A few clouds hovered above, shot through by black power lines. The sky looked like a vast sheet of music.

I don't know if Erik noticed all of this as he stared out his own window. He seemed absorbed in the idea of searching for Von Humboldt's jungle mazes without any competition.

I hadn't explained this to him yet, but I had decided that I had to convince Yolanda de la Rosa to guide us, should I need to go up to the forest to look for my mother. Yolanda was the only person I knew who could lead me through that wood. When she was just a girl, her father had taught her each of its paths, its secrets, the location of its bogs and fens, its burial grounds, its havens of tigers and birds. If my mother was there, Yolanda would be able to find her.

Though I hadn't seen her in years since she'd left Long Beach and returned to Guatemala, I was confident that her temper and her devotion to Tomas de la Rosa were just as scorching as ever. And even if she were still mad at me, I knew she also remained a fanatic for any clues that would help her track down those mazes and the Jade that her beloved father had failed to discover. She'd never turn down a chance to finish what he'd started.

I would tell her about Mom's e-mail, and if I had the slightest fear that she wouldn't help us, I'd imply that my mother had sent me information that would help her find the Stone. I'd tell her anything I had to. And if I did convince Yolanda, that would mean a pretty nasty bit of rivalry for Professor Gomara.

Whether it would be the best thing for me and my mom, though, I still didn't know.

CHAPTER 11

The Museo Nacional de Arqueología y Etnología, in the heart of the city's Zone Thirteen, is housed in a dove-white colonial palace built to harbor nineteenth-century Spanish ladies in white gloves. Its halls were once fragrant with orchids, ornamented by purebred dogs, and made humid by crystal fountains. It does not seem, then, a natural home for the weapons and fanged idols of pre-Columbians, but as Erik and I climbed the steps leading up to the museum and entered through a doorway decorated with a brilliant mural of Maya warriors, it was just these sorts of mementos we glimpsed in the building's corridors and inner chambers.

We bustled toward the reception desk, which was tucked into a corner on the north side of the foyer. A woman cashier stood beside a small display of glossily bound books, coffee cups, and T-shirts, the latter bearing color photo decals of images taken from the Flores Stelae. We paid our *quetzales* for our entrance fee, shelved our two backpacks and suitcases behind the desk, and made our way into the galleries.

I had been here several times as a girl. I knew the general layout of the place, which hadn't changed so very much in the ensuing decades. I remembered precisely the location of the one treasure that I wanted to see there besides my father.

Erik did too.

"Come on," he said. "You're going to love this."

Steering me by the elbows, he walked as if by instinct toward a particular back room, which held the most beautiful and occult piece of art in the museum's collection.

My shoe heels made an echoing sound as we rushed through the first rooms of the museum. From behind the polished glass of the display cases I could see the skulls of antediluvian humans, adorned with mosaics of bright blue turquoise and leaf gold. The jeweled heads stared out at observers, grinning and luminescent. Human teeth glittered in the dioramas, too, displayed in little clay bowls or spread out on white pieces of linen. Primitive but unexpectedly luxurious dentistry was evident from these remains; the cavities of these forefathers had been drilled, then filled with what appeared to be tiny stopper stones of lapis lazuli or jade. There were startling ithyphallic sculptures as well, and basalt-stone bowls where the blood of sacrificial victims once welled. And in the far corner of the room we saw a preserved *tumba,* or tomb, uncovered years back in a cave in the remote Peten. Inside lay a child's skeleton, with bones the color of vellum, and whose concave skull bore witness to a heavy blow. The curators had surrounded the body with pots containing grain and jewels, much as it had appeared when first excavated.

"Look at the stelae—the stone stelae," Erik said as we moved into another room, this one opening into a garden space and stocked with the tall basalt pillars carved by the Olmec and the Maya. These stood up to twelve feet and were incised with the delicate curving images of kings and scribes and slaves. "Most of the picture stones we've found have been made purely of basalt, in some cases granite. The majority of these are from Tikal. The Flores stones are the only ones known to be carved entirely out of jade, and blue jade at that."

"I haven't seen them in person in a long time," I said. "Just in books."

We entered La Sala de Jades, the one chamber of the museum devoted to the jade relics that have been discovered and retained in Guatemala. In the center of the room, displayed on lucite stands, stood the pièce de résistance.

The Flores Stelae consist of four different panels of carved blue jadeite, each approximately one and a half feet tall, one foot wide, and half a foot thick. Illuminated by small spotlights fixed to their bases, the stones shimmered like extraordinary stained glass. Each of the panels had been chiseled with hieroglyphs crafted in the shapes of dragons, maidens, jaguars, and dwarves, detailed with intricate cross-hatchings, geometric flowers, and obscure medallions. Fierce grotesques also stared out from the panels—hunched hissing vipers and gargoyles with wild eyes and bared teeth, mixed in apparently random order among other abstract signs, such as circles and rectangles, slashes and diacritical dots. The marks, however haphazard, were arrayed in a series of lines, an arrangement that had led all Mayanists to believe the stones could be read like any other book, until Tomas de la Rosa's 1967 talk at the El Salvador conference successfully destroyed that theory.

Standing there, I could see the attraction of the meaninglessness thesis. There was something relaxing about this incoherence. The ineffable hunchbacks and women and serpents floated within the rich iris color, which transmuted into different shades and opalescent depths according to the angle of the windows' light. The sun pouring through the stone fell upon us while we stared at the carvings. When I looked over at Erik, I saw that his face and white shirt were covered by a thin blue veil.

"My mother really wanted credit for interpreting these panels," I said. "I wonder if she'd published her article before de la Rosa, she wouldn't have felt like she always had to go running out into the jungle to find things. And then maybe . . ."

"She wouldn't be lost now."

"Right."

"Probably not," Erik said. "Look at de la Rosa. He was always getting into trouble—with the army, first. They say he bombed that colonel's house in the mid-seventies, after slipping past the military guards dressed as an old peasant woman. He killed an accountant working inside, maybe even on purpose. And he injured a lieutenant, too. I've forgot his name, but the colonel—Moreno, that's what he was called—

punished the kid for not guarding his home well enough by training him in the interrogation methods they used on the Marxists. The boy wound up becoming one of the worst butchers in the war—"

"Not exactly the effect de la Rosa would have been after."

"Which may be one of the reasons he had that breakdown," Erik said. "But I really think he went crazy because his friends were killed by those guerrillas. That's when he got out of the resistance. Started to focus on foreigners in the jungle—then he was looking for the Queen Jade, and everybody thought he'd lost his mind because he was scaring the competition to death. Like your father, right? With the quicksand pit."

I nodded. "That happened on an expedition. De la Rosa dressed himself up as a sherpa, and my dad didn't even recognize him. He led Dad's team off-trail, and when they were completely lost, he just slipped off into the forest. Dad went chasing after him and fell into a pit. Right about when the quicksand reached his chin, de la Rosa showed up on the edge of the swamp, called him a couple of filthy names, and pulled him out."

"That's some story."

"It's why we cut off contact with their family. I had to stop writing to Yolanda a few years after she moved out of our house. We used to be best friends, though she wasn't anything like me. Her father taught her to climb, track, hunt, fight, even disguise herself—when she lived with us, she liked to put me in this choke hold and play around with punching me a lot, and then sometimes she'd dress up in these costumes, like Magua, the villain from *The Last of the Mohicans.* She'd come running at me, yelling these Indian curses. Just to keep my wits sharp, she said."

"*The Last of the Mohicans?*"

"She's kind of unique."

"I'd guess."

"But then Tomas hurt my dad. It was my mother's idea that I distance myself. It was very important to her. My father's had kind of a psychological problem with the jungle ever since the quicksand. It was a question of loyalty, she said." I felt a smile waver across my face. "But I know now it was a mistake, my not writing to Yolanda. She kept writing me until the late eighties. And in the last years, the letters weren't so nice. She let me know pretty clearly that I'd betrayed her, and that she hated me. I hadn't spoken or written to her for twelve years until two weeks ago. I sent her a note when I heard Tomas had died. You know— something abbreviated and totally inadequate. 'I'm so sorry to hear about your father. All condolences. Lola.' But she hasn't answered, and I can't say that I blame her."

We both grew quiet after my confession. The stones shimmered before us like water. Erik reached up and touched the hieroglyphs.

"De la Rosa," he said. "In my business, you almost can't get away from hearing that guy's name in every conversation. He's our sacred monster. But for me, he was always the least interesting part about the Stelae. When I was a boy, I didn't care *what* they meant. I just wanted to know all about the adventures of the person who found them. That is, Tapia. He was on the scene fifty years before Tomas de la Rosa. Oscar Angel Tapia—"

"You talked about him at the house. And I've heard my mother say his name."

"He was the one snatching the stones under the Indians' noses. He's what piqued my interest in turn-of-the-century antiquarians. And led me to Von Humboldt."

"What's his story, exactly?"

"Oscar? Poor old man. He thought he'd made it when he came across the Stelae. In 'twenty-four. He was a coffee magnate, lived in a mansion on the island—Flores—and once he'd made his fortune, he decided he'd spend it collecting antiquities. He kept an encrypted journal of his adventures. In his diary, he writes that he liked to use his servants as guides, to help him collect from the surrounding areas. And he made a few good finds—amphora, flints, little idols—all of them are in the museum now. But he wasn't too happy just digging up scraps and bits. He asked his servants if there wasn't something really big to be found in the jungle. And you see, there was." Erik gestured at the Stelae. "The locals kept the panels very secret. The legend was that they were cursed. So none of his maids or lackeys said a word about the things because they thought if they did, they'd drop dead. Except his cook turned out not to be so superstitious.

"This cook, under the presumption that a nice handful of change could be forthcoming if she so divulged, told him about these panels just sitting up in the southern part of the Peten. 'I have heard the greatest rumor today from my chef d'cuisine. She speaks of a blue stone folio, of delicate proportions and craft, which is simply moldering in the forest.' He wrote that in one of his journal entries, backward. As I was saying before, he fancied himself a follower of Leonardo."

"You've memorized his writings?"

"I was interested in him for a long time—because of his cryptographer's bent. Anyhow, Tapia had a difficult time getting his servants to help him on the expedition, at least at first, but then he paid them so much money that the whole curse problem didn't really seem so bad anymore. The cook, however, was *not* paid, as the story goes. So up Señor Tapia and his serfs scrambled into the forest in the southern Peten. Tapia crosses a waterway and loses two men. Then he finds the panels on the banks. He has his servants rip them from the ground and somehow gets them back to his mansion, after which they were inaccurately named the Flores Stelae. And then the curse hit. Or so they say."

"What happened?"

"Nasty disease. Every single one died within the year of the same symptoms—turned blue, rolled around the floor screaming in agony. All the locals fled the island for fear of catching it themselves." He shrugged. "But something tells me it wasn't because of any curse."

I smiled. "The cook."

"She must have put a nice drop of poison in their lunches one day, then collected what she believed to be her fair share of pay—or more—and run like the wind."

"No wonder you were so fascinated."

"It was years before I even began to think about the stones themselves. It wasn't until I was nearly twenty that I read de la Rosa's *Meaninglessness in Maya Iconography*."

"The hieroglyphs are all that my mother was interested in."

Erik squinted up at the carvings. "I've got to tell you something, though. I've never been a fan of the theory that they don't mean anything."

"I didn't know there were any dissenters left."

"Well, I've always had a fantasy of proving your mother wrong."

"Any ideas how?"

He shook his head and smiled. "Not a one—but that doesn't mean I couldn't still do it."

"Dream on—"

As I said this, I felt small wiry arms wrap themselves around my shoulders, and whiskers brushing my cheek.

I turned around and saw the burning gaze, the luxuriant mustache, the impeccable tweed suit with the Windsor tie, and the brave smile of Manuel Alvarez, my father. From his collar to his wing tips, he looked strong and collected. No one would be able to discern any sign of the troubles he'd seen in the past days unless they knew him very well and could read his eyes.

"Lola," my father said, then hugged me again, pressing his face to mine and murmuring my name several more times. "Thank God you're here."

CHAPTER 12

N either the police nor the army have enough men to look for her in the jungle, which is where I am afraid she might be," Dad told us in his office fifteen minutes later. "Why she would go up there, I don't know. Vacation, is what she told me, though I'll confess I didn't have a very good feeling about it. . . . As for the police, I've called them thirty times, but whole villages have been swept away out by the Rio Dulce, and people are starving. Not that you would know that by looking around here, but in the northeast, the suffering's terrible. And she said that she was going up into the forest six days ago now. I've been sitting here ever since, just waiting and waiting for her to call."

While I listened to him, I wondered if I should say anything about my mother's e-mail, but I didn't see how it would help yet, and she had asked me not to. Erik also appeared to have remembered my mother's secrecy, because he didn't disclose anything as my father continued to talk and pace about the room.

Erik and I sat on two Victorian slipper chairs arranged in front of my father's desk, and he busied himself by making coffee from a little plastic percolator he kept in a corner. I could see that he labored to hold up under the horrors of the last days, yet I still knew how frightened he was even before I felt his cold fingers when he handed me my mug.

"I'm sure she's just in Flores, Dad," I said.

"She's not in Antigua," he said. A vein stood out in his forehead. "I drove around there two days after the storm hit, and I couldn't find her. I looked in all her regular hotels. And then I couldn't get to Flores. The roads are blocked."

"Erik and I are going to look again. We'll go south from here to Antigua, and if she's not there, we'll head up north to Flores. We'll find some way to get up there. And . . . you remember how she gets. This is nothing new."

"Yes, sometimes she does run off on her expeditions and never leaves us a word—"

"Actually, on the subject of jade expeditions, Señor Alvarez," Erik said, "I would like to ask you about what's going on in the mountains."

My father held on to my hand; he did not appear to have heard Erik. He brought himself up to his full height and touched my cheek.

"But this isn't like the other times, dear," he said. "And I'm afraid you know that." He chucked my chin and then looked back up. "And yes, Erik—it looks like there *has* been a jade strike. Farmers up in the Sierras discovered scads of it. Speculators are already running up to the mountains, along with innumerable university men. In the midst of this hurricane there's some hysteria over a possible jade mine. Nothing's certain yet, understand. But one of the scientists over at the school has sent me some samples, and they seem genuine enough." My father moved over to his desk and picked up the specimen box, which he opened. "It's all a very big occasion, if you haven't lost your— your—wife. Which is how I think of her, though we're not married. So now I don't give a damn about any of this. Though you can see for yourself that it's the real thing."

He handed Erik the box. I banged my chair as I slid it close to his and looked inside.

The plastic container had several small compartments, each with its own sliding cover. Erik pressed a slide and opened one of the cubbyholes, which contained a rough flint of nearly perfect indigo jade. The rest of the cubbies held piles of chips, rough hunks, or small uneven marbles of the same material. Erik picked up the flint and held it against the beam of the mica lamp. It glowed cerulean, and was riven with threads of peacock and near-purple.

"It's the real thing," Erik said. "The blue. I didn't believe it, really. Not until this minute."

"Yes, yes, it's all real," my father said. "But never mind that now. Lola. You're going to have to get yourself a guide, especially if you have to head up north. But they're not very easy to come by now, as they all seem to have gone running up to the Sierras."

"A guide?" Erik asked.

"Well, you aren't thinking of going up there alone, the two of you?"

"If you aren't going with us . . ."

"Who, Dad?" I asked. "Oh, no, he's not going."

"As she says, that's impossible," my father said. "Or—doesn't he know? About me?"

Erik cleared his throat. "I heard you had an accident once, in the jungle."

"An accident? It was no accident. It was de la Rosa!" My father's ears grew pink at the tips. "And I've had something of a . . . hesitation about going back into the jungle ever since. Actually, it's more than a hesitation, I'm afraid. I tend to have something of a collapse when I even smell a swamp. So thanks to Tomas, I might hurt the search more than help it."

"No, you wouldn't," I lied.

"That sounds very hard, Señor Alvarez," Erik said, after a pause.

"Yes, it is, my boy. Yes, it is. Yet one must accept certain facts about oneself. It would be better that I feel ashamed here in this office than go barreling out north and make a mess of things. So. We need not linger on it." My father let go of my hand. "But it will be difficult traveling. You may have to get up to the Peten—far north, which is woolly country, now. And as I was saying, you'll need a guide, as I don't think it's necessarily the best idea that you two go by yourselves."

"Why?" Erik asked.

"Why? Because of your reputation, sir."

"Dad."

My father fanned out his fingers. "My good man. I haven't been living under a rock, you know. Whereas you've heard these embarrassing stories about me, of course I've heard so many bad things about *you*. For years Juana has been telling me the most shocking stories about your conduct—I expected some sort of blundering Priapus. Though I must admit that looking at you, you're not quite what I expected. You're very human. You don't have a tail. But I can't imagine letting you run off with my daughter into the jungle by yourselves."

"Dad, I think I'm a little too old for you to worry about me running off with boys—"

My father trained his burning gaze on Erik's, doing an excellent job of ignoring me. "I know your tendencies with women—problems keeping your belt buckled. And then how, when you're finished with them, you simply race away as if you were in Pamplona. But I know you'll behave yourself with *her*. For if you don't, then—well. I may be of a delicate constitution, but these things can be overcome. If they have to be. My daughter's happiness, you see, I cherish it. I'm sure you understand."

Erik looked down at his coffee cup, and then up again.

"Yes, I think I do," he said, unhappily.

"Don't get excited, Dad," I said.

"I'm not excited," he said. "I'm not excited yet. Later, maybe. Now, no."

My father stared at Erik. Erik stared back. Here passed an uncomfortable silence.

"So what do you have to say, son?" my father asked. "Speak up."

"I just want to make sure you're not going to—challenge me to a duel or anything first."

"Oh. Well. You have nothing to worry about now."

"That's good."

"I'll make it very clear if anything of that nature becomes necessary. Yes?"

"I'm glad to hear it." Erik was holding up under my father fairly well.

"Getting back to the business about guides," I said. "I'm assuming Yolanda is still in town."

"Who?" Erik asked, looking back and forth between us. "What did you just say?"

My father nodded. "She is—though I've been thinking. You should consider getting someone else—"

"But you said it would be hard to find any guides, and if she's here—"

You're talking about Yolanda de la Rosa," Erik said. "About her guiding us?"

"Yes," I said, shaking my hands at him so that he'd calm down.

"Absolutely not." He looked at me. "I thought we already talked about this."

"You may want to listen to your promiscuous friend, Lola," my father agreed. He searched through his desk, then picked up a piece of paper and handed it to me; I saw that it contained, among other listings, the address of a bar called The Pedro Lopez. "Though your mother doesn't like it, I've been keeping my eye on Yolanda. She's been a mess since Tomas died. She hasn't frequented the more reputable places lately, either." He pointed to the address of the bar. "I've had to bribe the bartender here just so he won't give her too much to drink."

"That's just great—but it doesn't matter. I'll get her to come with us." I took a long breath. "We should probably get out of here and start looking."

"Don't get your hopes up about Yolanda, darling," my father said. "I don't think she'll come with you."

Erik remained fairly quiet, for the moment kept his thoughts to himself.

He stood up. "Are we off?"

"Yes."

Out we all went, into the museum proper, past the mastodon molars and the glittering skulls, and the tombs, the stelae, and the jade room. Manuel escorted us back up to the reception desk, with its display of books and mugs dealing with the Flores Stelae. He pressed some of these upon us as gifts, handing me a new second edition of my parents' book on the stones, *The Translation of the Flores Stelae.* He also gave us two of the T-shirts with their color decals showing images from different panels.

"I want to give you—something," he said to me. "I wish I could help you more."

"Thank you for everything, Señor Alvarez," Erik said, holding the bundle in his hands.

Manuel smiled up at him. "You're a good man, Erik—on the inside. You're listening to your better instincts. That's nice. You care for my daughter, I can see this. That's nice too. Maybe she likes you, even— but no, probably not. Yet you shouldn't feel bad. And remember, behave yourself."

"I—will, sir," Erik said.

"Very good," my father said. "Now please leave so I can say good-bye to my daughter."

Erik looked at me and raised his eyebrows. Then he went outside, and my father and I were alone.

I put my arms around him. "Dad."

"Dearest. Lola, my angel."

I squeezed him harder. Since my parents hadn't married, and I stayed with my mother, I had never lived with my father for very long. But it didn't matter. I take after the man; I inherited from him the great gift of desiring books. And the love I harbored for him had always been so large that sometimes it felt too big to contain. This feeling, along with the fear I had for my mother, was wild enough to stagger me in front of that museum. I just clung onto him and couldn't say anything.

Then he took a step back.

He was standing very straight, squaring his shoulders. His eyes brimmed.

"Good-bye, darling," he said.

"Bye, Dad."

I kissed him, picked up my luggage, and waved good-bye. I felt him watch me while I passed through the foyer, and I had to brush my sleeve against my face as I moved beyond the door of the museum and into the afternoon light.

CHAPTER 13

Walking into the pale sunshine, I squinted and looked for Erik. As soon as I appeared, he stood up from his seat at the bottom of the museum's steps. He held his bags in his hand.

"I would very much prefer it if we didn't contact this de la Rosa woman," he said. "For reasons I've already explained. Everyone knows you can't trust that family."

I began tugging my hair into a neat and orderly ponytail. "I have to go looking for her anyway."

"Why?"

"Because you don't know the jungle well enough—not as well as my mom—and we need Yolanda. If she'll help me."

"I'm telling you, I can get you through the bush. I've done it—"

"Once or twice before."

"Right. Twice."

"With help."

"With some help, yes. But I can do it, with maps—I can get us past the Rio Sacluc. *You don't want to bring a de la Rosa.*"

"Erik—" I looked up at him. Both of us were hot, perspiring, already tired from the overnight trip. I put my hand on his shoulder. "I have to bring her. She'd be the best guide. Just don't argue with me about this."

But of course, being Gomara, he did. He mustered all of his manly skills against me, and so sentenced himself to lose at the intergender battle we proceeded to wage in the shadow of the museum. He would lob some perfectly formed and beautifully conceived reason for avoiding all contact with Yolanda, and I would destroy it using the most powerful weapon in my arsenal, which was to simply stare at him with an implacable expression, cross my arms, and say, "No." Or, "Because."

He soon tired out.

Erik sat back down on the steps and clamped his mouth shut. He gazed out onto the street, and then peered up at me again.

"You know what?" he asked.

"What."

"All right—all right." He opened his arms. "That's it. You beat me— you—you—*Sanchez*."

"Good," I said. "That was easier than I thought."

"Don't rub it in."

"My father must have scared you."

"He had his persuasions, certainly. The giant eyes were a nice touch. The threatening was even better. He must have learned that from your mother."

"Get up."

He sighed and brought himself slowly to his feet.

"Besides," I said, "Yolanda probably won't agree to help us."

"We can only hope," he grumbled. "A de la Rosa."

"And if she does—you should know that the last time I saw her, she was very beautiful."

He crossed his arms, disgruntled. "Oh, well, then. Yes, that changes everything. And from what we just heard, she hangs out at bars. So that can't be too bad, can it?"

I looked out onto the city, and scanned the white and yellow taxis skidding through the flooded streets.

"Actually Yolanda de la Rosa can be a lot worse than you think," I said.

CHAPTER 14

The dusk had deepened into a thick purple nightfall when Erik and I came around to The Pedro Lopez saloon. We'd already visited it before in the afternoon, around four o'clock, and though its inebriated customers claimed to know Yolanda, she couldn't be found sitting on the stools lining its small wood bar or at the tables strewn across its floor. Erik had not been sad to leave. Zone One, on the eastern side of the metropolis, is not much commended in most guide-books, which describe the area with vague yet spasm-causing warnings about robberies and adjectives like *tawdry* and *seedy*. I'd say that it turned out to be a more populous and confusing place than that.

We taxied, then walked, soaking wet, along the flooded cinder-colored streets as shadows fell across stores and saloons. The lights of the shopfronts brightened the evening air, so that the alleys shimmered in front of us, black and gilt and crimson. The flooding from the storm didn't seem to have discouraged much in the way of social commerce. Women and children made their ways down the sidewalks, holding grocery bags in their arms. Homeless men in rags and bare feet loitered in alcoves; twenty-something boys kicked at the water with their boots and called out brutal fashion advice to Erik, who thanked them for their concern and kept walking. Three men thrashed around in a bout of roughhousing or an actual fistfight down one side street, one of them falling into the water, only to be jumped on by his friend or foe, I couldn't tell. And two elderly women in indigenous dress cleared off debris from the floor of a grocery store with shovels, heaving the junk onto the road.

Erik and I hurried past these people, the floods, the broken glass, the drowned blocks, until we again reached The Pedro Lopez and opened its front door.

Twenty men looked up when we appeared. Some of their faces were blurred with drink; others were blank, unreadable; still others smirked or raised their eyebrows. I heard obscenities and some laughter.

"As I was telling you this afternoon," Erik said, "I don't think this is a place where we want to spend a lot of time."

"We're not here to socialize."

"That's good to hear. When I was younger and fancied myself a real toughie, I used to run over to this part of the city to take a look at the girls. But I didn't make many friends. I found that I didn't fare very popularly in establishments like this."

"Is that so?"

"These kinds of boys and I don't seem to get along. They always think I talk too much."

"We all do, Erik."

"Yes, but these sorts tend to express their critiques by bashing my head in."

"We'll just see if she's here, and if not, we'll run right back out."

The Pedro Lopez was a large crowded box of a saloon. The floor was damp and muddy, littered with sawdust, peanut shells, smashed glass, and cigarette ash. The bar was carved of wood, with a backsplash mirror, which revealed a row of drinkers' faces hovering within a vapor of blue cigarette smoke. A line of men sat on oak stools avoiding their reflections and passing one-liners to each other out of the sides of their mouths. One of them was an old grandfather with a face like a walnut and stray puffs of white hair that floated over his great planet of a head like tiny clouds. He took sips from his beer, tasting it with a connoisseur's manner while humming a tune to himself. The old man's song wasn't easy to hear over the low grumbling voices that filled the air, which were in turn interrupted by the bellowing of the younger men sitting at the tables and the laughter of their lady friends. Most of the drinkers were civilians dressed in work shirts and jeans, and I saw, with some delight, that many of these men qualified as muscular firefighter types. Standing out, at the center of the saloon, were two men in army uniforms, drinking steins of beer at a large table that might have seated six.

The older of the uniformed men was a soldier in his sixties, and of high rank, as he displayed several enameled rectangular pins and stars on his green uniform. His silver-and-black hair swept back from his chiseled features. A neat black mustache sparkled above his white teeth. He had small sloping shoulders and delicate hands, one of which held a cigar that danced in the air when he gestured. His companion, however, was less prepossessing. This other soldier, perhaps in his middle to late forties, was large, tall, very brawny, his square face disfigured by a scar that extended from the left eyebrow down across the nose and toward the right cheek. His lower eyelids drooped slightly and formed tears in the corners, but this did not soften his appearance. His cheeks were flushed, and his upper lip drew back over his square teeth.

The two soldiers talked to someone in a cowboy hat who sat at a smaller table nearby. Tall and lanky, this person sipped a Coke and shielded their face with a wide-brimmed black Stetson. The hand that cupped the can was brown, slender, and tough. Under the hat hung a long black ponytail.

As Erik and I slipped through the crowd, I saw the younger soldier reach out, take hold of the cowboy's shoulder, and shake it violently so that the ponytail shuddered.

"Get out of here!" one of the bar patrons yelled at the soldiers. A few others joined along. But none of these people got up to help.

"Well," Erik said. "At least we tried to find her—time to go back to the hotel."

"We found her," I said.

I began to walk toward the soldiers. Some of the lady patrons, who were mostly very beautiful and garbed in astonishing low-cut dresses, lit up at the sight of Erik as he followed along. One woman with ebony hair and another with large green eyes shimmied their shoulders in tandem when they saw him, and this motion triggered startling repercussions within their blouses. He sauntered by them, laughing, until the younger soldier pushed the cowboy to the ground. I couldn't yet see the face under the Stetson's brim. But I still went running.

"What are you doing?" Erik yelled after me.

"I know I've seen you before somewhere," I could hear the older soldier say to the figure on the floor. "I have a wonderful memory for faces, and yours is not one I'd likely forget."

The figure replied with something I couldn't quite make out. The older soldier smiled with one half of his mouth, so that the precise curve of his mustache tilted. He glanced back at his companion.

"Are you going to do anything about this?" he asked.

"One more drink, and I just might," the younger soldier said. His drooping and watering eyes moved over to the Stetson, stayed on the face beneath its brim, and then shifted back again.

"I can tell you remember this little creature from somewhere," the older soldier said to his companion.

"Back off," the other one grunted.

"I'm not going to back off, and you're going to do what I say, aren't you?"

"Yes," the soldier replied, after letting out a breath.

"You know, my friend here would have been perfectly useless in the world if it hadn't been for me," the older soldier said to their victim. "Can you imagine giving a person that kind of gift—a purpose in life? Though I expect you never had that problem, did you? You had some purpose, I'm sure. I'm positive I once saw you working the wrong side of the war."

"Leave the kid alone," one of the men sitting at the bar called out.

The older man's mustache twitched. "Do you have something in your eye? Don't worry, I'll remember your name soon. See, I *know* you've done something you shouldn't. You used to be a troublemaker. No need to lie about it—I'm just curious, for old time's sake."

"Stop that," I said. I stood in front of them and peered down to see the face of the person on the floor, but still couldn't because of the Stetson's brim. The soldiers flicked their eyes up at me, then back down again.

"You should go away," is all the younger soldier said.

Erik had now reached the center of the room.

"Take another look," the older soldier said to his partner. "Don't get distracted by the girlishness—how tiresome, crying—look at the face and help me out. You must remember."

The person on the floor attempted to stand up and was pushed back down by the boot of the younger soldier. I heard a vivid profanity.

"Oh, you do me too much honor," the older one said. "And—actually—I hope this does not sound too indecorous, but you are a tad too grubby for my taste. Though perhaps not for my associate. He has a somewhat more base temper. Really, sometimes I can barely restrain him."

From behind me, I picked up the surreal sound of the old man humming at the bar.

"I would just love to leave now," Erik whispered into my ear. "I think these men are going to do something—bad. Come on."

"If you don't listen to your mate, we will give you a very stimulating evening," the older one said to me.

I ignored him and stepped between the figure on the floor and the two soldiers.

The black brim of the Stetson lifted, and I saw her face.

I felt dizzy when I looked into the black-green eyes that I hadn't seen since I was thirteen years old. There were now lines around her eyes and her wide lips. Her sharp cheeks looked wet and pale. She'd been crying. But her voice was as steady and edgy as always.

"Oh, God," Yolanda said.

I crouched down and put my hand to my mouth.

"Hello, Lola," she drawled. And then she whispered, "Don't let them hear my name!"

I pulled her to her feet and held her. I put my face into her shoulder.

"We have to get out of here," I said. "I have to talk to you."

"Let—go—of—me," she grunted.

Simultaneously, to my left, I heard Erik talking with the soldiers.

"No, no, don't do that," he was saying.

And then I heard him say, too: "I'm not much of a brawling type, especially with members of the army."

When I turned, I saw the younger soldier with a slow and dreamlike clarity. He wore a green uniform that fit precisely on his bulbous frame. He swayed toward Yolanda, his legs bowing outward, his eyes tearing, and his scar mantling with blood. She pushed me to the side but did not otherwise move. Erik, though, took a neat step sideways and wedged himself between them. The soldier halted in a great jerk. His forehead shone like a coin in the dim light of the bar as he leaned back and brought his arm forward in an imperfect gesture. His elbow stuck out, his body turned at an awkward angle. The fist cracked into Erik's cheekbone, whose head snapped to the right. Then Erik fell down.

I screamed.

The soldier with the mustache stood back. The other one hovered above his victim. I threw myself on top of Erik, and he frowned under me as if he were contemplating a difficult mathematical problem that he would rather not have to solve. When I peered back up, the soldier with the scar looked terrible. His eyes began running with what appeared to be real tears. He seemed exhausted, and his face began to twitch.

"I used to be really good at this," he said to me. "I'm the best there is. You'd better run."

"Get away from us!" I shrieked. I reached up, clutched the soldier's arms, and slapped at him so hard my hands burned. I began to randomly shake his arms until one of his legs buckled at the knees. He slipped sideward, hitting one of the chairs before he smacked hard onto the ground. Then he focused his attention on me. In my shock, I felt his right boot ram into my right leg.

"Don't touch her," I heard Yolanda say, in a remote, stretched-out sounding voice.

"I'm the best there is," the soldier croaked again.

All the men in the bar stood up and began to yell.

"No need to get excitable," the older soldier said. "My boy here lost his temper, that's all. He had too much to drink."

The younger soldier wiped his face with a battered hand and swore. The shouts of the rest of the men in the bar became deafening.

"It was beginning to get dull in here anyway," the older soldier said, as the men around him began spitting threats.

He began to walk out of The Pedro Lopez with quick clacking steps. The other soldier took a blood-eyed glance up at Yolanda. He rose to his full, slightly unsteady height, and followed his friend.

Yolanda pulled at her hair in frustration and turned sharply back to her seat. I helped Erik to his feet and led him to the table. A bloody lump was swelling on his cheek, beneath his left eye.

"Are you all right?"

"I am not all right," he said.

"Oh, Erik."

"No, don't look at me like that. I'm fine."

"Are *you* all right?" Yolanda said to me.

I said yes. My leg was nothing compared to my nerves.

She looked over at the soldiers leaving, and her mouth jerked. "They get like that sometimes. Doesn't matter that the Peace Accords got signed. Thirty years of war doesn't end so neatly."

"I know," Erik said.

None of us spoke for a while after that. We sat back down, gingerly, and Yolanda sipped her Coke to control her breathing. We avoided each other's eyes. General conversation in the bar also halted, and the drinkers glanced over at us, though they indicated no interest in approaching our table.

CHAPTER 15

Yolanda's face flushed red as she struggled to pull herself together.

"Who were those men?" I asked.

"I don't know." She squeezed her Coke can, working it into a little piece of foil. "I've never seen them before. But that one with the mustache must have spotted me with my father. When I used to help him out during the war."

"The big one can hit," Erik said.

Yolanda waved her hand at me. "So. Lola. Glad to see you, thanks for coming by, and all that—*but I want you out of here.* I'm not talking to people right now." She tossed the can to the floor. "I'm in mourning," she said flatly.

"Mom's lost," I blurted. "Maybe in the jungle."

"Manuel told me," she said, slowly. Her face was thinner and more serious than I remembered. "I am sorry to hear it."

"What are you talking about, you're sorry to hear it? My mother's lost!"

"And my father's dead. I won't ever see him again."

"Yolanda—"

"You cut me out of your life a long time ago. You don't know what things have been like for me here."

"I know," I said. "My father—"

"Your father," she said. "Don't bring fathers up to me. Or mothers. Because it was your mother who told you to stop writing me, wasn't it?"

I rubbed my hands across my eyes.

"That's what I thought."

I stayed quiet for a long moment. "I'm so sorry," I told her, as I took hold of her hand.

Her irises were ebony with an inner star of emerald, and I saw bruise-colored patches under her eyes.

"I don't want you to touch me, Lola," she said. "Not you or anyone else."

But I didn't let go, and she didn't pull away, either.

"You look older," she said then, and sighed.

She did too. I knew she had turned thirty-three last August. I bent down and hugged her tight and hard.

"Stop it," she said, though she still didn't smack me off. I felt her press her cheek into my neck, but not enough that it would be obvious to anyone looking on. "Go away!" she said in a fierce voice. She took my shoulders in her hands and moved me away, until she was holding me at arm's length in too tight a grasp. She was shaking.

"Yes, well, I'm getting that this is very awkward," Erik said. He cupped his bad eye with his hand. "I for one vote to go back to the hotel. Let's talk about all this there. I don't know if anybody can tell that I'm in serious pain."

"Excuse me, but who in the hell are you?" Yolanda asked him.

"I'm Erik." His right eyebrow rose slowly. Despite his discomfort, his neurons had begun firing again at the sight of her lovely face.

"You're what?"

"I'm—I'm—a Guatemalan," he said.

"He's Erik," I said. "Gomara. A friend of mine."

"A Guatemalan?" She scanned her eyes over him. "Are you quite sure about that?"

"What does that mean?" Erik asked. His right eyebrow went back down.

"You don't seem very Guatemalan, my good man. You look like *her*—pure North American—"

"I look better when I don't have a concussion."

"Yolanda, my mother went up to the Peten for the Jade," I cried out. She just looked at me.

"Did you hear me?"

"I heard you fine."

"She thought it might be up there. *The* Jade."

" 'The Jade'?"

"De la Cueva's Jade."

"You mean my father's Jade?"

"Yes. It looks like he could have been right about it all along. They've been finding blue jadeite in the Sierras—"

"I've heard all about that," she said. "Everyone's yelling about a jade mine. Well, they can take it if they find it, can't they? They can choke on it."

"Those reports might prove the old stories," I said. "About the Stone. If we have to go to the forest to look for Mom, it could—it could—be worth your while."

"You want me to guide you," she said, thrusting her thumb toward the bar. "Pick one of the drunks here, they'll take you."

"They're not as good as you."

"Why should I go? Are you going to pay me? I don't care about money. What else could you offer—a new car? A plane ticket out of here?" She closed her eyes. "Old times, maybe?" A few more seconds passed, and I didn't understand exactly what she was asking me. It only occurred to me much later that I had made a bad mistake in not answering this last question.

"Yes, that would be stupid," she said then, in such an acid voice that I was sure she hated me; I should have never, never stopped writing her.

But I was also certain that I'd only have one chance at getting Yolanda to come along.

"I can give you a shot at finishing your father's work." I hesitated. And then I began to lie to her. "I haven't told you everything. My mother found something—a secret map, in some Spanish archives. And it's just come to light."

"So?"

"It gives the exact location of that Jade. And I have a copy of it, which I'll show you. If you come with me."

"You're trying to fool me," she hissed. "There's no secret map."

"We're going up there to find her—and the Stone, if you want," I said, clasping my hands together. But in the next second I felt my desperation kick loose for the first time since I'd heard my mother had vanished.

"You have to help me!" I nearly shrieked at her. "Not because you like me. Not because you care about her. Because I'll give you whatever you want—*I have a map*. And I'll help you find that rock. I swear it."

She leaned forward and took hold of my right hand in hers. She touched it to her cheek with a brutal pressure.

"My father was probably—no, he *was* insane. At the end. Can't you see how it hurts me? *There was nothing to find.*"

As she said this, I could hear the chatter of the customers, and beneath that, the constant uneven droning hum of the old grandfather at the bar.

"No—you always believed in your dad," I said.

"I'm too tired for that stupid dream now, Lola." She put my hand down. "Just leave."

She turned away from me. The party swirled around us, and beer steins floated overhead. Patrons swung in and out of The Pedro Lopez, and the line at the bar grew thicker, until a crowd formed.

"I just had my lights punched out," Erik said to no one in particular.

"A song," someone said then, over him.

"A song! A song!"

"Give us one there, Felipe," one of the barflies said. "Help us shake the blues off now that those bastards are gone."

In the backsplash mirror I could see the grandfather smile.

"No," he said. "You young buggers leave me alone."

Eventually they did get him to turn around on his stool, and a few men whistled and swore, and told him to start up.

The old man began murmuring in that same off-key voice, though in my daze I could barely hear what he was saying. The crowd surrounding us grew quieter. Yolanda drew her hat down over her head.

"What's he doing?" I asked.

"I've never been hit like that before in my life." Erik opened one eye. "Did I hold up all right?"

"Yes."

"Did you get hurt?"

"I already told you I did. Listen, is that man singing?"

"Who?"

"The old man."

Erik peered at the bar with his good eye. "Yes."

"What? I can barely make it out."

"Agh, it's a song," Erik said. "Maybe it's our musical cue to leave."

"What song? Have I heard that?"

"It's an old song."

"It's one of the oldest, around here," Yolanda said, and then she began moving her lips to the words.

The grandfather closed his eyes and continued to talk-sing. It took me a while before I could understand the lyrics; it took me even longer to realize that this tune was one that my mother knew. The last time I'd heard her hum it was on the evening of her trip.

While I applied more ice to Erik's cheek, I listened to the old man's grumbling, fractured voice as he sang to the familiar melody:

> My queen, my beauty
> What have I done?
> Why have you left me?
> To live in this world
> So cold and so empty
>
> I lost you, I lost you, my darling.
>
> My treasure, my charm
> Do you forgive me?
> Stay safe in my arms
> Where I can kiss you
> Where you will stay warm
> I lost you

I lost you
I'm lost, too
I'm lost, too
I'm lost
without you

My darling

The ice rested in my hand; my leg no longer hurt, absorbed as I was in the old man's awful singing. The song made something terrible inside me begin to expand. I could hear my mother's voice in my ear, and I felt a cracking, a breaking.

Yolanda did not appear much better. Her jaw remained clenched, but the muscles in it trembled. She wouldn't look at me at all now. I remained invisible to her even when the ballad ended and the men at the bar applauded their friend. He nodded and turned back to the counter so that he could resume downing his beer.

"Good-bye," she said, when I tried to slip my hand inside hers again.

"We should get moving," Erik said, after another minute. He touched his face with his fingers. "All I want to do right now is go back to the hotel. This has all been supremely interesting, but I would really like to never come here again for as long as I live." He stood up and took hold of my elbow and moved me toward the front door. "Come on. Let's go."

I took one more look at Yolanda, but she turned away from me. There was nothing else that I could say to her tonight.

"All right," I said. I touched the sore spot on my leg and nodded. "We're out of here."

On our way back across the bar, though, I glanced back. And even if she jerked her eyes away from me, I gathered that Yolanda was sufficiently interested in what I'd had to say to watch me carefully from under the brim of her hat as I walked out.

But I would have known that anyway.

CHAPTER 16

We'd reached our lodgings at the Westin Hotel, in Zone Three, by ten o'clock. The Westin towers over Guatemala City's palm trees and black mesh of power lines is a particularly complex example of modern architecture, as its facade is composed of hundreds of white triangles suspended in the air, like a colossal white web spun by a pretentious spider. All allusions to the twentieth century end, however, once you're inside. Erik and I limped into a rococo foyer groaning with bronze sculptures of boys in Shakespearean dress, white marble, erupting flower arrangements, and murals of sylphs and Greek goddesses. We staggered up to our separate rooms. I bathed, then changed into jeans and the T-shirt of the Stelae that my father had given me. I made my way up to Erik's suite, bringing my bag of books and maps so that we might plan our search in Antigua and possibly Flores.

When I knocked on the door, he opened it dressed in sweats and giant fuzzy socks.

"I thought I'd send up for a treat," he said, holding a glass of wine. The mark beneath his eye had spread a little, though the color appeared slightly less raw. His hair was a wet mass of curls combating for turf all over his head. His bad eye winked; the wine swirled in its glass high in the air. "This is to commemorate my first terrifying and extremely painful fistfight, which I've decided will also be my very, very last."

"Great idea."

"Have a wine." He thrust the glass into my hand.

"Even better idea."

"Time for food, too. You see I've ordered."

"Yes—yes—smells great."

In the green-and-pink sitting room of his suite stood a chintz-covered sofa, and in front of that a cherry wood table. On this table rested a silver platter crowded with four covered dishes and a bottle of Spanish Rioja.

"I'm hoping that if I drink enough of this I can forget what happened tonight," he said.

I sat down on the sofa as he uncovered the dishes. Surrounded by the velvets and flowers, we dipped our huge spoons into a risotto, pink and white with butter and crayfish, while Erik talked about sixteenth-century Italian sea captains who had sailed to the Americas in search of gold and mermaids, but found instead only these tiny dragons crawling on the shores, which proved such a savory addition to the rice dishes beloved by the Medici. On the heels of this indulgence, we ate half a cake frosted with burned caramel sugar. This pastry was molded into a small mountain, crested with apricots, and out of its center oozed dark chocolate. The menu called the confection "Hot Burning Love."

"You would order that," I said, getting the last of it from my spoon.

"And you would eat it—stop gobbling all of it. The more I eat, the better I feel."

"Does it still hurt?"

"My eye? It's deadly. Though I remember that you—helped me."

"Yes. I helped you."

"I saw you when I came to."

"You did faint."

"I didn't faint. I did not faint. I was registering my surprise. *And* when I chose to get back on my feet, I swear I heard you babbling something outrageous to that Yolanda. You said your mother had found a map, and that she could use it. Or hopefully I was hallucinating?"

"You were not hallucinating."

"Do you have a top-secret map that you didn't tell me about?"

"No."

"So why did you tell her that?"

"So that she'd come with us. I know she won't otherwise."

"If she does, she'll probably strangle you when she finds out you lied. Frightening woman." The chintz upholstery appeared to surround Erik with a garden of roses and blue lilacs and irises. He leaned back and began comparing Yolanda's charms to those of the executioners in ancient Istanbul, but then, after some minutes, became distracted.

His eyes had traveled down to my shirt, and stayed there.

"Erik?"

"What?" He glanced back up at my face, then looked back down.

"You didn't seem too put off when you first laid eyes on her."

"She's attractive. Very, very, very attractive, when you first look at her. Though something tells me that she and I might not get along so well. And contrary to apparently everyone's expectations, I don't always run wild after every difficult woman I faint in front of."

"Don't you?"

"Well, at least I'm considering amending my habits. Being attacked by a sociopath has changed my perspective on things. I think. Besides, even if it didn't, I still wouldn't be interested in a person like her."

"Why?"

"Not my type."

"No? So what's your type like, then?"

"What?" he asked softly, still looking down at me.

"Your type?"

"Oh," he said. He edged closer. Involuntarily thrilling and ill-advised chills began to radiate through my chest, and I could feel my pulse thud in a weird quick way. He moved forward on the sofa again. He edged toward me closer still. Then he said, "Blondes."

He peered up again at me and smiled; back down went his gaze.

I realized that Erik wasn't really staring at my figure, as I'd thought, but instead at the icons on my shirt.

"Look at this dwarf," he said.

"What?"

"Look at this dwarf."

"Excuse me?"

"On this T-shirt. There's a very clear image of a dwarf. Very finely cut. Beautifully done. It's embedded in a text that, as far as I can read, is completely jumbled—but we already knew that."

I looked down at the picture of the blue images of the Flores Stelae displayed across my shirt. I had some training in the reading of Maya hieroglyphs, though I couldn't read them upside down.

"It's right here," he said. Erik reached out and touched one of the icons, on the spot right over my collarbone. "Let me see if I can read this passage." He examined the string of hieroglyphs, then shook his head. "No, I can't. It looks like it should mean something. As if it's all scrambled up."

I got hold of myself. "That's why Mom said it was just ancient wallpaper."

He nodded. "Meaningless."

"Right."

"That just doesn't convince me—like I said before. I don't believe the Maya thought that way. They were too pious. It's like Gothic architecture—have you ever looked at it? Every symbol on Notre Dame signifies something. Something religious. It's the same way with Maya architecture, Maya books. The temples are all carved with hieroglyph prayers—everything we've ever excavated has a coherent text carved into it. Meaninglessness is just a bone to throw to the theorists."

I shook my head. "You're wrong. The Maya practically invented the idea."

"What do you mean?"

"They discovered the concept of zero, for one."

"But a zero isn't meaningless. Add a number to zero, and it's magnified by ten."

I propped my face up with my hands. I was exhausted, but I couldn't help but remember a relevant reference in a completely different source. There was a chapter in de la Cueva's own papers that would support my point.

"Here, hold on, I've got you cornered." I reached down to my canvas bag, where I'd put my books and maps and copies. I'd Xeroxed not only the *Legende* but also all of de la Cueva's *Letters* before we'd flown to Guatemala. I began to sift through the pages until I came across a particular passage. "De la Cueva wrote something about this." I held up a page with the telling paragraphs. "In one of her letters to her sister, she describes how she found out that her lover—Balaj K'waill—had been lying to her about the Jade. How he'd been trying to trick her and lead her off into the forest so that she'd get injured, or starve, and die—"

"So?" Erik yawned.

"—and from the sound of it, when he realized that he failed, he had a pretty clear idea that his life didn't amount to anything."

"I'll bet not."

"The poor guy knew that everything he'd done added up to a big, empty zero. . . ."

December 15, 1540

    . . . I have written you, Sister, that two weeks ago we had found the First Maze. The Maze of Deceit! This Labyrinth is as unreachable as heaven, as deep as hell, and built curiously from blue jade that has been tortured into circles and traps that we wandered through at our great peril. For this past fortnight I have struggled to pierce that puzzle. I tested its curves, studying its feints and its dead ends. But I could not crack it. As we worked to plumb its secrets, we began to run out of food and water, and my men commenced dying of fever at some twenty a day. Balaj K'waill counseled me to have patience and I held out as long as I was able. But eventually I had to admit that we must return to our city—a proposition to which my lover reacted at first with teasing humor, and then, when he saw that I would not change my mind, with the most bizarre and tragic melancholy.

    "Darling," I said, "you are wasting away from your gloom. Before we leave, let us you and I go to the river and take some rest that you so well need."

"You should push on, Governor," he replied, and his face was ash-colored. "I am sure we have almost solved the Maze."

"No, I have decided," I told him. "And you know I am not a woman to change my mind. Yet let me hold you and bathe you. We will joke and play, sweetheart. We must restore your strength."

I took his hand and led him down through the forest, toward a river that runs through the wood, and by that water we took our leisure. I rubbed him with balms and I sang in his ear; and then, in order to lift his heart, I thought I would entertain him by teaching him our country's dance, the Sarabande.

"One, two, three, four," I whispered in his ear. "Those are the maneuvers of this game we are playing, my dear. One must go forward, forward. And move smoothly, like a European."

"La, la, la," he said, laughing and singing songs I could not understand. He grew berserk, spouting nonsense words, numbers, and rhymes.

"To dance in Goathemala, my sweet," he said, "one must move roughly, skipping every other *trac.*"

"Every other what?"

"That's the French for 'track,' my beloved thickwit. And as you have noted that we are quite backwards, you must follow our reversed native steps, which are four, three, two, one, zero." Balaj K'waill swung me wildly to and fro, jumping, skipping, and pushing me back, all the while shouting, and mixing these freaks with obscenities, then laughing some more.

"What does all this mean?" I demanded of him.

"*It means nothing!!*" he said.

"What means nothing?"

And here he began weeping. "None of it. Not one word nor deed of mine has had any significance."

"But we have come so far to find the Jade."

His tears turned into a sour laughter. "The Jade. The *Jade.* You once told me that the English word for jade means a woman of perverse morals. And so you are the only Queen Jade in this jungle, Beatriz."

I felt myself sicken. "Are you saying that you lied to me?"

"Yes!"

"But we found the maze!"

"This?" He pointed at the monstrous labyrinth. "This is nothing but a dream. You will find no riches in there—and if there *were* a Jade, I would not ever bring you to it. For why else would I lead you to the jungle, except to destroy you? And yet you survived this starvation, this searching without food and water, without rest, which has nearly murdered me these past months. *Will you Europeans not ever die? Is there nothing that will kill you?*"

"Stop talking. Say not another word."

"I am sure that soon I will cease talking forever," he continued, looking at me again with his beautiful eyes.

"Why do you say that?"

"Because you will not let me live. A European cannot brook being bested by a savage."

I did not answer him at once. I gazed at him and thought how he had taken my love for a toy. And then I discovered all of my affection burgeoning into venom, for an awakened woman betrayed is a dangerous thing.

"No, I will not let you live," I said. "But not because you are a savage. Because you have broken my heart."

And I did not.

Agata, I could not toll his treachery. He has been taken by the gendarmes, who have treated him as we do all traitors.

My lover is now dead. But sister, I swear to you, I think that I am also one who belongs in the grave.

What is that song the old bards sing around here?

I lost you I lost you my darling . . .

Dear God, I murdered Balaj K'waill. And I see now that I have as good as kill't myself.

"All right—all right," Erik said after a minute or two of silence, while he ruffled through the photocopies and yawned again. "Meaninglessness—it's all here. What with crying, the strange dancing."

The dancing *was* strange, I thought. "Those numbers—what do you think he was trying to say with all that?"

"That he's depressed. He doesn't see the sense in things anymore. So you're right."

"I'm just showing you it's not a very modern concept," I said. I had a very clear image of the gaunt way that Yolanda had looked at me in that bar tonight. "Everyone loses faith once in a while."

Erik peered at me. "I'm going to order up more room service if you keep making that face."

I rubbed my nose. "All right. I won't get soggy. Just no more food."

"More wine?"

"Okay."

He leaned back and closed his eyes. He looked happy, despite having been smashed up a few hours before.

"Erik?"

"Yes."

A few more seconds passed. I realized that my mouth was gaping open, and I shut it. The wine was doing a good job of relieving our pain. "Okay. We know about Balaj K'waill's lie to de la Cueva, but there's still the primary source to study. We should look at the *Legende* before we get any further. It's what my mother was using as a guide."

"Yes. That's a good idea. You do that."

"You're *sleeping*."

"I think you're the one who's sleeping."

"No, I'm not."

Pause.

"What?" I asked.

"What do you mean, what?"

"Nothing . . ."

"Can you move over a little to the left?"

"*You* move over." I forced my eyes open. "And wake up."

"I'm comfortable."

"No, seriously." I smacked him on the thigh. "We still have things to do. We're going to study the *Legende*. I'll read it to you."

"I read it when I was a kid. Know the story by heart. Scary rock. Obsessive kings. Curses."

"Not good enough. But don't worry, you'll love it. Though I think we should probably have some coffee first."

"Just a little nap."

But next came a call to room service, a tray, a carafe.

"This had better be good," he said ten minutes later, grumbling into a cup of black joe.

"Oh, it's good," I said, unrolling my Xerox of the *Legende*, then spreading the papers out onto my lap. And in fact, few other books could have kept me conscious at that hour. "Erik, trust me. De la Cueva's the best."

THE LEGENDE OF THE QUEEN JADE
*(As rendered from Beatriz de la Cueva's journal,
dated October 3, 1540)*

In our world's earliest age, when the new-born earth was still pure and unsullied by the foolishness of man, one great old King ruled the entire land. He governed the Valleys and the Seas and the Sky and all the Plains. He mastered squalid cities and bounteous shires. He owned the meager coasts. And he presided over the princely Jungle, with its sacred Dragon Tree, which is possessed by a spirit such that it bleeds like a man when cut by an axe. Yet of all his possessions, he enjoyed his reign of the lofty blue Mounts most.

The mountains glowed like the sky itself, for within their crags hid precious jade, as clear as water, and as hard as a woman's heart. One fleck might be worth the lives of one thousand miners, and so the king's fortune was most assured. Nonetheless, it was not these rivers of jade that secured his power. Instead, his sovereignty was preserved by one particular Gem that the king warded upon the advice of his necromancer, a crouchback Dwarf, who had been told of the Stone by the gods in a Dream.

For no mere piece of Jade do we describe. This was a charmed and magick jewel, the Queen of all Jades—so named as the blue rock glowed as fair as a goddess, stood as tall as an Amazon, and ruled over men's greed with its terrible glory. Any who owned it (the Gods had said in the Dwarf's dream) would rule over all Enemies. The old King had never known danger or defeat on account of this monstrous weapon, and had raised two strong sons in the hopes they would govern the country together.

So the King was happy until the day he felt approaching one Villain. And he knew that not even the Stone could help him then.

The Villain was death itself.

"It is time for me to pass my scepter to your two right hands, my sons," the King said to the princes. "You shall govern together, and in peace."

"But I wish to govern alone, Father," said the Eldest.

"And I will not share my power with this knave," agreed the Younger.

The King and his sons argued, with much weeping and roaring, until the Sovereign understood that no words would thin their fat wits, and so he Split the Kingdom and forced them to choose:

"One man shall rule the rich jungle, where the blessed Dragon Tree stands, as well as the Princely cities and the lofty blue mounts, but shall not have the one Jade," he said. "And the other shall govern the base coasts and the basins, the deserts and the swamps, yet shall call the Talisman his own."

"I shall have the lofty blue mounts, then, and do without the Stone," said the Eldest.

"And I shall have the base deserts and the basins and the swamps, and call the Talisman my own," said the Younger.

And perhaps it might appear from these choices that the Younger boasted of a stouter heart than his brother.

But as you shall see, it was not so.

And so the King died.

The Younger, before inheriting his Throne, knew that no good

king could serve his country without a fine wife, and he selected as
his bride one round-faced Sorceress who had been his sweetheart
since his tender years.

For her part, the Sorceress loved the Younger Brother for his
warm eyes and his soft slow hands. And she burned for him with a
passion that was not diminished by her understanding of her
husband's weak nature. His flaw was an excess of Curiosity, as he
fixed his mind too much on that which was strange, beauteous, and
queer, even dangerous.

But as all men are the stuff of debility, the Sorceress thanked the
Gods that her lover proved only a Dreamer, a flaw much more be-
nign than Lust or Greed or Gluttony or Stupidity.

And so she was of good cheer when they married. The Younger
Brother gathered to him his Wife, his Servants, and his Prize, being
the Queen of all Jades. Together with these he trod off to the base
deserts, where they would live in happiness and peace.

But not for long.

Rather than govern his realm with the craft of his Father, the
Younger Brother succumbed to his weak quality. He grew bewitched
by the beauty and Charms of the Jade, which he bade his Servants
bring to his Private Chamber so he could look upon it in secret.
What mysteries did it hold? He wondered. What powers did it wield
over him? Day after day he gazed upon its blue glory, and soon he
could think of nothing else but its sheen, its pure clear color, its
shape, its startling perfection. So entranced did he become, and so
jealous of its company, that he forgot all other things. Like a Lover,
he remained in his Private Chamber and worshiped the Gem. So he
mused, and he brooded, and thought, and desired with a terrible
greed, and malingered from this new condition.

And soon enough he became as thin as a ghost, and toppled over
in his Bed, while still stroking his Treasure, and Died.

Which left the Sorceress alone to Rule the droughty deserts and
protect the Jade by herself. She grieved much for her husband.

"We are all tempted by the things we love, and we all must pass
from the world," she said, as she fixed the crown to her head, and

watched as the ragged masses bowed to Her Grace. "So now, my husband, you have left me alone except for the protection of the Treasure. But for what reason should I be protected now, and continue to live? All my days I desired no one else but you. And yet, for the weal of these people, I will try not to fail."

Meanwhile, in the empire of the princely jungles and the lofty blue Mounts, the Elder Brother beheld his wealthy dominion, and all his silken wives, his jade-adorned slaves, his palaces and libraries, his legions of poets and Soldiers, and his rich jungle, with its spirit-possessed Tree, and knew himself to be the most Magnificent Prince under the sky.

But he could not be happy.

Like his Younger Brother he desired the Jade. Like that King of the basins and the deserts and the poor coasts, he cherished the image of the brilliant jewel. And his desire increased day by day, until he thought himself the poorest man in the world.

Still, he would not have moved in Treason against his Brother's kingdom had it not been for the counsel of his Dwarf, who had also served his Father. This Dwarf fathomed better than anyone else in the land the dangers that came with two Rulers.

"The old King knew not so well what he broke when he sundered this country," the Dwarf told the Elder Brother one day, as the two men walked in the Royal pleasure gardens, which were sweet with myrtle and marigold, and alive with butterflies and the whispering mahogany. "I have had a Dream of great trouble. In the night came to me a vision of a Tempest and a War between your Realm and that of the Younger Brother's, and these things will destroy our cities down to the last child."

"My Brother," the Eldest brooded, "we have heard the news that he has died."

"He expired from idiocy, my lord."

"Yet his retainers continue to possess what we do not."

"It is so. They possess the Stone. And we must take it from them, King."

"But it is their inheritance."

"And it is your *death. Should we take the Jade, none of those beggars might harm us. Imagine their fear at what we might do."*

"They would shake and cry, and never raise arms."

"They would remain mild as kittens and meek as women."

After one evening spent in bloodletting and prayer, the Eldest agreed with his Dwarf's counsel.

"Attend to the Army so that they might fetch the Stone from my brother's kindred," he ordered the Dwarf. "And if they do not gift it to us from suasion of coin and kindness, do not be shy to gain it by less pretty methods."

"Such as?"

"Take care to keep the Jade intact. But as for what folk might resist you, rip the Jade from their cold hands if you like."

And so the Great War began.

Down from the lofty blue Mounts, through the lush and dark Jungles, marched a Legion of Soldiers armed in jade breast-plates, holding gold spears, and guarded by Silver Helmets worked into the snarling face of the Jaguar. As they made their way across the country, they were horrible, bristling, and a Terror to See.

Descending to the deserts and then to the poor coast, the warriors gathered upon the white cliffs. Glaring down upon the kingdom of the Younger Brother, they began to roar like Beasts and shake their spears and their shields.

The Witch, sitting upon her wood Throne, startled up at the bluff. Upon seeing her enemy, she raced through her City, calling for her strongest men and her most stalwart women, and her sword.

The Foes battled for days. And the strongest, to their surprise, found themselves in a rout. Women soldiers of the Coast, in their rags and their streaming hair, fought off the gold spears and jade blades of the Eldest King's warriors with mere sticks and fury. The men, equally valiant, wrested the silver jaguars off the heads of the Eldest's halberdiers, and tore their throats with their bare hands, or lopped their skulls with their farming scythes.

The Eldest's Army lashed at the poor people of the Coast, their axes dripping, their jade breasts crimson, blood on their armor, blood in their eyes.

But the blood was their Own.

On account of the Jade, they could not master this war.

And yet, what is the power of a Talisman in the face of evil and cunning?

On the Fifth day, when the Witch's victory was nearly secure, three of the Eldest's best warriors gained good luck and struck at her until they broke her shield. She fled into her palace, running through the halls, through the plain rooms, through the meager gardens, until she reached the Chamber that was the safe-keeping of the Jade.

And here she saw the Eldest Brother waiting for her with the Dwarf and one tall, thin, sad-eyed Priest.

"I understand that you have been left a Widow, and so now are the proper owner of the Jade," the Eldest said. "If you are good enough to let me keep this Trifle, I will let you keep your life."

"No enemy can Destroy me while I own that precious Thing," the Witch said. "It is mine alone."

The Eldest laughed.

"It has come to my understanding," he said, "that if we two Marry, you could not name me as your Enemy, and what should be yours would be mine."

"But I do not like to take you as a husband," the Witch screamed.

"Yet you must," the Dwarf said. "There is one cleverness of the world that you have forgotten: Women are below men, and so do not have the power to refuse an offer to wed."

Guided by this bit of wisdom, the Eldest now ordered the Priest to perform the Rites. So this man of the Gods draped the trembling Witch with flowers, and chanted prayers above her head, and caused her to take the hand of the Eldest.

"You are now his Bride," he said, as he was about to anoint the Witch with oil.

But then one thing happened that was not foreseen by either Dwarf or King.

As the thin, solemn, and—it should be said—lonely Priest bent over the Witch to touch her face with the Holy oil, he peered into her dark eyes and fell in love.

Of course, his companions noticed nothing of this as they rejoiced over their dominion of the Jade, and listened with delight to the sounds of the Coast warriors dying under the thrusts of the gold spears.

The Eldest stood victorious on the bloody mount of his brother's land. By his side quailed the Witch, his new wife. The Stone, magnificent, beaming its blue light, had become his own. It would protect him.

It would protect him from all save himself.

Years passed.

In Due course, the Eldest King proved much like his brother, for the charms of the Jade made him, too, grow mad.

Ensconced in his Castle on the top of the lofty blue Mounts, he looked upon the Queen of All Jades and turned into an idiot from his greed.

Soon, he could bear to look upon nothing but Jade, and ordered his architects to build him a great City made of the glowing Blue boulders in the Jungle, within the shade of the blessed Dragon Tree. And then he ordered them another plan as well:

"Hide this City within a Winding Jade Maze, made of curves and circles, which we will know as the Labyrinth of Deceit," he said. "For I possess such a Treasure that it may only attract Foreign Thieves and Murderers. You must do this, and keep me safe."

So the Mad Blue City was built in the shadow cast by the great Tree that bleeds ruby sap. And it was hidden within that colossus of a Labyrinth formed of diabolical jade passages and maelific stanzes and Confusion out of which there would be no Express.

The Eldest King brought his Stone and his people to the city within the Maze. He brought his Bride too, but blindfolded, so that she could not find her way out.

When the mask fell from her eyes and she gazed at her cage, the Witch saw she could never read all the labyrinth's dangers and escape.

The moon waxed, shining down upon a city where dark plans hatched. The moon waned, and the black shadows of the eve concealed subtle minds.

The calendar turned again.

There were whispers. Some said there were shadows on the walls of the Maze, wherein lay the corpses of royal enemies, and where rebels practiced treasonous arts. Gossip held that a secret and mutinous force had been raised against which the royal arms would fall. Others agreed among themselves that the Eldest Brother had entered an early Dotage, as he could think of nothing but his Stone.

The wise wizard Dwarf, much older now, realized that a crosseyed Ass could have given the Eldest Brother better counsel than he. Yet he still tended what remained of the kingdom and pursued all rumors of sedition. Thus, when he heard of the larks in the Maze, he left the Palace one dark night and traveled toward the Labyrinth's riddling routes.

In the shadows, the Dwarf leapt easy and soft through that Labyrinth, as he knew each curve and folly of its Design. Past its dead-falls he slipped with little dread, though there were perils that faced him toward the North Star, toward the Sea, toward the Sun, and toward the Heat of the South: sucking marshes, and red-eyed jaguars, and roaring rivers. Past all this he ran, and he ducked, too, the rocks and mire thrown by the shrieking gobelyns that lived in its dizzy heights. He pushed; he pressed. He cast out his eye and his keen ear until he saw shadows of twisting limbs on the Walls of the maze. He heard the moaning breaths and the obscene, murmured oaths. Peering deeper into the Puzzle, he roamed its circles. He reached a moon-flooded spot and observed there the Witch and the

Priest married in an embrace, with wet lips and gleaming teeth, moving and biting like serpents.

"We have had no trouble breeding rebels in the forest," he heard the Witch cry, at the same time she dispatched her warm deed. "The Eldest Brother proves too feeble to remain King."

"He has turned many against him," said the Priest.

"He loves what he cannot own," she said. "And we will raise our Army against Him and crush this city into blue dust."

"We will," the Priest wept.

And as he peered through the night's gloom the Dwarf saw this man looked sallow and dazed.

"When the sun rises twice more, we will bring our Force to lay siege upon his Castle, and leave no enemy of mine alive."

"Yes."

In the shadows of the Labyrinth, the Dwarf trembled.

Back to the Palace he flew, under the moon that would grow thinner and lighter until it vanished like smoke under the Sun. The Dwarf entered the blue castle and pushed through the doors and past the jade-breasted guards. He discovered the Eldest Brother hunched on his shining throne, his indigo crown tilted on his head, and his purple sword within its scabbard. His eyes were glazed and gawping blind at his Court of Knights, who kneeled before him and waited their orders.

"King," the Dwarf said, "it is time for you to rise from your throne and throw off this Pallor."

The Eldest Brother said nothing, but only blenched and stared.

"There is Treason afoot. There is a plot for your Death."

The King seemed still to have a child's mind, though he did frown at this.

"There is a plan for your Murder, at the Order of the Witch, who even now puddles your Bed by her sweat mixt with the Priest's."

"I know it," came at last the answer, but the King remained soft-brained and mild.

So the Dwarf mused upon this trouble for one more hour. And in the red dawn, he knew it was himself who must call the order. Striding into the Court once more, he said, "There are traitors in our midst, and so we are to arms!"

The Knights happily agreed. Gathering the King to his feet, the Army stood, roaring as it once had down at the poor country of the Coast. Then these horrible men marched upon the Witch and her Lover.

In the King's own blue bed, wrapped in cambric windings and with their lips red and sore from kissing, the two betrayers were discovered. And when the Eldest Brother looked upon his wife in such disgrace, he cast off his Dotage at once, and drew his sword, and slashed it down.

But he only slew the Priest, as the Witch proved too fast.

Down the halls she flew, shouting for her rebels until her mutinous friends emerged from the corners and shaded nooks of the castle, and from the deep black folds of the forest itself.

A second battle commenced, though from the first the rebels buckled beneath the royal force. Jade blades slashed through the air, dripping, plunging, and terrible to see. Women and men, still clutching their weapons, fell to the ground and watered it with their blood. Halberdiers stood above the begging forms of the insurgents, shouting out the King's name. The Witch, leading this war, was one of the few untouched by the soldiers' wrath. She raced to the vanguard until she reached the Eldest Brother and raised her sword against him.

But he proved the more apt killer.

He drew his knife and murdered her with one swift stroke.

As the Witch felt her life escape, she turned her beautiful face to her husband. Remembering once more the dark eyes and slow soft hands of the Younger Brother, she wept.

"I curse you," she said. "I call upon the great powers that have shaped all that is fell, and all that is fine, to cast the King into ruin, and all that he divined. None of your kin shall be safe from my spell, for the angels shall burn your blue city with fire, drown it with

water, and commit you to hell. And any man who seeks anew to claim the Jade shall suffer that same fate. Each soul tempted by the Stone's beauty shall smother in flood, and be eaten by storm, until he wakes within Hades' gates."

She took one more breath.

"But you shall suffer worst of all, my husband, my devil, the master of my bed. For I destroy you and all you love. You are dead. You are dead. We are dead."

And then she was silent forever.

The King went cold with fear.

"The Jade!" he screamed, rushing about the palace to find any sanctuary where he might retain his Gem. But there was no such safe place there.

Commanding his slaves to collect the Queen of all Jades, he fled his Mad city. He passed the Dragon Tree, which poured a river of blood into the earth, as he continued to run far, toward the East. Here, he hid within a second Maze of his own making. He called this the Labyrinth of Virtue.

And of what was this crazed Puzzle composed?

Of nothing more than a riddle:

> *The Roughest Path to Take*
> *The Harshest Road to Tread*
> *Is the one We must Make*
> *Tho' our Hearts fill with Dread*

> *The Hardest Pass to Walk*
> *In these Days foul and Fast*
> *When crooked sin us Mocks*
> *Is ours to Brave and Last*

> *He who steers due from Hell*
> *For he who bears the Waves*
> *The Jade waits in her Dell*
> *And the Good Man is Repaid*

In this secret lair, the Eldest Brother hid with his Stone. For days, he gazed upon its blue splendor, and stroked its glittering form with his shaking hands. He whispered to the Talisman as if it were alive and thought himself the most happy man.

Yet this King was deceived in his Faith.

The Gods had heard the prayer of the Witch, and it alone was in their power to confound the Protection of the Jewel.

So in that high place that exists beyond the world, past the doorway of the Smoking Mirror, the Deities cast their eyes on the Kingdom and the Covert of the Eldest Brother and wished it gone.

Down came the wind like a great Hand, and it smothered the City and its people and its Ruler and the Jade with its wild fingers. In that crushing force, the temples became dust, and soldiers, who stabbed at the enemy air with their knives, were sucked into the heavens as if swallowed by God's throat. Blood filled the gardens, and bones cluttered the courts, and the lashings of this Weather wiped away the Vanity of Men.

And the King, with his Jade, was made also to vanish by the howling Tempest. He clutched onto his Fortune with his dying hands, until the strength of the wind ripped them away.

The kingdom of the Eldest and the Youngest and their father disappeared. And how quiet were the forests and the mountains after these days! In this time, no bird, no dragon, no gobelyn, disturbed the cracked blue palace with their furtive work.

More years passed.

But as the earth is built to be the home of Man, in its kindness it grew green things over the remnants of the blue city, the old bones and the blood, and began to feed new life again.

Villages were built. Children were born. Grandfathers took the Tale of the King and his Deceit to their graves. Danger, too, breeds. From progress Stupidity has risen anew, and the Gods, in their Wisdom, look down upon us and wait.

Sons and Daughters, we must not forget our failings. We must

not forget that beneath all this pretty world lie still the bones of your
ancestors, who died so hard on account of that Temptation.
    Remember always that under the skin of your City rests still that
one parlous Gem that seduced men to their Deaths.
    Your life has been built on the Tomb of the Powerful Jade.
    Take care to learn from this Tale, then.
    Hark this:
    Do not seek the Stone, or Disturb it Again.

"Erik," I said. I was bending over the pages of the tale which I'd spread out on the coffee table, underlining a particular paragraph with a pen. "Look at these lines."

"Hmmmmm." He stretched out on the sofa, folded his hands over his chest, and peeped at me from half-shut eyes while I read aloud from the *Legende.*

The Eldest King brought his Stone and his people to the city within
the Maze. He brought his Bride too, but blindfolded, so that she
could not find her way out.
    When the mask fell from her eyes and she gazed at her cage, the
Witch saw she could never read all the labyrinth's dangers and es-
cape.

A few days before, I had noticed that quirk in de la Cueva's writing style, when I'd examined her letters to her sister, Agata. There, she described to her sister Agata how the Maze of Deceit was a "difficult bugger to scan," and I'd wondered how exactly one should translate that phrase. In these lines from the *Legende,* I had just come across a similar sort of question.

"It's the word *read,*" I explained. "It's a strange usage. The word has a complicated etymological history. The Spanish verb *leer,* 'to read,' is a derivative of the early Latin *legere. That* means to 'gather' and 'collect,' and also to 'speak' and 'tell.'"

"Very, very, *very* interesting," Erik mumbled.

"It's a mother word to the later Middle English *legende,* or legend—

the tale—and the old French *legion*, which means 'the gathering of men.' I think that de la Cueva's playing on the word, here. The witch is plotting to gather her rebel army, while she's being led into the labyrinth. So de la Cueva is probably trying to convey the idea that she can't marshal her forces. *Or* she might mean that the witch can't read the labyrinth, as in 'reading the situation.' I'm thinking about translating this text into English—but it's difficult because of her linguistic games. What I'm wondering is whether 'read' should be translated literally."

His lips began to flutter halfway through my speech.

"Erik. *Erik.*"

"Yes, yes. I'm just concentrating."

He concentrated while I scribbled down notes, and I'd filled up three pieces of paper before the coffee wore off and I felt my eyelids dropping, too. I leaned over onto what I thought was a pillow, listened to the sounds of the city traffic outside, and tried to puzzle out my questions about the tale. I wondered if my mother had also found the writing strange when she'd studied the legend. I wished I could ask her.

After a while, I heard the tumble of papers as they fell to the floor. I turned over and arranged my elbows in a jutting position so that I might get a bit more room on the sofa. I was going to go to bed in just one minute.

I could swear I felt Erik's hand stroke my hair right before I fell asleep.

CHAPTER 17

Six A.M.

The xeroxed pages of Beatriz de la Cueva's *Legende* and *Letters* spread out on the dark hotel carpet in white scattered drifts, where they caught the sunlight misting into the windows. The light also wafted onto other jumbled remnants from the previous night: empty wineglasses and plates of disintegrated cake, and the sock that had slipped off Erik's behemoth foot.

I leaned up on an elbow and looked at him. I brought my face closer up to his, curiously inspecting, not quite sure what I was doing. His face looked slightly mashed and creased, and his surprisingly long lashes fluttered against the cheek stained with the purple bruise. His cheek flickered when I nudged him. And then nudged him again.

He opened an eye, like a large overfed lion snoozing in a zoo.

"You dropped off," I said. "You didn't go to your room."

"This is my room."

"Oh. Well, never mind that. You'd better get up. We're going to Antigua this morning."

"Coffee," he said.

"You get it." I leaned down and touched the sore spot on my leg. "You crushed me to pieces on this thing all night."

"What?"

"You had your head in my lap."

He sat up with his dented-looking hair waving around. "Oh. Sorry."

"So you get the coffee."

"All right."

He heaved off and padded toward the phone, so that within twenty minutes we were both sipping from a Turkish-thick brew and nibbling on fried bread glittering with sugar.

We packed our books, pens, my etymological notes. But we didn't feel human until we had showered and dressed—me in Wranglers and a sweater with a big pointed collar and red sneakers, Erik in his jeans and the large T-shirt with the decal of the Flores Stelae. The T-shirt was slightly too tight, and the icons on it stretched out across his chest. We walked out through the gilt-and-velvet trappings of the Westin's foyer, sidestepping the other, posher guests. Then we went out to a nearby Budget office and rented ourselves a small blue Jeep.

Erik launched us forward, speeding, braking, chatting about the risotto of the previous night, and steering in his customary one-finger fashion down the highway. I looked out the window at the city and the encroaching grasslands, toward the hillsides flashing past, and the chicken buses with their rainbow stripes hurtling through the splashing high water. I rolled my window down to feel the wet breeze on my cheek and my arm. A dark arrow of birds marked the sky above us, and I watched them until they were out of sight.

Before us lay the road to Antigua.

CHAPTER 18

To reach the city of Antigua from the capital of Guatemala, we had to take southern side roads to avoid a washed-out section of the Pan American Highway. Alongside our Jeep, vans and trucks pushed through the mud and rain, while one notably battered brown sedan continuously veered behind us. Long, wide, and surrounded by new marshes and heaps of trash that had collected since the storm, the road jagged up through the highlands and toward the three sister volcanoes, the Fuego, the Acatenango, and the Agua. Green hills bordered the road. Dinosaur-tall banana trees sprung out of the wet banks alongside ferns, mesquite trees, and periodic dazzles of red bougainvillea. On the hills, I saw the sienna and pastel stucco houses that industrious folks had built on tall, impressively sound stilts.

These homes, and the scatterings of shops visible along the way, had survived the most recent of the country's catastrophes, as they appeared here after the 1920s, when the U.S. Corps of Engineers began to lay down the tracks of this thoroughfare. The PAH—also known as the Carretera Interamericana or (as it is also called) the "Highway of Friendship"—had been approved in 1923 at the Fifth Conference of the Pan American States. At that historic meeting, ambassadors from the Americas had passed a resolution calling for the construction of one massive avenue that would stretch from Alaska to the tip of Tierra del Fuego in Argentina. Visionary and adrenaline-charged engineers soon began to blast their way through the wilderness. They pushed their tractors past the endangered jaguars and rare plants, ignoring the fearsome screams of the howler monkeys and the environmentalists, and carved the thin glossy road through the continent.

In Guatemala, this link of the highway hugs the lakes Atitlan and Amatitlan, much as had the routes of de la Cueva and Von Humboldt, who survived their droughty treks by sucking the dewdrops off the fronds of river-fed flora and hurling their shriveled hides into the aqueducts, when they were lucky enough to find them. Later came the tar and machinery, and infant, slippery suburbs sprouted among the hills. The road fed commerce, merchants, industrialists. And it had seen other, more desperate inhabitants, as well.

Sitting in the Jeep's passenger seat and watching the arrow of birds shoot farther down into the sky, I thought how four decades after that historic assembly of the Fifth Conference, when civil war was raging in the country, the Indian rebels had begun to bomb out pockets of the highway. After the disastrous U.S.-led or -aided coup of president Jacopo Arbenz, in 1954, rebels destroyed sections of the road with hand-made dynamite and other home-cooked explosives that they used to burn the cars of the crossing army. The soldiers then chased the insurgents up north, back into the Peten forest, where they shot them beneath the wet dripping leaves of the banana trees that shaded the moldering Mayan ruins. One hundred and forty thousand civilians died in the war, which spanned from the 1960s until a peace treaty was signed in 1996. And during each of those years archaeologists like my mother, Tomas de la Rosa, and (for a while) Manuel Alvarez had traveled the cracked avenues to reach the jungle, often crossing over patches scarred by crossfire or explosions.

"My parents became friends with de la Rosa on this road," I began to tell Erik. "In 1967, the year before I was born. They'd driven him back from the symposium on the Flores Stelae."

"In El Salvador, where de la Rosa surprised them with his paper on the hieroglyphs?"

"Yes. My mother later said that she couldn't drive along the highway without feeling sad—a few years later, she'd come back and saw that it had been bombed. She knew that bodies had been found here, too, after they'd been dumped by the military."

"The Disappeared. That kind of thing was sickeningly common during the war. The army murdered a lot of folks before the truce." He squinted into the daylight coming through the windshield. "And I don't know if the country's ever going to get over it."

I looked out the window and saw two bright chicken buses, several pickups, trucks loaded with shivering plants and strapped-down heaps of scrap metal. All the vehicles sprayed rainbows of floodwater. I again noticed that brown sedan driving at a steady speed about one mile behind us. The car was a large, four-door, later-model Toyota, dripping with rivulets of greasy mud. The license plate was dented and illegible. The muzzle of the car was striped with sludge that crawled up the hood in snaky forms. The spattered windshield had two fan-shaped clearings carved by wipers, but I could barely make out the driver. This person was obscured in shadow and wore some sort of a wide-brimmed hat; he or she looked cut out of black paper.

"Who's that?" I asked.

"What?" Erik swerved around something. "Just give me a minute. The road's difficult here."

As we drove farther along, we came into view of brown cliffs strung with green trees, and a light silver rain began to fall. Behind us remained the brown sedan. The dark driver's hands beat on the wheel in a particularly impatient and agitated manner, and then they reached up to squiggle off some fog that had collected on the windshield.

Watching this, I felt something nervous and electric pass through my chest. But Erik, not noticing anything, pushed on the gas and bent around the drive until we came into view of the volcano Agua.

"Now what were you talking about?" he asked.

I took another look behind me, but I still couldn't see the silhouetted figure in the sedan well enough to tell. And so, until I could be sure, I wouldn't say anything to Erik.

"Nothing," I said, looking up at the magnificent Agua before us, which was wreathed by blue and black clouds.

But inside I knew—I could feel—that the person following us in that car was Yolanda.

CHAPTER 19

I did not catch sight of any Stetson-wearing enemies when we first entered the Hotel Casa Santo Domingo, as so many other details caught my eye. My mother abhorred paying over fifty dollars for a room, so Erik and I had spent the past two days searching through colonial Antigua's budget motels before wandering into this graceful baroque resort. The Casa Santo Domingo, a rambling half-restored ruin of a seventeenth-century monastery, is a place of long, dark, shadowy stone hallways illuminated by beeswax candles. This network of chambers leads down into an actual catacomb, where the orderly tombs of the higher priests and the jumbled bones of the lesser friars have been excavated. Above, the monastery opens out into voluptuous atriums filled with violet hydrangeas and scarlet poppies, arrayed in still-perfect rows.

The staff had worked quickly to erase any signs of Hurricane Mitch—the toppled palm trees had been cleared, and one or two broken windows were even now being repaired. Moreover, there was no sign of a lack of business: when we arrived to talk to the concierge, a concert had just let out, a travel group had just arrived, and the foyer was filled with many elegant people.

We had been waiting for a word with the busy concierge for about an hour when I began to hallucinate Yolanda. Erik and I stood in line at the reception desk, surrounded by women dressed in tulip-tinted shifts and vertiginous heels. The men wore three-piece suits, with the corners of peacock handkerchiefs emerging from their pockets. Peering between these shimmering bodies, I thought I detected a flash of bright black hair, and heard a familiar laugh. I was sure I saw a figure stamping through the crowd with a gait that I recognized. But when I went searching through the throng, I saw no signs of anyone that I knew.

Before I became completely obsessed by the hope that Yolanda might be following us, my attention was distracted by the concierge.

She had an elfin face and coffee-colored eyes. She wore a dark green suit with a rectangular brass nameplate pinned to her chest. It read "Marisela."

"Juana Sanchez was here one week ago," she said, glancing at Erik and then back down at her computer.

Erik and I shot looks at each other.

"Finally!" I said.

"Did she leave a message?"

"I don't believe so—but please wait one moment while I check."

"That means we'll have to go to Flores next," I said to Erik.

"There is—something here," Marisela said. "A note on the computer about her stay."

"What does it say?" I asked, in a louder voice than I'd intended.

Her dark gaze fluttered over at me, then back again at Erik.

"Could you read us the note?" he asked.

"No, there's just an asterisk by her name," she said. "We usually mark a guest's file when they leave items behind, or if they do leave messages. I'll have to ask the manager. Though I don't have time at the moment. You see how busy we are. Perhaps you could wait in the bar."

I nodded. "All right."

"First thing we've found since we got here," Erik said to me.

"I just wish it had been *her,*" I said.

"Would you happen to know if they have any good champagne in that bar of yours?" he asked the concierge. "I think we're both feeling a little ragged right now."

Marisela assured him, with another mothlike flutter of eyelashes, that they did. Little else was needed to persuade him. He led the way, and I scrutinized the ladies around us as we made our way through the perfumed crowd. In the next few minutes we found ourselves in a very swanky saloon, attempting to relieve our anxiety with a good strong drink.

The bar was dark, fashioned from mahogany with rich gold and brass fittings. The light was almost a burgundy color, but a television hung above the counter, showing bright and distressing images of the ways that Mitch had ravaged the country's north and eastern areas. Up in the north, there were helicopters, people starving, and villages that had been swept away by the storm. Next we saw pictures of blue jade tumbling from a landslide in the Sierra de las Minas, which had been detected by resident gemologists in the days after Mitch. A Harvard Peabody scientist held a cobalt boulder in both hands, revealing its purple and gold veins, and the light glanced off the patterns in starlike rays. The television reporter said that the geologists studying the matter were still confused as to the exact source of the stone, though they expected there would be some breakthrough soon.

All these pictures together had the effect of making me feel sick.

"Could you turn the TV off?" I asked the bartender. Without looking up from the paper he was reading, he raised his hand and flicked the knob on the box so the screen went dead.

Erik squinted at the wagon wheel under the western-inspired glass tabletop. "I can't believe she stayed here. She usually prefers grubby little motels and yurts."

"I know."

"Not that I mind. The beds here are supposed to be fabulous. But a thread count over one hundred gives her gout."

"I have no idea what was going on with her."

After some minutes of mulling over this mystery, Erik shifted in his seat, so that the hieroglyphs on the decal of his T-shirt caught the chandelier's light, and my eye. I knew how to read hieroglyphs, though I was no expert. And I'd seen the images of the Stelae many times before because of my mother's work. But I thought I detected some pattern in the jade pictures there that seemed newly familiar. I saw images of sun gods and of holy men. My attention locked on these pictures for a moment, and I stared at the decal.

"Well," he said. "We should talk about something. If I'm just going to think about how we've missed your mother and about how a bunch of Harvard idiots are getting all the jade and glory while I sit here staring at wagon wheels, I'm going to lose my mind."

"How about this?" I brought my hand up and began to touch the icons on the shirt, pressing Erik's large and plush chest with my fingers. I think he liked it.

"What are you doing?"

"What *is* this?" I asked, pointing to the image of a male or female face in profile. "That's the symbol for jade?"

"Oh. Yes." He nodded. "That's it—that's good."

"I remember reading about this image in one of de la Cueva's letters to her sister Agata," I said. "She wrote about a lesson where Balaj K'waill taught her this hieroglyph. He was tutoring her in the Maya language, and said this was an important image in their language. Then she made this joke about how 'jade' in the European tongue had a double meaning. How it's a word for a bad woman."

"I've read that passage," Erik said. "In graduate school—it's famous. It's one of the first documents ever used to decipher Maya writing. Back in the 1800s decoders were already referencing it. And your mother used it, too—at Princeton. To help translate the Stelae."

"I don't think I knew that," I said.

Erik put his hands on the table and laced his fingers together. "That's how these things happen. Clues found here to be applied there. It's another form of detective work, decipherment. Which I used to be really interested in—I told you that already, didn't I? I mean the classic form of decipherment—the breaking of concealment codes, not of other languages like this."

"You told me a little bit about it. Not everything."

"I started out studying the Roman ciphers, but after a while I became interested in the Maya's language code. And I think I became an archaeologist on account of the Stelae—their hieroglyphs. The translation problem."

"Because of my parents' writings on it?"

"That's part of it. Like I said, I always thought that they—and de la Rosa—had gotten the translation wrong."

"Did you ever tell my mother that?"

"First time I met her—and you can imagine how well that went off." He laughed. "Actually, why don't we look at them? The Stelae. To pass the time. I have the paperback your dad gave us in my bag."

Erik began poking through his stuffed knapsack and pulled out a copy of my parents' book, which detailed the markings of the Flores Stelae.

"Again, the Stelae aren't in cipher. One or two scholars played around with that idea for a while, in the sixties, but they turned out to be wrong. Neither the Maya or the Olmec used puzzles of that kind, because logographic writing—hieroglyphs, of the sort used by the Maya and the Sumerians, and the Egyptians—just isn't flexible enough for ciphering. That's an invention of the Greeks and Romans, who used alphabets. Caesar used a device called a transposition code. And then there are the stream codes—complex riddly things. But all language is a kind of code, and so are the hieroglyphs of the Maya and the Olmec. No one could read them at all for centuries."

"Why were you so interested in ciphers?"

"One of my first papers was on Oscar Angel Tapia and his mirror writing—but I began working on those sorts of problems as a kid. Lewis Carroll's bizarre little puzzles. The cipher of Augustus. Morse code, Mary, Queen of Scot's puzzle-embroideries." He cocked his head. "Am I rattling on?"

"No. It's good to talk. And I love ciphers—when I was young, for me, it was the scarabs in *She-Who-Must-Be-Obeyed*."

"By Haggard?"

"Right. The Greek uncials that he starts that story with. Also, Poe's *Gold Bug*."

"Your mother probably got you started on stories like that."

"Probably so."

"My father introduced me. He was a mathematician. A widower. Spent his life untangling riddles like these. I picked it up after him."

"So, it's kind of similar to how I became interested in them. Because of my folks."

"Probably not as much as you think—nothing adventurous, really, in it."

He paused. I waited. He ate some of the Japanese mix the waiter had brought over, then said, "I was a bit of a solitary kid. Nothing like the heroic and very muscular Casanova that you see before you today. Do please take that look off your face, you maddening feminist, because I am only joking. What I mean is that I was this awfully fat little child prodigy, very emotional and brainy and lonely, and once my father told me that one day I'd crack the riddle of my loneliness—that's how he put it. He said that—the heart was like a puzzle. You just need to put it together. I didn't happen to know that he was talking to me in metaphor, so I took his advice very thick-wittedly and literally. I began reading all his books on cipher, and by the time I was twelve I was studying Lacedaemonian military code instead of going to those sweaty school dances. Which turned out to be exactly the wrong move, as far as girls were concerned. Didn't get much in the way of dates until I was almost twenty, and we moved here."

"I can barely believe that."

"Yes, ha. Funny what growing a foot will do. Getting away from the war probably didn't hurt, either." He drank some more wine and slipped his eyes over at me. "Though I'm happy enough about all that now because being such a mole meant I was able to spend all my time with my dad when I was a kid. I didn't really meet someone else that I could work on ciphers with until I met Dr. Sanchez." He took another sip, then hunched his shoulders up around his ears. His mouth drooped. "How did we get on this subject? Oh—codes. Codes."

"Erik, I want to thank you again for coming with me." Huge unexpected feelings of friendship began swelling in my chest, and I had to flick my fingers around my eyes as if I were batting off invisible midges. "I want to thank you very much."

He tucked his chin down. "Yes. Well. You're welcome. Your mother—you know—she's a pain in my neck. But I don't mind her that much. I'm happy to have come."

I stared at him. "You really came here for her, didn't you?"

"What?"

"For her. Not for jade."

"Oh, let's not get into that now."

"You did—you did. You came here because you really care about her."

He paused, then: "It *might* have been one of my reasons."

"The others being?"

Erik met my eyes and smiled. "I thought we were reading this book."

"Were we?"

"Yes, so come on."

"Erik."

"Concentrate."

"All right."

While we waited for the concierge, we flattened out the paperback on the table and examined the translation my parents had written.

"This really is a beautiful edition," Erik was saying.

I looked down and touched the glossy paper of the *Translation*'s new printing, then studied a fragment of the Flores Stelae's first panel:

> *The of story the Jade once was I king Jade*
> *You without lost I'm too lost I'm too lost*
> *Fierce king true a jade under born noble and jade*
> *I'm you lost I you lost I warm stay will*
> *The of sign the jade possessed I serpent feathered Jade*

"This is so strange," I said. "You do feel as if you might be able to read it . . . wouldn't it be interesting if it were a code, like you were talking about?"

"Sorry? I wasn't paying attention."

"That the Stelae really were written in code. You said the Olmec and Maya didn't use them. Puzzles and ciphers."

He turned another page. "That's right. The Greeks and Romans did. In alphabet languages."

"Wouldn't it be amazing if the reason no one could read the Stelae was that they *were* ciphered?"

Now he glanced up at me. "What?"

I repeated what I said.

He looked back down at the book and blinked.

"But I told you already. The Maya didn't use ciphers."

"I'm just saying, what if they did? Wouldn't it be amazing?"

He blinked again, still staring at the book.

Yes," he said after a few seconds.

"Hello? Madam? Sir?"

Suddenly the silky-haired concierge had come into the room. She said that she had a free moment and could speak to us.

We rose to follow her. As I hastened out of the bar, I could tell by the way that Erik rolled his eyes that he was still pondering something. But my focus grew clear and narrow. I became so consumed with the possible news about my mother that the Stelae and their translation were immediately removed from my thoughts.

CHAPTER 20

Marisela, the attractive concierge, told us that not only had my mother stayed at the Casa Santo Domingo the week before, but she had also left a small duffel bag behind. Should we be able to prove our relation to her, through documents or some other source, then we would be able, she said, to take this bag and give it back to Professor Juana Sanchez, as she had given the hotel no indication of where it should be sent.

"You see, we are not a storage facility," Marisela said. "The bag is very safe here, in our storage room, but we will have to mail it back soon if it is not reclaimed. Or throw it away."

Marisela smiled as she said this, so as to remove any possible hostile interpretation that her words might be given. And indeed, I think that they were not so interpreted by the soul to whom they were directed. Though this person did not happen to be me, even as I was the person who promptly offered up handfuls of papers and wallet-sized photographs that would verify my familial link to Professor Juana Sanchez. Marisela, because of the fact that Erik and I had arranged to take two separate, though communicating, rooms at the Casa Santo Domingo, had come to the conclusion that I was some sort of spinsterish sister or cousin. She thus felt quite free to flirt with Erik in a very subtle and professional fashion, mostly through her eyes and her puckered lip and the exquisitely suggestive modulations in her voice. After some minutes of this she also, through a quick maneuver, slipped a piece of paper that I saw bore her own personal telephone number into his pants pocket. My reaction to this was not to be threatened—as I explained to myself, of course I would not be threatened, as Erik Gomara could never in this lifetime be a firefighter and would never be any kind of policeman. I told myself that my only real problem with this scene (besides the fact that I was itching to get hold of that bag) was that I had been resigned to the spinsterish-sister role, and so was beginning to feel something like the Mexican-American version of the governesses and secretaries the actress Maggie Smith occasionally plays in Agatha Christie book-to-film masterpieces.

Erik did not respond to the comely and aggressive Marisela much. Rather, all of his previous vulnerability, his gentleness when he spoke about his father, his bafflement over the Stelae, his boyish vulnerability and chattiness, all of this vanished when he now turned to me, saw the expression on my face, and began to smile in this very wicked and happy way at what he apparently mistakenly regarded as my jealousy.

"Ha!" he said.

But I just frowned at him, took a good firm hold of Marisela, and said that he could look after the rooms while we two girls frisked down below and got hold of my mother's bag.

I liked Marisela much better after she had led me down to the storage room of the Casa Santo Domingo, adjacent to the preserved catacombs and the ossarium. We walked down cold steps toward hallways carved of stone that glowed copper and gold as it took on the color of the candlelight billowing from the brass votives strung along the corridors. The lower sanctums of the monastery were no ordinary administrative area. They still have their medieval bones, both architectural and human, with beautiful low stone doors and chilled flag floors, and the shadows that moved across the walls evoked the ghosts of the monks buried here five hundred years before.

Marisela unlocked a door with a set of iron keys; it opened into a room filled with cardboard boxes and sacks of stuff, items lost and found, and a supply of candles and canned food. The space was lit by fluorescent cylinders running across the curved ceiling. She stood in the door and waited patiently while I searched through the bags until I found the one belonging to my mother. It was the buff-colored vinyl Hartmann duffel bag that I had watched a driver throw into her taxi cab's trunk only a week and a half before.

I crouched in front of the bag and zipped the duffel open. My heart began galloping in my chest. In the bag, wrapped in clear plastic, I found clothes, a hairbrush, toiletries. And underneath all that I also discovered a small salmon-colored book, hinged with a shiny brass lock, which I recognized immediately as the diary I'd seen my mother pack just before she'd left. As long as I'd remembered, my mother had always bought the same kind of journal, with this pinkish binding, and when work put her in a bad temper she'd ram her pen into its pages as if she were assassinating some torpid and loathsome animal. Then she'd lock it with its tin key.

I rummaged around, but there was no key in the bag.

"Yes, that's it," I said to Marisela. "Thank you."

"Anything else I can help you with?"

"No."

"Should I lead you out?"

"I can find my way. Though it would be nice if you could tell my friend I'll be up soon."

"Your—friend?"

"Yes. My *friend*. My very very good friend."

Her eyes widened slightly as her cerebral cortex painfully expanded with the idea that I was not quite the virginal sister she had imagined, and then she whisked off and left me down below. Standing there with the bag clutched to my body, I heard a smattering sound, a scattering wet noise, which meant that it had just begun to rain again.

I began to walk around, hoping that a little ramble through the catacombs would help calm me down.

The catacombs of the Dominicans were composed of small hollow cells, where archaeologists years back had excavated the bones of the monks who once lived in this monastery. It is one of the most astonishing features of the Casa Santo Domingo that a person may simply wander about the lower regions of the hotel, enter the excavated rooms, and see these ancient graves and bones. The rooms are lit with subtle electric lights and miniature torches. Some of the biers are marked with bilingual explanatory plates, and many are not. These uncovered graves are so small, and wedged into such tiny cavelike hollows, that they bring to mind the cave burial sites of the ancient Maya, who buried their dead in similar holy caverns. Many of these, like the tombs of the monks, have not proven extraordinarily hard to excavate in the rare cases they have been found at all. Some solitary archaeologists, or those working in twos and threes, have come across such tombs in the jungle, though the monks are buried with crosses and the Maya with their heads pointed east.

I wandered back into the darkling corridor. The torches' golds and opals burnished the monastery walls.

A murky figure emerged from the shadows, passing into the firelight.

I heard a rustle, the stamping of heels. She appeared from one of the cells. Her Stetson was tilted back on her head, and her dark hair fell against her shoulders.

I began to shiver with the same old delicious panic I felt when I was a girl and she'd jumped at me, dressed like a monster, then put me in one of her choke holds.

"Hello, Lola," Yolanda said, in a conversational tone, then in two swift steps she stood behind me and wrapped her arms around my neck and shoulders. "Let's see if I've still got the touch." She squeezed me. "Yes, it all comes back now." She squeezed again.

I struggled once to try to wrench those arms off, but I couldn't.

"You're being ridiculous," I said in Spanish, and pulled on her roughly. Then I stopped. "You're scaring the life out of me. What are you doing?"

"Paying you a visit."

"You didn't seem much interested in that before. In the city."

"You said something very intriguing right before you left. So I decided to drop in on you."

"I thought you might."

"I'll bet you did."

"Why have you been slinking around the hotel, then?"

"I preferred to see *you* before you saw *me*. I wasn't even sure that I could stand the thought of listening to your babbling—but then I realized that I had no other choice."

"Don't lie. You're here because you want to talk to me."

"You'd like to believe that, wouldn't you? The truth is, I don't care if I ever see you again."

"I don't believe that."

"Why should I? You're not my family."

She labored to cover up the emotion in her voice; her arms twined around my chest a little harder.

"From the looks of things, I'm the closest thing you have," I said.

"That's just an insult to my father—and you know I can't have that. He'd never have left me dangling the way you and your mother did, all these years."

"That's not—"

"And that's because you forgot me, Lola. You *forgot me*. Though then you conveniently remembered."

"Your father—" I started.

She squeezed me again. "What about him?"

"Okay—for one thing? He almost killed my dad. He *hurt* him! Which is why we haven't talked in fifteen years. And for another, he *wanted* you to live with us. It wasn't him taking care of you when you were a kid—that was Mom. And I know there was a part of you that liked it."

I heard her swallow. "Why talk about ancient history, anyway? I'm not here for that. *Where is it?*"

"The map?"

"Don't play with me."

"Hidden."

She began to jostle me. "Well then, why don't you just take it out of its hiding place and show it to me, because you know I need to see it."

"Come with us, and I will."

"Come with you and help you look for your mother, you mean."

"She went up to Flores—that's where we're going tomorrow. You help me, and I'll give you that map Mom was using." I stuttered, only for a second. "I swear."

"Lying to me would be *such* the mistake," she said in English.

I thought to myself that even if I didn't have any sort of specific detailed map to give her, I did have de la Cueva's sketched chart. But the fewer details I gave her, the better. I mumbled something incoherent and made a gesture with my hand.

"And as for your mother," Yolanda went on, "I already know she's not here. All I had to do was look around for half an hour to figure that out."

As she talked, Yolanda maintained her old choke hold on me, which was just as much an embrace as it was any kind of attack. She put her chin on my shoulder.

"And by the way, I did see that you're still with that chatty big-boned boy."

"Yes."

"I'm sorry to say I'm not surprised your tastes have run to paunchy teachers."

"Paunch can have its charm," I said, shocking myself.

"Yes," she laughed, pretending to give me the Heimlich but actually more smash-hugging me. "It is very charming on you."

She smashed me some more, and for a second neither of us said anything.

Then I said: "Yolanda, I didn't forget you."

"Oh, no?"

I put my cheek on her bicep. "How could I?"

She knocked our heads together with a gentle *cloc*. "Actually, I'll bet you didn't. I'll bet you still have the odd nightmare about how I used to beat the feathers out of you. Because I really did let you have it—didn't I? Remember that time—remember that time when I dressed up—"

"Like some crazy Indian, and you talked in that scary voice—"

"And you *screamed*—you just lifted your hands up and shrieked so I nearly went deaf, and all I had to do was push you with my little finger and down you went tumbling. Something like *this*."

She slipped off her shoes.

"What are you doing?"

"I wonder if I'm too old for this now," she said.

"What do you mean?"

"I wonder if I can still give you a good whipping," she said.

She began to wrestle me.

In the gold and black of that corridor, now busy with our antic shadows, Yolanda's quick hard arms clung and slipped and twisted me into all sorts of shapes whose one constant was that they ensured I was at her mercy. Half-guffawing and half-swearing, with one or two sobs breaking into our din, we cursed and sweated as we began grappling with each other. I bent down quickly and heard her hack out a breath, then I tossed my mother's bag on the floor so I could tear myself away from her. But her forearms only squeezed tighter against my chest and slid up toward my throat.

With one big heave the two of us fell onto the floor, feet kicking. She wangled her arms around my waist and brought me down, sitting on me. She let me wrench about until I scrabbled out from under her.

"*Get—off—me!*" I blathered.

"Come on, *that's* not wrestling. You're not trying hard enough."

Some multisyllabic profanities were exchanged here as she insulted my posterior, my clothes, my taste in men, my brain capacity, so that we were laughing and weeping as we simultaneously tried to bash at each other.

Yolanda lifted me up by the waist and began jumping up and down before her eyes caught the bag I had tossed on the floor. She let me go and stooped to pick it up. But I grabbed my mother's duffel and pushed her, roughly.

She fell, hard, onto her side. When she looked at me through her hair, I saw that her lips were quivering. She gripped her left wrist, which was scraped somewhat badly.

I had never hurt Yolanda before.

"Yes, I'm too old for that now," she said after a few seconds. Even her voice sounded scratched and damaged.

"Yolanda—"

"Don't."

"I just—"

"There's just nothing that you can say," she said, still looking at me from under that curtain of hair. "Though—you're right. He wasn't the best father. And I did like living with you. Though none of that matters to me now that I can't see him again. I didn't even get to go to his funeral. I don't even know where he's buried!" She rubbed the injured part of her arm. "And even if you are not my friend anymore, I hope that you do find your mother. Because I don't want anyone to feel like I feel. Even you—I don't want you to know what it feels like to really be alone."

In that light Yolanda's face was starved, terrible. Her lips continued shaking, and a vein streaked her forehead. I thought about telling her again to stay with us, and come to Flores.

But she stood up, picked up her shoes, and walked back down the corridor until I couldn't see her anymore, though I could hear the echoes of her hard breathing for a few seconds after she'd disappeared.

I stayed on the ground and rubbed the sore spot on my leg as the rain began to dash harder against the shell of the monastery.

I put my hand to my eyes. I had heard in that splitting voice of hers how angry she was. And even though I wanted to shake her for being a stubborn ass, I knew well enough that she had a good reason for it, too.

The light ebbed in the hall, the candles disturbed by a wind that had sneaked inside.

It took some time before I was able to get back up.

CHAPTER 21

Once back in my suite at the Casa Santo Domingo, I called my father to tell him where Erik and I were, and also explained that we were probably going to have to venture up to Flores in the morning. After he gave the name of a hotel there, we hung up. Then I staggered to Erik's room. His quarters, like mine—visible through the open and communicating doors—were in a gorgeous cavernlike space, spare as cloisters are, with antique brass fittings on the walls. There was an upholstered sofa, as well, and in the hallway a small oak bureau.

So as not to completely bias him against Yolanda (should she yet agree to guide us), I gave him a severely redacted description of our encounter, which was still sufficiently stimulating that he became quite upset. I also surprised myself by not describing the full contents of my mother's precious bag. This duffel was the only physical and textual link I had to her, and so I had filled it earlier with everything I had brought with me that was fragile and crucial, like my de la Cueva materials and my Fodor's maps. Now it sat next to the oak bureau, where I could keep my eye on it. If I had explained to Erik what I'd found in the Hartmann, I worried that he'd recommend we read Mom's diary together, so as to learn where exactly she had gone. But a secreted diary usually doesn't get rifled through by the likes of Yolanda or Erik or me until its writer dies. And I wasn't prepared to deal with that possibility.

So I wound up, in the end, telling him very little of what had just happened.

Nevertheless, he could tell that I wasn't feeling that fabulous.

"Sit down, sit down," he said. "You just relax. I've already ordered food—Armagnac . . . bread . . . those tasty little olives . . . two plates of rabbit in mustard sauce. It'll be coming up any minute."

I had showered and changed back into my sweats, and so had he. He sat next to me on the sofa, and we watched the sparkling fire very comfortably, though both of us were busy with our thoughts and did not speak for a few minutes.

"Maybe we should watch TV?" he asked, flicking on the contraption.

The dark screen lit up. On it appeared the smashed houses, flooded plains; army rescue helicopters dispatched to the remoter northern regions of the Motagua Valley, and by an area called Rio Dulce. Up high on the plateaus above the cracked banks of rivers were tarp-covered settlements of the new homeless, and here were some raw new graves. We even saw pictures, taken several days before, of terrified women and men and dogs and cats stranded on the roofs of their homes, surrounded by green rising water that flooded into the area my mother had planned on trekking into.

"Oh, Jesus God," I said.

Erik flicked the television off and glowered down at his knees until another thought occurred to him. He snapped his fingers. "I know what to do."

"What?"

"I know just what'll fix you up. Or me up, at least."

As he walked to his closet to fetch something, a knock came at the door and a short maid came stamping in, bearing the platter of mustard rabbit and Armagnac. The maid looked as if she were about forty years old and had a mass of shaggy black hair flying around her face. Her bent and wide-hipped frame was clothed in a blue uniform with white piping.

"Good evening, señor," I heard her say, while I closed my eyes and fended off the afterimages of the destroyed homes and floods. She shuffled around for a bit and clattered the plates on the bureau, with her back turned to us, though we could hear her muttering complaints about her feet. She had an oddly masculine and wheezy voice.

"Wouldn't that be better on the coffee table?" Erik asked.

The crone only glanced at him over her shoulder and grouched some more, then resumed rattling the crockery and in general making a nuisance of herself.

Erik shrugged and made his way over to his closet, where he dug out that stuffed knapsack of his. Crouching down to rummage through it, he extracted a squat, blocky book bound in red, a black-and-white decal from the UCLA library adhered to its spine.

"Ahh—the *Narrative!*" I said. "The purloined Von Humboldt. I was wondering if you might have that book in there."

"You said you wanted to see it, and here it is."

"You're such a thief—you said your research assistant had it."

"Yes. Sorry. Lied. I couldn't let just anybody take my Von Humboldt."

"And now?"

"And now—now—it's fairly appropriate reading, considering we're heading north," he said. "Your mother's read and practically memorized the same material, as I should know well enough from all those savage edits she gave me on my book. And those jade stones that they were showing on the television earlier—Von Humboldt wrote on similar stones when he described his Guatemalan travels, so we might want to look them up. And besides, you've been reading to me such awful things about de la Cueva and spinning such outlandish theories about the Stelae that are still twanging on my nerves that I'd like just to get back to some familiar territory, or I'll never get to sleep. I'm tired of all those deranged Spaniards. I'd much prefer to spend my evening with a nice, romantic, weirdly fearless German. Wouldn't you?"

I took one more look over at my mother's duffel bag, which sat in a lump by the maid's sneaker-shod feet. Then I thought about Yolanda's face again, sad and harsh in the stone halls. But Erik was paging through the red book, finding the right place, and began to read to me with relish and much feeling.

The maid dropped a spoon, and with a great deal more cursing and complaining, she bent to whisk it up before she gathered her trays together, stamped out of the suite, and banged shut the door.

I leaned back and listened to Erik's voice telling me Von Humboldt's story, reassuring myself that Yolanda and the diary could wait.

"You see, Von Humboldt thought the Jade was a giant magnet, and he hired six Indian guides to help him find it, as well as a slave named Gomez, who was some kind of genius expert on the Stone," he said. "Von Humboldt, for his part, thought that the Stone would have great scientific uses. But he almost died in the process—the Indians weren't very amenable to the idea of Germans and Frenchmen tracking around their jungles. Still, I actually think that he was less interested in magnets or precious gems than simply going on an adventure with Aimé Bonpland—his closest friend."

"Sounds like more than a friend."

"Von Humboldt was in love with him."

"And Bonpland?"

"I think he'd have to be in love with Von Humboldt to go racing through the jungles after him, wouldn't he?"

"Well, if we don't find Mom here, you just might be racing through the jungles with me—"

"Don't interrupt. So both of them had this amazing curiosity in common—they went all over the Americas studying the fauna and the geology. Their search for the Queen Jade—that was in 1801—was probably their least successful expedition, on account of the jaguars and the poisonous snakes and the peevish Indians. But it makes for good reading."

Erik and I spent the next hour leafing through Von Humboldt's diary, focusing our attention on the chapter where he claims to have stumbled across the same Maze of Deceit described by de la Cueva two and a half centuries before.

"They were on the trail of the second labyrinth, the Maze of Virtue, when they ran into a little trouble," Erik went on. "Von Humboldt believed he was very close to finding the stone . . . but he didn't want to risk Bonpland's life. Start here. *This* is where they find the first maze."

"*Dear Alexander*," *Aimé Bonpland said, when we reached the first threshold across the river Sacluc.* "*We must be very careful. This is a most magnificent find, but the Indians are beginning to exhibit a rather bad temper.*"

"*Never mind them,*" *I blurted out.* "*Look at this prodigy!*"

For the Labyrinth of Deceit was, indeed, an architectural marvel of the first water. A colossally winding temple made of the most perfect blue jade, and once entered, seemingly endless, this maze proved the most astonishing of any discovery we had yet made. And also the most dangerous. We might enter one of the sapphire passages, grow confused by its signs, and become so baffled by its convoluted express that we could not take a single step forward. Once having braved this foray into the maze, however, we could discover ourselves not at the other end of the puzzle, but instead mired in a dangerous terrain of jaguars or floods or sinking marshes, from which we would never return.

Such hazards, then, were ours in the wood, as we, with our six Indians and mulatto navigator, stood before the Maze. And so it was well within our luck that when we traveled forward and gazed upon the worked rock, this Gomez, our friendly guide, attempted to explain to us some barbaric formula of the puzzle's markings, based upon some combination of the "number zero" (so he said), and which did not make much in the way of sense. Better still, he mentioned in his next breath the nearby presence of an even more practical artifact than this labyrinth—that same masterful and Magnetic Queen Jade sought by the once and great Governor de la Cueva.

"*I am only leading you on this path because you are a scholar like myself—yes, believe it—I, too, have a scientific inclination, which has been fed by my slave owner's library,*" *said our Gomez as he led us through the wood.* "*It is a rare thing for me to talk so candidly with a white man as yourself, but because we two are brethren in the Science, I must show you that I, the Great Gomez, have discovered the little plot of these Heathen. I believe that the Stone is up here, Señor Von Humboldt, through this passage of the Deceitful Labyrinth, and then past a second maze.*"

He paused for a moment to point out the correct directions. And this was much to the apparent distaste of his colleagues, who began to speak to him in a brutal-sounding tongue.

"Alexander," Aimé said. "We must be careful. I no longer know where we are going."

Yet I tugged my friend along the Maze's rough path, and we continued wandering until I too realized, with a shock to the nerves, that we had become quite lost.

All about us were what appeared to be an everlasting chain of identical shrubs, trees, bosks, heaths, fens, and quagmires, and this change in our conditions seemed aptly described by our Gomez when he began singing a curious tune:

> I lost you
> I lost you
> I'm lost too,
> my darling

"I told you!" Aimé Bonpland whispered, holding on to my hand.

"Do not worry, we are not lost, as I am making a joke," Gomez said. "According to my calculations, we must only follow the Dwarf."

"What?" I asked him.

"The Dwarf. Can you not understand good Spanish?"

I replied that I could, although it became evident almost immediately that I was not the sole man who had some skill with languages, for the Indians once more abused Gomez, clearly enough voicing their distaste at this important disclosure. Yet their protests came too late, for Gomez had led us to the place he had promised.

A tall, crumbled, fantastic blue city rose before our eyes, all spires and turrets, with great devastated keeps and eroded ramparts, even as it now sank into the muds and soughs.

"The kingdom of stone!" Aimé Bonpland cried, as the Indians continued their dark cursing. "The prison of the Witch, and the *house of the jealous King. Just as de la Cueva wrote. You have done it, Alexander!"*

I discerned a glint in Aimé's eye—in the past hour he had become the more reckless of our pair, for I found myself less fascinated by the jade kingdom than the glowering of the savages.

"That's all quite wonderful," I said, "but perhaps we should be going now."

"We are so close—we should brave death to discover the great Jade!" he shouted at me, flailing his arms about in excitement. "We need now find the dragon tree, then solve the Maze of Virtue, and then the Treasure will be ours!"

The Indians began emitting certain bird-like whistles, and queer calls, and a horde of primitives all at once emerged like a hallucination from the bush with their rude weapons drawn, to deter us from further investigation into their sacred jungle. Thereafter we were greeted with a volley of arrows, one of which found its way into the torso of our Gomez, who briskly died.

"I think not," I said, then grabbed Aimé Bonpland by the arm and forced him to make a swift exit from that particular patch of the forest.

Though my companion was much disappointed in our failure to secure the Stone, I did not share his discontent. As we dashed past deadly snakes and man-eating swamps, and heard the fell sound of murderous Savages racing behind us, I reminded him that he might have shared the fate of our good Gomez. That he did not was my best fortune.

Those Readers who possess an agile heart will know what I mean.

Erik stopped reading the *Narrative*. He had read the entire chapter while I lay on the sofa, quietly listening. We had already drained the last of the Armagnac; the candles flickered and shed their light. The fire crackled and burned blue and diamond colors in the hearth.

"That last sentence is why I love Von Humboldt so much," Erik said, and looked at me.

I looked back at him, too. Our eyes held.

To my great consternation, a queer and violent blush began to spread through my body, and despite nearly thirty years of intensive training in English, Spanish, Latin, Italian, and a bit of the German language, I found myself at an utter loss for words. I opened my mouth, closed it; I attempted to compose myself, but a wild erotic demon seemed to be controlling my limbs so that I very nearly swooned into the warm and capacious lap of the infamous Erik Gomara.

And then our dignities, such as they were, were saved. For my hot and irrational glance was diverted by an unnerving sight. Perhaps on account of some atavistic modesty, I had turned my cheek away from Erik, so that I looked over at the oak bureau by the communicating doors. I glanced down at the carpeted floor beneath this bureau, where I had, an hour before, placed the Hartmann duffel bag containing Mom's diary and my maps and papers. This is where, also, that noisy maid with the stamping gait had been clattering around with our dinner plates.

My mother's bag was gone.

CHAPTER 22

S low down, Lola, slow the hell down," Erik said, looking up
from the pages spread out on his lap. He was trying to write on
them by the illumination of a small flashlight, as it was still
dark out.

It was five in the morning, and we were in the Jeep, on the Carretera al Atlántico, about seventy miles north of Guatemala City. A
heavy rain slowed our progress as we chased Yolanda down through
the Motagua Valley of central Guatemala. We hadn't come across
her, yet.

"You're going to get us into an accident," he went on. "I've been on
this road plenty of times before—in far better conditions than these—
and even then it wasn't safe. There are potholes, gaps in the road.
When I was about twenty years old, I drove the Atlantico when it
wasn't even flooded and almost broke my neck. And you don't even
know if you're right. Maybe you lost the bag somewhere else, maybe
that really was just a maid. Yolanda might not even be here. And we
have to seriously consider if we want to find her in the first place."

"*I know that was her!*" I howled. "My God, I can't believe I fell for
that bad wig. And she *took* it—the bag—and she's bringing it up here.
She's got all our maps!"

"And your mother's journal," he said. Though I hadn't wanted to
mention anything about that book back at the hotel, once I realized

that the duffel had been stolen, I broke like a dam. I'd told him everything about the diary.

"And my mother's journal." I pushed the Jeep through water and the
shadows. "Yolanda thinks she'll find the stone, and that's up north.
That's the best guess that I have about where she's run off to. So that's
where we have to go."

The Carretera al Atlántico, known in English as the Atlantic Highway, stretched before us in our headlights. It peeled off from the Highway of Friendship after Guatemala City, where it would continue to
push north through the Motagua basin and dip down toward a town
called El Rancho and Rio Hondo, until it connected up with another
road that leads to the Peten and Flores. We had been driving for more
than four hours, taking turns at napping, and navigating the Jeep
through onyx water and floating branches and wedges of trash that
Mitch had hurtled from eastern villages down to the drain of the valley. Our headlights glittered over the flooded parts of the route, and
when gusts of wind parted the showers, the unexpected starlight
transformed the rain into sequins and the mountains into bronze and
silver. Mud slid from the surrounding banks before us and into our
wake. Deep ditches along the road were filled with rainwater and more
mud. Other vehicles occasionally skidded past us, despite the insane
conditions, though these were mostly huge olive-colored army trucks;
we had learned from the news already that the military were making
their way from the city to the Peten region to bring panicked evacuees
armed order, food, and building supplies for the emergency encamp-
ments.

I glared out into the woolly air and still didn't see a sign of that
blasted Yolanda. I pressed my foot on the gas to speed our chase, but
this was not a good idea, for I almost immediately heard a churning.
The Jeep shuddered and slid to the left. Erik and I jerked in our seats,
and his flashlight spattered light into my eyes. I coughed and righted
the car again.

"Damn," I said. "Sorry."

He bent down to get the pen that had fallen to his feet. "I'm telling
you, you're going to get us killed."

"*What* are you writing?"

"I thought I'd take a look at what we were talking about before. I'm—working on the Stelae."

"The Stelae?"

"To see if it's encoded, like you were saying. It's a very interesting idea, and I was just thinking, what if you're right? What if it is a real code? Not an obscure language. Not wallpaper. A cipher."

I had to fix my eyes back on the road. "That was just an idea. I think we've got more important things to think of right now. Like this high—medium—speed chase."

"No—listen, like I've told you, there's no evidence of the Maya ever using ciphers, but what if they did? I mean—the Stelae read so strangely, it might just be because they've been scrambled. Maybe they're not supposed to be read, except by certain people. I've been trying to think of any kind of formula that might work, testing out a few lines in my head while I was driving. But I think I'd need a computer— and years, probably—not just a piece of paper and a pen. There's no reference point, I don't even know where to start. The only codes I could think of were European, Middle Eastern. Just for practice, I've been trying the Caesarian transposition code—the one that Caesar used in the Gallic wars, where he shifted every character up five times. I've tried stream codes, a more complex version based on Caesar's, and I also gave a shot at *atbash*—I heard once of an ancient Roman practice, where no ciphers were used at all, but the real meaning of a message would be written on the shaved heads of servants, whose hair would later be allowed to grow in. Then they'd travel through enemy territory to their general or king, and shave their heads again so the words would be revealed. I'd shave my head right now if it would do any good. I just feel as if a light had been turned on in my brain when you said that—and then everything went dark again."

The Jeep slid to the left a second time, and the tires grazed a rough patch that bordered those grisly ditches. I pressed toward the right and tried not to speed too much, though I was happy to notice that the starlight was just beginning to fade in favor of the slightest suggestion of gray dawn.

"It could be a substitution code," Erik went on. He didn't appear to have noticed that we had nearly gone rocketing into that ditch. "Or it could be an *ephor*—the Spartans used those. It's where you write a cipher on a strip of paper that has to be wrapped, in the Spartans' case, around a staff of specific dimensions; without that you had nothing but gibberish. Perhaps the text needs to be written out in some similar way, a paper of a particular size, or wrapped round. Or it could be a transposition code, after all. Just not like Caesar's."

"What is that, exactly?" I asked, only half concentrating on what he was saying. "Is it where you arrange words in a block? And then scramble them?"

"Yes. You transpose them in a numerical order. The Romans used that. As did the Greeks. That one's found all over the ancient world— so if you had, I don't know, six, one, five, two, four, three, and the letters S-G-T-H-S-O, that would spell *Ghosts*."

"I'm not really a math person," I said, distractedly.

"But I tried out a few versions of it, and no go. So then I tried out this version of a stream code developed in the 1500s by this man named Blaise de Vigenere. He'd shift up the letters according to a pre-arranged random order, and the trick was, you didn't have to remember the order at all. You just had to remember a word. Say, if the order was: the first letter shifts by five, and the second by fourteen, then the next by twenty-three, and the fourth by four, and the fifth by eighteen—this is the famous example—you wouldn't have to remember that at all. You'd just have to know the word *foxes*, because that's what *aaaaa* translates into under that scheme."

"You're getting a little ahead of yourself, I think," I said. "You're applying the principles of sixteenth-century cryptography to a pre-Christian text."

"It's just that I can't think of anything else *to* apply. It's like what Tapia wrote in his journal, about the first time he saw the panels—'this book has no rhyme nor meaning that I can discern, and perhaps can be read not by any living man at all, but only by those who have long been dead, and busy themselves now with the dark and busy translations of Hell.' "

"Not too cheerful," I said. But at this point I had more or less stopped paying attention.

Ahead of us, a flickering light ornamented the black air. It veered behind the curtain of rain.

It was just a tiny blur of red in the thinning dark, like a flame. And then, as I hurled closer, the blur separated into two trembling disks.

Those were the taillights of a car.

CHAPTER 23

L ola?"

"What?" I was spying out the windshield but had no idea what kind of car we might be trailing.

"Are you listening to me?"

"Yes, yes. Or, no. Sorry. What were you saying?"

Erik shuffled the papers on his lap and tried to smooth them out with his hands.

"I was telling you about Tapia. And his ideas about the Stelae."

Keeping my eyes on those tiny blurred stars of light, I maneuvered past a fallen branch, then asked, "Where did Tapia find the panels again? It wasn't Flores, if I'm remembering. It was in the forest, somewhere. Around water."

He looked down again at his notes. "Codes—codes—codes. If this is encoded, what would they want to encrypt?"

"I don't know, but I was asking you—about the panels?"

"Oh, yes—he found them in the forest, the southern edge of it, before it clears and ascends into the plateau. I told you this, remember. They were originally right by a waterway—a river. The river Sacluc. Where we might be going, actually. It's miles long, and a lot of relics have been excavated there. Here—I'll show you."

He began sketching out a map for me on a piece of paper, but the rain battered the Jeep's rubber windows, and I had to work at evading yet more branches in the highway, as well as some deeper flooding. The wind rushed toward us harder, and the growing dawn revealed that mud oozed out in larger doses onto the highway from the surrounding hills.

Some of these banks did not look altogether steady, as they were slough-ing large chunks of themselves onto the pavement. The taillights skit-tered and jumped about a mile or two ahead. When the gloaming lightened further, I could make out that the car was long and low, though I could not tell what color or make it might be. I narrowed my eyes at it.

"Could that be her?" I asked.

Erik looked up from his notes and drawings. "What?"

"Is that *her?*"

"Oh, look at that. Well. I can't see anything from here—I don't know." He squinted too. "Maybe. But—no, stop that—don't speed up."

I continued driving in an involuntary serpentine route over the slick road; the car before us veered slightly and righted itself in the mud. The rain pounded down. Several minutes passed, and then I re-alized I had to push the speed slightly higher than was advisable to make sure that was Yolanda's car. While I edged forward over my steer-ing wheel, Erik finished his map and waved it in the air.

"This is it, this is where Tapia found the Stelae," he said.

I glanced over to see what he'd drawn:

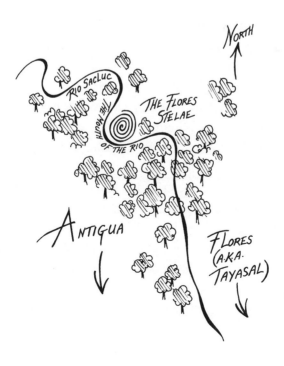

I looked down at this chart, then back at the road, and at the car. Then I looked at his sketch again.

And this is where I began to understand.

"I've seen that map before," I said. "Tapia wasn't the only one who explored there."

"That's true," he said. "Like I was saying before, a lot of people have found relics here. Even Von Humboldt traveled along the Sacluc for a while."

"No, listen. De la Cueva made a map *just like it* for her sister, Agata. When she was in the forest looking for the Jade. And that's Von Humboldt's trail too? So they were all in the same place as Tapia, right?"

Just as I was saying this, and making all the deductive correlations, I realized that this wasn't really the best time to discuss it. I had just come into complete view of the long brown car, and saw the outline of a cowboy hat within its cab. A massive jolt of adrenaline thrashed through my body and sent its electric impulses down to my right foot, which smashed the gas pedal down to the floor of the Jeep. Yolanda did the same, so that we were both barreling through the marsh at about fifty miles an hour, while another section of the hillside smashed down between us. The landslide sent out a large sticky wash of stuff onto the highway and down its rain-filled ditches, along with heaps of mud and rock that our Jeep flailed up and over, wheels madly spinning. Erik and I heaved back and forth in our seats. Yolanda's car slooped around in the sludge and nearly tipped into one of the ditches.

"Erik." I was hunched over the steering wheel. "I'm going to get her."

He had gone as pale as a flounder, but his academic hysteria compelled him to yell at me some perfectly grammatical argument that had something to do with the Stelae and the river Sacluc and how there was a vast tract in the area described by the map that had never been perfectly combed by any of the explorers.

"It is interesting, though," he said. "Now that you mention it, it is slightly weird that no one, including Von Humboldt or your de la Cueva or anyone else for that matter, reports seeing the Stelae until Tapia does in the 1920s—"

I saw the long brown old car skid onto the mud that had spilled onto the highway, and I saw too the car plummet, quick and rough, into the ditch off the side of the road. The front of the car crumpled and began to plunge into the mud, which began to cover it as it continued to slide down the mountain. It engulfed the woman inside.

"Oh—no no no no," I heard myself screaming. "We've got to help her!"

I slammed on the brakes, opened my door, and raced out into the mud as fast as I could toward Yolanda.

CHAPTER 24

The car had fallen on its driver's side into the ditch, and already the landslide covered half of it in a thick and rocky mud. Rain surged down, helping to speed up the burial. Erik, having bolted from the Jeep at the same time as I did, began shoving away the stones and sludge with his hands and forearms. Through the smeared glass we could see that Yolanda—unmistakably her, from the twisting face I glimpsed through the dirt—was mired in rising black water that entered from below through a shattered driver's-side window. Though I was nearly blind from the downpour, I saw that she was hoisting the filched duffel bag above this pool. Hauling back more rock and dirt that continued to fall in a slow ooze from the hillside, I grasped onto the handles of the two passenger-side doors, but my fingers slipped away from them; she had earlier locked them, and so was caught inside.

"She'll drown in there!" Erik yelled at me.

I moved more mud and yelled at her through the window. "Yolanda! Open the car!"

But there was no answer as the rain kept hammering down on us.

"Yolanda, move it!"

"What is she doing?" Erik yelled.

"Yolanda!"

Still, there was nothing.

But then here, very dimly, very faintly, came her voice, like a cat yapping in its cage.

"What in the hell ARE YOU DOING?!"

Down in the bottom of the car, Yolanda's body began to move around with increasing violence; she seemed to be struggling with a safety belt. The car was flooding with water and mud.

"You ran me OFF THE ROAD!" she hollered at us again.

I raised my arm and with rapid violent strokes brought it down on the glass of the front-seat window. I was really hurting myself. I hit at that window again and again, and Erik bashed at the glass too with both fists. The window cracked into a net, and when I hammered down on it again, a section of it gave way and fell inside the cabin of the car. I reached in and flicked up the door's lock. Erik and I shoved aside yet more mud and with a great slow creak opened the door. We could see the filthy, soaking, bedraggled and behatted Yolanda floundering in the deepening well of the car as the water crept up her chest, toward her chin. Beneath the brim of her Stetson, blood seeped down. She was also still trapped by her seat belt, which was hidden from us well below the rising black water. Her right arm stuck out from the water as she held the duffel above her head.

"Take it!" she screamed. "Or else you'll never be able to find your mother!"

I reached in, grabbed the duffel, and threw it at Erik.

"Now get me out of here!"

I peered down and wiped the mud and rain off my face.

"Hold me by the waist," I said to Erik.

"What?"

"Just do it! I have to lower myself into the car, and I don't want to slip."

Erik reached down and got a firm grip on my jeans' belt, and I began to crawl down into the car. The water had filled the bottom third of the cab, and Yolanda thrashed in her seat while trying to extract herself from the belt. In her dazed state, hampered by the mud in the water, she couldn't find the button to press. I hung down while the landslide continued to pour sludge into the car, which sank deeper into the ditch. I grabbed the part of the belt crossing Yolanda's chest.

Her lip was cut; her eyes shot over to me. But she spoke in what was now a calm sounding voice. "Get it off. Get that off me. The water's coming—"

"Hold on."

I thrust my hands into the water, toward her waist, and followed the line of the belt. The seatbelt's plastic latch lodged under her hip, and because of the coldness of the water I had trouble feeling exactly where the button might be.

"Cut me out," she said. "Do you have a knife?"

I tried to look back up over my shoulder. "Erik. Do you have a knife?"

"No," he said, after a hesitation. "I didn't buy one."

"I thought I wouldn't be so afraid of dying like this," she said, evenly.

"Just hold on," I said.

"Here, let me get in there," Erik said.

"I've got it—I've got it," I said. "Just don't rush me."

"Get me out of the belt, Lola," Yolanda repeated.

I closed my eyes and plunged my hands deeper into the water. I closed them around the belt's lock. The water still rose from beneath and also poured down from above. Mud, too, slid into the car, onto my back and neck, down onto Yolanda's face. The rising water passed her neck and reached her jaw. She flailed about, once, so that I lost my grip. I could barely see anything through the rain.

"Stay still! Move up," I yelled.

My fingers circled the lock again, beneath her body, and I fumbled around under the water with my eyes closed until I touched the button. I pressed it, but nothing happened. She and I looked at each other, and I felt myself begin to go to pieces. Yolanda leaned away from the side of the car, pulling herself up by gripping onto me, and I pushed the button a second time. It gave, and the seatbelt unlatched.

"Get up, get up, move up!"

I slipped my hands beneath her armpits, and she pressed against the car door with her legs, so that I lifted her, slippery as a weasel, from the black pool of water.

I hauled Yolanda out of that car, pulled from behind by Erik, and she came, coughing and sliding and bleeding. The car had sunk three-quarters into the ditch and was nearly filled with water. Clay slid down Yolanda's face, and she shouted into the rain, saying something I couldn't hear. I saw that her legs moved in a dancy, jerky way when she stepped away from the ditch onto the mud-slicked highway and then tumbled onto the pavement, bringing me down with her.

We sat on the highway, covered in mud and battered by the rain. The pale walls of rainwater caged us. Yolanda's shoulders began to move, and when I looked back I saw her white teeth and her streaked face—but she wasn't crying, or cursing, like I'd thought. That girl was laughing at me.

"Hi, Lola," she said. "Good job with the not killing me."

"God!" I said.

"Let's go!" Erik said, hunching under the rain and reaching for me. "Let's get to the car!"

I took another flabbergasted look at her, and then we stood up, slipping and staggering in the mud. All of us ran to the Jeep.

CHAPTER 25

I can't believe how long it took you to start following me," Yolanda said once she'd crawled into the back of the Jeep. She spoke to me in English; her voice sounded raw and hoarse. She started to fling our knapsacks and duffels around to find a more comfortable spot. "I mean, I was relieved that you weren't making a nuisance of yourself. But later, when I thought about it, I was a little surprised. I mean, you'd think—"

"I know, I know," I said. "Just shake some fake hair in front of me, and I'm useless."

"And I can't believe, once you did find me, how quickly you nearly murdered me. You're the Conan Doyle fan. Seriously, Lola, it's embarrassing."

"I think I'd rather have a chat about how you're a thief, and how you're also mentally . . . bananas," Erik suggested, in the driver's seat. He pressed on the gas and pushed the Jeep out of the mud in slow turgid starts. Around us we could hear the rattle and plashes of the rain and the deep grinding of the mud under the tires. The Jeep swerved slickly. Then, with a sucking pop, it broke free of some hindrance and began to roll unsteadily down the highway.

"Excellent," Yolanda said. "Get us out of here."

"Hey—that duffel bag," I said, reaching behind and taking up my mother's Hartmann. For Yolanda had already gotten her hands on it. "Don't steal this from me again!"

"I already looked inside. I read everything except for that diary—your mother's, right? I was saving that one for last—but the rest of it's useless. Is the map in the journal?"

"No." I clasped the bag in both arms. "It's—it's in the rest of it."

Erik looked over at me, then back at the road.

"You just have to know the right way to piece things together," I said, extemporaneously. "You just didn't read the maps carefully enough."

"I always read carefully," she said. She leaned back. "It's got to be in the journal."

"Just keep away from my things, Yolanda," I said. "I mean it."

"Oh, I'll behave until you turn around." She shrugged. "But I'm patient. I'm willing to wait. I just want to make sure that you were telling me the truth about—all that nonsense. My father's work."

"You just want to preempt us on a dig," Erik said.

"We're not here for a dig," I said.

"What do you know about it?" Yolanda asked him.

"I know what I know. I've heard about you and your—"

"Yes, you've heard about Tomas de la Rosa, I'm sure. So—right. I'm here to preempt you on a dig, as you see it." She made a wide-arcing gesture with her hand. "What are you going to do, throw me out of the car?"

"Of course not," I said.

"What are you talking about?" Erik asked.

"I'm just checking," she said. I turned around to find her staring at me, and then she lowered her eyes. She touched a line of blood that came down from her head and examined her red finger. "Sorry," she said. She cupped her hand to her forehead; her face buckled for several seconds before smoothing out again. "I suppose I sound paranoid. I think I hit my head."

"Yes, so enough with that," I said. "And yes, your head's bleeding." To Erik I said, "Watch the road."

"I'm watching it."

I pulled a tissue out of my mother's duffel and brandished it at Yolanda. "You don't look so good."

Mud and weedy matter covered her hair in clumps, and her high-boned face had scratches across the left cheek, and one small gash on the left side of her lower lip. Dirt striped across the nose, and under her filthy bangs her eyes glistened. I pressed the tissue onto her injured forehead.

"Don't fuss all over me," she said. But even while she grumbled, she closed her eyes and let me clean her up.

"Stop moving."

"What are we going to do with her?" Erik said.

"Take her with us."

"That's obvious," she said. "You just trashed my car, for one thing."

I pushed some of the hair out of her face. "Didn't look like much of a car to me, you kleptomaniac."

"You know you wouldn't have got very far without me, anyway."

"You'd better be worth the trouble," I said, furious about the whole business.

"I know you're happy I'm here," she said. "It's written all over your mug."

Angry or not, I wasn't able to deny that, and so I rubbed her whole face briskly with my tissue instead.

"Then again, if my father were here," she went on, darting away from me, "no, if my father were here he wouldn't be caught dead with the likes of you two. A gaggle of north Americans running around the Peten, hunting and picking and poking around—he wouldn't have put up with it for even half a day. He'd run you out in a minute."

"Are you starting on that again?" Erik asked, bristling. "I'm Guatemalan."

"And I'm—Mexican," I said. "American."

"Not here, you're not," she replied. "You both look and talk just like Staties."

It is an uncomfortable fact for many U.S. Latinos that they seem very brown in the States, but can appear less so once they cross the border. So Yolanda was very cheerily trampling over our delicate racial psychology.

She grinned, and Erik growled something under his breath. I was still having some intense flashbacks to the near-drowning and so was able to ignore her.

"In any case," Yolanda went on, "back to our main subject—you're lucky to have me along. Plus, it's as good a time as any for us to be looking up in this area. Before anyone else does. Because now, you're going to have to pay attention. They really have found something in the Sierra de las Minas."

"Right—blue jade."

"But it's an even larger strike than I first—than any of us—first thought. Yesterday some men uncovered several huge veins of it in the mountains. I think that the mine's going to be massive once they track down the source. And the quality—I've gotten hold of samples of the stones. I've never seen anything like it."

I told her that my father had shown us a store of blue jade chips when we had seen him last.

"In the city you said they could choke on it," Erik said. "The jade."

"Did I?"

"Yes, you did."

"Well, never mind what I said. I was not . . . in the best mood. But now—who knows? If they found the mine that's described in that old story—that legend—then there might be a Queen Jade up in the forest, like he thought. My father. He always focused on the western side of the forest, though I thought we should head east—toward Tikal, the ruins. But that's neither here nor there, if you really do have a map. You have to give it to me."

"If you help me, I'll help you," I said.

"So—when do I get let in on the big mystery?"

Erik looked over at me, and I raised my eyebrows at him so that they disappeared into my hair.

Did he suspect a connection between the quests of Oscar Tapia and Beatriz de la Cueva, too?

"A day or so," I said. Though I wasn't sure what exactly I'd be able to show her then—if anything at all. "When I feel more sure that you won't—"

"What—*abandon* you?" Her voice quickly turned hot. "Is that it?"
I hesitated. "Yes."

"Like you abandoned me?"

She stared at me from under her hat, but when I flinched, something changed. The light in her eyes dimmed.

"I won't do that," she muttered. "Ditch you, I mean. Now that I'm here, I'll stick—as long as you don't give me another reason to distrust you." While I continued to watch her, her mouth began to struggle in her face. I could swear that I saw some revised and furious love in her expression. Then she turned away. "And so—that's what we're agreeing. A day or two until you show me that map. I'll help you find Juana, and then I'll go looking for the Stone, specimen, Jade, whatever you want to call it. But the bargain is, if I find it, it's mine. My father's—I'm not having any Statie steal it. So it's not *his*." She looked at Erik. "And not yours. Not Juana's. Mine. By rights."

Erik rolled his eyes at me on this, silently explaining that Yolanda de la Rosa would be sorely disappointed in these expectations should any discovery be made, but I shook my head at him.

"You know I don't care about any of that," I said. "You can have it. I just want my mother."

"All right," Yolanda said. "We have a deal."

She leaned back again in her seat and then touched the tissue to her forehead, which had begun bleeding again.

Erik wrinkled his nose at me but stayed very quiet, and pressed the Jeep forward through the shoals of mud and the downpour that was so thick it was white as steam. I looked back at Yolanda, and when I saw that she had belted herself in and was keeping quiet, I relaxed a little. I reached down and touched the fabric of my mother's bag, listening to the sound of the plastic crackle inside until I felt a hard rectangular object. I touched the outline of this for a while. I had it back, and it was safe with me. Erik tried the radio for some news or music, but only received static. No other cars were visible on the road, not even a bus or an army van, though after a few miles I saw a settlement of plastic huts shivering on a far plateau. I knew these to be some of the relief camps we'd seen on television the day before, and that they were filled with people evacuated from the regions most severely ravaged by the storm.

The huts stood on a promontory elevated from the banks of the highway about five miles off, and were built on hastily constructed wood foundations. The settlement was so far away from us and visibility so limited that I couldn't see very much, except for the green shapes of the little dented tents arranged in a half-circle within the mud. Two brown vans were parked to the left of the huts, but I couldn't make out any people or animals. The flashing rain looked as if it would erase the little sanctuary.

I looked at these awful houses for a long while. They were a horribly clear reminder of why I was here.

I retrieved Erik's copy of Von Humboldt from a bag at my feet, then unzipped my mother's duffel and began to unfold the origami of clothes and paper and Xeroxes. As I tucked the *Narrative* between two of my mother's shirts, I found it at the bottom. I lifted up my mother's journal from its plastic wrappings; it was still dry.

Erik glanced at me, but I didn't say anything to encourage his interest. Yolanda peered at me too, but I wasn't about to open up my mother's secret book for her greedy gaze or anyone else's.

I only wanted, I said to myself, to hold it in my hand and feel part of her close to me.

CHAPTER 26

Erik, Yolanda, and I continued to descend into the Motagua Valley, which extends from the southern highlands of the country, down past Guatemala City, and into the plains that stretch beneath the eastern Sierra de la Minas until it reaches the outskirts of the Peten and Belize.

In the thin light of the morning, I could see that we weren't in the deepest part of the valley yet. Our slow pace was telling: what should have been a ten-hour journey north would take much, much longer. Still, the constant dark-and-pale presence of the rain fell on land that changed with a terrible alacrity. The hurricane had done its worst in Honduras and Belize, rushed northwest through the forest, and then stalled in the higher regions of Guatemala. But the effects here were still severe. The highway flooded with high and shining water, out of which stretched the black arms of tree branches. The rain cleared for several minutes at one point, so that we could see the road filled with drowned wood boards and unidentifiable crushed masses of plastic and metal, perhaps from homes or other buildings that had been torn up by the storm, then carried over the desert on the wind.

"Farmers grew coffee here," Yolanda said suddenly. "And they grew tobacco, and cardamom, and lower down they grazed cattle. But all that's gone now."

"Everything looks . . . *dead*," Erik said. His profile was clear and sharp against the gray window.

"Except there," she replied. "Those settlements."

Farther up to our right stood another land projection, upon which stood another camp of perhaps one hundred tents, fashioned out of more dark green tarp. They trembled against the gray and white sky, and the flooding waters ran around the plateau, met in one stream, and came tumbling over down to the highway where we drove. The camp was mudstained and drenched; I could see several bent figures hurrying from one tent to another, holding baskets in their arms, or shielding their heads from the deluge with their hands. Dogs scampered after them, jumping and snapping at each other in the puddles. I couldn't see any children. Some of the tents looked as if they might collapse from the weight of the water.

"I heard on the television that there were almost two hundred thousand evacuated," Yolanda continued.

"From . . . Honduras?" Erik asked.

"No. Guatemala. The lowlands—mostly eastward. But of course, it's the lowlands where we're all going."

"Where are the rest of the evacuees?"

"Not in the cities. I think camps have just been scattered all over the valley, like this."

I sat there quietly, not moving or saying much for another hour. We drove, and drove. Yolanda eventually fell asleep in the back seat, and Erik had to concentrate so much on the road, he didn't notice what I was doing.

Afternoon began to approach; the light lowered in the sky. I looked down at the recovered prize I held on my lap, on top of the crinkling bag. I rubbed the rough pink cloth covering the journal. I rasped my finger against the edges of the pages shut tight, and I tapped at the tin lock with my nails. The face of the lock was pierced with a small keyhole. I ran my thumb over its contours.

"What are you doing?" Erik whispered. "That's your mother's, right?"

"I'm just tinkering with it," I whispered back.

"Well, tell me if you find anything in there."

I ran my fingers around the lock's small metal square. I lodged one of my fingernails beneath the tin face of it, and pulled. Nothing

happened. I tugged a little harder. I heard the sound of paper ripping.

And then the lock broke loose. With a yank, I snapped it off.

The diary opened.

Erik couldn't have known my clenching panic as he edged the Jeep
over rocks and gaps and whirling water. A shallow though deepening
river stretched in front of us, and more heaps of black and gold debris
collected in jagged heaps on the higher sections of the highway. A sign
that was still standing said we were forty kilometers away from a land-
mark called Rio Hondo. My heart pushed against my ribs, but not because of the water rushing onto the Jeep in streams and waves.

I lifted the pink shell of my mother's journal and ran my hand over
the first page, which was embroidered with her Gothic script, its letters
like delicate leaded windows.

I began to read.

CHAPTER 27

A fter sixty pages filled with my mother's difficult mathematical formulas, notations on obscure archaeological theorists, and complaints about academic politics, there came a long gap, lasting about a year, where she hadn't written anything at all. And then I found this:

October 13, 1998. My work on the Stelae has been interrupted by the news of his death. I have not been able to concentrate on my refinements of the Labyrinth of Deceit ever since.

Pneumonia, I heard. Though others have said malaria.

I had hoped to send my work out for publication this week, I can't get organized. All I can think about now is the past.

October 15

I've spent days incapable of concentration on my Puzzle. Perhaps it if I write my memories down in their entirety, I will be able to release myself from them.

The '67 Symposium on the Flores Stelae was the first time we met Tomas.

We'd been hearing stories about him for years, however: Of his discoveries of rare jade pieces, his interest in the Witch's stone, his work in the Resistance and his sabotages of the army's death squads. Later, we'd add to these tales the rumor that he bombed an army colonel's house and killed an accountant. And he disfigured a guard, as well, a kid lieutenant—whose negligence was punished so effectively he grew into one of the bloodiest killers in the war. . . .

All of these events helped to make de la Rosa notorious. But it was his paper on the Stelae's meaninglessness that would make his name. And we were undeniably jealous, as we'd thought we'd come up with the idea first.

As soon as we walked into the El Salvador conference room, I saw a giant, ugly man, grave-faced, dark-eyed, black-hatted. He was tipping back a whiskey and surrounded by apoplectic and conservative scholars Drs. Guillermo Saenz and Gregorio Rodriguez. He was not handsome—no. Not gentle-looking. But there was something about him. Something attractive.

The next thing I knew, that man turned and stared at me.

I swear, he looked at me in the most indiscreet way.

"You must be the kids who nearly beat me with your article on the Stones," he said, after unraveling himself from his colleagues and walking up to us. His gaze did not veer from my face. "Hell, I'd rather talk to you about our crazy hieroglyphs than get yelled at any more by those old coots"—here he pointed to Saenz and Rodriguez—"who are my best friends in the world, even if they are damned capitalists."

"Well, yes, it's very nice to meet you," Manuel said, as polite as always.

I'd nearly forgotten he was standing next to me. He put his hand on my shoulder.

"Juana?" he asked. "My dear? What's wrong?"

"There's nothing wrong with her," Tomas said, too boldly.

I looked away from him; he and I had already communicated everything to one another. And this is when I told Manuel the first lie.

"Nothing, sweetheart." I smiled at him. "I'm perfectly fine."

Manuel was so trusting, he suspected nothing. He even invited de la Rosa to accompany us on our drive back to Guatemala City.
I could feel the man's eyes on me the entire drive.

October 16

I'm going to stop scribbling these memories down and get back to my work! I'll never get it done at this rate.

I king jade fierce king true a jade
under born noble and jade the of sign jade

I have to concentrate. I must make sure I translate the lines of the Maze perfectly.

My right hand pressed against the leaves of the journal while I read that last line again.

I took in a breath; I found almost everything in these entries baffling, but I knew that sentence was critical.

I flipped back to the beginning of the entry:

"My work on the Stelae has been interrupted by the news of his death. I have not been able to concentrate on my refinements of the Labyrinth of Deceit ever since."

It had seemed strange to Erik and me that Beatriz de la Cueva and Alexander von Humboldt had described a labyrinth, but never mentioned Oscar Angel Tapia's Stelae, even though all three adventurers had canvassed the same area. It also appeared very odd that my mother had scribbled down fragments that I recognized from the Stelae, and had written here also of "translating" the maze.

Was it because the Maze of Deceit and the Flores Stelae were the same thing?

"That's it," I whispered. "That's what I thought."

But neither Erik nor Yolanda heard me. Nor did I have time to react to the other strange passages I'd just read.

For here there came a bump, a jostle. I was thrust forward and crumpled the diary's pages. The sides of the Jeep creaked.

And then came a harder jolt.

CHAPTER 28

"Oh, no," Erik said.

"What's that?" Yolanda said behind me. I didn't know how long she'd been awake.

I closed the journal so she wouldn't see what my mother had written. The rain thrashed against the sides of the car, sounding like rocks thrown onto the metal hood; water dripped down in streams onto us from openings in the Jeep. Steam and the white water made it difficult for me to discern what was in front of us. I put my hand over the book and shook my head.

"It's nothing," I said. I wrapped the journal back up in its plastic. "I'm just reading—"

"What are you talking about?" she asked. She hadn't even noticed the diary; she was poking her head through a vent in one of the Jeep's rubber windows.

"That doesn't look good," Erik said. He stuck his head out of his window, too. "All right, it's okay, I can maneuver through this."

"You can? We've got to get out of this car. Where did all this come from?"

I peered up through the windshield again. "I can't see anything. What's going on?"

"That," she said, pointing.

I unzipped the rubber window on my side of the Jeep, peeled it down, and squinted through the storm to see that we had reached the outskirts of the half-submerged town of Rio Hondo. And I saw, too, that the road we had been traveling on had disappeared.

From our right-hand side, green-white water poured around us, frothing, curving, slamming into the highway, having burst through dams constructed days before. The Rio Hondo, which runs parallel about a kilometer southwest of this small village, had flooded on account of Mitch and the ensuing days' rain, then broken through the sand bags that the townspeople had piled up on the banks. The bulwarks were ripped and draining sand into the river, so empty burlap sacks floated by us in the rushing pool that gathered about the Jeep, smacked up at its sides, and poured water through the doors before it pummeled past. Yolanda, Erik, and I yanked down our windows to get a better look at the situation. To the west, there was nothing but high and leaping water. Directly to the east stood the town. Here we saw a desolate gas station, a quarter of it covered by the water already, as well as vacated convenience stores and some homes with half-shorn roofs. I also saw one small, very pretty church built from clay and stucco and painted white, so that it resembled a delicate porcelain sculpture. It didn't bear any visible damage, though the storm had pushed up mounds of dirt, broken tree branches, and rocks against its sides.

We zipped up the windows again.

"Is there any way to get up to that church?"

"I'm having trouble controlling the Jeep," Erik yelled. "The back wheels aren't turning—the road—"

She widened her eyes at him. "Can you reverse?"

"No!"

"Wait, wait," I was saying. I gripped onto my mother's wrapped journal; I tucked it back into the bag and buried it within another layer of plastic. "I've got to think. When did it get this bad?"

Erik was sweating. "Pretty much now."

"Where is everyone?"

"I don't know. Trapped in their houses. Or evacuated."

The Jeep jerked forward once through the water, which spread around us tall and dark and deceptive. For we didn't see what work it did beneath. The oncoming river ate at the road so its banks extended far past its borders and created a cliff that swept to the deepest and hungriest reaches of the waterway. Underneath us, the tires of the Jeep skittered and jumped. Water continued flowing through the cracks of the doors and the windows. Erik grappled with the steering wheel in an attempt to maneuver the Jeep east, until he was sure that he was not steering on much of anything, as the tires only sporadically touched the highway.

Yolanda brought her head forward, and I could feel her wet hair on my cheek. I could hear her breathing.

"Yolanda."

"Don't be afraid," she said.

"Get out of your seatbelt," I told her and Erik.

"Good idea," she said, unlatching herself. "We could be headed for some—swimming."

"I hope not," Erik said.

"We'll be fine," she said, as tough as possible. "We'll be all right."

She put her hand on my shoulder. I put my hand on hers.

"But if it's not, I want you to know—" she said, hesitating.

"But if it's not what?"

"But if it's not fine—then I want you to know—"

The car began joggling beneath us. She gripped onto me even harder with both of her arms, in an unmistakable hug, and pressed her face close to mine again and closed her eyes. "*That I—can't—stand—you.*"

"*I—can't—stand—you—either,*" I bellowed.

"Hold on," she said. "Something's wrong. The Jeep's moving down."

"Hold on."

"Hold on!" Erik yelled. "I can't make it move!"

He reached out and grabbed me too; I held onto his hand. The cabin shifted and groaned. We jerked. We heard a long, scraping, sliding noise as a section of the road fell into the water rushing westward. And then the Jeep lost its ground completely.

It rolled over slowly, and did not stop, and as I held onto my mother's bag I was hurled up and on top of my head with my face and shoulders against the roof of the Jeep and choking on foul black water. Everything was dark and very cold, and I couldn't see either Erik or Yolanda, except that I felt their bodies struggling above me. I began kicking at obstructions, and struggling up through some barrier made of mud and cloth, and somehow pulled the upper half of my body through an obscure vent, but when I reached my hands out—one still holding onto the duffel—I felt nothing else but more water, and when I opened my eyes everything around me was black. A piece of canvas, or weeds, or sheets of plastic had wrapped itself around my torso, and my feet were trapped inside what I thought might be the rubber windows of the Jeep. As I thrashed inside that disaster, I had the freezing and immediate sensation that something familiar, final, and inevitable reached up through the water to greet me, as I had always known it would. It was my own personal death. I moved left. I turned right. But I couldn't breathe. I was eating water.

And then something reached into the place that I had fallen to, and put its arm around my chest, and it dragged me up, pulling me out of whatever windings I had become caught in. I found myself above water, and in the rain, and relieving myself of some of what I'd swallowed.

And then I inhaled again.

Erik had me by an arm. His face was white and twisted behind the rivulets pouring over him. He began to yank me out of the slipping burgundy-colored cliff of mud that had just minutes before been the Carretera al Atlantico. I opened my eyes and saw Yolanda, smeared with muck and streaming with water and also, improbably, still wearing that infernal black hat of hers. She yelled at me from the higher reaches of the bank. She moved back down the ravine in quick lunges and splashed into the deeper stretches of the water to help him drag me out. All three of us swam and clawed away from the drowned Jeep and up the sheared bank until we felt the hard edge of the remaining sections of the highway. Erik took hold of me by the waist, and then my rear end, and pushed me up until I could crawl onto the flooded road, while keeping the duffel bag stuffed under one arm; he then attempted to do the same for Yolanda, who informed him with complete dignity that an ass like him wasn't going to touch hers. I threw the bag at my feet, leaned down, and on the unsteady bank wrapped my hands around his arms. I pulled as hard as I could and he slipped and kept sliding away from me so that I heard myself shrieking, until he propelled himself forward through the water and scrambled up. Next he bent over the remaining side of the road, and while I held onto his belt he gripped Yolanda up from under her armpits and dragged her out of the water as well.

Mud covered our faces and our eyes; we wiped away the red pieces from our mouths; I saw red streaks on Erik's chin and began to brush these off until I realized that they were blood. Then I found that I was just standing there, and not doing anything but gripping his arm, as I had a crazy sensation that if I didn't, he would go sliding back down the ravine and I wouldn't see him again.

"You okay?" he yelled.

"Yes. Yolanda?"

"Are you breathing all right?" she asked; she had both her hands on my arms, and looked terrified. "You took in a lot of water."

"I'm fine."

"You're sure?"

"I'm sure."

"I'm not. That was sickening. But—wait." She jerked her head back at me.

"What?"

"Where's the map? Where's the map?"

I brandished the Hartmann. "It's here."

"Show it to me!"

"You girls give it a rest," Erik said in English, then examined a cut on my cheek with his fingers. "Just remember—we could be extremely extinct right now."

"Show it to me," Yolanda said again.

"No, no, no," I said. I clutched it to my chest, but not just because of Yolanda. What had I just read in that diary about my mother? "Don't ask me again."

She stood there in the rain, looking down at the bag. She touched her hand to her mouth.

"I don't see why you won't just give it to me," she said, slowly.

"The Jeep's dead," Erik said, peering over at its hull rolling in the water.

Yolanda stared at me and did not appear to have heard what he'd said.

"Yolanda?"

"Yes, what? Oh, all right. Then let's just go." She pointed east. "Up here."

We waded through the water, past a bodega with its red-painted Coca Cola sign, a Ford abandoned to the storm, and into the evacuated village until we reached the white church. I climbed its brick steps and pushed open the wooden door.

Inside, the church was flooded several inches, yet remained dry enough to shelter three pigeons, at least two mice, a cabal of birds, and one orange salamander that crept along the white plaster walls with its sticky toes. A faint light passed from a high window and glimmered on the water surrounding the altar. It also shone on some long wooden pews, upon which we all collapsed.

CHAPTER 29

I'm wiped out," Yolanda said an hour later. We were still in the church. "Has it stopped raining?"

When we'd first entered the building, she'd hugged herself tight, and wouldn't speak. At last, she'd taken off her hat. I was sitting on the driest bench. She came over and sat by me, but hadn't rested her head on my lap until she fell asleep and didn't realize what she was doing. I petted her hair only as long as I was sure she was unconscious.

Now awake, she moved off, and I stood up and waded to one of the windows.

Erik sat three pews away from us. The poor guy looked as if he'd been flattened by a giant hand. "What do you see?"

"Nothing," I said. "That is, no rain." The sky had grown paler, and from above the clouds thin edges of sunlight appeared. Painful aftershocks of terror kept shooting through my body, and I could feel a sharp bruised spot on my head from the accident on the road. "It's clearing up."

"Try Manuel again," Yolanda said. I opened up the soaked cell phone that Erik had pulled from his pocket. "Or dial emergency. There has to be someone around here who can help us. Weren't there cars driving down the Carretera before?"

"Army trucks," Erik said. "We passed at least two on our way down. Probably traveling northeast—to bring people supplies."

She closed her eyes. "I won't be getting inside any army truck. Not with those murderers."

"You might have to," he said.

"See—that you could even say that proves that you aren't really from here."

Erik glowered and pushed back his hair from his forehead.

"I can't get anything on this phone," I said.

Erik's face began to turn a rough shade of red, and without saying anything he stood up and walked outside of the church. Now it was just Yolanda and me.

"Leave him alone," I said.

She shrugged. "He's almost adorably easy to irritate. Though I guess since he's your boyfriend, I'll do you the favor of laying off."

"He's not my boyfriend."

She sat up in the pew. Light came in through the glass and fell across her face. She seemed to have given up yelling at me about the duffel bag, which was good. I wasn't ready to think about its contents yet.

"Oh, relax," she said. "It's obvious, if distasteful."

"We're not together. I like—firemen. And policemen."

"What?"

"It's a long story. The short answer is, he's not my type."

"Fine. Have it your way."

The corners of her mouth flickered up. I thought then that she was a lot like my mother. After she got over the shock and the hypothermia, being on the weirdest of adventures could put her into a good mood.

"So . . . ," I began.

She raised an eyebrow at me.

"So how have things been for you?" I asked.

"Been for me?"

"Your life, in these past years."

She waved her hand. "Hard as a brick, Lola. As you can see."

"But you must have had—friends. There must have been some times when you were happy." I paused. "That is, I hope so."

"Happy—oh, you mean, with men?"

"Among other things."

Her smile concentrated itself on the right side of her mouth, and she nodded a little. "I've had some nice times. I've met some very decent, very good men. But . . . I never got married. As you probably suspected. Certainly there's no law that you have to. It would have been nice, it just never happened. I was always working with my father—though I don't know if I should be blithering to you about all this." She grumbled out a laugh.

"Why not?"

"I'm a private person now. That's one way you could put it. That's the way I put it. I'm more careful about who I—" She left that last sentence unfinished.

I waited, listening.

"Did you think that we were friends?" she asked abruptly. "Back when I lived with you?"

"That was a long time ago," I said. "I was nine when you first showed up. And you were a scary little eleven-year-old."

"Right—so, did you?"

"Think you were my friend? Not at first, no," I admitted.

"No, not at first," she said. Her eyes looked emerald in the church's light.

"Later, though, I did."

She nodded, not looking at me.

"Later," I went on, "I saw that it was probably one of the best friendships of my life." When I said that, I felt my arms fling out at my sides for a moment, uncontrollably, because I wanted to hug her. "I never had another friend like you. I never had that *thing* with another person again."

She passed her hand over her hair. She looked naked without her hat.

"About men, you know," she said, changing subjects again, "don't get Oedipal or electrical or whatever on me, but I never felt much of the need for them, actually. One of those domestic arrangements. My father and I were so close that I suppose it got in the way. I enjoyed his company. Does that make sense?" She shrugged. "And then he died!

And so . . . that's why now I don't seem to have much of anything at all. I'd begun to think I'd made a mistake—or that I hadn't—because I'd taken advantage of my friendship with him when he was alive." She shook her head. "I still haven't answered that one completely, for myself."

Her calm expression didn't change much while she told me this, except for just the slightest lowering of her eyebrows.

"But then you showed up, talking about your mother. *And* about this map. The only thing I could think of to do was go off hunting after you so I could find that rock Dad was always nattering about. It sort of feels like this is the last trip I'll ever take with him. And all of this running around has made me feel better. Don't feel quite so much like drinking myself berserk." She coughed. "And look at me now. Being *congenial* with a Sanchez. The old family enemy. Who thinks we might have been friends once. I don't know—either things are looking up for me, or I've . . . swallowed too much acid rain today. What do you think?"

"Too much acid rain," I said.

She chuckled for a little while, looking at me in a cock-headed, funny way.

"But you had still better not be lying to me about that map," she said then.

One of the birds, sitting in a window, began to flap its wings and shake up rain and gold-colored dust into the deepening light. From outside, I heard a splashing and a prolonged, curious grinding. But the rain and heavy winds hadn't started again.

"I just hope you didn't lie to me to get me out here," she said again, slowly, with an edge sinking into her voice. "Because then I will not be . . . congenial."

I held her gaze.

I didn't have much in the way of a map yet, just an idea, a few clues. But the floods had made the country rough, and we'd had two accidents in one day. I was beginning to understand in a clearer and colder way that if I told the whole truth and Yolanda left us, it could mean my mother would die.

"I have a way of getting us to the labyrinths," I said

"I'm glad to hear it," she replied, over a loud, sharp sound that came from somewhere outside.

The bird in the window took flight toward the rafters.

"What's that?" she asked.

The splashing and grinding noises had grown even louder, and there was a metallic clanking as well, so that I had an image of some great beast pushing through the mud with iron feet. Then came the sounds of men yelling and talking.

Erik popped his ruffled head through the church door, and then the rest of his soaked bulk appeared; he regarded us for a second.

"Time to go," he said.

Yolanda threw her hands up. "What?"

"Time to go."

"I don't understand—"

"The hour for departure is nigh," he said. "Please hoist your buttocks into the air and begin to move your feet until they miraculously convey you outside of this church, after which you may deposit your fundament once again in one of the nice cozy trucks that are presently waiting to take you all the way to Flores."

We just stared at him.

"And don't think I like it any better than you do," he said to Yolanda. "But it is the army."

She turned away from him and her lips formed silent and hell-raising suggestions until she looked at the geckos swimming around at our feet. Then she put her cowboy hat back on, and followed me through the church door to face the soldiers waiting outside.

CHAPTER 30

On the outskirts of Rio Hondo sat five olive green army flatbed trucks covered with tarps and filled with provisions and stoic uniformed men. Because of the last day's violent wind, it had been difficult for helicopter pilots to transfer supplies to the north, where thousands had been left homeless by the storm. The army sent out these caravans in their stead. Traveling across the Carretera al Atlantico, the soldiers were not deterred by the washouts on the highway, as they employed pontoon bridges made of durable buoys that could be thrown up over the landslides and gullies that now pocked the country's roads. About twenty men sat in the back of each truck, half obscured from our view by the tarps, though we could see their knees nudging up on the boxes and sacks of water, meat jerky, medical supplies, and tinned vegetables. One of the soldiers standing about told us to take our seats in the last van. The three of us approached it, and its tarp was partially lifted by an unseen hand. We gazed up at the dark interior of the truck and its huddle of soldiers; the men at the very back remained indistinct in the shadows, but those we could discern had rifles leaned up against their thighs as protection against any bandits or looters.

Next to me, Yolanda stood upright and still. I could hear her breathing.

"I can't go up there," she said.

Erik had already begun climbing into the truck's hold—but he, too, had gone quiet and tight-mouthed. He turned around and reached his hand out to me. Two of the other soldiers also extended their hands to help lift us up.

"Come on, Yolanda," he said, in a calm and unhappy voice. "We have to get out of here."

She stayed rooted, staring up at the men. About thirty seconds passed like this. Then thirty more. A minute. Two.

"We have to leave," Erik said.

"What's the hold-up?" one of the soldiers asked.

"Oh, they're just scared," another voice said from the back of the truck, where we couldn't see.

"Scared of what?"

"Go get my right hand, Rivas," the voice said. "Tell him to come over here."

One of the soldiers came leaping out of the truck, and splashed back toward the rest of the caravan.

"Excuse me, ma'am," Rivas said.

We made way for him, then I put my arm around Yolanda's.

"We have to go," I said. "Erik's right."

"These people are assassins," she murmured to me. "My father used to tell me that the world would be better if they were all dead."

"Come on, girls," said one of the soldiers; he was small and dark, with a bilevel haircut.

In the same low voice, she said, "I'd rather ride with the devil."

I just stood there and let her think it through.

"Plus there's also the fact that if these boys knew who I am, they might not seem so friendly," she continued. "Which wouldn't be the safest thing for you, either."

Erik still had his arm outstretched, and he opened his eyes just about as far as his eyelids would allow. "Lola? What's going on?"

"What's wrong with that woman?" asked the soldier with the bilevel. "The one with the hat."

"Many things," Erik said. "Many, many things."

"What are you talking about?" he asked.

"My friend is trying a joke," I said, trying not to sound nervous.

"He's being funny." Then, to her: "You have to make up your mind now, Yolanda. And I'll stick with you, whatever you decide."

She looked over her shoulder at the flooded town and the creeping, moving river. "Not much of a choice, I can see that," she said.

"Five seconds, Lola," Erik said. "No more. Then I'm going to have to *insist*. Besides, I don't think our friends here are as patient as I am when it comes around to waiting for ladies."

Ahead of us, we could hear the trucks starting; some of them began to slowly drive through the water and toward a sound part of the highway.

"Give the order, son," said the officer we couldn't see.

"Saddle up!" the soldier with the bilevel yelled. "Heading out!"

Yolanda looked at me. She pulled hard on the brim of her hat.

"All right," she said. "So much for principles. But they'd better not touch me."

She took Erik's hand and hurled herself over the side of the truck. I climbed up after her, still holding onto my mother's bag. Two men grabbed onto my pants and my elbows to help boost me. I looked around and saw that we were surrounded by soldiers.

The truck shook about in the mud and, with more grinding and slow heaving, began to move. Erik and Yolanda sat on either side of me on the small bench in the truck's cab. We pressed up next to the men, who had crushed together to make room for us.

Then the soldier named Rivas came running back, gripped onto the truck's backside, and hauled himself on board, too.

"Well?" came that voice from the back. "Where is he?"

"He's with Villaseñor's crew. Says he's busy."

"Busy?"

"Yes, sir."

"Well, I'll have to talk to him about that on our next stop."

The soldier with the bilevel looked toward the back of the truck, then turned to Rivas.

"Pull the tarp all the way back, Private. Too dark in here."

"Yes, Colonel."

Rivas began to yank at the green canvas so more light seeped into the truck.

It was at that instant we recognized the person giving orders.

His face was half in shadow, and he looked smaller than I remembered him. But there was no mistaking the soldier with the mustache and delicate hands and the suspicions about Yolanda, whom we had met a few days back at The Pedro Lopez saloon in Guatemala City.

CHAPTER 31

Inside the truck, it was humid and silent and filled with a ghastly pearl-colored light.

"Are you sick?" the soldier with the bilevel asked Yolanda.

Yolanda's right cheek flickered. Erik wrapped his hand around my arm.

"No—I'm fine," she said, looking over the side of the van. There was nowhere for us to jump down except into the rushing water.

"She's just scared, as I was saying before," said the man—evidently a colonel—whom we knew from The Pedro Lopez. He sounded cool, and weirdly easygoing. "These people and I met a few days ago. We had something of a disagreement, over a bar tab, I believe it was. I'm afraid I was drunk and can't quite recall. But it was my sidekick who made such a fuss. Had too much to drink and became belligerent."

"You mean, Estrada started a fight?" one soldier asked.

"Precisely."

"He can do that sometimes," another soldier said. He had a shaved head and a round face. "He give you that?" He pointed to the bruise under Erik's eye.

"Yes, he did," Erik said.

"Gave me one once, too," the other replied.

"Yeah, well, we're all learning how to live with the changes," the soldier with the bilevel said, presumably about the Peace Accords. He looked up warily at the colonel and cleared his throat. "Estrada's had more trouble than most. Especially lately."

The colonel began stretching his fingers like a violinist warming up for a concerto. "Exactly, my boy. We must teach him to behave himself. Sometimes he needs—correction. That's all. It could happen to anyone."

"I would like to get off this truck now," Yolanda said. She pressed her hands on her thighs, very deliberately, to keep them still.

"Sounds good," Erik said.

"There is no need for such dramatics," the colonel said. "I assure you, we aren't quite the gargoyles you might think, miss. And sir. No one's going to bother you. Things just aren't done that way anymore. There are checks on such behaviors."

Some of the soldiers shifted about in their seats, as if they weren't so sure.

"And besides—what's a little bar fight?" the colonel went on. "Nothing. Completely forgotten. We're all here on a humanitarian mission. As you are, we understand."

"We're here to find my mother," I said, as controlled as I could. I don't think they could see I was shaking.

"Exactly. You're here to find your mother. We're here to convey supplies. Nothing more. So just sit back down. Or get off. What do I care?"

"Are you serious?" I asked.

"Yes. What do you think this is?"

The three of us continued staring at him, uncertain what to do.

"What's your name?" Rivas now asked Yolanda, in a friendly way.

"Suzanna Muñoz," she said.

"Doesn't ring any bells—but you look familiar. We met before?"

"That's exactly what I thought when I first saw her," the colonel said.

"I think I *have* seen you somewhere."

"She has one of those faces," the colonel said. "Just reminds you of something."

I squeezed Yolanda's wrist.

"I swear I've seen this girl, sir."

Yolanda sat there with a frozen face and her arms tensed, as if she were preparing to flee or possibly even attack Rivas. But then she relaxed with a sudden jerk of the shoulders and took on an altogether different pose. In one moment her eyes looked haggard and dull; in the next she broke out into a bright, not too obviously false smile, and I saw her transform herself into a charming and slightly ditzy character who talked with her hands and smiled a great deal.

"I sell things on the street," she said. "You must have seen me around the City."

"What do you sell, food?" Rivas asked.

"Or—flowers?" the colonel said. "Roses, perhaps."

But nothing alarming showed on his face when he said this.

"Toys," she said. "Children's toys. Games."

"And you're friends with these North Americans?"

Erik's eyes bulged out slightly.

"Mexican-American," I muttered reflexively. "I am, that is."

"What?" Rivas asked, wincing.

"Don't pay attention to her," Yolanda said. "They are *so* very gringo I can't even tell you. But yes, we're friends"—she pointed at me—"I've known this one since I was a kid—she sells books—and the other one's her boyfriend. He's"—here she gave him a look that was almost tender, and then winked at him—"he's an . . . idiot."

The men in the truck laughed at this. Erik and I just sat there, strained and watchful.

"Anyway," Yolanda went on, "I just came along with her to help."

"That explains everything," the colonel said. "All enigmas solved, all conundrums unraveled."

"The colonel knows a lot of words," Rivas said.

"The colonel's got a lot of tricks up his sleeve," the soldier with the bilevel said. "Respectfully speaking, of course."

"Of course."

The soldier with the bilevel looked over at us, sharply, closely. "So there's no problem, then, right, Colonel?"

"No problem at all," the colonel said, smiling at us too before tucking his chin into his chest, as if getting ready to take a nap.

"See," the soldier said. "So there's nothing for you to worry about."

"There's nothing for us to worry about," Yolanda repeated, in a cheerful voice. But when I placed my hand on top of hers, I felt it had gone completely cold.

"Everything's just swell," Erik said, looking out at the miles of flooding around us.

From a makeshift window created by a tied-up piece of tarp I could see the landscape descend and grow ever more swollen and wild with floodwater.

We were trapped. Or we were saved.

The wide water shattered past us; the wet air clung to our limbs; the men around us had illegible faces. There was nothing else to do but pretend to be calm.

Lurching in the unsteady truck and stealing nervous glances at each other, we steadied ourselves and entered with these new and troubling companions into the heart of the Motagua Valley.

CHAPTER 32

The line of army trucks dipped into the hollow of the valley. The great dark walls of the northern Sierra de las Minas and western Sierra del Espíritu Santo rose around us. We lowered into a basin flooded with fresh water that created hard driving for the trucks, but in some of the valley's empty draining patches we could see that pale tall grass covered the depression, and the flora was ripped here and there by the rigors of the hurricane. Many trees had been stripped entirely of leaves, and their naked curving branches looked like lines of dark calligraphy against the pallid backdrop of the basin. Pieces of broken wood and heaps of torn bush floated in the road, but the trucks had less trouble passing over that than through the higher water, which could reach halfway up their sides.

Most of the soldiers slept upright, with their lips and nostrils quavering, though the colonel alternated between taking short naps and continuing to examine Yolanda. Erik leaned against me lightly and rested his chin on his chest just like the others. Yolanda nudged up against me after he did. She tried to keep awake, but her body grew heavier and looser. After a while, she fell asleep too.

We were all exhausted. But I couldn't rest. It occurred to me that during the commotion, I hadn't said anything to Erik about my mother making a connection between the Stelae and the Maze of Deceit. I planned on telling him later, and I wanted to tell Yolanda too, though I worried that she'd figure from that information that I'd lied about the map. Regardless, all decisions about disclosures could be put off for the time being. And I could read my mother's disturbing book again, privately. After some delicate maneuvering to get hold of my mother's journal, tucked in the bag that sat at my feet, I started to look through the diary while trying not to disturb my friends leaning on me.

In the cramped quarters of the truck, their touch was my only comfort.

October 18

My affair with Tomas began two months after the conference. This was in Antigua, in a beautiful hotel that once was the monastery of the Dominican monks.

There's nothing like making love to a grim-faced man with large, slow hands. Afterward, we lay in bed, drinking brandy and talking.

He told me about his friends, Drs. Saenz and Rodriguez. Though they were conservatives, they'd helped hide him from the army after there were those rumors that he'd bombed that officer's home (I did not ask him if those rumors were true). He talked of his wife. And of his interest in finding Beatriz de la Cueva's Jade.

"But The Queen Jade's *just a child's story," I said.*

"So's the Bible, and so is Le Morte d'Artur, *but we still do excavations for Christ's body in Jerusalem, and for Arthur's tomb in Glastonbury—"*

You're looking for the Witch's Stone." I laughed. "That's insane."

"I'm looking for Guatemala," he said. "Which is lost. Don't you understand that?"

I was stunned into silence by the fever in his voice.

"What are you looking for?" he asked me then.

I stared at him, very intently, at his eyes and his mouth.

But I could not say out loud that I had been looking for him.

He left me, not a year later.

He went back to his wife and his daughter. And I went back to Manuel, who eventually did forgive what I'd done.

Fifteen years passed, and we still kept in touch, occasionally even working together. And he didn't mind leaving his daughter with me when he'd go off on his jaunts, on account of the army's too-keen interest in his family. I didn't mind having the girl at our house, either, as I thought it was good for Lola to know her.

Meanwhile, Manuel and I resumed our romance on its old, idiosyncratic patterns, and seemed happy once more.

For his part, Tomas devoted himself to the rebels, even after they were nearly obliterated by the squads. But he abandoned the cause just as suddenly when he found that Drs. Saenz and Rodriguez had been killed by a guerrilla, probably for their rightist leanings, in that ancient cycle of revenge.

After that he changed. Without the war to consume him, his interest in the Jade became an obsession. And he grew distrustful of his foreign colleagues working in the jungle. He now took to calling them colonials and meddlers, even thieves.

I didn't hear from him after he called Yolanda back home in the days following his wife's death. I thought about that man every day, though I'd never lay eyes on him again.

Manuel did see him one more time, though. He had one last conversation with Tomas when he was chin-high in that quicksand pit.

Tomas fooled poor Manuel so that he almost died in the forest, and he has never been the same. I gave this as the reason why Lola should not write to Tomas's daughter anymore.

But when I am honest with myself, I have to admit that I didn't separate those girls because of Manuel.

I kept Yolanda and Lola apart because I have never been able to get over the hurt that Tomas did by leaving me.

I put my hand over my eyes.

A bad spasm went through me. Disbelief, and then, when I read that last line again, I had an awful, cold feeling. *I kept Yolanda and Lola apart.*

If I had been certain my mother were safe, I might have allowed myself to entertain some very dangerous thoughts about her just then. I think I would have frightened all of those tough soldiers with the words that filled my mouth.

But I didn't know if my mother was safe. So it didn't matter. I tried to tamp that feeling down; I wouldn't so much as describe it to myself.

To this day, I still have difficulty talking about it.

CHAPTER 33

L ola," Yolanda said. She had just woken up. I was still laboring to repress the shock at what I'd just read in my mother's hand, and Erik remained leaning heavily against me. I pressed the book to my chest.

"What?"

"Did I fall asleep?" She rested her head on my neck and twined her right arm around mine.

"For a minute."

She glanced over at the colonel, then at the soldier with the bilevel haircut. "Please don't let me."

"It's all right. He's not doing anything."

"I'm just so tired."

"Take a nap, you'll be fine."

"What are you doing?"

"Reading my mother's journal."

"The one with the map."

"Yes."

"Anything in there about me?"

I paused, and felt my chest clench. "In a way."

She pinched my arm gently. "Perhaps you shouldn't tell me about all that. I think I know how she felt about the de la Rosas." She pointed at the scenery. "And why ruin an otherwise perfect day?"

My heart crumpled. To hide my face from Yolanda, I looked up toward the landscape. Through the gaps in the red tarp I spied the burgundy ridges of the northward Sierra de las Minas, and I couldn't see the dark green pools that were the last stretches of the Motagua Valley anymore. To the south lay the red extensions of the Sierra del Espíritu Santo, which was stained with the afternoon sunlight slanting downward, onto the mounts and the dell. It turned everything from the combes to the coming river into shades of ocher and blood, scarlet and wine and rust. We'd passed the flooded ruins of Quiriguá and approached the Rio Dulce's bridge, which had held despite the swollen waters that had consumed six different villages during the hurricane. The Dulce is a high silver river where Guatemala's wealthy usually keep boats, but no schooners or yachts were to be found. Trash was scattered on the higher ground, along with crushed trees and planks from some of the houses that had been swept away. Up on the highest and driest areas stood more small settlements made from corrugated tin, and children ran in the muddy patches that might have served as front lawns. Several of the army trucks began to shear off from the line and toward these people, but we continued on our way to Flores.

Yolanda stirred again. She was staring out at the children running around the settlements.

"Yolanda," I said.

"Yes."

"I want you to forgive me."

She didn't say anything.

"Do you think you could do that?" I clenched my molars so hard my jaw popped. "For not being there for you. For not writing to you."

She stayed quiet for a few more seconds.

"Yolanda?"

"Yes, I heard you." She continued gazing at the children outside, and the black trees and the flood and the poor huts. "You know why I was so angry?"

"I think so."

"I don't know if you do. Because I certainly never told you. It's because you were the"—she hesitated here—"best friend I ever had. That's why I felt so much about it. Even though we hated each other sometimes. But that's how it was for me, too. I haven't had too many people I could count on, you see. It meant a lot to me. And when you wouldn't write back to me, and then I got that note of yours, last month—'All condolences'!—I didn't think that I could ever *not* be angry at you. And now it's just . . . gone. All of a sudden, like I just cut it out of me." She looked at me sideways. "It surprises me. But I like it."

"You just forgive me," I repeated, and gripped onto her hand. "I made a mistake."

"Yeah, well, I don't care about that anymore," she went on. "I'm even glad I'm here. With you, that is, not with the army"—that she whispered in a lower voice, glancing at the colonel. "You don't think he'll give us any trouble?"

"I don't think so. Not here."

"He recognizes me."

"I know."

"Just keep an eye on him. But . . . as I was saying, I'm glad. That I'm here."

"Me too."

"I'm feeling so generous, in fact, that I may even be warming up to your—your—you had some sort of unbelievable explanation for who this fellow Erik was, exactly. What was it again?"

"My friend," I said.

"Yes, fine. . . . But anyway, this will be good. The two—three—of us. We're going to go find your mom, and that thing my father wanted."

"We'd better," I said.

We both watched the tents and the mercury blur of the water flash at us from the window.

"When you wrote me that note after he died," she said, "I ripped your letter up. All in pieces. Then, after, I dug each piece out of the trash and pasted it back together."

"That sounds like you," I said.

"Then I set it on fire."

"Even more like you."

She squeezed my arm, and then she pressed her head back onto my shoulder. Erik mumbled something into my hair, woke up with a start, and attempted to arrange himself in a more gentlemanly posture, but then fell asleep again with his hand once more under my arm. His head tilted back, and he began to snore.

The river swept by, gold and brown and green and blue, with a fine smattering of rain and the splashing and calls of birds. And then the river ceased moving. Or rather, the truck did.

A soldier was saying that there was a problem with one of the vehicles, and another answered that the truck directly behind us had a flat tire (there were only three trucks left in our company, as the remainder had continued shearing off to their own destinations as we neared Flores). Though the colonel persisted in his dozing, several of the others had been roused by the truck's stop, and a number of these decamped to see what was going on.

I craned my neck to get a better look outside, but I didn't really care where we were at that moment. I was still dazed by my mother's journal.

When I glanced over at Yolanda again, I saw that she was peering over my shoulder. I'd let the diary fall back from my chest, and she was reading the exposed pages.

CHAPTER 34

"So, why don't you tell me what's in there now?" she asked.

"Oh—well—*no*," I said. I snapped the book shut. I was ready to hug and kiss Yolanda and ask her for forgiveness, but I found that I was really not at all prepared for her to read my mother's bitter secrets about disgracing my father.

"Like it or not, I did read something there," she said. "Something about—was it *me*? Did I see my name? Come on, let me look at it. I won't tell anyone."

"Let's keep talking about old times. I'll just put this away."

Erik woke up when my elbow stuck him in the ribs. "What's going on?"

I stood up and looked over the side of the truck. There was firm enough ground, covered by about eight inches of water. The trees bristled before us, just off the road, extending into a soggy and grassy long grove. A ways down from us stood the stalled truck, with one of its wheels removed. A small crowd of soldiers milled about, discussing what to do. Some kicked at the water because they were bored.

"I need to be alone for a second," I said. I grasped hold of my mother's duffel and jumped off the truck.

Yolanda slammed her hat back onto her head and followed me out, and Erik came bungling down, too.

The colonel followed.

"You're being stupid," she said outside, frowning a little. "You're not still trying to hide something from me, are you? Because"—her voice hardened—"please just tell me that you're not."

She continued peering down at me, and then, with a nimble and shocking flick of the wrist, she gave me a push and snatched the diary from my hands.

"Just to put you in your place," she said. "I just told you about my *feelings*, all right? And I *never do that*. So don't make me regret it."

"Give that back to me, Yolanda," I said, as calmly as possible. "I can't let you read that—*I* shouldn't have read it."

"Why? What's in here?"

"That's just—Mom's—private—*agh*." I raised my voice and struggled with her for the diary, though she was able to keep it from me by holding it over her head. One or two soldiers told me to quiet down.

I looked up again at the crowd of soldiers around the truck. In their midst a large and broad-shouldered soldier turned toward us, slowly. When he came into full view I noted the scar across his face and the rigid jaw and the problematic tear ducts.

This was the younger soldier who had given us so much trouble at The Pedro Lopez.

But he wouldn't do that again. He'd been drunk, right?

Yolanda looked up too, and stopped what she was doing.

I grasped the diary and stuffed it into my mother's pack.

"You two look bizarre grappling around like that," Erik said, still sleepy.

Yolanda and I looked over from the soldier to the colonel. He glanced at us from the edge of his eye and then approached the other. The colonel began to talk very gruffly to the scarred one. To the side, the soldier with the bilevel haircut blinked in a hard and nervous way.

The colonel turned from his colleague and started walking steadily toward us. The scarred one followed him. Then came the nervous one with the haircut.

Yolanda and I both moved apart, and took a step back.

"He said he wasn't going to do anything," I said. "They're on a humanitarian mission."

Erik turned and saw the approaching men.

"No," he said. "Wait a minute."

"It's all right," I said.

"What does he think he's going to do—he's going to try to fight me again? He can't—there are soldiers everywhere. They won't let him."

"He said he wasn't going to do anything," I repeated.

Yolanda continued staring at the colonel. He made his way slowly over to us, but fingering a small knife that hung from his belt.

"He lied," Yolanda said.

"No."

"Yes. He lied. He's going to hurt us."

She turned and began to walk quickly across the road, toward the trees.

Erik began to jog in her direction. "Yolanda, stop."

"Don't go that way," I called after her.

She turned around. Her face had turned the color of birch, and her eyes were a sharp hard green.

"Follow me!" she yelled.

"What?"

"Move, dammit! I know what I'm talking about!"

She turned, and then slipped into the dark covert of the mahoganies.

CHAPTER 35

I saw Yolanda's black hat like a sharp shadow against the glimmer of the woods as she disappeared into the grove. The three soldiers moved after her, quickening their pace.

I ran into the trees, with Erik fast behind me.

I could hear the smashing rapid footfalls of the men chasing us.

"Yolanda! Yolanda!"

We raced into the dense shifting patch of forest. The sunlight struggled to work its way within the clinging leaves and the clouds of bugs that ate the fragrant air as we slogged through the mire. Ahead of me, Yolanda darted forward and nearly disappeared into the forest's black and mint-colored shadows. The trees, dripping with moss and rain and choking with flowers, crawled around my head and attached their root fingers to my feet; they snagged on my mother's heavy duffel bag as I tried to rip through the bush. I was confused, but I still ran for what seemed a long time, far from the trucks on the highway. Erik wheezed behind me, grunting a complaint about women—and behind him, I heard the voices of the soldiers. The man with the bilevel haircut yelled something; he sounded frightened. The colonel barked at him to shut his mouth. The one with the scar kept silent.

We crashed into a dip in the forest. Here, the trees parted onto a small pond surrounded by a muddy bank laced with crabgrass and willow; the thicker hedge of trees curved around the basin. On the far side, the mahoganies looked so tightly knit together that a person could not fit through them.

Yolanda splashed through the water, scratched her way up the bank, and began to jolt up the thicket by hooking her feet and hands into the dents and crotches of the trees. She grappled up to the branches of a mahogany while her breath came out in quick hard contractions. Then she slipped over to another nearby branch, apparently planning to make an escape through the canopy of trees.

"Hurry!" she yelled. She glared down at me, surrounded by leaves.

I slid into the water; Erik half fell into it beside me. We watched, dumb, while Yolanda reached down to give me a hand. But we were too far apart, and she was too high to reach.

"Jump!" She looked up and past me.

We heard the heavy steps of the men behind us. They clambered and smashed through the wood. Then they stopped.

"Can you make it?" Yolanda hissed.

I gripped onto my mother's duffel bag.

"I do not believe your friends have quite your acrobatic skills," the colonel said, in an eerie, calm voice.

We all knew he was right.

"Just go, Yolanda," Erik said. He turned around to face the soldiers.

"They don't want us," I said, though I wasn't really sure of that.

But Yolanda didn't go. She grimaced and climbed down from her tree, half cracking one branch on her descent.

Her shadow cast a long dark line in the pond where Erik and I stood. The colonel's reflection reached up into the green water from the opposite direction: the two lines wavered, breaking apart when I moved my leg.

"Who are you?" Yolanda asked.

"I know you who are," the colonel said.

"Get the hell away from here," Erik yelled. "You're scaring these women."

"You should be scared too, my dear man. Or don't you remember the conversation you and Estrada had before?"

"I remember it."

"Once he gets started, there's really nothing I can do to stop him, you see."

I looked up from the reflections in the pond, up to the men on the other side of the bank.

The soldier named Estrada remained farthest back, still in the thicker part of the wood. The soldier with the bilevel haircut stood to his left. His cheeks shuddered, and he seemed terrified.

The colonel stood above me; his hands were cut by the branches he'd run past. His elegant head, clean triangular cheekbones, and small mustache formed a smooth, almost pleasant facade, until his mouth opened into a wild gape. He let out a strange and short sound, like a cry.

"Your father," he said to Yolanda, "your father killed my nephew."

"What are you talking about?" she yelled.

"Moreno," the soldier with the haircut said. "Calm down."

The soldier with the scar still said nothing, but his right eye winced and began to tear up.

"My father never killed anybody," Yolanda said.

"Your father killed my nephew," the soldier repeated. "With an explosive."

"Moreno," the soldier with the haircut said again. He hunched in the mud.

"De la Rosa's only been accused of one killing," Erik said. "That accountant."

"My nephew," the colonel said. "Nearly my son."

"Moreno," Yolanda murmured.

"Then that's—I've heard of this man," I said, looking at the scarred soldier, and remembered the stories about de la Rosa blowing up an army colonel's home. His bomb had scarred a young soldier who'd gone on to do terrible things in the war.

"Many have," the colonel said. "Estrada is my protégé."

"That's the lieutenant," Erik said. "The killer."

"Help us!" I screamed, toward what I thought might have been the place where the trucks had stopped.

"I wonder if they can hear you through all this?" Moreno said, gesturing at the web of trees around us.

I screamed for help again.

"Oh, God," Yolanda said, bending down at her waist. I thought she began crying, but when she looked up, a scowl tore over her face. "Your nephew was an accident! He was a mistake!"

"As if that matters to me?"

"And he was—*just one person*. And you've killed—"

"I'm sure that you understand that my little world means more to me than the whole universe, Señorita de la Rosa. As these things always do, to all people. My sweet nephew was more wonderful to me than any village. Certainly much more than your insignificant little head. Though I'm sure your father would disagree, if he were still alive—*if* he were still alive. Is he? I heard such bizarre things about his funeral."

And now Yolanda did begin to cry.

Moreno walked toward us, slipping ungracefully down the bank until he half fell into the water at my feet. Erik yanked me away from his path and dragged me to the other side of the basin. I dropped my mother's duffel on the shallow end of the bank.

"Go away," Erik said to Moreno.

"Get away from her," Yolanda commanded. She did not sound afraid.

Moreno stood knee deep in the water, smeared on one side of his flanks by mud. The third soldier remained on the banks, useless and sniffling. Estrada, who had stayed silent and still on the far side of the pond, began to make his way down.

"It was her father who gave you that scar," Moreno said.

"De la Rosa did hurt me, Colonel Moreno," Estrada said. "You're right."

I slipped out of Erik's grasp and jolted over to Estrada, though again, when confronted with so much mass, I barely knew what to do. I gripped his shirt and his shoulder and tried to shake him; I was half hanging off his torso and trying to make him fall down, but he didn't. My nails were scratching at him when Erik began to pull at me from behind.

"We—have—to—go," he grunted. "He'll hit you. Or worse."

"Don't touch her," Yolanda said. "I won't let you do anything to them."

"Is that so?" Moreno asked. "And how would you do that?"

"I don't know—Lola—leave . . . But you—yes, you—why don't you come over here, Lieutenant Estrada? Pay attention—that's right—let me see how ugly you are, *hermano*. My father did an excellent job on you, didn't he? You must be the absolute filthiest cuss I ever laid eyes on—I'll bet you never get any attention from the ladies, you poor thing. Though there are still uses for you, aren't there? We could put you in the circus? Or you could play monsters in the pictures—"

Moreno had climbed the bank and stood in front of Yolanda. While she spat her insults at Estrada, she also was trying to pull off the branch of the tree that she'd cracked. Estrada continued to make his way up toward her through the water, and Erik and I wrestled him and punched him, so that he walked unsteadily through the pond and up the sliding bank. He was magnificently strong.

"Stop it," he said, to us, irritated. He hit Erik across the face with the back of his hand. And then a second time. Erik staggered back, coughing, and gripped onto him harder again.

He hit Erik again, this time with such force that we both fell back. Estrada and Moreno stood in front of Yolanda, who had cracked the branch off the tree and began to swing it at them.

The stick hit Estrada hard on the shoulder, but he only grasped onto it with both hands and ripped it from Yolanda. He hurled it to the side. The two men took another step closer.

Yolanda stood on the bank defenseless, but perfectly still and ready for their attack.

The soldier on the other side of the pond remained there, gulping with fear.

"You make me sick, with all your talking," Estrada said to Yolanda.

"You make me *so* sick," she whispered.

Estrada put his hands, slowly, on either side of her face.

A moment passed. I had no idea what was happening.

He stroked his thumb across her cheek. He touched her lips with his fingers. A terrible expression scorched his features. He bent his face close to hers.

And then he kissed her on her mouth.

Erik and I went totally silent at this, in shock.

"Don't lose your temper, my boy, and do anything disgusting to her," Moreno said. "You know—I just can't control him sometimes when he gets angry—"

Estrada turned from Yolanda and raised his left hand. He brought his fist down onto the head of Colonel Moreno.

"That's enough of that," he said, hitting him. "That's enough of that."

The soldier with the bilevel haircut leapt to his feet and went scrambling in a random direction, into the farther reaches of the jungle. Moreno lay on the ground below Estrada.

Estrada hit him a second time. "That's—enough."

The beating went on for several seconds until Estrada looked up at us. A filament of blood ran from his jaw to his neck.

"I'm returning a favor," he said to us, in a soft voice. "I'm going to kill him like he killed me. He killed me. Do you understand?"

"No," Yolanda said. "You're crazy. *You're a butcher.*"

"Maybe. But do you know why?"

"Shut up!"

"Because of your father. Because I let de la Rosa get past me and blow up that house. *This* is what your name means to me." Estrada pointed to his scar, and his cheeks were wet. "And look at *you.* I've been wanting to kill you since I first heard your name. But now that I see you . . . I want—" His face was thrashed with emotion. "Women are harder."

He turned away from us and looked back down at Moreno, who was moving.

"Come on, let's go," Erik said, tugging at the two of us. "Jesus, let's get out of here."

"You'd better," Estrada said. "I don't know what I'll do if you're still here when I'm done."

Moreno lifted up a hand in the air and dropped it back down again.

I saw that he had a severe cut on his face, and he did not appear to be breathing normally. He tried to say something, but he could not enunciate any words. He sighed deeply, as if he were sleeping and dreaming.

I grabbed my mother's duffel bag from the bank and began pushing Yolanda into the pool. She had a horrified expression and violently wiped her mouth.

Then the three of us bolted away through the trees.

CHAPTER 36

For an hour, Erik, Yolanda, and I pushed through the layers of the wood until we reached another stretch of the Carretera al Atlántico. We had wandered so far from the resting point of the army trucks that we could no longer see them, and we thought we were probably safe from the reaches of Estrada.

We found ourselves alone on a section of road, and began wading through the water while monkeys capered above in the bush. The moonlight fell very pale and thin over the long highway, turning it into a skein of moving silver. The Peten, with its black and ragged forest, mounted all around us.

I hiked my mother's heavy duffel bag up onto my shoulder.

For hours, we walked upon this road; sometimes our teeth chattered, or our voices caught in our throats. But mostly we kept our thoughts to ourselves.

Around midnight, we reached the section of the Carretera al Atlántico that forks off into a sand spit and extends to a pair of islands. The sand made rustling noises beneath our shoes, and a breeze swirled over our heads. We were encouraged by the sight of the streetlamps. Walking closer down the spit, we saw the village that emerges as a small, knobbed, bungalow-covered patch of land in the center of the lake known as Lago de Peten Itzae.

"There's Flores," Yolanda said.

I nodded. "Thank God."

"It's also known as Tayasal," Erik said. "That's its fifteenth-century name."

Neither Yolanda nor I said anything to that for a second, but we looked at each other.

Then Yolanda said, "Oh, Tayasal?"

"Yes."

She raised her eyebrows at me; she was being nice to him. "I think I might remember that name—was that it, exactly?"

"That's what the Peten Indians used to call it. This is the place where Cortés left a white horse, and they wound up worshipping it as a god for the next hundred years or so. Well, not the actual horse, obviously, but after it died they made a stone idol of it. And then around 1618, missionaries arrived—white men hadn't been seen here again since old Hernán Cortés. But they were not very *nice* white men. Apparently, they weren't much intimidated by the fact that the Indians could have chopped them up into stew or whatever, because as soon as they saw the horse god, they just crushed it to bits. The Indians, for their part, were apparently far too gentlemanly to register their dissent with a hasty bit of decapitation or disembowelment, which was too bad, because they were promptly pacified and enslaved, and . . . can you tell that I'm wholly traumatized and talking like a deranged pedant just to keep myself sane and awake?"

"Actually, yes."

"But don't stop now," I said. We continued lugging our way toward the blue-and-gold lit houses and the little winding stone streets, which were not flooded on account of the incline of the island. "Come on, tell us the story about the white horse—it was Cortés's, and it was lame when he left it here, and when it died the Itzae took its bones and buried them in sacred ground, and erected a stone in its place—"

"Over which the unintentionally ironic Spaniards later built a church, and this town," Yolanda said.

"Yes, but before that the Franciscans smashed the idol, and it looked like the Indians were not going to make much trouble about it," Erik went on, "until the very bad day in 1623 when the Itzae started to feel upset at the priests, and so belatedly rose against them and killed them all in a massacre, after which they were forced to run up into the hills beyond the lake and were never seen again."

"And here we are," I said, hiking my mother's bag up.

"Yes," he sighed. "Here we are."

We stood at the edge of the village of Flores and looked up at the gold lamps shining through the blue air, and the stars that sparkled down, casting reflections in the surrounding lake, which dazzled back up again.

And even though I was so sad, the sight suddenly pierced my heart. It was a shock to me. Despite everything that had happened, and that I had read, the world was still beautiful.

I took a breath and tried to see that, as hard as I could.

"I can't wait to go to bed," Yolanda said.

CHAPTER 37

I n the gloom of the night, we could barely make out Flores's street signs and numbers. We wound our way through the stone-covered lanes and past the mysterious moon-glimmering views of the lake, until we stumbled across the hotel that my father had mentioned to me when I last spoke to him on the phone. The Hotel Peten Itzae proved to be a tiny, slightly ramshackle bed-and-breakfast, hung with pots of gardenias and ivy. The owners decorated the place with plain upholstered furniture and an old-fashioned stereo with pine-wood veneer. A broad wood common table dominated the kitchen, crowding an old wood-burning stove that was about the size of a sofa. The host was a lanky dark man; he and his pocket-sized wife, as well as his four nightgown-clad teenage daughters, had all climbed out of their beds to greet us in the hall. They spoke to us quietly, as five other boarders were sleeping in the house. Erik, Yolanda, and I, dirty, exhausted, and still very scared from our brush with the soldiers, gawked back at our hosts as a terrible hunger hit us—we had not eaten for hours. But the landlord, behind whom stood his girls, all of them waking up at the sight of Erik, only shook his head and said, "We don't have anything ready for you, sir. Our stores are poor. There isn't much coming into Flores, because of the hurricane."

"Was there much damage here?" Erik asked. "The streets aren't flooded."

"Not so bad as in other places," the host said; "only one person has died."

"One person?" I asked.

"We got lucky," his wife said. "People are starving in the east, and so most of the supplies are going there, not here."

"We don't even have chocolate," one of the daughters said.

"We don't have Zucaraias," another of the daughters said, meaning the Spanish version of Frosted Flakes.

"We don't have any Pepsi, either."

"Or orange soda."

When we looked at the woebegone girls and their haggard parents, the terrible feelings we'd been trying to fend off with crayfish risotto in Guatemala City, Armagnac in Antigua, reconciliations in Rio Hondo, and stories about holy horses just a few minutes ago threatened to come down on us with more force than we could manage. Even Yolanda looked as if she were ready to simply lie down on the oak floor and weep. The girls also appeared close to tears, from the look in their gigantic eyes, and the husband and wife, glancing at their daughters, began to press their lips together very hard, as if they were trying to keep their composure.

"We've had a rough week here, see," the landlord said. "My girls here, they don't understand."

"Somebody died," the smallest daughter said, from behind her father.

"A lady died," said her sister.

"What lady?" I asked.

"Ssssh, honey, we don't talk about that," said the mother.

"We're looking for a woman named Juana Sanchez," I said. "We're here to find her—maybe she took a room here, in your hotel?" I described my mother, down to her hairdo and her grumpiness and her job as a professor.

But the landlord said: "Not here, ma'am, and I never heard of her, sorry."

"Let's just go to bed and forget that today ever happened," Yolanda said.

None of us moved, though, and everyone grew quiet again. We all just stared at each other in the hallway under the glare of the ceiling light, until Erik—who until that point had been looking very bad, with his hair standing up straight on his head and mud still on his bruised cheek—glanced over at me and grinned in that way that I remembered when he'd been flirting with the hussy librarians at the Huntington Library a thousand years ago.

"Okay, I think I'm going to have to take charge here," he said. "We'll have to postpone that bedtime, Yolanda. It appears clear enough to me that a little sticky debauchery is in order. Otherwise we're going to go out absolutely, clinically—*nuts.*"

"You're the boss," I said.

"Really?"

"No, but go on."

"Fine," he said. "You know what we need?"

"Yes, a long, cold, nasty, chewy, stiff drink," I said.

"Stiff as a board," he said.

"All right," Yolanda said. She wouldn't let Erik look tougher than her. "But don't forget the hors d'oeuvres."

"That doesn't sound so bad," the landlord said.

"All we've got is pancake mix," his wife said.

"And we've got a little rum," the landlord said.

"What do you mean, we've got a little rum?" his wife asked.

"Rum will do," Erik said.

So we all went into the kitchen with the huge stove and started to mix up some booze, and the wife of the landlord sat down at the long oak table and put up her bare feet while Erik wrapped an apron around his mud-splattered pants and whipped up Bisquick pancakes. Yolanda went out into the living room and found, among the landlords' extensive collection, some old vinyl Liliana Felipe records. Soon the maracas and horns and thumping drums and Felipe's dangerous and sly voice began to bang through the house like a wonderful calamity, causing these little Hummel figurines on the top of the stereo to shake and shudder. It also caused the other up-to-then-sleeping lodgers to slump out of their rooms, though they perked up quickly enough when they smelled the pancakes and the six bottles of Bacardi that Erik discovered in the very back of a cupboard, at the sight of which the wife registered shock and indignation until she had consumed four glasses of the stuff at the urging of her new Guatemalan-American bartender.

"Drink up, you glorious beauty queen," Erik said. "You have the eyes of a starlet and the legs of a fawn, and your daughters are going to break the hearts of a million men."

"Okay," she said.

Until dawn, Erik displayed the talents that had melted the chastity of the postdocs at UCLA, driven my mother to distraction, and ecstatically corrupted the university deans until they slid under the tables in the faculty lounge. For one night, his mastery of the saturnalia allowed everyone a respite—and in my case, I could forget what I had just read in my mother's journal. By two in the morning I saw the daughters of the landlords whooping and swinging from his elbows, and the wife tangoed with her husband and bawled out Felipe lyrics in his ear. The drunker Yolanda became, the more stiff and proper she looked, as she sat at the table very rigidly, with the increasingly perfect posture of a Russian ambassador or a corseted duchess and the haughty expression of faux soberness. But when I came over to hug her, she was not so formidable after all; she pressed the knuckles of my hand very hard to her face and kissed them.

"I love you and I hate you," she said. "But I actually don't hate you at all."

"You're my best friend, Yolanda," I bawled. "I was a horse's ass."

"That's right," she sobbed back, in complete inebriated agreement. "You have the ass of a horse."

The rest of the lodgers, as well as a half-dozen other men, sat with Yolanda at the long wooden table, where everyone laughed and wept inconsolably at the horrors of the hurricane and the war and the wide, incomprehensible void left by all the dead. Periodically the landlord's wife hauled her daughters back to their bedrooms, but within minutes they reappeared in the kitchen, barefoot, munching on pancakes and taking curious sniffs at the rum. Meanwhile, in a gluttonous and life-affirming effort something like an old biblical story involving loaves and fishes, Erik managed to make the bottles last all night long and baked as many as eight different courses of pancakes, which he cooked in an old black frying pan and toasted by flipping them up in the air so that they performed several less-than-perfect aerial loops. Dancing, swigging, sweating, and telling the constantly reappearing girls riddles and jokes at the stove (where the landlord got the wood to fire the behemoth up, I don't know, but I did think that I saw him drag out a couple of nightstands toward the backyard and return with sufficient kindling), Erik finally at six in the morning tiptoed over the sprawled forms of the daughters, picked the stiff-backed Yolanda straight up from her chair, and began to waltz with her to "San Miguel Arcangel" while they traded more insults and guffawed and bawled in each others' faces. And then, after that, it was my turn.

"Get up, Cleopatra," he said, leaning over me. "Come foxtrot with me, my gorgeous blue-stocking, my dolphin, my sweet fury, my mermaid."

"You must be drunk," I said.

"Perfectly so," he replied.

"Oh, do it, for Christ's sake," Yolanda said. "It's so short."

"What's so short?"

"Life," Yolanda cried.

So we did begin dancing within all that somnolent madness. Erik put his arm around my waist, then bounced me about to the mambo of Celia Cruz's "Burundanga." I was hurled up in the atmosphere by giant hammy hands and hauled around so that my limbs were flailing and my hair scattered everywhere, and my boots wouldn't even touch the floor as he swung me and flung me all about the whirling, colored kitchen, and when I held my head back stars sparkled behind my eyelids and I laughed for the first time in eight days, which is when this nightmare had started. After an initial blast of discombobulation, as I'd never danced with anybody like that before, I didn't have any trouble digging down deep into my crumbling heart to find all the explosive and hysterical stuff that makes up the best of salsa and rock-and-roll. When he started swinging me up and down the way the bobby-soxers in 1950s movies do, I bellowed out the half-memorized lyrics with a rapturous dyslexia, and Erik laughed so hard he nearly choked. The partiers gave me a few manic *Arribas!* between cup and lip.

When the music stopped, all I could hear was the rush of blood to my head and the sound of the needle skidding like a runaway car on the vinyl. Erik's face turned plum-dark while he roared, "You are the absolutely best *worst* dancer I've ever had the pleasure of destroying a kitchen with, my excellent flat-footed beauty." I opened my eyes and discovered that we hung onto each other as if the ground moved beneath us, while all around the others enjoyed this fantastic alcoholism that for a minute had wiped every bad thing from our minds.

And that's when I heard it.

"Here's to the lady who died," said one of the neighbors, a handsome older man who had consumed most of the rum and so enunciated his words with a laborious accuracy.

I heard the clinking of glasses and smelled the spilling of more rum. Yolanda presided at the table like a queen, her Stetson at a perfect jaunty angle and her hands dancing in the air along to the music, and she nodded, only half comprehending this toast.

"What lady?" I asked, remembering that detail again.

"There was that lady who died, man," the neighbor said.

"You mean 'lady,' " another neighbor said.

"What do you mean, 'lady'?"

"What?"

"I said there was that lady who died."

"You said, 'There was that lady who died, man,' when you meant 'the lady who died, lady,' because *this* girl here's a lady."

"Yeah, well that's what I meant. The lady who died."

"Lady."

"Lady."

"What in the hell are you people talking about?" I asked.

"These North American girls got a mouth," someone said.

This was one of the other neighbors, or perhaps a lodger, who also had his head down and began weeping afresh. And then the rest of the neighbors' eyes started to fill up with tears, which fell down their faces in streams, and the landlord too, and they started talking once more about everything that had been lost in the hurricane and the meaninglessness of life, and how all of the people who disappeared would never come back ever again.

"Somebody died," Yolanda said, mournfully.

"Don't get my kids upset," said the landlord's wife, looking suddenly completely temperate and grabbing three daughters from their truant positions in the kitchen doorway, and a fourth who was sprawled out in the living room. "This subject is bad for their emotional health."

"Mine too," the landlord said.

"Who died?" I asked in a whisper.

"Was it a local?" Erik asked.

"Oh, no, thank God."

"Bad fortune even to say that."

"It was a North American, like you."

"Like me?" I asked.

"No, not so much," one of the lodgers said. "She was dark—she was a Latin."

"I'm a Latin."

"More of a real kind of Latin."

"Not Hungarian?" one of the neighbors asked.

"No, a Mexican?"

"A Mexican from America? Or an American from Mexico?"

"I think she was a teacher or something. A professor. She was going up to the forest, I think, or coming back down from it."

"Anyway, that poor woman bit off a piece of bad luck. She was hit by a tree when the storm came, and then they brought her up here."

"She's in the morgue, madam, from what I hear," said the handsome older man to me, carefully and clearly.

"I see," I said, and then it took all of my concentration to keep my body and mind together, and to keep calm.

"He's not talking about Juana," Yolanda said. She focused on me very hard with her too-steady eyes and began to sober up through sheer willpower.

"No, it's not her." My voice sounded queerly flat.

I felt Erik take hold of my hand.

"No, it can't be. It's not her that died here," I said.

"What's wrong with your face?"

"She's fine. Lola, don't worry."

"Is she going to faint?"

"No. She's not going to faint."

Unfortunately, Yolanda was right, as I didn't faint. I stayed very conscious.

The men at the table went back to their drinking, but I just stood there for a long while, uncertain what my next move should be.

I couldn't arrange my thoughts in a linear order. I went over to one of the chairs and sat down on it, and didn't speak a word.

But I knew what I'd have to do.

CHAPTER 38

Four hours after the fiesta at the Hotel Peten Itzae had ended, and when the businesses and government buildings had opened, Erik and I walked into the thin light of Flores, through the stone pathways and past the blue- and rust-painted houses.

We made our way in total silence; I could hear only the ghostly sound of the lake's waves on the shore, and the echoes of our shoes on the cobblestones.

We were heading to the police station, and the morgue.

As we made our way through Flores, we saw that it had been washed by the hurricane, and in the hour after sunrise the island took on colors of pale blue and ivory and a light, stony pink. Yellow, green, and turquoise hotels and houses lined the small streets; their buffeted facades peeled back in places, exposing a crumbling stucco, or delicate layers of colored paint. The lake surrounding the island was a dark blue mercury; it spread out into shades of cobalt and periwinkle and was bordered by poke boats painted marigold or bright green. A few men and boys rowed their boats over the lake and made their way to the nearby island of Santa Elena, with its language school and famous caves.

Erik and I had left Yolanda behind at the Peten Itzae. I'd deposited my mother's bag there, too, and I hadn't brought anything with me but that diary and my identification papers. This small load was tucked under my arm as we moved east and north around the island and crossed over the central square that is made up of, of all things, a basketball court. And then we headed west, turned right, and reached the Gobernacion Departmental, the large building that houses the governmental offices for the department of the Peten. The office was lit and open, and from behind the glass doors we could see officers dressed in blue uniforms behind a counter, and beyond them a warren of rooms.

"I can go in with you," Erik said as we stood outside the doors. "Or I could just go in alone, if you like."

"No, but thanks," I said. "I'll do it myself."

"What are you going to do, exactly?"

I looked across the street at more of those placid blue houses. "Tell them I need to see that woman. To see—"

He nodded. "If you can identify her."

"It's not likely that it's Mom," I said.

"That's right."

"We don't even know if they'll let me in," I went on.

"We don't even know if those men at the hostel were right—we were drinking. They could have made a mistake. Maybe no one died here at all."

I nodded. "There's that, too."

But as I was soon to learn from one of the officers—a friendly woman with curly hair and in one of those neat blue uniforms with a very stiff collar—someone was killed around Flores after being hit by a tree in the hurricane, and the victim was female, and a foreigner. The officer also informed me that she would let me in to see if I could identify the body, because up until now no one had.

After a bit of a wait, during which time Erik and I sat next to each other on benches in total silence, I was led into a room.

The room that constituted Flores's morgue was small and buff-colored, with one metal table, a sink, and two file cabinets. Something was happening to me so that instead of being struck with hysterical blindness, which I would have much preferred, I was instead inflicted with a sort of hysterical alertness I observed with a surreal clarity the black wavy speckles in the floor's linoleum, which was cut into flat black tiles. A white plastic trash can stood behind the metal sink, and on the wall were signs in black and red Spanish script that I had trouble reading. Beneath the ceiling hung a row of scuffed yellow cabinets, and above them stretched long rectangular fluorescent lights.

A male officer with papyrus-colored hair wheeled something into the room on a metal rolling table. This mass was covered not with a white sheet but with a cotton blanket, woven in marigold and black designs. It was something like a blanket for a bed, or a very large shawl.

He turned it back, gently, so that I could make the identification.

The woman underneath the blanket had dark hair and a face of indeterminate color, with high cheekbones and a brutally sculpted jaw, made severe by the drawing back of the skin. I saw the precise fringe of the eyelashes and eyebrows that had been plucked into a delicate arch. Her thin lips distended in a dissatisfied expression. The hair fell back from her face; her nose was long, not hooked like an eagle's, thin at the bridge and flaring at the nostrils; she had pierced ears but wore no earrings. Her neck was long and pale above the shawl-like blanket. Peering closer, I saw that on the far side of her face, which I couldn't make out too well because of my angle, there was a bruise.

A few minutes later I left that room and moved again through the corridor, covered with more of that black-speckled linoleum and abraded by white lights. I went back to the waiting area with the bench where Erik waited with my papers and my mother's diary stacked up next to him in a neat pile.

He looked up.

"It wasn't her," I said.

"Let's get out of here."

"It wasn't her."

"I'll take you somewhere, Lola," Erik said. "Somewhere you can rest. You look terrible."

"They said they thought she might be Hungarian," I said.

And now my body and my hands and my face were moving all by themselves, and I couldn't do anything to control them or stop it.

CHAPTER 39

Erik hired a cab that took us across the spit to Santa Elena Island, and the cave of Actun Kan. The cavern sits behind a patchwork of hills, half hidden, and is famous for its burial chambers. Limestone formations score its walls; the Indians believed that some of the patterns looked like their snake gods, which is why its Spanish name is La Cueva de la Serpiente, or the Cave of the Serpent. Other visitors have said that the limestone shapes favored the rain god called Chac, and the Europeans believed they intuited the face of Saint Peter there.

The cave glimmered with small electric lights strung within its hollow; the hurricane's rains still soaked the ground, and in some places the water stood several inches high. Erik had the driver maneuver us up to the small lot before its mouth, and when we emerged from the cab the opal sky descended onto the small buttes, stained dark burgundy and iron from the rain.

Erik put his hand on my hand, which still gripped my mother's journal. "I thought this might be a nice place to bring you after that scare. Someplace peaceful."

"It is."

He looked back at the car, a small green pirate cab driven by a spiky-haired teenager wearing an AC/DC T-shirt.

"You want me to wait for you here?" the cabbie asked.

"Just a second," Erik said. He looked at me. "What would you like to do now, Lola? We can do anything you want. We can relax here for a while, and have the driver come back. Or we could go looking for your mother in town. Or we could talk. About whatever you like. Your mother. Or—I don't know—the Stelae. We were talking about codes—I have some ideas; it might take your mind off the last couple of days."

But I wasn't ready to talk about jade yet this morning, or Von Humboldt, or how my mother had written about the Stelae and the maze and its decipherment.

"We'll do all that, Erik," I said, "but right now I'd like to be alone. Just for an hour or so. To be by myself and think."

"You sure?"

"I'm sure."

"An hour, all right. I'll go into town and scramble around a few of those B & Bs to see if anyone's heard of your mother. Maybe get some supplies. And then I'll come right back here and get you."

I smiled at him, and he squeezed my hand.

Above us, a light drizzle began to pluck at the wet mud at our feet. The sky looked heavy, and very low; magenta and coral streaks brightened the clouds.

The cabbie slid off in the green car with Erik in tow. I watched them leave and pulled my collar up against the rain. Then, tucking my mother's book under my arm, I went off by myself into the cave.

The dark cavern rang with the sound of insects and my own footsteps as I slogged through the wet pools that had flooded the threshold. The electric lights cast a brassy glare on the limestone walls, which looked smooth initially, but then revealed themselves to be formed of intricate layers of dripping stone, as if that limestone was once a substance as soft as water. As I went deeper, the grottoes grew blacker and the water colder, but the lamps shone bright enough so that I could see stalagmites growing out of the floor in the white twisting shapes of wax. I also glimpsed the bumps and ridges in the stone walls, which didn't look anything to me like snakes or gods or saints, but more like writing in a foreign language, or random scratches and ridges made by someone's hand. I ran my hands over the limestone, and when I did, grit came off on my fingers. I wandered through the black and bright tunnels and rooms of Actun Kan, and did not understand any of the marks that I passed by, until one of the signs on the walls did look familiar. Tromping through the water, I leaned forward and peered at the scrapes on the wall. It seemed that I was staring at a very old hieroglyphic language. The marks were nearly rubbed away, though still embedded in the stone; almost illegible. But when I brought my face closer, and ran my fingers over the characters, I made them out:

Marisela y Francisco 1995

And that pretty much ended my experiments with cave paleology. I continued walking, holding my mother's journal, until I reached a high-domed chamber in the cave, which was well lit enough to read by. I sat down on one of the higher stones on the edge of the room. Green and brown lizards danced over the stones and up the walls; insects flew in small storms that I batted away with my arms. I sat with my knees up to balance Mom's journal on them, and my thoughts were accompanied only by the eerie *tink* of swimming salamanders and the echoes of pond-diving toads. The shock of thinking that I had just been about to identify the body of my mother, and the hard jolt of seeing that other woman, combined with my earlier panic at having read Juana's confessions, made me feel lightheaded.

I looked down to steady myself. The journal remained on my lap; the tin lock hung broken from the boards; water damaged part of the spine, and there was a rip in the salmon-colored binding cloth.

From far off came the splashing sounds of animals swimming in the pools that lined the cave. A small brass lamp, fixed into one corner of the cave's ceiling, sent out light that fell across my legs and my arm like a stroke of gold paint.

I opened my mother's journal again.

October 19

Next day. Spent the morning looking at things I've written in the past week, and it strikes me how hard it is for anyone to ever forget their past no matter how much they'd like to.

Though forgetting de la Rosa is probably beyond my talents.

Lola's always reminding me of him, for one. The strange thing is that I think she takes the most after Manuel. Not just that she's a bookish thing, or sometimes a little shy, but rather that she has his same constancy and stubbornness and timidity—she never did take to life out here with me in the bush, like Manuel with his maddening phobias.

I'll have to face it, eventually. She's an armchair creature. She'll never come out to Guatemala with me now.

I chuckled, and my laughter bounced back to me from the cave walls. I knew that in my last few days of tracking, flood-jumping, car-crashing, Yolanda-surviving, and army-caravanning, I was setting some kind of *macha* record the likes of which the great Juana Sanchez would find hard to beat herself.

Then I began reading again and stopped laughing.

But still, she has the other's hair, his build, his face, his hands, his eyes, doesn't she?

It's funny how someone can appear exactly like someone else you hate, and you can love them so much that it justifies your whole life.

Because I think that my loving Lola has justified my life. It's the one really good thing I think I ever did. Even if Tomas never loved me.

Still, I have my regrets.

What's that old song again?

> *I lost you*
> *I lost you*
> *I'm lost, too*
> *My darling*

Nevertheless . . .

I should perhaps remind myself that I have another consolation, in addition to our daughter.

And I believe that it is time that I turn my thoughts to that sub-ject, again.

For it is no small matter that I, and not my beloved rival, have cracked the puzzle of the Queen Jade.

I gripped the diary with both hands and read these passages again and again.

And the strange thing is that I think she takes the most after Manuel. But she has the other's hair, his build, his face, his hands, his eyes. It's funny how someone can appear exactly like someone else you hate . . . Our daughter.

There seemed no other way of interpreting these writings. Tomas de la Rosa and my mother had an affair in the year before my birth. De la Rosa was my father. Not Manuel Alvarez.

CHAPTER 40

Perhaps the human heart should only confront a few revelations at a time, but in the gloom of my cave I was learning secrets. And I was starved to understand the rest.

As I read, my back grew stiff, and my neck as well; it became increasingly humid in the cavern. The light from the brass torch attached to the wall broke into glistering coins of gold that swam on the surface of the pools. Mosquitoes hovered over the water, and on account of the torch these too turned burnished and oddly lustrous. I turned the pages, and that crisp flicking of the paper echoed clearly and precisely in the stone chamber.

Then I came to an entry written just before she'd left on her trip to this country I now found myself in.

October 20

I've decided to leave for Guatemala in two days to locate the Stone, despite the gloomy weather reports on the news.

It no longer seems adequate to me to simply publish my findings concerning the Maze of Deceit. Rather, I would prefer to go alone, and finish Tomas's work. This will be my way of paying my respects.

What findings on the Maze of Deceit? I continued paging through the book, at a quicker pace.

October 25; 8:00 P.M.

In Antigua now, and the rain's getting worse by the second. Just in case I run into a squall while out in the jungle, I'll write down here a copy of the decoded text, for safekeeping. And I'll keep my diary at the Hotel Casa Santo Domingo.

THE MAZE OF DECEIT

Half a year ago, I was obliged to take on the task of editing a monograph authored by the insufferable Erik Gomara on Alexander Von Humboldt's Personal Narrative of a Journey to the Equinoctial Regions of the New Continent. *Though I dreaded to take on this interminable job, it turned out to hold for me the most marvelous consequence: for when I reread the German's telling of his efforts to capture the Queen Jade, I found that certain descriptions of the Maze of Deceit bore a strange resemblance to the images on the Stelae. Von Humboldt's report of the labyrinth's confusing "passages" and "signs" recollected for me a haphazard pattern that Manuel and I had translated from the Flores panels back in the early 1960s.*

Could there be a relationship between them? As I tried to recall any other accounts of patterns that related to the mazes or the Jade, I remembered also some fragments from Beatriz de la Cueva's Letters *that might shed some light on this fledgling theory.*

I ran to the U's library and paged through de la Cueva's correspondence to her sister Agata. In them, I returned again to the stories of Balaj K'waill, the Labyrinth of Deceit, the deadly trek through the jungle, and the murder of the beloved slave.

I did not at first understand what relationship, if any, this history might have to the Stelae. And for several weeks, I shelved my ideas and suspicions at the back of my brain; whatever trail I had been on seemed to have gone perfectly cold. But the entire time, something was forming in my mind: An idea. An insight.

And then, like a light, on it came.

I woke up one night, just before dawn, and the notion struck me full force:

*In the 1920s, Oscar Angel Tapia found the Stelae at the mouth of
the Sacluc, which is exactly where de la Cueva writes that she saw
the maze of "clear blue stone." We'd all thought of the first labyrinth
being some gigantic Coliseum-like edifice winding its way through
the trees,* instead of a stone book placed, so precisely, at its threshold. *In the* Narrative, *Von Humboldt writes about this too, describing blue carved stones and the first maze. And he recounts also
"sapphire passages" where one grows "confused by the signs."* All of
this is his description of the Maze of Deceit, which is what the
Stelae are.

*That is, at the border of the Sacluc sat the maze, which was made
up of both the Stelae and the jungle itself, and through which no one
could find their way without its deciphered guidance.*

*And what is of even greater import—as I continued to study
Beatriz's correspondence, I found within it the key to the ancient cipher. The Secret to the Code!* **The key was in one particular letter,
dated December 15, 1540, describing a bizarre dance lesson between the governor and her comely slave.** *In this epistle, Balaj
K'waill appears to succumb to a fit of madness, but I found the
method in it. Scholars have read of their famous duet with blind
eyes for centuries. No one before me has known that the answer to
the mystery was there the entire time.*

What key? I wondered, slapping through the pages of the journal.
It looked as if she hadn't transcribed the code itself—but I had no
trouble recognizing her description of that letter. I'd read it out loud
to Erik a week ago. This was the epistle where Beatriz de la Cueva
recounts for Agata how she had tried to teach Balaj K'waill how to
do the Spanish dance called the sarabande, but that he'd had an insane fit where he begins shouting nonsense words, numbers, and
rhymes.

Apparently the solution to the Stelae-Maze was to be found there.

*For the next four days, I applied this key to the Stelae, and found it
easily cracked. I had written the first, roughest draft of the Flores*

Stelae. And thus I was also the first modern person to understand the precise nature of the Maze of Deceit:

Though this Maze has been called a Coliseum, or a Colossus, its gigantism exists in the mind, not in space: The winding and baffling passages that de la Cueva and Von Humboldt describe are passages not that one walks through but that one reads.

Months passed after this revelation had come to me. Keeping my own counsel, I gloated over my accomplishment. On account of my concerns that I had not yet deciphered the Maze-Stelae with complete accuracy (for I will never reveal my work until it is Perfect) I had not yet revealed to a single soul, not even my daughter, what I had found.

I was just about to do so when I heard the news of Tomas's death; after that, everything changed. I kept the Secret to myself, resolving to go in the forest alone to look for the Stone, and finish my old lover's work.

So here I am, back in Guatemala, and that journey begins today.

My first task will be to use the Maze of Deceit as a map in the forest, employing also some clues I've found in Alexander Von Humboldt's Narrative. If I do come across the city, my second step will be to look around for a dragon tree, according to the records.

As for the next riddle, the Maze of Virtue, I think that's fairly straightforward.

And if I am correct about both, perhaps I will discover the Jade.

Later today I'm heading for the Maya Biosphere Reserve, coming as close as I can to the mouth of the Rio Sacluc, where Tapia found the Stelae. From there, I'll have to follow the route (insofar as it qualifies as one) that is described in the decoded Maze of Deceit. In so doing, I know I'll be following the paths already hewed by Beatriz and Von Humboldt.

Perhaps I'll get lucky.

I won't even stop in Flores, as the weather continues to get worse and worse.

And the last thing I'll do before I leave is write out a clean copy of the Maze-Stelae.

THE MAZE OF DECEIT, DECODED

I turned the page. I turned the next. But all I found were the stubby remnants of several leaves that had been ripped out of the journal.

And then:

There now. That's all done. I've shipped the thing off to Lola in Long Beach, for safekeeping. She'll get a kick out of my theories when I finally explain them to her. I think they would particularly appeal to such a bookish girl. What's that queer line from de la Cueva's Legende?

. . . the Witch saw she could never read all the labyrinth's dangers and escape.

Indeed.

Now off I go to the jungle.

Hunching over the diary, and sweating in the cave, I shook my head and groaned.

The cracked Maze of Deceit was in Long Beach!

And the only clue my mother had left us for its decipherment was a reference to a dance lesson that took place nearly five hundred years ago.

CHAPTER 41

I had reached the maddening end of the journal. Sitting on my stone
and encircled by the brandy-colored light, the glistening water, the
warm air filled with gold motes, and the dragon-eyed creatures, I
felt these secrets work their way inside me and alter my fathoming of my
whole life. I looked around me. Unseen fish and lizards continued to
dive and leap into the pools, and drops of water falling from the dome of
the caves and its stalactites chimed as they slipped into the ponds, creat-
ing an exact music within the cave, to which I listened for a while.

Then I slid off my rock and made to leave.

Moving back through the tunnels and rooms of Actun Kan, I ran
my fingers again over the graffiti hieroglyphs carved in 1974, 1983,
1992, 1995. As I worked through the passages toward the cave's mouth,
the stone corridors began to take on a natural light, so that it appeared
as if a thin copper leaf had been applied to the stone by an adept
mason. The light grew brighter, falling across the cave's hall in a soft
line. After this I heard the sounds of footsteps, and Erik appeared, dark
against the glare.

"Here you are," he said.

"Oh, Erik . . . you'd better be good."

He stopped walking. "At what?"

I looked at him until I could see his eyes and his mouth in the
shadow. I reached up and touched his jaw, and I kissed him.

He brought his arms around me and bent down to hug me as he kissed me back.

"At breaking codes," I said.

"What?"

"Breaking codes—*hey*, you're shaking."

"Yeah."

"Why?"

He looked down very seriously at me. "Because I'm crazy about you. I mean it."

Little fires were thrilling through me, too; my face and fingers felt electric when I pressed them to his body. My breath flew out of me, and I laughed at the sensation.

"They were right about you," I said. "You're dangerous."

We held on to each other hard, as if we were half afraid our dizzy heads would make us tumble.

"What does that mean, I'm dangerous?" he asked, smiling into my hair.

"It means that you're for me, aren't you?" I asked. "I can feel it."

"I think I am."

"Here, touch me, touch me."

We ran our hands over each other, shivering. We kissed again; for a moment my fear whited out, like the color of the sun shining through my closed eyelids. He slid his hands under my shirt and gripped my waist.

"Like this," I said. I was showing him how to hold me. "Hug me, Erik!"

"I'm here, it's all right."

The fear came back again, and I thought about my father, Manuel. "It was so bad in that morgue."

"I know. You're here now."

I put my face against his chest and waited until the harsh feeling passed. "You're a good person."

"I hope so," he said. He almost sounded frightened. "Maybe I wasn't before I met you."

For a while after he said that, we didn't speak at all. We caressed and kissed each other and pressed close in the chiaroscuro of the cave.

I stepped back only when the fever dimmed a little. The light shining into the cave grew more golden. My mother was still waiting for us to find her, and we could both tell it was time to stop.

"We have to go," I said. "I found things out in her diary. I think I can find her."

"What things?"

"She wrote here that she didn't stop in Flores at all."

"She went up to the forest, then."

"That's right. And she writes about the path she was taking, so I have a pretty clear idea where we should be heading."

"We'll start up there today. What do you say? Tomorrow at the latest."

I nodded. "I found other things out, too."

"Yes . . . ? "

"I think that maybe they should wait."

He leaned his head closer to mine. "What is it?"

I hesitated. "I'll tell you when we go get Yolanda."

"All—right. What exactly are you talking about?"

"It has something to do with the Jade. My mother figured the puzzle out. But I'll explain it when we get back to the hotel."

"The maze? Then we'd *better* get back." Mirth rippled over his face. "You're too much! This whole thing is cocked."

"I think you like some of it, actually."

"I'm ready to do what it takes, let's put it that way."

On the way back in the cab he grasped my hand, and I saw the trees flashing past. I leaned my head back and pictured him, my mother, Manuel, and Yolanda someday in the future, all of us having dinner together, and a quick bolt of happiness shot through me.

And then I had a broodier, time-twisting thought that mixed in with my hope: my future depended on what I found in the jungle, and I was excited and terrified to go there with Erik.

Perhaps this mixture of emotion was just how Beatriz de la Cueva had felt when she embarked on the journey for the Jade with Balaj K'waill so many centuries ago.

CHAPTER 42

e arrived back to the Hotel Peten Itzae by two o'clock. That morning Yolanda had taken a room on the building's first floor, while Erik and I had been led up to two apartments on the second by the landlord's very tired wife.

I walked up to the door of Yolanda's room and knocked. No answer. I knocked again.

"Anyone in there?" Erik called out.

"Hello?" I said.

But when we opened up the door to look inside, she wasn't to be found.

"She must be—I don't know, taking a shower?" I said. Yet I didn't hear any running water. A light effervescence of angst shot across my collarbones; I felt like something wasn't quite right, despite our reconciliation. I remembered our childhood together, and how she would first disappear from view before springing upon me in one of her wrestling holds. And a tweaking nerve ending that had frayed in my youth was warning me that perhaps I might expect some similar ambush now.

We walked up the stairs, which were made of a soft and polished wood adorned with a runner made out of a red textile. I reached the other apartments, and the one bathroom. They stood empty. I turned from that door, walked farther down the hall, and opened up the blue-painted door to my room.

Yolanda was sitting on my bed. She wasn't wearing her hat, and her black hair fell in a tumble over her shoulders and down her back as she bent over my mother's duffel bag, which she had rifled through. She'd scattered about the room all the atlases I'd brought and all my books and papers.

"I've been looking for that map you promised me," she said.

I stayed in the doorway. The light feeling I'd had in the cab went away completely.

"It isn't here, is it?" she asked.

"Yolanda."

"Do you *have* it?"

I closed my eyes. "No. Not exactly."

"God, Lola." She shook her head.

Erik walked into the room.

Yolanda's cheeks and nose were turning red; the corners of her eyes sparkled. "He told me not to get angry at you, but now that I know it's true, I am. I really am very, very angry."

"Who told you not to get mad at me?"

"I'm in a frenzy," she said, in a cold and very calm voice.

"I'm not exactly sure if I should say anything right now," Erik interjected. "But Yolanda, you're obviously upset. A person might think that you're going to hurt yourself, or . . . someone else." He paused. "In particular, I'm not wild about the word *frenzy*."

"Tell him to shut up."

"It's all right, Erik."

"There's nothing here," she said. Her voice burned across the room. "You lied to me."

"Of course I did," I said.

"*What?*"

"Of course I lied to you. *I don't know where my mother is, Yolanda.* She could be dead. Do you know what I'd do to find her? A lot more than tell a lie to my good friend."

"Agh—you—"

"You wouldn't have come along if I hadn't told you what you wanted to hear. And later, you would have left us if I'd told you the whole truth."

"I should leave you right now then, shouldn't I?"

From below, I could hear some men talking, and then footsteps walking toward the landing before the stairs. Was that the landlord?

"I've found out something, though," I said. "For real. And if you'd just give me one minute—"

I heard the downstairs footsteps rise up to us, and a familiar voice. Manuel suddenly appeared, poking his withered-looking head into the room. He stepped inside. He was wearing one of his tweed suits, and had his hair half-combed across his pate. His shoes were shined, his eyes were large and bright. But his collar was kinked, and he looked like he hadn't slept in a week.

"Are you two having that conversation, dear?" he said to Yolanda. Then, to me: "Hello, darling."

I stared at my father who was not my father and wiped away the tears that began to run immediately down my cheeks.

"Honey?"

"Hi, Dad."

"Hello, Erik," Manuel said.

"Hello, Señor Alvarez. How did you know we were here?"

"I'm the one who told my daughter about this hotel."

My father looked between Yolanda and me, and a brief pained expression flickered across his face. And this made me remember again the reason why I had cut off contact with Yolanda in the first place—because my friendship with a de la Rosa had hurt him. Or at least my mother had said so. And I'd decided to pick family first.

My stomach and throat clenched at that thought.

"It appears that you and Yolanda have had a—misunderstanding," Manuel was saying.

"It's a little more than a misunderstanding," I admitted.

Yolanda sat on the bed and stared at me with her rough eyes without saying anything.

"How'd you get here?" I asked Manuel. "The roads are blocked."

"A helicopter, of course, my love," he said. "I've learned a trick or two from your mother. I certainly wouldn't bother myself with that God-awful highway."

"Oh."

"So, we have more things than a squabble to deal with today," Manuel said. "Are you ladies going to be able to make up?"

"No, Manuel," Yolanda said.

"I can make it up to you," I said.

She didn't respond.

"And how so?" Manuel asked me.

Erik looked at Yolanda. "I think she's got some good news for us."

"I've found some things out," I said. I wiped my wet cheek again. "I got hold of one of Mom's diaries, and she writes in it that she went to the forest over a week ago, so we have to head up there as soon as possible."

"Oh, Lord," Manuel said.

"And she also writes about the Jade. I think she figured out part of the path that leads to it. She found out what the Maze of Deceit was— and we can use it as a kind of guide to find her. The maze isn't completely . . . decoded . . . but Mom writes about the *key* to it in her journal. I think I know where to look for it. And if we find it, we can decipher it, and find out the way she went."

Manuel frowned. "That's all a bit much for me. Are you saying she found the maze? That doesn't seem like her—she didn't say anything about this to me."

"I know."

"You must be mistaken."

"I'm not. I can show you."

"So you're talking about *deciphering* the first maze. . . ." Erik folded his forehead into an accordion as he pondered this. "What does that mean, exactly?"

"The Maze of Deceit wasn't a structure—a building—like we'd imagined. It was the Stelae. The panels."

"The Stelae?" Manuel asked.

"Oh—no—hold on," Erik said.

Yolanda still sat on the bed glaring at me, not uttering a word.

I looked from her to Erik. "It's true—she decoded it. Though we don't have the deciphered version here—she sent it back to Long Beach for safekeeping."

"No—wait," Erik said. "I was thinking that—before—in the car. That the Stelae might have something to do with all this . . ."

"Yes, all right," I said.

"No, I'm just telling you that I seriously was. Before Yolanda smashed her car up and distracted me—"

"Yes, yes—I believe you."

"Okay," he said. "You're making me crazy right now."

"Apparently it is all very clear to the two of you," my father said, "but I would like more of an explanation."

"The Maze of Deceit and the Flores Stelae *are one and the same*," I said, describing how the stories of Tapia, de la Cueva, and Von Humboldt fit together. I took out my mother's journal and opened it to the pages where she described her discovery. I also showed them Mom's calculations, and her description of the route she'd planned to take through the forest. The copies of the documents we'd been traveling with were scattered all over the floor, and I snatched these up, riffled them together, and thrust them under my friends' noses as further proof.

From Von Humboldt's *Narrative*, where the German describes his first encounter with the Maze of Deceit, I showed them this line:

We might enter one of the sapphire passages, grow confused by its signs, and become so baffled by its convoluted express that we could not take a single step forward.

And from the *Legende* itself, I read out the following quote:

So the Mad Blue City was built in the shadow cast by the great Tree that bleeds ruby sap. And it was hidden within that colossus of a Labyrinth formed of diabolical jade passages and malefic stanzes and Confusion out of which there would be no Express.

"It all makes sense now, if you look at what's right in front of you," I said. "The words *passages* and *express* were meant literally by Von Humboldt as *written* passages and *expressions*. And we'd been confused by de la Cueva's use of the word *stanze* before, because it means 'room' in Italian. But *stanze,* etymologically, forms the root word for a poetical stanza."

They stared blankly at me.

"It has something to do with a stanze—the room—being called a 'standing' or 'stopping' place. And a stanza—the division of a song or a poem—is described by its stop at the end."

"How do you know all this?" my father asked, after a few seconds.

I extended my arms, a little wildly. "A lot of reading."

Eventually, they believed me.

"My goodness," Manuel said, putting his hands in his pockets. "Juana kept all of this so close."

Erik said, "She did it. The old girl did it!"

I pointed to the correspondence. "Mom says in her diary that the key to the Stelae is in one of de la Cueva's letters. Written December 15, 1540. It's where she writes about this dance lesson—Erik, do you remember it? We were looking at it in Guatemala City? We need to start going through it."

"I know the letter you're talking about," Erik said. "It's the one where Balaj K'waill spouts gibberish. And where he admits that he lied to de la Cueva about the Jade."

"Right. So we'll study it, and find out how to decode the Stelae. And when we do, we'll know where to go in the forest."

"Those are a lot of ifs, Lola," Manuel said.

I turned toward the bed. "But I really do think we have a map now, Yolanda. Or at least the beginnings of one—we just have to solve the cipher. If we crack it, everything that I said will have been true."

I approached her, holding the *Translation* and the *Letters.* But she remained on the bed and put her head down, looking up at me in a very baleful and frightening way.

She shifted, grimacing, and made a menacing gesture. It seemed she had not heard what I'd said.

She did not care at all about maps, letters, the routes, or the Stelae. She stood up and walked toward us. She remained staring at me, her eyes like hot glass and her lips completely white.

She walked until she stood behind me, and then with a quick flickering movement brought her arms around me so that they circled my chest.

My grip on her arms grew tighter, as well, and my heart started jamming at my ribs.

"Don't do this, Yolanda," I said. "You wouldn't have helped me go get Mom."

She continued to hold on to me, her arms embracing me like a vise across my chest.

"You could have hired anyone else for that," she said, in this awful, tender voice. "You didn't even try to find another tracker, and they were all over the city. If you'd just looked. What *you* wanted was forgiveness from me. And I would have given all of that to you. If you'd shown me. That you were sorry. For cutting me loose. But all you did was try to fool me." She began to loosen her grip. "Over the years, you've been teaching me a hard lesson, Lola. But I've got to learn it. I've got to learn it. You're teaching me that I'm all by myself. Everyone that ever belonged to me is dead."

"Oh, no," I said. I went limp and felt her words just hollow me out.

If I were to claim her, I'd have to disclaim my father. And maybe she wouldn't want me for a sister anyway.

She dropped her arms, turned around, and walked out of the room.

CHAPTER 43

A mazing," Manuel Alvarez said, as we talked later in my room. He still sat on the bed, and looked at Mom's key to the Stelae. "The stones come down to a five-number cipher. Not meaningless at all, were they?"

We were alone; I sat next to him, my hand on his shoulder, and read along. "Doesn't look like it, Dad. Though we still have to decode the panels."

He shook his head. "She didn't tell me, Lola."

"I know—she didn't tell me either."

He turned the pages. "It looks like it might be fairly simple to solve—that is, unless you haven't the brains to see the obvious in the first place. Leave that to your mother."

"She was surprised at it herself, I think."

"The Stelae and the Jade—the two things were connected the entire time, and none of us knew. Though it isn't clear how far that gets you."

"Why not?"

"What if we decipher it and it still doesn't make sense? Or the landscape has changed? Or your mother reads it differently than we do?"

"Well . . . let's just take this slowly and worry about those things if they come up. We won't be able to solve everything today—that's all we know for sure."

Manuel read for a little while longer and then closed the book. He reached up to touch my hair.

"Dad."

"I had to come here, you know. Couldn't let the old fear stop me. After all, I thought your mother might be amused if I were the hero for once."

"Dad, it's all right."

"I waited by that phone, darling. I was sitting there, trying to act like a normal person—all you could see on the news were pieces on the jade they keep finding up in the Sierras—more and more of the blue every day. But what did that matter to me? If they find a mine or not? She's really taking so much longer to get back to me than she ever has before—the longest we've ever gone without speaking is three days. And then it occurred to me that perhaps she was trapped somewhere or . . . something. I saw that it simply didn't matter if I got swallowed up by a swamp or shot or nibbled on by crocodiles if she—if she needed a little bit of help in coming back, you see. So here I am. And in that helicopter, no less. Hideous things, helicopters. Smashing about in the air like I don't know what. Thought I was going to be hugging a mountain at any minute."

I rubbed my hand on the bedspread in a nervous gesture. The red cloth, similar to the runner on the stairs, was embroidered with blue stars, green doglike animals, blue men, and tiny yellow flowers.

"Yolanda really is quite upset, you know," he said.

"Yes, she is."

"She won't come out of her room, and she won't even say if she's coming along with us. Though she *must*. You'll have to patch it up with her sooner rather than later."

"When she'll talk to me. It's all a mess."

"She'll calm down, in time. The two of you have always had that, what should I call it—connection. You were—friends." He looked down at the journal and touched the salmon binding, fingering a rip in the fabric. "So you read your mother's journal—"

"I did, Dad."

He stared blankly ahead for a moment or two, and then tried to smile at me. "I hope that wasn't a mistake. Do you think it was?"

"How do you mean?"

"Well, if she finds out, she might be—a little angry. She likes to keep things to herself. And I've always respected her in that. Did you—did she write anything too personal there?"

He wasn't smiling now, and his mouth bent down into a long, hard dent. He didn't look like he usually did; his face was emaciated and wary, as if I were about to hurt him.

I shrugged.

"There really wasn't anything but notes on the Stelae," I said. "Scholarly writing, things like that."

"Scholarly writings."

"Oh, yes. It was actually fairly boring stuff until I got to the part about the panels—then, obviously, it became very interesting. But the rest of it was a yawn."

"Really."

"The *most* boring. She knows how to yammer on."

He stared at me a few seconds longer to make sure. When his face relaxed, it sagged a little. "I don't think we have to tell her that when we see her." He took my hand. "Like I said—she's a temperamental one. And she'd get awfully upset if she heard that criticism about her writing style, wouldn't she?"

"She'd probably start stomping about and roaring about my lack of taste, yes."

"Absolutely. You never want to get my angel in a bad mood. That's one lesson I've learned. Always best to remain on her good side—though on the other hand, maybe you should tell her when we see her. What do you think? Maybe she deserves it for all the trouble she's putting us through."

I laughed. "All right, then."

He lifted up my hand, and in a gentlemanly, fatherly, and very tender way he kissed the back of it with his small dry mouth.

"I adore and love you so much, Creature," he said. "I need you and your mother so, so much, my dear."

I put my arms around him and rested my head on his shoulder. "We need you too, Dad. And I love you!"

CHAPTER 44

The four of us spent the rest of that day and the night in the Hotel Peten Itzae, with Erik studying Beatriz de la Cueva's correspondence, and my father and I waiting for Yolanda to emerge from her room and say whether she would come to the forest with us. Day turned into afternoon, and the sky darkened into tin and lead colors that were reflected by the waters of Lago Izabal. The poke boats with their roughly painted green and yellow trim skidded across the swollen water; boys and fishermen worked the lake, dressed in baseball caps and white shirts or T-shirts displaying everything from *Charlie's Angels* logos to portraits of Rigoberta Menchú. Women bent down on the banks and washed shirts and khakis against the stones, so that foam formed traceries of delicate white on the surface of the lake.

The afternoon deepened further; evening came on. Manuel drank a few rums with our fellow lodgers and then retired for the night. Yolanda had still not shown her face or given us one sign. Erik and I parted in the kitchen, remembering our kiss again and so awkwardly saying good night before the smiling landlord's wife and their watchful daughters. Then I retired to my room and went to bed. I couldn't sleep at all, though, with the moonless night rushing through my window like a mass of black birds, and the sounds of the men's talk floating up through the floorboards.

An hour later, at eleven o'clock, I couldn't stand it anymore. I sat up and kicked back the covers on my bed.

In my nightgown, I opened the door of my room and waited to see if anyone was around. Not a sound; not a footfall; everyone had retired for the evening. I slipped into the hall. I padded through the blackness of the corridor until I reached the place where he'd sleep that night.

"Erik?"

I turned the door handle. Inside, I found him working at a desk under a dim lamp. My parents' *Translation* was opened to an analysis of the Stelae's first panel, and next to the book he had placed a dictionary that he'd borrowed from the owners of the hotel. Spread all about were sheets of paper, upon which he'd written an ever-growing list of words and mathematical solutions.

He looked up and smiled. Half of his face was visible in the light, and the other remained in shadow.

"It looks like you're getting lucky," I said, putting my hand on his shoulder.

He raised his eyebrows at me.

"Your work, your work?" I asked, pointing down to the books.

"Ah, well, yes. I am getting somewhere with this." He looked back down at his writings, and his bangs fell over his eyes.

"Show me."

He began to shuffle around the papers and then found the section in de la Cueva's letters that my mother had focused on.

"I found the passage she was talking about," he said. "The December fifteenth letter, describing the dance lesson."

I took his hand and led him down through the forest, toward a river that runs through the wood, and by that water we took our leisure. I rubbed him with balms and I sang in his ear; and then, in order to lift his heart, I thought I would entertain him by teaching him our country's dance, the Sarabande.

"One, two, three, four," I whispered in his ear. "Those are the ma-

neuvers of this game we are playing, my dear. One must go forward, forward. And move smoothly, like a European."

"La, la, la," he said, laughing and singing songs I could not understand. He grew berserk, spouting nonsense words, numbers, and rhymes.

"To dance in Goathemala, my sweet," he said, "one must move roughly, skipping every other trac."

"Every other what?"

"That's the French for 'track,' my beloved thickwit. And as you have noted that we are quite backwards, you must follow our reversed native steps, which are four, three, two, one, zero."

Erik stopped reading.

"That's it!" I said. "That's got to be the numerical cipher."

"Yes. But the instructions, as far as I can tell, have something to do with two different directions. I don't think the numbers alone are going to decode the Stelae. First, Balaj K'waill instructs us to 'skip every other *trac*,' and for a while I wasn't quite sure what he meant until I began to puzzle over that word—"

"Track," I said.

"Right. *Track*, as we usually use it, refers to marks made by feet on a path, or wheels in a rut. So he's saying that they should skip their dancing steps, it seems. But the word's related to writing as well, in a remote way."

"Track," I said. "Trace?"

"Yes, there's some connection between the two, in Old French. *Trac* and *Trace*. Both meaning a beaten path. And tracking the path becomes a means by which to trace it. *Trace* is another old term for dancing, as it turns out, and it's also a word that we use when referring to clues, in detective fiction—"

"Vanished without a trace, and so on—"

"—but it also comes from the Latin word for drawing"—he flipped a page of the diary—"*trahere*, as in drawing something behind you, like a cart. Which leaves a mark. A very specific sort of mark. The kind that you make when you draw with a pen."

"A straight line."

"Exactly."

"But if I'm getting you right, all this is assuming that Balaj K'waill was playing intentional word games. That he was a punster who knew the French terms for *track* and *trace*—"

"Or, in the sixteenth century, maybe this was all common knowledge. He was a linguist. And I think that I am on to something. Just listen. The way I'm reading this first part of the cipher is that when he says we should skip every other track—"

"It means that you should skip every other line of text."

"Which is what I've been doing here." He shuffled through the papers before him and showed me a leaf. "This is a few lines of your parents' translation, from the first stone of the Stelae."

The of story the Jade once was I king Jade
You without lost I'm too lost I'm too lost
Fierce king true a jade under born noble and jade
I'm you lost I you lost I warm stay will
The of sign the jade possessed I serpent feathered Jade
You where you kiss can I where arms my in
Earth over power all Jade man and sea and Jade
Safe stay me forgive you do charm my treasure my
My of account on Jade it gift great one Jade
Darling my you lost I you lost I empty so
To destiny my was Jade for land this rule Jade
And cold so world this in live to me left
In years thousand one Jade Soft every Peace perfect
You have why done I have what beauty my

"Right," I said. "Incomprehensible."

"But this is what you get if you separate out every other line. I blacked out the rest of it. Remember that paragraph I showed you before? The text that I now think we're supposed to be reading looks like this."

The of story the Jade once was I king Jade
Fierce king true a jade under born noble and jade
The of sign the jade possessed I serpent feathered Jade

Earth over power all Jade man and sea and Jade
My of account on Jade it gift great one Jade
To destiny my was Jade for land this rule Jade
In years thousand one Jade Soft every Peace perfect

"Do you think that it makes more sense?" he asked me.

I squinted down at it. "I think it *might*."

"Me too. And assuming this has worked, then I just have to apply the numbered cipher. Four, three, two, one, zero."

We continued to stare down at the pages and the black writing on them that glowed nearly bronze in the lamplight. Silver specks of dust circled in the air; I turned and saw that Erik still had a bruise beneath his eye, and he hadn't shaved in days.

But he looked wonderful to me.

I put my hand over his and rubbed his palm with my thumb. I could feel the pulse in his wrist and hear his breathing. All discussion of cryptograms and signs faded away.

I reached down and turned off the light.

"I guess I'm done with my labors for the night," he said.

"Not exactly."

I couldn't see him or myself in the dark, and after I had hauled us over to the bed I had a bad moment when the things I had learned in the last day began to crowd my mind. I hovered over him, not speaking, touching the hair falling away from his forehead. But my worries continued to struggle inside me, and I wondered if I really could do this at all. So I hesitated; the shadows continued to fold around us, and I could hear us breathing, swallowing. He did not press. He kissed my fingers; he kissed my palm and wrist bone.

"It's all right," he said. "This is enough for right now."

But I didn't want it to be enough. I bent down toward him.

"Oh, no," I said, "you won't get off so easily."

"Ah, the dominant modern woman," he said in a teasing tone. "You know, in the eighth-century Maya tradition, it was very common for the man to take the courtship lead, as Central American maidens were supposed to be very docile and innocent, and liked to run shrieking from their suitors, though obviously today that would be somewhat tedious or even frightening—"

"Stop talking," I said.

Then I took his hand. And I was so gentle. At first.

A chatty, sexy, maddening, Latin, and very large man must be made to know who's boss right away, in the first seduction. First teasing, tickling, and very slightly scratching, I took a furious joy in stripping him of all available language until he could only answer me with his hands and his treelike thighs. There were certain moments, I'll admit, when he was the one getting the better of me, though I was not one to complain too much when I discovered myself aloft in the air a foot above that narrow bed, wildly moving my elbows as if they were wings that might keep me afloat. I heard his devilish chuckling somewhere in the nether regions around my hips. And then all was soft—all tender soft, I found he could be—though his raspy pelt rubbed against my ribs, my chest, giving rise to the most heavenly of inflammations. I wrapped myself around his massive waist; he curled himself about me, head to tail, and nudged his muzzle onto my cheek.

There was a moment, right before, when he reached up his hand and cupped my face.

"My beauty," he said. "My beautiful girl."

Then I held him tighter and tighter, and I was smiling and moving like a porpoise. I think I surprised him by how strong I was, and how I wrangled him about and made him yelp with happiness. The floorboards shook beneath us, and the bed half-hopped about the room like a colt, and I took that man and pressed him to my breast, and I kissed the breath out of him so that he lay back, stunned. From my pillow, I felt this tornado of laughter come out of me. Everything lifted, I was happy; though I tried to keep quiet enough so that no one else in the bed-and-breakfast could hear.

And then it happened again. And again.

CHAPTER 45

TWO A.M.
As I walked softly back through the halls, which were inky black and full of obstacles, I could hear a faint rain tapping on the roof.

I walked down the stairs; I felt the runner's rough cloth under my feet.

Then I found my way to the door of Yolanda's room. I knocked.

"Yolanda?"

She must not have been sleeping. I started and jumped back when she opened the door. The light had been turned on in her room, and she was a dark daguerreotype in front of the lamp.

I waited, and she didn't say anything.

"Are you coming with us tomorrow?" I asked.

"You mean today."

"Are you coming with us today?"

She kept on staring at me with such an angry look.

"I—I know how you feel about your father. Or at least I'm starting to. I'm this close to being in the same position as you. So don't turn away from me."

"I told you once before not to talk about my father."

I paused. "Fine." I stared at her. "Are you coming with us?"

"What do you think?"

"Yolanda, I'm so sorry about everything."

"Go back to your boyfriend," she said.

She shut the door.

But in the morning, she was packed and ready before all of us. She put her hat back on; she slung a heavy pack over her shoulders, along with some other items we'd need for the trip. She'd spent the day before not just in moody hiding, as we thought, but in shopping via the credit card she found in my mother's duffel bag. New rubber tarps and metal spades, flashlights and two machetes, snacks, painkillers, the antibug spray called DEET, and synthetic fiber hammocks stacked up against the foyer wall. In the kitchen, she stamped about in her big suede hiking boots, disturbing Erik as he sat at the breakfast table scribbling rapidly over a rustling sheaf of paper. She intimidated the landlord's daughters while she slammed down some coffee and ate an apple with noisy bites. (The daughters were also, I will say, shooting curious and somewhat scandalized glances at me on account of the involuntary joyous sounds that had escaped from me in the night; I tried very hard to ignore the shocked and newly intelligent expressions on their smooth faces.)

"If there is anything to find out there with this new map of yours," Yolanda said to Erik, "I'm going to find it."

"I have to figure it out first," Erik replied, not even looking up. "Though I think I might be close—even if what I'm deciphering doesn't . . . doesn't quite . . ."

"Doesn't quite what?" I asked.

"I can't say yet—just give me a little while longer," he said.

"If you're really interested in finding Juana, you'd better hurry up," Yolanda grunted.

"He's working hard, dear," Manuel said. "We can all see that."

She frowned, though at least she was talking to them; Yolanda wouldn't even look at me. When I tried to touch her arm, she stepped back. Then she walked away.

Within the next hour, we were on our way to the Peten forest.

CHAPTER 46

At noon on November 6, we found ourselves on the road that stretches northwest from Flores, through the small riparian town of Sacpuy, and up through the part of the Peten forest called the Maya Biosphere Reserve. This passage forms the initial part of the Scarlet Macaw Trail, a byway that cuts through from Sacpuy, past the large and splendid Laguna Perdida, or Lost Lake, and into the first reaches of the jungle's buffer zone, a ten-to-fifteen-kilometer-wide swath of land where the government continues to permit slash-and-burn farming. We planned to stop at the Lost Lake, leave our car by the side of the highway, then cut on foot northeastward through the buffer zone until we hit the mouth of the river Sacluc—the same tributary over which de la Cueva and Von Humboldt had crossed, where Oscar Angel Tapia discovered, or stole, the Flores Stelae, and where my mother intended to travel in the days before Mitch hit. By that time, we all hoped Erik would have unraveled the Maze of Deceit from the clues left by my mother, and we would be able to discern the correct jungle path upon which to proceed. If we then found anything that looked like a ruin of a city, we would see if we might find the "dragon tree," or *Dracaena draco*, which both de la Cueva and Von Humboldt wrote of as a key signpost in their letters and journal. And after that we'd have to puzzle out the second maze, the Labyrinth of Virtue, being the riddle that begins with the gnomic lines *"The Roughest Path to Take/The Harshest Road to Tread/Is the one We must Make/Tho' our Hearts fill with Dread"* . . . hoping all the time that my mother was following the same clues.

But all of that was far ahead of us, as we had miles to go before then.

The road that runs northeast through the jungle of the Peten showed signs of recent flooding, though much of the high water had already drained into the rivers below. Shaggy olive bushes and char-treuse palms lined the road, along with remnants of banana farms and wet acres where farmers once cultivated corn, beans, and chili. Manuel drove us down the pocked and marshy highway, occasionally with such trepidation that he pressed his chin nearly up to the driving wheel of the Ford Bronco that Yolanda had somehow rented the day before. She sat beside him in the front, jostled by the thwacking of the wheels; Erik and I remained in the back. He was still working on his decipherment, scoring the paper with his pen and spanning the pages with arrows and cross-outs, as well as numbers and words.

"You're getting it, aren't you?" I asked.

He nodded. "I *think* I am. I was just confused at first."

"What does it say?" Yolanda asked.

"It's complicated," he said. "The text, I mean. The way it reads. I'm still checking my work—I have to make sure that I'm doing this correctly."

Yolanda slapped at the rearview mirror so that she could take a good look at him. "Let's hear it."

"I said I was still checking my work—"

"Is there a problem?" Manuel asked.

"It's—well—look," Erik said, shaking a handful of papers at me. "The maze—the Stelae—it's made up of . . . *tales,* or some-thing."

"Tales," Manuel repeated.

"What's he talking about?" Yolanda asked.

"I certainly couldn't tell you," Manuel said.

"Stories—I'm deciphering *a handful of stories,*" Erik replied. "And they're all related to the legend—they have the same characters. You're supposed to use the tales as guides when you get to the mouth of the Sacluc, where Tapia found the maze—or, the Stelae. Lola, last night I

showed you a part of the text before I started working on the num
bered cipher."

"Where you skipped every line."

"Yes, and after I did that and used the cipher, I translated it into this.
I think it's written in the voice of the Eldest Brother:

THE STORY OF THE KING

*I was once a true King, fierce and Noble. Born under the Sign of the
Feathered Serpent, I possessed all power over Earth and Sea and
Man. On account of my one great Gift, it was my Destiny to Rule
this land for one thousand years in perfect peace. Every soft girl I desired would call herself my wife, and embrace no other. Every strong
man would bow before me as a slave and despair. . . .*

He read this out loud, and everyone went very quiet for a long, tense
minute.

This was our map. But there was no "X marks the spot." There was
no description of a specific cave like in *The Count of Monte Cristo,* no
pointing skeleton like in *Treasure Island.*

I think that I can speak for all of us when I say that the morose complaint of an extinct king was not quite what we'd been hoping for from
the decoded Maze of Deceit.

CHAPTER 47

The Story of the King'?" Yolanda blurted out, in the car.

"Could you repeat that?" Manuel asked.

" 'Born under the sign of the Feathered Serpent'?" Yolanda exclaimed again.

Manuel frowned over his shoulder. "Erik, you're not making any sense."

"Oh, I'll explain it to you," Yolanda said. "Though you won't like it. That's not a map."

I raised my hand like a crossing guard. "There's no option. We *have* to make sense of it."

"I'll show you how it's a map," Erik said, "if you'll just give me more time to make sure I'm not missing anything—"

"I can't use that to get us through the jungle," Yolanda answered. "That's a practical joke, not an atlas. No . . . forget it. I've decided. We're going to have to go east once we hit the Sacluc. It's the only rational choice."

"Why east?" Manuel asked.

"I was telling them before," she said, batting her hand in our direction, "my father always thought he might find something in the west, but my idea was that closer by Tikal, and those ruins—eastward— we'd be more likely to find some sort of structure."

"Perhaps," Manuel said. "But on my last trip to the forest I—I lost my compass. So I'm really not sure how to find the landmarks."

"I'm very confident that the way is east," Yolanda emphasized.

"Just hold on," I said. "Erik, how did you figure this out? Could you be missing something?"

He shook his head. "I don't think so. As far as I can tell, it's parsing perfectly—the numerical cipher's a transposition code."

Erik explained to Manuel and Yolanda about how he'd skipped every other line of hieroglyphs, and then said: "The text is divided up into units of five symbol-words. In de la Cueva's letter, where she describes that dancing lesson with Balaj K'waill—the one that Juana writes about in her journal—K'waill mentions the numbers four, three, two, one, zero."

"That was when he was jeering at de la Cueva," Manuel said. "When he said that Guatemalans were backward, he was teasing her with the clue."

"That's right. The only thing I couldn't figure out at first was what the zero stood for, until I realized that each zero corresponds to the symbol for *jade* in the text."

"What does that mean?" Yolanda asked.

"That the symbol for *jade* is a dummy. It's means nothing—and everything, at the same time. You can only understand the text if you cross out each instance of the word. So the first sentence of the uncracked text, once you parse it into the units of five, becomes—

> *The of story the jade*
> *once was I king jade*
> *fierce king true a jade*

and then, striking out all the instances of the word *jade* and reversing the passages, like Balaj K'waill instructs you to—"

"Four, three, two, one," I said. "It's backward, so you reverse it to one, two, three, four."

"Yes—"

> *The of story the*
> *once was I king*
> *fierce king true a*

becomes—

The Story of the King
I was once a true king, fierce . . . and noble, etc.

"It *was* so easy to crack," Manuel said, though without bitterness.

"Yes, it's not very hard, now," Erik said.

"Well, as to the bit about the zero blotting out the symbols for jade, that's an ancient trick," Yolanda said. She turned in her seat, directly toward Erik. "It's old hacker's wisdom. You know: 'In a riddle whose answer is 'chess,' the only word that must not be used is *chess*.'"

"It's amazing!" I said.

"It is clever," Manuel agreed. "Excellent, Erik. You've done it. And so . . . maybe my daughter was right to bring you along, after all. I might have to revise my opinion of you."

"You will, I guarantee it," Erik said, his head still bent over the pages. Mine was too. "In a couple of days, you'll be crazy about me, Señor Alvarez."

"Oh, dear," Manuel said. And I could tell from his tone that he wasn't responding to Erik; nor did he sound as if he were even talking about the maze.

"I'm not going to revise my opinion of—" Yolanda was saying.

"Look," Manuel interrupted.

Erik, Yolanda, and I gazed up and through the windshield, and stopped discussing codes and keys.

The landscape had deteriorated mile by mile, and this far north it had turned into a flooded disaster area. We passed by patches of forest that were nothing more than scorched, dripping lands, fringed by shattered homes and trees with lime-colored bark and yellow leaves. We maneuvered past caved-in sections of the road; here chocolate-colored earth, streaked with lime and pebbled with stones, extruded into the paved areas, thick, deep, and making exhaling sounds when the car's wheels crushed on by. We saw people picking blown litter off their *milpas*, or farms; two women and a man stood in front of shattered huts and simply cried.

"Terrible, terrible," Manuel said.

"It used to be beautiful here," Erik said. "My father used to take me out around this area, during the summer. . . . I don't recognize it now."

I pressed my hands on the window glass. "It's ruined."

"Stop," Yolanda said. "This has something to do with me."

"What do you mean?"

"Just stop right here. I'm getting out."

"Just for a minute, Dad," I said.

"All right."

"Give them some of our supplies," I said.

But Yolanda had already thought of that.

She dug through one of the knapsacks, pulled out several containers of dried fish, and ran out into the mud to give these packages to a woman standing before one of the huts. The woman had very long dark eyebrows, and dead, set eyes that stared out at the settlement with a jolting expression of total, wise, but unaccepting comprehension. While Yolanda handed her the packages, she asked her a few questions; the woman shook her head.

Then Yolanda ran back to the car and slammed the door. "Twenty people died in that woman's village."

"Did you ask her if she'd seen my mother?"

She had been ignoring me for a full day, but talked to me now.

"Yes, she hadn't. And she told me she hadn't seen her family in days, either. She's . . . in shock, I think."

In the rearview mirror, her eyes met mine for a second.

Her face twisted before she looked away from me again. "She says that even more people died farther north."

We stopped talking; Erik kept scratching at his paper. I had a momentary vision of my mother's eyes as Manuel pressed the car down the shifting road. I could sense the weather getting warmer, and even more moist than before. The burned and green and wet fields passed us by. Birds clawed through the thick air. The remaining bronze leaves on the mahoganies shuddered in the wind, like hands on long thin arms that made unintelligible signs.

Our car passed two, three, four more destroyed towns. We drove on.

CHAPTER 48

A t three in the very hot, very humid afternoon, the four of us reached the outskirts of the Lost Lake, the point from which we'd agreed to begin making our way into the bush. I'd been hoping to see a car parked along the road, as a sign that my mother might have been here in the days before. But there was no such indication. The rain forest thrust abruptly from the ground, incongruously, green, woolly, and empty of any visible human habitation. The air felt thick and swarmed with bugs and hot mists; our clothes hung heavy on our bodies, and our shoes stuck in the mud when we stepped out of the car. The light had begun to dim. The sky turned slate-colored and appeared full of rain; the deeper reaches of the forest seemed very dark indeed.

"There's no path to take the car on," Yolanda said as she opened the back of the Bronco and began to drag the packs and gear forward. "We're going to have to leave it here."

"Are we just going to walk in now?" I asked her.

"It's getting dark," Erik said, squinting up at the trees.

Yolanda and I stood side by side at the back of the car, grabbing the bags and the bottles of water. I wore a long-sleeved shirt, jeans, high boots, socks, but I already felt the bites of the mosquitoes, so I took a bottle of the DEET and spread the cream on my neck. Next to me, Manuel worked to put his own pack on, though his hands had begun shaking.

"Yes, we're going in," she said. She glanced at me. "If you really think

Juana is close by, we're on the clock. It wouldn't have been easy for her in there."

I squinted up at the sky. "You're right."

She crammed her pack down and stuffed her hammock and mosquito netting more securely in their places. Next she took out a giant black Maglite from the pack's side pocket, and pointed also to one of the two machetes she'd bought in town. These were fearful-looking knives, sheathed in leather, with brass studs on the scabbards. "We'll make our way through the forest with these."

My father dropped his pack and cursed; he sweated and continued shivering.

"Let me help you with that thing," Yolanda said. "It's . . . heavy."

"That's all right," he said. "I can do it." He forced the rucksack on.

No one mentioned my father's hands at all.

"I guess that's it, then," Erik said, taking up one of the other packs and slinging it over one arm. "No use in stalling or fainting or fleeing, is there?"

"Exactly," she said. "Oh, and by the way—have you been to this part of the forest before?"

"This part?" he asked, then shook his head. "No, not here. Farther south, just around Flores."

"Well, then—there's a nasty regional mite that you should watch out for. It crawls under the clothes, and bites. The privates, mostly."

"Are you playing games with me?" Erik asked

"I don't play games in the jungle," she said. "And I don't hold grudges in it, either, even if I want to. It's too dangerous." She looked over at me with steady dark eyes, and her cheeks were red. "We're here for two reasons only. Your mother—"

"Yes," I said.

"—and my father. My father's work." She shifted her gaze over to Erik. "But it's going to be hard, and you'll all have to look out for yourselves. So you should listen to me about the bugs. And there are a few other things, too. We might run into some of the big cats, in which case you should probably just run and scream your head off. You might also trip up on—sorry—sink holes."

"Yes, fantastic," Manuel said.

"And then there are these nasty feral pigs. Watch out for the machete blade as well, as it's very sharp. I'll probably be asking you to take over the bushwhacking when I get tired. Remember water, of course, or else you'll get dehydrated quick and be no use. And just . . . follow me. Don't get separated from me. It won't be very safe if you do."

I tried not to think about what these cautions might mean for my mother. And it seemed the same thought occurred to Manuel. He hesitated for a second, but then tugged down his shirt and nodded while clearing his throat.

"That sounds like very good advice," he said.

He went over to the car, and he and Yolanda locked it before walking across the road and entering the forest.

Erik and I watched them as they parted the trees with their hands.

Yolanda took out the blade and stood before the bush, and though Manuel had turned waxen and more fragile since entering this atmosphere, I realized that it had the opposite effect on her. In the tawny light, in the presence of the jungle, her face flushed and a watchful private expression settled on her features. She raised the machete and swung it in a fierce and graceful arc. Thin precise muscles appeared in her neck. It occurred to me that she was as fluent in that gesture as I tried to be with words, because her father had made her an expert in how to survive in this wild place.

Manuel followed her, brushing away some of the leaves with tentative fingers. Then they disappeared.

"All right—you ready?" I asked Erik, hiking up my backpack.

I was covered in sweat, but undeterred by the mosquitoes frolicking around my extremities. A frightened excitement moved through me. I felt as if I could have pummeled down Yolanda's path all night long until I found my mother.

He looked at me and nodded.

"I'm ready to go with you, Lola," he said.

I smiled and touched his chest, once, with my hand. And then we turned from the road, toward the blue-dark trees, and went in.

CHAPTER 49

We entered the forest, batting away the mosquitoes and large buzzing flies, and stumbling over the low-lying brush and the great roots of mahoganies, which extended up thirty meters into the air and sent their large shoots into the ground. These roots ramified and formed a network of hard gnarled tendrils among the ferns and sedge and waterlogged mud that laved the jungle's floor in waves. The air was very moist and hard to breathe, as it felt so thick in the lungs and the mouth. Also, the heat, which I had noticed before in Flores, had reached upward into the high nineties and moved over us with a rank force.

It took time to adjust. Every time we took a step, we landed in a plush and sucking mud that threatened to pull off our boots and crawled onto our legs, doused our pants, and otherwise maneuvered itself almost immediately up onto our chests and faces and hands. The mosquitoes evidenced a particular attraction for any protuberance on the body of special sensitivity, so our attention was very much involved for the first hour in the Sisyphean task of removing the living black layers of insects by swiping at them with our useless hands. Though no one said anything much during this initial period, that does not mean it was silent in the forest; the air was busy with the movements of the jungle's inhabitants, mostly spider and howler monkeys. These creatures, dancing in the tree canopies and springing with big-toed feet from vine to vine in a kind of crazy play, shrieked at us in almost human voices. Then they'd shake the trunks and branches, breaking off branches to actually hurl them down at our heads, apparently in some kind of editorial concerning our unwelcome status there. What was all the more unnerving and wonderful about the spiders and howlers was the freakish way their faces looked, human and mobile, with the jaws moving and the lips grimacing, so that they seemed just on the verge of shouting at us certain extremely articulate profanities. When I saw them do this, I suddenly understood with a discomposing lucidity how related we all were to the beasts.

Until I heard something leaking and felt a wetness on my shoulder.

"Is it raining?" Erik asked behind me.

"What is that?" I said.

Yolanda began guffawing.

"Pretend it isn't happening," I heard Manuel say.

When I had the brilliant idea to look up, I realized that the monkeys were peeing on and very anthropomorphically laughing at me.

Beyond the racket of hominid urination and giggles, however, there were other, less compromised fascinations and pleasures in the jungle.

The orchids were as lithe and fresh-colored as girls; the trees were magical, leafy, woven with fuchsia blooms and white petals. At times the electric music of the insects would be broken by the thundering noise of the birds. These were red and green creatures with large hooked bright yellow beaks and thrashing wings. And there was also the rushing timbre from unseen rivers, the ingurgitational sound of our boots in the mud, and the efficient ripping of the machete as Yolanda hacked an emerald path for us through the bushes and the flowered vines.

She looked taller and stronger here than she did in the city. She swung that weapon so swiftly, it seemed more mercury than steel as it sizzled through the greenery. I could hear her steady breathing, like a pulse; her lithe arms moved with rapid and savage strokes. The severed heads of scarlet blooms marked her wake, and the reflections of the bush walls that she carved tinted her black hair with the shades of sap and sea glass, apple and holly.

This rough glowing corridor that she fashioned with her blade would eventually cut toward the famous river Sacluc.

After an hour hiking through the rain forest, I had no idea where we'd just been or where we were.

"Is it close?" I asked. "I can't tell. Are we far away from the road? Are we almost there?"

"We aren't almost there," I heard Yolanda say. "It's at least ten more kilometers to the Sacluc."

"Do you want me to take over?" Manuel asked.

"I'll do it," Erik said.

"There will be plenty of time for that, but I'm not tired yet," Yolanda said.

"Ten more kilometers," I said. "How long will that take, do you think?"

"Maybe another whole day. And drink some water, all of you. I won't be able to carry you around this place."

Pieces of sky were visible between the trees' leaves, so we could see canary and gray clouds hanging overhead. The light in the lower wood grew more obscure, turning green as it reflected the color of the brush and the moss that crowded onto the bark of the mahoganies. The rainwater caused everything in the forest to glisten, and its flora proliferated around us, heavy, glazed, and so luxuriant that it seemed it might swallow us up in one great moist gulp. The trees' branches and trunks were huge, sometimes as big as six times my body around, and they extended up into the air in curving lines; ferns and mosses curled in their furrows, orchids and lianas ran down from them like streamers. And some kind of chemical process was performed in the hot mud, which created mists and other vapors that rose from the ground in thin white billows.

We passed through a cloud. I listened to Erik's tramping and breathing, and watched Manuel in front of me stagger occasionally, then right himself by pressing against the trees. Yolanda would wait for him sometimes, but she remained so busy cutting us the path that she didn't even seem to notice us that much. She kept her eyes on the brush ahead and gave no sign of any hesitation about her direction, other than one or two consultations with the compass she'd kept in her pocket. But I don't know how she managed it. I couldn't have even led us back out if I'd tried.

The afternoon wore on. None of us talked. It didn't take long for our muscles to begin aching, or our backs, or for our feet to hurt. But instead of this distracting me from a gory bout of self-reflection, I found that my thoughts sprang around in wild and unamiable directions.

Before night fell, it occurred to me with a nice neurotic twinge, which hit me like an attack of sciatica, that I understood almost nothing that had happened in the last few days. I didn't really understand Guatemala City, with its guards and soldiers wandering around with rifles stuck in their pants. I didn't understand why anybody thought it might be a good idea to worship a horse in Flores, or what sort of peyote the authors of the *Rough Guide* or *Lonely Planet* were taking. And, more nerve-rackingly, I didn't understand what had become of my taste for firefighters, or why I was more Mexican or Latin back home than here, or how I had been ripped from my soft cozy armchair to dally among incontinent monkeys, or what had happened to my connection with Manuel Alvarez. I didn't understand (or didn't want to) the meaning of one bloody word in my mother's journal. And I sure as hell didn't understand why she would come out here all this way and not tell me exactly what she'd discovered, or why.

And then, on top of all of these invigorating metaphysics, I realized that I could also barely fathom that woman's face in the Flores morgue, which had looked carved out of ivory, and was so still because she wasn't alive anymore, as she had been killed by a tree. It was when this image came to me that I found myself stumbling suddenly over not only roots and orchids and slippery frightening snakelike creatures gliding through the mud in front of my feet, but also an extremely confounding fact that disturbed me more than anything else. I thought: *Even if my mother didn't die in Flores, and even if I find her out here, somewhere, alive—someday she will die. Someday I'll never see her again.*

This idea had never come to me before with such clarity.

So here I was in the jungle, thinking of all things horrible, incomprehensible, void, and nonsensical as I climbed past ferns twisting in a breeze like acrobats, and maneuvered past majestic trees wreathed in mist. I looked behind me, but Erik was communicating violently with some spotted centipede that had become suddenly interested in crawling up his leg. Ahead I saw Manuel, smaller than me and lighter, and the tall, elegantly boned frame of Yolanda. Out of all of this, every person I was with, every fact and datum that I'd run across, I wondered if the only thing that I thought I could possibly ever puzzle out with the aid of my million misfiring synapses and whirligigging gray cells was the story translated by Beatriz de la Cueva five hundred years ago about a King, a Witch, and a Jade.

We were following Beatriz de la Cueva, Balaj K'waill, Alexander Von Humboldt, the unlucky Oscar Angel Tapia, Tomas de la Rosa, and Juana Sanchez by heading north through ten to fifteen miles of buffer zone in the Maya Biosphere Reserve. Directly past the river Sacluc we would wind our way through the Maze of Deceit (which apparently was composed of stories) toward a moldering kingdom and a magical tree, and then crack the Maze of Virtue (nothing more than a riddle). Only then would we find a stone that some called a magnet, others a talisman, and still others a queen. And maybe, as well, we'd find my mother.

Ahead of me, Yolanda stopped in the forest's dusk and lifted her face toward the canopy. She turned around and looked at me for a second, but didn't smile. I stopped walking too. Then she reached behind and pulled her flashlight out of her bag. She switched it on.

The cold, white, brilliant light lit up the jungle like a flare. The beam blew through the shadows hanging from the boughs and covering the monkeys and the birds. And all about us there were fogs and wings of dark air, and the sounds of coming night, and the trees like giants closing in.

"This is where we'll camp," she said.

CHAPTER 50

The jungle's dusk moved down over us quickly, and we turned on each of the three flashlights Yolanda had brought along, so their beams moved in crisscrossing patterns over the rough clearing where we'd decided to rest for the night. To my left, Manuel and Erik labored to set up hammocks and pulled out filmy white sheets of mosquito netting. I trained one of the torches onto the ground where Yolanda worked, with sure and fast digs of a spade to remove the mud and tussocks, and tried to dig a hole and level the surrounding earth. She still wore her hat at an angle over her eyes, and in the ebbing light I saw the scratches on her chin and her jaw, and the grime swiping at her cheek and across her nose. She pushed the spade into the ground, but the wet earth continued to cave in and she couldn't get any leverage, so eventually she smoothed the whole area as level as she could make it. Then she began to cover the area with a nest of soaking leaves and ferns that I had gathered, as well as half of a crimson bromeliad plant.

Next she brought out of her backpack a stick of magnesium with a flint attached to one end, and took a small silver knife from her back pocket. With the knife, she whittled off a few scraps of the mineral stick and sprinkled them on the wet leaves and wood.

She struck the flint on her knife until a spark came, and the scraps of magnesium caught flame and the whole pile of wet steaming stuff began to move and crackle and radiate heat and gold light.

The four of us crouched about the fire for a while, our figures rose-colored against the forest, which grew gray, then black.

When night had fallen completely, I looked at my friends, and they seemed so lovely and wonderful that my heart expanded. I watched the red light play against their faces, and the shadows cast by their bodies. Manuel looked old, tired, and beautiful; Yolanda sharpened her machetes with a stone. Erik sat on the far side of the blaze and tinkered with his decipherment with a pencil, frowning in concentration while a blue light glimmered like a jewel within the deepest part of the fire.

Then he put his pencil down.

"Lola?"

"Yes."

"I've got it," he said. "I've deciphered it."

Yolanda threw her machete to the side. Manuel sat up straighter and pressed his hand to his chest.

"Tell me that you decoded a map," I said.

He didn't answer at first.

"Is it a map?" I asked again.

"In a way," he said. I could see from his face that he was excited. "It does give directions that we're supposed to take once we hit the Rio Sacluc, where Tapia found the Stelae. And like I was telling you before, the stories are related to the legend. You've got the same characters . . . but . . . it's a little complicated. Just don't—get upset."

"What do you mean?"

He spread out the pages before us.

"It's another puzzle."

THE LABYRINTH
OF DECEIT, DECODED

The Story of the King

I was once a true King, fierce and Noble. Born under the Sign of the Feathered Serpent, I possessed all power over Earth and Sea and Man. On account of my one great Gift, it was my Destiny to Rule this land for one thousand years in perfect peace. Every soft girl I desired would call herself my wife, and embrace no other. Every strong man would bow before me as a slave and despair. Cold dark deep and absolutely pure, that holy rain would make rich my Gardens, and I would walk in my fields like a Fearsome Lord. When it was time for me to depart from this world, I would rise with the Sun like a God, and take my place beyond the Smoking Mirror of the sky.

But nothing but my death came to pass. At the end of my days, I was a pauper but for one Treasure, and alone. I dwelled in no rich Gardens, where the soft girls once sang to me. I walked through no fields like a Fearsome Lord, nor smiled upon my slaves trembling with dread.

It was a Witch who destroyed my life. The most beautiful woman I ever saw.

My last Wife, whom I conquered as the most terrible of all foes, brought me fame and a dowry of land. And yet it was none of these virtues that I most cherished. I had made her mine so that I might own her one Fortune, but when it was in my possession the perfection and splendid horror of the Gem drove me mad.

This Treasure consumed my days. My heart cracked with love for it. Hour upon hour I gazed and mused upon it, and soon my fine gardens withered. The fields grew fallow. The slaves began to look me in the eye. And I cared for none of this. For I had discovered all happiness in that rare Prize.

So my languor persisted until the day my Dwarf whispered rumors of lust and betrayal in my ear, and I woke from my sleep. I stole from the chamber of my long rest and began to creep about my Palace, searching and listening. And upon reaching my own bed, I surprised her in her lover's arms.

The Priest.

I knew one more moment as a King when I killed them both, but with her curse I understood all was lost. I flew from that place. I gathered my Treasure and prepared for my death. With one last look at my home, I escaped the City, and entered a second Covert of which I will not tell here.

Where is that fine Kingdom of old now? The blue city I once ruled? You, the Knight, the Traveler, the Quester, the Reader, seek my shining palace and my Jewel.

Yet the way will remain hidden from you if your heart does not dwell on the faith of our fathers. Consider the sun, and the Smoking Mirror beyond that sky. Remember the holy morning of Heaven, which all Kings enter when they die.

And so, if you seek my Treasure you must, too, begin with the path that tracks the day's first rays.

Three of the paths you may choose from will contain no Jewel, but danger: At one way lies a maelstrom in the hour of winter; at another lies the fierce jaguar protecting their young in the spring; at a third lies the drowning marshes during all seasons; and at the fourth, should you choose correctly, you shall find what you seek.

Trust me.

I, the King, am no liar.

Should you seek the Queen, you must start toward the East, where the Gods and the penitent reside.

The Story of the Witch

They call me Sorceress, but I was once a simple person. If I were extraordinary, this was only because I harbored a passion for my small and poor country. Toward the West, where the sun sinks into the ocean, our soil grew few crops, and we lived off the fast and creeping things that roamed the great Deep. And yet, for a while, we did have the Treasure. We harbored in the protection of this tremendous Jewel.

Once, we were our own People.

And then we were no more.

After long years of peace and solitude, the day came when we saw our enemy on top of our cliffs, horrible with their armor and swords. Down these dire knights flew and crushed our life in their strong hands. And it was only when I was brought before my new King, and told to bow like a wife to my own killer, that I felt the monstrous change work within me. For he had stolen our Gift. He had taken our Gem.

Yes, it was then, only then, that I became this Witch.

Through evil glamour I made myself lovely. And with my body's charms, my tongue's magick, I converted a Holy Man into a monster and a traitor. I poured honey into a Priest's mouth and dreams of royal murder into his ear. I rubbed him with a balm that poisoned his mind with jealousy.

He agreed to help me kill my husband.

But it was not to be.

Before our plot was sealed in blood, my husband and his Dwarf discovered us, and though I flew to my soldiers the king trapped and killed me. And when I knew my death was near, I did not use my last breath to bless the fast and creeping things of the Great Deep that had once sustained us, nor did I look with pity at the men mired in their evil, nor the women trapped in their lusts.

Instead, I cursed my enemies, and became as hard and as wicked as my husband.

I killed them all with my last words. The gods' Storm took both the pure and the impure, and the old and the young.

And now I, too, have disappeared.

Yet it is only I, from the grave, who will tell where hides the Treasure.

Do not trust the words of men, kind traveler. For they seek to keep to themselves all power unto death. I do not hunger after such glories. I am an evil woman, the most terrible of all, and I seek my penance.

Three of the paths you may choose from will contain no Jewel, but danger: At one way lies a maelstrom in the hour of winter; at another lies the fierce jaguar protecting their young in the spring; at a third lies the drowning marshes during all seasons; and at the fourth, should you choose correctly, you shall find what you seek.

Trust me.

I, the Witch, am no liar.

Should you seek the Queen, you must start toward the West, from where I came.

The Story of the Dwarf

As all stretched men are born idiots, and all lofty women born fools, I am happy to have been made in neither of these forms. Instead, I remain myself, a Dwarf, born from the Great Northern Tribes, whose peoples may see into the futures with the aids of dice, dreams, and the craft of the stars.

These arts have been mine. Of prophets, our City has seen none finer. And through my skills, I had my first vision that we would all come to blood and death that first day I laid my eyes upon the Witch. Yet my good stupid King was so set upon his hunger for her Treasure that I did not warn him of the future I feared.

He conquered her seaside kingdom. They were married, against her word. And then he was happy. He could now take his Prize, the Great Jewel.

Heaven, my mother always said, is ruled by Dwarves, and Hell is governed by Hunchbacks, for both these holy tribes descend from the spirit of the blessed Northern Star. And it is thus that these races reign over the spirit world with perfect wisdom and peace. Only the poor Earth suffers its governance from that blundering clumsy race of Giants, who are born without the aid of the constellations. So perhaps it is no great surprise that my King's base greed, and the Witch's worldly wiles, and the Priest's silly cod, combined each of them to create disaster and thus kill us all.

During the first years of my King's triumph, when he grew ever more sick with his hunger for his Treasure, I counseled him to dash it against the rocks. Thus temptation would be gone. And we would remain safe.

But he did not listen to me.

More, he sickened. More, he hungered. He grew wan and pale with his passion for the Jewel's beauty and power. And so fiendish was this desire that it made him blind and deaf as the dead he would one day soon join. He did not hear the shouts and howls of his cat-wife, the Witch, as she drugged the Priest in his bed with her body. And he did not see the Priest suffered too from the pangs of love, despite the fool's white face and crossed eyes.

But I did. For I am a Dwarf, and sacred, and brave.

Into the forest I crept, to spy upon the lovers. The moon rose, the moon fell. After their ruttings, the Witch and the Priest crawled back to the City, and then straight I traveled after them, toward the North Star, which is the Sign of the Feathered Serpent and the guide of all good things.

I brought the King to his puddled bed. And what magnificent wrath did we see then. Half-jaguar, half-man he seemed, and bearing his blue blade. But the Witch proved too fast.

Though he did kill her, not even her death could quiet her curse.

When the trees began singing, and the sky swept down upon us, my Lord escaped from the city and into a second secret Covert that he hoped would keep him safe. But no more of that will I tell.

As I am a Dwarf, you will hear as much truth in what I speak as in all of my silence, for I do not possess the fork-tongued talents of the Giants. Believe my tale, then, as it contains no crime. Should you, too, Dear Traveler and Knight, have a hunger for the Treasure, I may call you Fool, and I will be right.

Three of the paths you may choose from will contain no Jewel, but danger: At one way lies a maelstrom in the hour of winter; at another lies the fierce jaguar protecting their young in the spring; at a third lies the drowning marshes during all seasons; and at the fourth, should you choose correctly, you shall find what you seek.

Trust me.

I, the Dwarf, am no liar.

Should you seek the Queen, you must start toward the North, under whose sign I was born.

The Story of the Priest

I, a Priest, was lifted to the sky like a God by my Lady's love. And yet I, the Priest, discovered that I was no God. When my Lady abandoned me, I came crashing to the ground.

An ugly man I was, fumbling and meek. I prayed to the Gods in terror, and my tongue stumbled in my mouth when I spoke before the King. He, seeing my weakness, raised me to the highest station, where he might use me as a doll.

When he offered me my price of girls and wine, I became his sword and his shield. I stood before crowds of men, and told them all that he had been chosen as their ruler by the Gods, though I knew it was not so. When he glutted himself while thousands starved, I explained to the people that such sacrifices were required by the spirits of Earth and of Heaven. When he stole the wives of men for his own. I soothed these husbands with the hope that they might be made holy by their suffering.

And all the time, I grew more weak and more foul, as the bane of power worked itself through my heart.

I only became strong and pure again when I saw Her.

The King sought the Treasure. But Priests have had enough of precious things. I cared not for any fine Jewel, but for my earthly Lady, who trod on the ground with no angel's feet, whose breath was no perfume, whose hand was rough, whose smile was bitter.

I loved her. I felt myself enter the sky when I gazed upon her. I floated above the mountains. The day she took my hand for the first time, my spirit leapt through the clouds.

I loved her to my death.

But when the King and his stunted Seer discovered us in our hot bed, my beloved knew me no longer. She turned from my side, and with what strange words did she curse us each. Knaves. Caitiffs.

Devils. Men. All of us were to be consumed by fire. All of us would die in dread and torture.

This is when I knew her falsehood, and her longing. And I felt myself tumble from the sky to where she had lifted me. Down, down, down, did I fall to the lowest realm in the Earth.

And here, I reside now, below. It is where all lovers go.

To Hell.

In my grave, the Jewel seems to me now not precious, but a cheap thing. For what reason might I hide it? Down here, where the sad and vile things writhe, we are all of us honest. For there is no art in Hades. And so it is with good reason that you should believe what I tell you: The Treasure is down here, where I live.

Take my counsel, then. Do not believe the others.

Three of the paths you may choose from will contain no Jewel, but danger: At one way lies a maelstrom in the hour of winter; at another lies the fierce jaguar protecting their young in the spring; at a third lies the drowning marshes during all seasons; and at the fourth, should you choose correctly, you shall find what you seek.

Trust me.

I, the Priest, am no liar.

Should you seek the Queen, you must start toward the South.

CHAPTER 51

orth, south, east, or west?" I said. "That's what we're supposed to choose once we hit the mouth of the Sacluc. Where
the Stelae were found."

"Right," Erik said.

"How do we know which way to go?"

"Perhaps the better question is, whom do you trust the most?"
Manuel replied. "The Witch or the Dwarf? The King or the Priest?"

"East," Yolanda said. "That's where we're going. That's—whom?"

"The King."

"Then I pick the King."

"I'm more partial to the Priest," Manuel said. "Poor fool."

"I don't trust any of them," I said. "But the Witch is my favorite.
She's so *strong*. She would have been my mother's, too—I'll bet she
chose that way. None of the others are sympathetic."

"Not sympathetic?" Erik asked. "How is the Dwarf not sympathetic?"

"He's too tricky," I said.

"He's responsible for the whole mess in the first place," Manuel
added.

"The Witch isn't strong enough to trust," Yolanda said to me. "She
surrendered to the Elder Brother."

"She didn't *surrender*—"

"Didn't we read something about this in Von Humboldt's journals?" Erik asked.

"What?"

He shook his head. "I can't remember."

"And the Witch tells us to go west," Yolanda continued, "but I already explained, my father's been all over that territory, and he never found anything."

"But maybe he was right, anyway."

"He wasn't," she said. "And he would never listen to me about that."

Manuel's eyes were dropping closed. "The Priest's only crime is falling in love, whereas the rest of them are liars, killers, or thieves."

We lowered our heads at this, thinking, and rubbing our sore necks.

"I'm too tired for this right now," Yolanda said. "That hammock is looking good."

"Just a minute," I said. "Aren't we going to decide?"

"We've decided east," she said. "The King."

"No, the Witch."

"The Priest."

"And I'm inclined toward the Dwarf," Erik said, "if only because I know that east's already been combed by archaeologists—because that's where Tikal is." He squeezed his eyes shut. "Though there *is* something else, but I've forgotten. I need to read through the papers."

Manuel yawned. "That's it, I can't stay up any longer."

"You're right," Yolanda said. "We'll need our rest for our eastward journey tomorrow."

"Westward," I said.

"Good night."

"Good night."

"Fine. Good night."

When the rest had ceased rustling about and begun their soft snoring, I crawled into Erik's hammock and pressed my ear to his chest. His heart was louder than the voices of the sleeping birds. Curling himself like a terrier against me, he slept too.

The forest was round and inky above us. The moving purple

branches of the dozing trees and the drowsy lizards whispered among one another; the dark was perfect and endless, though it was fringed with rose light from the fire and also busy with invisible eyes.

I swung in that hammock with Erik, and in my optimism I gripped his hand and tried to send myself out through the woods, into the blackness, and travel like the psychics and mediums to the region where my mother hid, to let her know I was coming.

I tried to feel her.

And then—I thought I did feel my mother somewhere, hidden from me in the huge wood.

With a leap in my chest, I was almost sure that I *could* feel her, because I loved her so much. My heart began to ring soft and clear, like a bell.

The night thickened and shifted; the wood extended its shadows to cover even the small roses of the fire.

North, south, east, west.

Which way?

I lay there, waiting for a sign. I couldn't sleep.

The next morning, at five A.M., we ate a breakfast of dried shrimp and bottled water, then set out for the mouth of the Sacluc. Heading north through the forest, we descended ever lower into the Peten, which sits on a declining stone peninsula where water from the earlier storm had pooled. For hours we pushed through the path that first Yolanda, then Erik, and later I cut through the woods. At every step, there was the constant pulling and sucking of the mud, which became deeper and higher, and more saturated with water as we made our way forward. The DEET covered our faces and hands, as did dirt and the unstoppable bugs; the lianas and orchids dangled in front of our eyes; the monkeys complained. Cacti scratched us as we moved past, and soon all of us had rents in our clothing, and notches in our arms, our faces, and our hands.

Soon, it was my turn to try the machete. And this was not one of those old-fashioned sorts of knives that I've seen in museums and antique stores, but rather an instrument that probably came out of a factory that year. It had an eighteen-inch-long blade of stainless steel, with a wood handle with a knuckle grip attached to the metal with three large rivets. The brand name *Ontario* had been stamped into the handle. With this frightening-looking gadget, I tried to copy Yolanda's style in cutting the brush, which was to grip the knife loosely between her thumb and index finger, and then swing the blade up in an arc. But I couldn't do that. I just hacked away at the bushes and the vines in a sort of random motion, using loops and crosswise cuts and vertical whacks.

"No, no, no, move it up," Yolanda said. "Oh, I can't watch."

"Or maybe more to the side, less spastically?" Erik said. "You look like you're trying to kill a kangaroo."

I looked at them and kept whacking.

"Just trying to help."

Yet I will say that even if I didn't have access to anything in the way of real skill, I still owned my indigenous reserves of Mexican stubbornness. And my flailing did do the trick. Eventually I cleared out a long path, before my arm felt as if it had been set on fire.

At one o'clock in the afternoon, we began to notice a greater degree of flooding on the ground; insects with velvety feelers and lobsterlike claws skimmed past us on rafts made of large leaves; the hanks of bush carved out by Yolanda's machete swam into the overflow, causing us to tread through standing water filled with scarlet and purple floating flowers in a hallucinatory version of Monet's *Water Lilies*. After half a mile, though, she had to strap the blade to the back of her pack, as we'd reached an opening in the wood that was hedged all around with mahoganies and filled with a high breach of water running off from a pond sitting to the east. The freshet exhaled a chill air, which converted into thin fogs; these vapors drifted to the towering mahoganies or traveled close to the surface of the stream, like a reflection of the intricate pattern the water made as it leapt over fallen trees and plunged into the dark part of the wood.

We entered the tall water and prepared to wade across it. Yolanda first, then Erik. I entered third, and Manuel walked behind. My father wore a large forest-green pack with a red handkerchief tied onto it. His shoulders bowed slightly beneath the weight; the soaked blue cotton fabric of his shirt puckered against his skin, pressing transparently onto his thin arms. The water reflected back his face, his moving shoulders. He did not look very sturdy. His small fine head, with its vanishing black and silver hair and large-lobed pink ears, barely reached above the vinyl back of his rucksack. Beneath the rising blue water, which reached to his hips, his legs moved uneasily. I turned from him and forged ahead—but then, when the three of us had passed already beyond the midpoint of the inlet, where the water was as high as our chests, I heard him slip and tumble into the stream.

"Dad!"

I jerked around to see him flailing in the water twenty feet away from me, grasping hold of a large rock close to the bank.

"I'm all right," he said, though I saw that the shirt fabric had torn from his arm and that his shoulder was scraped raw. He crawled away from us back through the pond and gripped onto the banks with his hands, pulling himself up onto the mud and turf that shelved away from the thick stand of trees.

"What's going on?" Yolanda asked. Close to reaching the other side, she half-turned in the water that extended to her shoulders.

"Señor Alvarez!" Erik yelled. He was chest-high in the water.

Manuel continued to climb up the bank, breathing heavily. He looked frail and his face had turned white.

"We shouldn't get separated," Yolanda said. "Cross over the water."

"Just give me a second," Manuel said. He had reached a flat, grassy area butting onto the wall of mahoganies, and remained on his hands and knees. "That winded me."

As we stood in place in the pond, watching him, our ears were filled with the dreamy, windlike sound of the water purling around us. But then came another sort of noise from behind the boles of the trees: a cracking, and a trembling of leaves. And next came an explosive sound of birds beating out from the shrubs.

"What's that?" Erik asked.

"I don't know," I answered.

We continued to watch, unsure what was happening. My father remained crouched on the bank, half covered in mud.

"Manuel," I heard Yolanda say. "Manuel, get over here."

My father turned his head. "There's something . . ."

Before our eyes, the bush parted with a tender rustling sound.

A huge, rangy, gold-furred cat with black markings and green eyes emerged and stepped onto the bank less than two feet from Manuel.

The animal looked to be almost two hundred pounds. It had long daggered teeth that would rip my father's flesh. The belly of the beast hung low and bulged and was covered with white fur; it moved with lithe slow steps, and lowered its head between its shoulder to hone in on its prey. From its throat came a rumbling menacing purr. And then it drew back its lips over its fangs. It hissed. It sounded as if it were screaming.

"Jaguar," Erik said, in a tight voice.

The cat's shadow cleaved Manuel's body. He looked up at its shining face and sat on his knees.

I stared at my father sitting in front of that monster, and experienced a moment of such perfect terror that I closed my eyes and imagined myself cowering back in the dusty peaceful aisles of The Red Lion, which was full of paper tigers and dead men who were made out of words.

It was where I had always hidden from my fears.

Then I opened my eyes again.

I raced toward Dad, through the swelling water that splashed all around with a great clashing sound, so the cat gave a startled leap in the air. But it didn't run.

"*Stand up and shout at it, Manuel!*" Yolanda yawled. She was scrambling about, trying to reach behind her to get a hold of the machete that was strapped to her pack. "It thinks you're food, for God's sake!"

My father's face tremored. "I'm afraid I can't move. I told you I'm not good at this sort of thing."

Erik ran beside me with deranged slow steps through the flood. We slipped, submerging into the pond, then heaved ourselves out of the firth again.

The cat stretched out its head and widened its eyes and roared. It swiped at the air in front of my father's face with its sharp massive paw. Erik and I shrieked to frighten it away. Yolanda was just managing to get the machete untied from her pack.

"Oh, it's pregnant," I heard Manuel say. "Don't hurt it."

"I can't let it get to you, Manuel!" she yelled back to him.

"She's going to be a mother," Manuel said.

"Get away! Get away!" I screamed. I'd nearly reached the bank. I could see the cat's pink teats poking out from her white fur, and for a second thought I might black out from panic.

Erik rushed past me and gripped hold of Manuel, trying to drag him back into the water. All of us were shouting at the animal while she shivered and growled and scraped at the mud.

And this is when we heard another rustling in the bush, and a noise like footsteps in the wood.

Yolanda had her blade out and raised it over her head, as if she were going to throw it at the cat. But the jaguar had stopped roaring; it flinched and turned toward the noise.

"Don't—don't—don't—Yolanda," Manuel yelled.

"Move!" Erik hollered. He and I had our arms around my father's shoulders, and we were dragging him into the water, away from the cat. Yolanda stood there, with her blade still poised in the air, and looked confused.

The cat moved away from us, padding in the direction of the trees; we could see that it was terribly thin. A ray of sunlight glinted over the gold fur, and then it slipped between the mahoganies and disappeared from our view.

A second passed; we were all in the water now. No one spoke. Another second passed, and another.

Then we heard the unmistakable sound of a gunshot beyond the trees. A second shot followed it. The woods shuddered and then were still again.

I jerked forward. "What's that?"

"A hunter?" Erik said. He gripped his arms under my father's armpits and was hauling across the water so that my father's body bobbed around.

"Just go!" Yolanda said.

"Erik—agh—" Manuel said.

"What?"

"—you're—squashing—me."

"Sorry." Erik removed his grip but kept a close eye on Manuel as he skittered into and across the pond.

"What was that?" I asked again. "Did someone shoot her?"

"I think I might have heard her run through the woods," my father groaned.

We slipped and half-swam through the pond, pushing each other from the back and pulling each other onto the other side of the bank. Erik reached the bank first and hauled me out by grasping around my ribs; he yanked Yolanda up, too, by the arm straps of her pack.

I bent down, grabbed Manuel, and helped lift him onto solid land.

Then we looked out onto the firth and the trees, and everything seemed peaceful and soundless again. There was no sign of the jaguar except for the scrapes and paw prints it had made in the mud. There was also no sign within the dark wood of a gunman.

We have four miles to go," Yolanda said, looking at my father. "Do you think you can make it?"

"There's not a question that I'm making it." Manuel was standing beside her on the bank and looking very white and grim.

"All right then," she said. She looked troubled but didn't press the fact that he had just frozen in fear and so endangered his life, and perhaps the rest of ours as well.

Erik and I stood up.

"We'll go when you're ready," I said to Manuel.

"I'm ready now."

We pushed on through the forest. But Manuel didn't look as strong as he claimed. As we started on the route again, I walked behind him and noticed every shake of his legs and the way he half-stumbled over the marshy sections of the forest. Though he'd kept up a decent stride before, the fall had hurt him, and he seemed to lack vitality and also confidence. He took slow, uneasy steps; we had to hold our pace to his.

I kept my eye on my father the whole next section, and every slip and hesitation, every time he reached out his hands to balance himself or hesitated, made me nervous.

On we trekked like this for another three hours, hacking away at the brush, worrying, half-lurching through the swamps and the meads. At last we hit the point that was our closest approximation of the place where Oscar Angela Tapia had discovered the Flores Stelae, and where Beatriz de la Cueva had found the Maze of Deceit with Balaj K'waill.

This point was the horrible and magnificent mouth of the Rio Sacluc.

"This isn't what we expected," Erik said.

"Oh, damn," Yolanda said.

CHAPTER 52

The Rio Sacluc reached much higher than the pond; it made the pond look like nothing. It ran through the jungle as a fury of ragged water, streaming in a torrent to the lower depths of the jungle. Through this we would cross to the other bank, which was half landslide, half soft mud, leading toward another outcropping of chicle trees that were shorter and thinner than the mahogany. Some of them had fallen in the storm, but when I squinted past the water I saw that three of the standing trees bore men high up on their trunks; these *chicleros,* or chicle extractors, were strapped to the trunks in leather cradles; working with knives, funnels, and buckets, they extracted the resin from the trees, which would later be used to make chewing gum. They weren't working at the moment, though—instead, they had stopped their labors to turn and stare at us as we contemplated fording the river.

One of them gestured at us to forget what we were thinking.

As we were too far to shout at each other, and the river too loud, I just waved back. Then I looked back down at the water.

I remembered that de la Cueva wrote to her sister Agata of a little stream that she crossed to get to the Maze: "The Sacluc is a very refreshing and lovely creek, which I understand is changeable, but today runs as the thinnest line of crystal water. The Maze of Deceit sits at its very mouth."

I winced. The four of us stood at that same bank of the white and moving deluge carving through the forest, and watched as the branches swept down in Heraclitean whorls of water. I thought how it was obvious from this evidence that the Sacluc was "changeable." It appeared that much of Mitch's fall had drained off from the forest, and entered here.

"I've never seen the high part extend this far," Yolanda said. "I've never seen it like this at all."

"Is there any way around?" I asked.

"There's no way to tell, though it doesn't look like it."

"We could track it down to see if it does peter out," Erik said. "How long does this stretch up?"

"Seventy miles or more," she replied. "It hooks up with the Rio San Pedro toward the west, and then a network of other rivers and lakes toward the east. It could take us days to find a better crossing than this. And this is where we're supposed to start, remember." She consulted her compass. "This is the original mouth of the Sacluc. And so this is the place Tapia found the Stelae, right across the water. It's from there that we'll have to choose a direction."

"We had better simply go ahead, then," Manuel said, "as I am still assuming that my Juana is down here somewhere, and I'd like to find her as soon as possible."

"I agree with that," I said.

"It's very high," Erik said. "Manuel, can you make it?"

"It's just—a little water."

"A little water," I said, "is not what I'm looking at. Dad, I want you to stick close to me."

"And who's going to stick close to you?" Yolanda asked.

"I will," Erik said.

"Don't worry about me," I said. "I'm strong enough to cross it."

"She'll have to take care of herself, the same as I will, and the same as you," Yolanda said. "That's the hard truth, Manuel. So if you want to go, let's do it."

We hiked our bags high onto our shoulders and began to move in a line down the bank and toward the rapids. It rushed forward in a broad roar, cresting in sprays and plucking off chunks of the shoal, which crumbled and melted into the river. The water rose much higher on our bodies than I had allowed myself to anticipate when I'd been trying to estimate it from our perch. It was cold, hard, fast, and did not allow much traction for our feet as they scrambled across the rocks littering the river's bottom. The weight of the packs, battered back and forth by the force of the waves, made us even less stable. Yolanda's black hat jerked this way and that, particularly when she reached back to check the machete that she'd restrapped to the outside of her rucksack. Manuel fared less well as he walked ahead of me. When the river reached only up to his hips, he stumbled several times. The red handkerchief that he'd kept tied to his backpack unknotted and then fell into the water. In a violent snap, it was sucked toward the west. The deluge moved so fast and loud I couldn't hear anything else—though I saw Yolanda turn her head over her shoulder and shout something before continuing. When I looked back, Erik yelled something at me as well and pushed his hands forward so that I would go on. I pressed into the deeper water, and then saw that my father's body canted toward the left, and his arms waved up crazily.

I called his name but couldn't even hear myself. I plunged through the river, reached out for him. He steadied himself; he put his thumb up in the air to signal he was all right.

And when I moved to grab hold of his pack, I felt my right foot glide against a smooth rock beneath me.

I slipped. Badly. I saw the water rushing toward my head.

The torrent thrust me off my feet, turned me around, and moved me with the same thrashing motion down its path as it had that red handkerchief.

I went down under the water, and the rocks jutting up from the floor of the river came up to cut me. My left shoulder and then both of my legs rammed and slapped against the sharp boulders. A roaring in my ears. I waved my arms around my head to keep my skull safe until water poured into my mouth and my lungs. I struggled up in the water; it was over my eyes, over the top of my head. The weight of the pack bearing me down in the river pushed my face under the surface. My feet kicked free in the river, and I heaved myself up once, twice, three times, to suck oxygen before I was slammed under again. I shrieked and grabbed at a rock and felt my fingertips slip. The deluge hammered over my shoulders. But I insanely kept my bag on my back—it contained the maps, my mother's journal, the other papers we'd need to find her. There was one moment when I looked up through a wave and saw Yolanda, Erik, and Manuel screaming at me from the river's bank, and then Yolanda ripped off her hat and crashed back into the deeper and more dangerous part of the water. I thrashed farther away from them, around a bend. I somehow righted myself, half cocked up through the water, and tried to drag my feet on the bottom, but they wouldn't hold. Seconds or minutes passed while all I did was swallow more and more water. I saw a rock coming toward me, bigger than the rest; I reached out for it, missed it. I reached out again.

And here, I grabbed Yolanda's hand.

"Hold on to me!"

"But you're—you're drowning!" I garbled back at her.

It was true; the two of us both were going under in that river. The water continued to blow past, and we pummeled through it. We gulped and kicked, then Yolanda gripped onto one of the huge rocks. Solid white waves smashed over our heads. Yolanda and I hung onto each other and pulled ourselves above the waterline to see that the rock she had grabbed was not so very far from the bank. We kicked off the rock and lunged toward the river's shelving, then half-ran and half-swam across that terrible channel until we landed on the shallower part of the river's bottom.

We dragged our way up it, and I still had the pack on; I unlooped my arms from its straps.

Then I lay down in the mud, and I worked to breathe, and it felt like my lungs had been torched.

I curled on the bank. It took me a few minutes before I could hear my friends' voices above the sound of the water. Then I jerked to a complete and lucid consciousness.

"Lola," Yolanda said. She huddled next to me. "Hold still. Just talk to me so I know you're all right."

I saw cuts on my arms and my legs and my hands. My shirt and my jeans had been shredded. Only one of the injuries felt serious, a contusion on my hip. The pack appeared to be just fine.

"Lola," she said. "Just say something."

I began crying. "I want to find my mother."

She looked up at Erik and Manuel. "She looks—all right."

"We're waiting here an hour to watch her and make sure," Manuel said.

I shook my head and wiped my face. My body felt full of panicked energy; I really didn't feel so much pain yet. "Okay—no worries—I'm fine."

"You are *not*," Erik said.

"I'd like to just keep going. I don't want to just lie around here."

"Sit back down!" Manuel hollered at me.

I stood up, and sat down again.

Yolanda remained by my side, with her knees in the mud; the skin around her eyes and mouth had turned gray.

"If she wants to go, we should go," she said.

"I do want to go," I said.

"Are you sure?" she asked.

"Yes."

"Good. Because that's why we're here, isn't it? So get up."

She stood to her full height and walked over to a boulder between the trees and the riverbank. She sat on it, apart from the rest of the group. She watched me.

I stayed on the ground. Sparkles of adrenaline rushed through me, though my legs did not seem to have any strength.

"So—get up," she yelled over at me.

"I'm trying to."

"It doesn't look like it. Do you think my father ever let me flop around like that? You think your mother took little naps in the jungle? And if she is here, you think she has days to spare? So if you want to get up, get up. If you want to do it—*do it.*"

"Enough! Be quiet, Yolanda!" Erik yelled back. "Can't you tell that she's hurt?"

But I saw her point. If my mother were really here, we probably did not have much time. I hauled myself to my feet and made myself begin to walk around.

"Fine, fine," I said. "I'm doing it. You're right."

Yolanda watched me carefully, and when she decided that I was mobile, she stood back up. She slipped her backpack on.

"That's how I learned from my father," she said, softly. "That's how he taught me to make it through the jungle."

She began to walk along the river toward its mouth, taking care to pick her hat up from where she'd left it on the bank. I put my pack back on, too, and began to move. Then Erik and Manuel did as well.

Now all of us set off again, back through the trees and past the loud, angry water.

I didn't get too far, though, before Erik lagged behind and pulled me back.

"Let me just—" he said. "Just give me a second and let me hug you." He put his arms around me and touched his cheek to the top of my head. "You scared me."

"It was bad," I said.

"Oh, Lola. Honey. Let me see what happened to your hip."

I unzipped my jeans; Yolanda and Manuel were ahead and couldn't see.

Erik crouched down and looked at the injury; the skin was banged and wounded above the hipbone, where the flank met the beginning of my waist. He peered down at himself, to where a rent had been torn in the lower sleeve of his left arm. He ripped off a piece of the cloth from his shirt and placed it over the spot.

"That'll help to protect you," he said. "More than just your underwear and your jeans."

He touched my hip very lightly with his fingertips; just a very small caress. Erik looked up at me. He picked up my hand and kissed it with a great tenderness, and I kissed him back and warmed my cold mouth.

"Erik."

He just smiled. He knew what I was thinking.

"Come on, hot stuff," he said.

"Okay."

I took his hand, and only then did we begin walking, swifter, to keep up with the other two.

CHAPTER 53

This is it, this is where we're supposed to start," Yolanda said, putting down her rucksack, when we'd reached our original destination on the other side of the Sacluc. She glanced up at the men working in the forest canopy, who were peering down at us with an Olympian detachment. One fellow inserting taps into a chicle tree with a large knot in the center of its trunk began to make circular gestures with his finger around his ear, letting us know that he thought we were severely deranged. Another man shouted down something in the Quiche Maya language, which I couldn't understand.

Yolanda shouted back; they had a brief conversation.

"What did he say?" I asked Yolanda.

"That we're—let's see if I can do an accurate translation," she said, bending down to check the holstered machete she'd tied to her rucksack. "Very complex language, you know. First, he hasn't seen your mother. And second—let me make sure I've got this right. All those gerunds and diphthongs, quite tricky. Ah, yes. He says that we are . . . stupid idiots. That it's. Stu-pid idiots."

"Oh."

"Forget that—this is the place where Tapia found the Stelae," Erik said.

"Here's my best guess, in any event," Yolanda said.

"Well, that's what we'll have to work with, then," I said. "And hope that Mom made the same guess, and so started from the same place."

"Has there been any sign of tracks, or anything like that?" Erik asked.

There hadn't been one sign.

"They would have all been erased by the water," I said. "It doesn't mean anything."

"Yes, that's probably right," Manuel said. "No use searching for footprints at this stage. We should be choosing which way to go. North, south, east, or west."

I began to pull the maps and papers and the journal from my pack; there had been some leaking into their plastic wrappers when I'd been in the water, so there was more damage on their edges and some slight smearing of the ink of the text, but everything could still be read. I picked up the pages where Erik had written his decipherment of the first maze, and leaned on Manuel because of the pain in my hip.

"The text here says that in three of the separate directions we'll probably run into some bad luck," I said. " 'At one way lies a maelstrom in the hour of winter; at another lies the fierce jaguar protecting their young in the spring; at a third lies the drowning marshes during all seasons; and at the fourth, should you choose correctly, you shall find what you seek.' We have to pick one of the directions, and then find a city, and then a dragon tree. And then we have to figure out the second maze, the Labyrinth of Virtue."

"Slow down," Yolanda said. "First things first. I think we've figured out which way is the maelstrom in the hour of winter. South. So I think that counts out the Priest. Sorry, Manuel."

Manuel nodded. "You're right. And I would prefer to avoid meeting more jaguars, and also skirt the routes with the marshes, if at all possible."

"So, now we're down to three directions—three characters," Erik said. "What I would like to do is take just a few hours so that I can go through the books and letters. I'm telling you, I remember something about this. Some detail I've forgotten. It's driving me crazy."

"There's no time to study," Yolanda said. "We have to make a choice now. Juana won't have the luxury of waiting if she's trapped out here."

"I actually agree, Erik," I said.

"Well, if we're going to jump into things," he replied, "we should probably head north. I think Juana would have gone that way. I've read a lot about dwarves before, they're very important in Maya literature. They were seers, counselors. It's an obvious choice. She would have picked that direction."

"But this is what I was saying last night—the Dwarf is wily," I argued. "Mom never would have picked him. He's a spy. My mother would definitely have picked the Witch."

"But the King's the owner of the Stone," Yolanda said. "And he's the one who brought it here in the first place. He's the only one who would know where it is. And this is apart from the fact that I've been studying this jungle for years, and I've got the best theory. It's got to be east, close to Tikal. What better place for a king to hide his treasure? That's the ancient city—it was probably his city. *And* jade's been found there, including the blue. It's the logical choice. Juana would have known that."

"Then why didn't you ever go there before?" I asked.

She crossed her arms. "Dad's the stubborn type, and he was so interested in studying the western part, the idea never caught on with him—he wasn't very flexible, sometimes, especially when it concerned his work. . . . But besides that, he's already been all over the west, so I know there are sinkholes there. I've also heard once of a big cat attacking a hiker in the area. And, as I think you've probably already figured out, the jungle is not neatly carved up into 'jaguar' and 'quicksand' territory. We have to go on more than these stories."

Manuel, Erik, and I regarded each other.

"We have to make a decision," Manuel said. He turned away from us and began to look around, until he fixed on the men working in the chicle trees; in particular he paid attention to the fellow strapped to the tree with the giant knot in the center of its trunk. The tree was approximately three hundred yards away from where we stood. "When I was a boy, and my friends and I had disagreements about whether to go to the cinema or play baseball, we used to have racing contests to decide who would win."

"You can't be saying . . ." I followed his gaze over to the tree, with the man dangling above the knot.

"I certainly am. It's a perfectly fair way to decide. My chums and I, we'd pick out some target, and whoever reached the mark first beat out the others." He pointed to the chicle tree. "Why don't we say, whoever touches the knot on that tree first decides which direction we'll take?"

"Whoever touches it first?" Yolanda asked.

"Yes. The first touch. And the rest of us will follow, without any arguments."

"I'd do it, Dad—but my leg," I said. "I can't run a race, I'm not fit for it now."

"She does have a point, Manuel, it's not really fair," Erik said. Though I noticed that he was already half hunching down into a sprinter's position. "I can run much faster than the women."

Yolanda did not enter the debate. Instead, she quickly bent down and unsheathed the machete that was strapped to her pack. Then she leaned back and raised the blade above her head. She flung it into the air so that it whipped like a propeller until it pierced the knot in the tree with a giant, violent *whang*.

"Aaaaggggh!" said the man working just above, in its branches.

"I touched it first," she said, looking at us.

"Dear God."

Erik stood back up. "You touched it all right."

The machete stuck out from the tree like Arthur's sword.

Manuel nodded, then squinted over his shoulder, toward the east. "Yolanda wins."

CHAPTER 54

We walked due east from the river for two hours, past the *chicleros* who continued to announce their critiques of our mental facilities in their complicated language, and then, farther on, through unpopulated areas filled with patches of gorse, more mahoganies, ferns that stood as tall as men, and mists of bugs. A few white-tailed deer poked their heads through the fern fronds, looked at us, and then disappeared.

"Tikal is a little over a day away from here," Yolanda said. "I think a path used by the Maya ran through this area, once. But with the earthquakes that have happened here, and then the hurricane, it's impossible to tell now."

The trees crowded all around us as we shoved forward, though in some patches several of the giant mahoganies had been felled by the hurricane, so there was no need to cut our way through. Quetzal birds sipped at the ponds that shone on storm-blasted ground, and flew away in a green explosion when they heard us approach. We climbed over soaked and spongy trees on the forest floor. The earth was uneven and pulp-soft, though Yolanda navigated the quags with quick steps. She continued to check her compass to make sure we headed due east, and kept urging us along.

At about four o'clock in the afternoon, though, Erik said, "Where does she think she's taking us?"

I looked behind at him, over my shoulder. "East, like she said. Toward Tikal."

"This doesn't look promising at all," he said.

"I don't know, my boy, I think she's on to something," Manuel said. "You shouldn't underestimate her. She's been in this forest far more than the rest of us have. She's a scholar of the region, and knows all the myths from Tomas."

"And she's done a great job of getting us this far," I admitted.

"She—has," he said. "But exactly how far are we supposed to go?"

"Until we find Juana," Manuel said, "or get nibbled on by jaguars or otherwise suffer the other curses warned of in those morbid little tales."

Of all of us, Manuel worried the most. He continued to walk ahead of me, but slower, and his face had begun to look sick. He was also sweating terribly, and twice I caught his hands trembling again.

Yolanda ducked beneath the low branches of the trees and light-stepped over the gnarled roots and the fallen trunks. Her black hat flashed ahead between the stands of mahoganies, and several times she had to hold up her stride so that we could make up the distance. She was half smiling.

"Finally—east," she said. "But I wish my father were here."

After three miles, the flora began to thicken before us. We reached a very tall, unscathed barrier of juniper brush, and Yolanda whisked her machete through the luminous green wall. We found ourselves, then, in a high corridor of brambly bush, filled with not only the ever-present bugs but also a clean sharp scent, like gin. My hip continued to hurt all this way, and occasionally I had to knead my flank to prevent the muscle from seizing up. Manuel moved in that slow stalky walk ahead of me, tentatively reaching out his hands to bat away the thicket.

"I have no idea where I am," Erik said.

"Just come on," I told him. "There's no use in tracking back now."

"I know, I just can't stand not being able to see where I'm going," he said.

"This is almost it," Yolanda said. "I think we're about to hit a clearing."

About twenty minutes later, we did.

The juniper forest opened into a low-lying savanna fringed by thin, lime-colored trees. The field bloomed all over with curling grasses and sedge bush and more ferns, as well as purple lilies that strewed their petals on the grasses. Needles of sunlight pierced through the treetops, burning the flowers with a hot color. Snakes slithered among the blooms. As we stood on the perimeter, we waved our arms to scatter the mosquitoes that congregated even more thickly in this area. A warm haze lifted from the forest floor, mixed in with the beams of light, and curled up into the gaps of the trees. In these gaps I thought I saw the glitter of yellow eyes.

"What's that?" Manuel asked, as we approached the clearing. "Did I hear purring?"

"No, those are frogs croaking and—burping, actually," Yolanda said.

"Oh."

"But this is *something*," she said, about the site. "I wonder if a ruin—a city—could be buried here. It might be the place."

"Then we should be looking for the dragon tree," I said. "The king—this is what I remember from the *Legende*—he 'fled his Mad city, passed the Dragon Tree, towards the East, and hid within a second Maze. . . .' "

"If we believe what de la Cueva writes," she said. "Then, yes, we should."

"Do you know what they look like?"

"Don't you?"

"Not much in the way of dragon trees in Long Beach."

"Look for a tree with red sap," Yolanda told us.

"Red sap."

"That's the signature of the dragon tree. The *Dracaena draco*." She walked ahead of us toward the open patch between the fringe of elms and mahoganies, and the sunlight barred her body. She took one step, another, and then we saw that the ground that had looked so firm began to flow up her boots, and toward her shins.

"There's some soft earth," she said, in a questioning voice, looking down—just as I heard a creaking and cracking in the wood behind us.

"Is that another jaguar?" I asked.

"Yolanda," Erik said. "What are you doing?"

"Dear girl," Manuel interjected. "Come back here."

"Seriously," I said, "did you all hear that?"

"What?" Manuel asked.

"There was a sound. Behind us."

Yolanda was still walking away, toward the clearing. She slipped and fell half into a substance more elastic and depthless than mud, and the three of us ran toward her. Snakes and dragonflies slid across the surface of the stuff. Yolanda tugged herself up out of the sludge and crawled over to a piece of firmer ground.

"That was disgusting, I can't even tell you," she said, but kept moving. "You people should be careful."

"And you?"

"I know what I'm doing."

We tried to maneuver around this plush earth, tripping over the lianas and ferns and avoiding the tendrils of mud that moved in a rippling fashion before they reared up and hissed.

"That's a snake," I said.

"Don't touch it," Yolanda said.

"You think?"

"How so very, very *National Geographic*," Erik said. "I'm so excited I could almost scream, and I'm not even joking."

"Perhaps we should give up on this direction," Manuel said. He was about thirty feet ahead of us, closer by Yolanda and the center of the clearing. Then he looked over his shoulder and stopped talking.

Yolanda now also stared in the same direction, and her face was set in stone.

"Is there an animal back there?" I asked again, and then stumbled.

Right next to me, Erik's foot slipped into some sort of sinking marsh. I was knee high in mud or sludge, and bent forward to test out some of the ground ahead of me with my hands. The area directly to my left did not feel safe.

"*Is this mud?*" Erik asked. He was looking down. "There are deep pockets all around."

"Jesus," Yolanda said. "*Go away.*"

I turned my head toward the stand of thin trees out of which we'd cut our path.

Lieutenant Estrada was standing behind me like a gruesome hallucination.

He was striped with blood, and thin deep strips cut across his right arm, which dripped darkly onto the ground. He was so close I could see the precise crimson zigzag of his scar. And in his left, uninjured hand he held a gun.

"That's who shot the jaguar," I breathed. "He followed us—that's who we heard before."

"I didn't get that beast—it got *me*," Estrada said, holding up his battered arm. He glared at Yolanda. "But you're not as fast as a cat, are you, de la Rosa?"

"I'm not either," I heard myself say in a low, warning voice. "But I'll do you worse than that arm if you get near her."

He held the gun to his chest. Black, with a long nose and a sleek handle, it looked surreal to me; I had never seen an unholstered gun up close before. His finger was to the side of the trigger. He was shuddering. "Been tracking you for days. But I just want to talk to her."

I reached up to catch hold of the weapon, but Estrada bolted away and headed toward Yolanda. She turned and dragged her feet through the mud in a stumbling race to the center of the clearing, with Estrada close behind. Manuel staggered after them until he reached a hard bank shelving down to the bare patch where Estrada and Yolanda stood, unsteadily.

"I'm going to hurt you," she promised Estrada. She was grappling at her back again, to get hold of her machete. "I swear to God I won't let you walk away from here." She got the blade loose and held it in her hands.

"Why did your father have to set off that bomb?" Estrada asked. "That's what I want you to tell me."

"Because you're a murderer!"

"Not before he got hold of me."

They stood about ten feet away from each other in the center of the glade, surrounded by fog and streaked by the eerie light. I stared at them, moving my mouth but not making any noise. They both started violently. As if mirror images of each other, they threw their arms up and looked down at their feet.

"Yolanda!" Manuel yelled. "Don't move!"

From where Erik and I stood in the bog, about fifty feet away from Yolanda, Estrada, and my father, we couldn't see what was the matter at first. The sedge glittered all around us as if it were scattered with gold flecks. Some of it, disturbed by footsteps, stuck up in peaks like the whipped whites of eggs. It was only when we continued to stare at Yolanda and Estrada and saw the mud crawling up their legs at an alarming rate that we realized that they had blundered into quicksand.

Both of them began struggling to reach the opposite sides of the pit, but the sand had already reached the middle of their thighs. Then their hips.

"I'm going to sink," Yolanda said. She was weighed down by her rucksack, and still held her blade in the air. "Lola, I'm going to drown."

"No, you're not!"

Erik and I were still on the edge on the swamp.

"We have to help them," I said.

He nodded. "Let's go."

"Don't come over here!" she screamed, and threw her machete onto the bank.

"She's right," Manuel said. "Stay put! This place is full of pits."

Erik and I took one look at each other and began to crawl over to where they were.

"Move, move, move," I shouted. "She might only have a few minutes!"

Ahead of us, Estrada was batting off the muck with his free injured hand; he did not let go of his gun.

"Take off your pack!" my father yelled, from his place on the bank.

Yolanda shrugged off her pack and placed it on the mud next to her, while Estrada struggled in the sand, sinking rapidly. The gun fell from his hand as he tried to swim and claw his way out of the bog; it landed on the top of the sand and glinted there, half submerging into the thick matter.

Estrada and Yolanda, both belly-deep, stared at each other across the bag; then they looked down at the weapon between them.

"That would make things easy, wouldn't it?" Estrada asked in a rasping voice.

"Oh, I'll make it easy," she answered. "I know what you've done!"

"Yolanda, just get out of there!" I yelled.

Manuel was sweating terribly, his face pale. He leaned down on the bank, threw off his backpack, and snatched his hammock out of it.

Yolanda and Estrada both began to lunge forward toward the gun, whose handle was sticking out of the sludge. Their movements were impossibly slow. Every fierce push through the sand only moved them forward a few millimeters—and deeper toward the center of the pit. Their arms shot forward in frantic gestures, but they remained nearly immobile except for their constant push downward into the quicksand. The backpack next to Yolanda sank into the bog and disappeared.

"Yolanda, stay put!" Erik yelled. "You're sinking faster!"

But she continued to push as hard as she could; their hands slapped at the muck that surrounded the gun handle. And then Yolanda's hand closed in on the weapon, and she pulled it up; it was dripping with the grainy stuff. She pointed it at Estrada's head, and he looked at her and winced. He closed his eyes.

She pulled the trigger, but nothing happened. Its chambers were clogged with muck.

"Aaahhhhhh," Estrada cried. He opened his eyes, and his scar was as white as paper. "Get out if you can. I'll die here, anyway."

The quicksand was nearly up to the soldier's chest. Yolanda was stomach deep and gasping.

"Were you going to kill me?" she asked.

"I don't know," he answered. His eyes were red, but dry now.

"Yolanda, stop talking and stay still," Manuel said. Erik and I were dragging ourselves through the mud and had nearly reached the bank where my father crouched. From my vantage, I could see that Manuel was shaking very badly, so that he had difficulty controlling his head and his arms. His hands and his thighs spasmed, and he stretched his face into a painful smile. His knees bent, and he sank into the mud, throwing his pack to the side. Squatting down, he began to curse at himself for his cowardice in a voice I could barely hear, but what I could make out contained language I had never known him to use. Yolanda didn't say anything. Neither did Erik and I as we scratched our way over the swamp. And then, still on the ground, Manuel mastered himself with a great effort, crying and swearing as he began to unfold the entire hammock. He sounded strange and terrible, and his face distorted. But he put his hands on the ground and pushed himself up. He stood on his feet. Then he flung the hammock over to where Yolanda half reclined in the quicksand, baring her teeth in a grimace.

"Grab it!" Manuel yelled.

As Erik and I reached Manuel, he threw the hammock a second time, and missed. He was not shaking anymore. He threw it again. Her arms lay on top of the fen, grasping with slipping fingers at the macramé loops while the quicksand slithered up and clutched at her back. Her lips stretched wide, and her jaw moved silently.

"Work harder!" Erik yelled.

She linked her finger around one of the loops of the hammock, which had begun itself to sink into the bog. She hooked her index finger into its circle, and got hold of it in her hand.

The three of us pulled and tugged. Hammocks stretch, and aren't as efficient as rope, but we kept on grabbing it and yanking it back, and then she did begin to move through the stuff, slowly, skimming through it while she hung onto the net. Estrada gazed up at us, his face fading into ash. We wrenched at the hammock until she slid closer to the bank. And just when she neared it, she stretched one arm back, toward Estrada. She didn't say anything to him as they looked at each other.

"Get yourself out of there!" I yelled at her.

She kept her eye fixed on her enemy. Estrada was sinking deeper, though his face had stopped twisting.

"You don't understand," he said.

She flinched. "Estrada."

He didn't say anything; he kept staring at her with huge eyes.

"Estrada! Grab hold."

And then the lieutenant heaved himself up. We had no idea what he was doing at first. We watched in shock as he plunged head first into the quicksand pit. For a moment, his back was still visible in the bog. Then it disappeared.

A deadly silence threw itself over the swamp; we could see the indentation in the quicksand quiver, move, and then begin to smooth itself out.

"Keep on pulling!" Manuel yelled.

We snapped our attention back, and Erik, Manuel, and I pulled until we dragged Yolanda's limp body out of danger. Erik wound his arms around her waist and helped her crawl up, away from the sand. She heaved herself between us.

We were all panting, and covered with thick sludge and dredged weeds. Manuel looked exhausted and ill. Yolanda hunched, dripping, in the middle of a circle we'd made, and eventually began to try to rub the grime off of herself, and off me. But the dark masses of it clung onto her clothes and embedded itself in her jeans. Her eyes were opened very wide.

"What did he mean when he said I didn't understand?" she asked.

"I don't know, sweetie," I said.

"What did he mean?"

"I can't tell you."

"It meant that he was insane," Erik said. "It meant that he was a killer."

"I'm not sure," Yolanda said.

Erik squeezed his eyes shut. "Oh, God, I wished I'd never seen that."

I had my arms around Yolanda. "What were you trying to do?"

Manuel ran his hand over his head. "Why did you move toward him? We almost lost you again."

She looked at me through the dark hair that streaked across her face.

"I was trying to save him, Lola," she said. "I was trying to save that man's life."

She put her cheek against my chest and began crying.

CHAPTER 55

I t took a good span of time before we could think clearly again, and only then did we haul ourselves out of the bog and push back through the corridor of juniper. Each of us had turned inward and quiet from the horrible thing we'd just seen. It took very little conversation to confirm that each of us now believed that east was not the right way to go, after all.

"I was wrong," Yolanda said to me, as we trudged side by side through the bush. "If my father were alive, I'd have to tell him he was right about not going that way."

"Yolanda," I said.

"It doesn't matter. What *does* is that we find your mother. And we know it won't be in that direction. That seems clear enough now."

"Are you all right?" I asked.

"No." She shook her head and paused as we continued trudging through the wood, back toward the river Sacluc. "I'm not all right. I don't know why I tried to help him—Estrada." She cleared her throat. "But I wish that I had."

"I'm sorry."

"Maybe it doesn't have to end badly, though. It could still be all right."

I touched her wrist.

"It could still turn out okay," I forced myself to say.

She nodded, and the four of us continued to hike until we returned to the area by the river. On account of the heat, the chicleros had gone. We washed ourselves and the hammock in the Sacluc and tried to lie out in the sun to dry, but the humidity was too great, and the mosquitoes continued to harass us. Manuel sat down and closed his eyes. He said that he'd had enough shock for six lifetimes and would just like a minute to collect himself, please. Erik sat by the bank of the river while Yolanda and I combed and washed the mud out of our hair. He pulled the papers and the journals out of my sack and began to look through them.

At a little after three o'clock in the afternoon, he did find that passage of Von Humboldt's he'd been trying to remember.

"I've got it." He walked over to us, with the wet and half-pulverized edition of the *Narrative* in his hand.

We looked up at him.

"You've got what?" I asked.

"This is the paragraph that's been in my head. It's from Von Humboldt's record of trekking through the jungle when he was looking for—what he thought was a magnet. It's the part where he writes about his guide. The slave, Gomez."

"You can barely read it," I said.

"I can still make it out," he said.

"What does it say?" Yolanda asked.

Now even Manuel opened his eyes.

The German's passage that Erik had recalled came right after the point where Gomez had teased Von Humboldt and Bonpland by suggesting they were lost in the jungle, and sang them a few lines of the old song.

"*I told you!*" *Aimé Bonpland whispered, holding on to my hand.*

"*Do not worry, we are not lost, as I am making a joke,*" *Gomez said. "According to my calculations, we must only follow the Dwarf.*"

"*What?*" *I asked him.*

"*The Dwarf. . . .*"

"It has to be the same thing," he said. "It's the direction they took to get to the blue city, remember. Gomez showed them the way."

"The way of the Dwarf," I said.

"It makes sense enough now, if any of this does," Yolanda said. She took the book from Erik and held it in both hands, fingering its broken spine. "I've been west, we've been south, now we've very certainly tried east. We might as well go north."

"You don't sound very hopeful," I said.

She gave me a small smile but said nothing.

"Should we stay the night here?" I asked. "Maybe we're too tired to do anything more today." My hip was throbbing with pain.

She passed her hand across her mouth. "I lost all the food I carried into that quicksand—"

"So we can't dally," Manuel finished the sentence for her.

Yolanda nodded. "And besides, I don't want to drag this out anymore. I want us to find your mom and go home."

"Yes, me too," I said.

"I agree," Erik said.

"I am getting so worried about Juana," Manuel said. "I'm more frightened of this place now than I ever was."

"But you've stopped shaking," I said.

"Yes," he replied, looking at his hands. "That's so."

The odd thing was, none of us moved, as some terrible depression seemed to hit the group. We sat down in another half circle, not talking much, and listening to the conversations of the animals and the murmurs of the breeze. We should have been off hiking by then. Even before we did that, we needed to dress and pack once more. From that same spot off the Sacluc, we had to set out again for the Jade in the last direction remaining to us.

But for a long while we sat there, coldcocked, too worn out to move.

CHAPTER 56

Few words were spoken between us during this hour, but I believe we were all beginning to doubt that we'd ever find Mom in that jungle.

As we lingered in the forest, that hopeful feeling I'd had when I lay with Erik in the hammock grew thinner. I couldn't feel my mother like I had then. And I thought that even if she had come to this forest and we *could* find her, there was a good chance she had died here, like that woman in Flores. Or like that terrible soldier who had drowned in the bog. It was November 7, and we had not heard from her in twelve days.

I felt a hard pang of very cold, very sickening reality as this occurred to me. The idea of our journey's futility propelled me to my feet. I didn't care if my logic was meaningless. It could happen. She was alive and here, and we had to keep on.

I stood and slipped on my pack.

"Let's go," I said. "Let's go get her. Now."

We headed north. This was thick territory, and woolly as any we'd seen before. Yolanda made hard use of her machete as she sliced through the bushes and the blood-colored flowers. Past the stands of chicle trees we found a ruination of tumbled mahoganies and marshes alive with butterflies and yellow-beaked birds. The trees reached down toward us, with their fringes of palms and their branches that were like the elegant arms of dancers.

We marched, my hip hurting so much that I worried that some serious and permanent damage might have been done to it. Yolanda's
black hat flitted ahead of us; I stared at the back of Manuel's small
poky head. Erik marched behind me. Together we passed ferns like im-
mense green cathedrals. Our boots sucked into the rich mire. To the
sides of our path scattered the severed limbs of the plants hacked
through by Yolanda, and before us spread the ever-deepening jungle,
with its broad glossy leaves as large as children. Occasionally there
would be a clearing where the hurricane appeared to have simply
peeled the whole skin of the forest floor from its rocky bottom, and
heaped up the remains in scattered piles.

We walked through this terrain for miles. Another hour passed, and
the sunlight dripping through the trees started to fade. At around six
o'clock, Manuel stopped walking.

"Hold on," he said. And then he just sat down on the ground.

"We can't go on for much longer," Erik said. "At least not today."

"I don't see anything," Yolanda said. "I don't know what we're doing
here."

"We'll go for a while longer," I said. "We'll go until we find my
mother."

No one said anything to that. A minute passed, then two; Erik and
Yolanda looked at each other and then up into the trees.

"I just need to rest for a minute," Manuel said. He was bending over
his knees and holding his face.

I sat down too. My hip was killing me.

For twenty minutes we stayed there, not talking. Erik dressed my
hip again.

"Maybe we should stop," he said.

I shook my head. "No. There's still light."

"Manuel's not doing very well."

"Manuel's doing fine, and does not like to be talked about in the
third person," Manuel said. "Lola's right. Let's get up and go a little farther until the light dies."

Yolanda smiled down at him. "You're getting tough in your old age."

"Yes, I am, aren't I?"

He looked better than he had a few hours before. She grasped his hand and helped him up, and they started to go off together, hacking through more juniper and ferns.

But I had trouble moving now. Erik had to practically haul me to my feet. He lifted me up by the ribs, and I *willed* my body to work. I took one step with my good leg, another with the bad. I pitched myself forward through the wood, traveling as fast as I could, afraid that if I slowed down, I'd stop.

CHAPTER 57

A thick dusk settled over the forest. The maze of the jungle flew out beneath our feet in circles and crisscrosses and dead ends of brush that we cut through with our flashlights and our blades. Bromeliads opened up in the mists, orange-red, lime-yellow, with spiky black-green hearts and leaves so sharp they'd slice flesh. We passed another run of trees, which ended in a shattered clump of wood where three other mahoganies had toppled in the winds. Farther on, another section had been ripped open, and all the tufts of furry grass and bush and the layers of mud had been stripped off, but in this neater space there stood a hump of earth, and what appeared to be some rocks.

Yolanda, Manuel, and Erik stopped walking.

"Oh—my—" Yolanda said. "This is it."

"Just hold on," Erik said, excited. "Just wait."

"No, you can see," Manuel said. "A tumulus; it could be something. A mound of earth—that's how Maudslay knew he'd stumbled on Quiriguá."

I knew that he was referring to the nineteenth-century scholar of Maya ruins in the Motagua Valley, but otherwise I didn't know what they were talking about. I couldn't read this place at all. Von Humboldt, writing in the 1800s, had described finding the Elder Brother's blue city after following the direction of the Dwarf: "A tall, crumbled, fantastic city rose before our eyes, all spires and turrets, with great devastated keeps and eroded ramparts, even as it now sank into the muds and soughs." If this was it, then it had sunk almost completely into the swamps, as here only mounds of mud dipped into lower shallows, and in dug-out sections rocks were strewn about with bits and crags of timber from the broken trees. We walked toward the clearing, picking through muck and deepening shadows. Above us, the chattering of the animals sounded loud and insistent. The air pressed against us, hot, full, and very wet.

Yolanda crouched down by one of the rocks, and I recognized the old adventurer's expression passing over her face; she was nearly happy. She turned her Maglite onto the site. "This is it! It's a line of carved stone!"

We all bent down, grabbing at the broken rocks that appeared in the mud; some were very large, too big to dig out, and as we heaved off as much mud as possible, we saw underneath what appeared to be a large flat rectangle of basalt that stretched through the area. We started to dip our hands into water that stood in pockets in the ground and splash it over the stone.

"Look, look, look, look!" Erik belted. "It is—it's been hewed. It's man-made."

"What is it?"

"I can't tell yet."

"This is it. This is what he was looking for." When Yolanda said "he," I knew she meant her father.

"It's a foundation," Erik said. "It looks like a foundation for a temple. Like the ones they found at Quiriguá and Tikal."

"Could it be part of a city?"

"I'd say it could."

"I can't believe it!" Yolanda said.

"I think it looks like Classic Maya," he said.

"Then where is she?" I yelled at them.

Erik looked up at me. Manuel already stood on the outer edge of the clearing, staring through the violet light. Yolanda stayed crouched on the ground, pouring handfuls of water over the stones and picking through the dirt with her fingers until she had cleaned off yet more sections of the rock foundation. It emerged from the mud in precise, artistic geometric shapes, forming hard-edged rectangles and squares through the sodden jungle floor. As she danced over the sumps and leaves, heaving the vegetation off this buried structure, more networks of stone appeared. She uncovered vertical lines of thick rock so exact that they could never be the creation of nature; here were angular depressions descending into a carved stairway; beyond that sat a fallen column of stone incised on every millimeter with delicate images of flowers, priests, women, words, stars, and suns.

She sat back, exclaiming. "I think it runs as far as we can see. The foundation. It could go miles through the forest—there could be an entire palace here, under the swamp. And Erik might be right—I think it could be Classic Maya. We need to be able to read these markings, though. It's too soon to tell. And—" she was looking around. "It's all basalt. But it looks like there's pieces of jade facing. We'll have to test it to make sure."

"But we might have found the ruins of a city, is what you're telling me," I said.

"That's right."

"Then where is she?" I asked again. "She should be here—do you see any tracks?"

We all looked down, but if someone had walked through in the past few days, their footprints wouldn't have held in that soft mud.

"Okay," Erik said. "We have to find that tree, right?"

"Right," I said. "The dragon tree. My mother would have been looking for it. And then she would have tried to solve that—that riddle."

"The second maze in the story."

"Yes."

"So—what does a dragon tree look like?" Erik said.

"I told you," Yolanda said. "It has red sap. That's why it has that name. People used to think that the sap was blood, and the dragons were men who'd been cursed by witches and turned into trees."

"All I see around me are trees," I said. "Help me look for it!"

"All right." She stood up. "What have we got here . . ."

But Manuel had thought ahead of us. He was on the far eastern edge of the clearing, standing next to one of the trees that had been half torn down by the storm.

"This is it," he said, in a quiet voice. "I already found it."

"Are there any tracks?" I said, walking over to him. "Is there any sign of anything?"

"Not that I can see."

"It does have red sap," Erik said, looking down at the broken tree and touching the bark with his fingers, which came back stained a dark burgundy color.

Next to me, Yolanda pressed her hands to her heart. "That means— it means we could find—"

"The Stone?" Manuel said.

"Juana," Yolanda said, uncertainly.

Manuel nodded. "Perhaps she has found it first."

Again, silence greeted that prediction. We stood there, not looking at each other; I refused to see the expression on their faces.

But then Erik said, "That wouldn't surprise me at all."

He leaned back his head and called out my mother's name, several times, in his loudest voice. I did too. We walked back and forth, through the clearing, shouting out for her. Then Manuel did as well. And Yolanda.

There was no response except for the shrieking of the birds and the spiders above.

I sat down on one of the trunks of the trees, and took off my pack; I held on to my hip, which was burning.

"Lola?" Yolanda said. "Can you make it?"

I didn't say anything.

"Lola?"

"I'm fine," I said. "Let's take the next step. We have to figure out which direction to go."

"It's time to solve the Maze of Virtue," Erik said.

"Yes," I said. "It is."

CHAPTER 58

I reached into my pack and took out the papers and the journal that I'd wrapped and wrapped again in that plastic to keep it safe from the rain. But the Xeroxes were more damaged from water than ever, and they stuck together in clumps; some of the ink had not run down the page, but just washed off. I picked through the papers until I reached the section of de la Cueva that I was looking for. The muddled type would soon be nothing but a smear, but with the aid of the words that I'd memorized, I could read the bleary lines to my friends:

> . . . he fled his Mad city. He passed the Dragon Tree . . . toward the East. Here, he hid within a second Maze of his own making. This, he called the Labyrinth of Virtue.
> And of what was this crazed Puzzle composed?
> Of nothing more than a riddle:

> > The Roughest Path to Take
> > The Harshest Road to Tread
> > Is the one We must Make
> > Tho' our Hearts fill with Dread

> > The Hardest Pass to Walk
> > In these Days foul and Fast

When crooked sin us Mocks
Is ours to Brave and Last

He who steers due from Hell
For he who bears the Waves
The Jade waits in her Dell
And the Good Man is Repaid

A round of mute stupefaction greeted my reading of that riddle.

"Well, does anyone know what that means?" I asked.

"Let me think," Yolanda said. "I'm drawing a blank. Manuel?"

"I have no idea," he said. "Let's see—'the roughest path to tread.' Sounds like what we've been on for the past three days."

" 'The hardest pass to walk . . . , ' " Erik recited. "Maybe it means we have to go back the way we came—that'd be the hardest pass for *me*. Or it could mean a circle, or it could mean going downward, into Hades. It's the labyrinth that Odysseus traveled through. Or it could mean a straight line. The Greeks had a theory about a labyrinth made up of one continuous plumb path."

"Odysseus, the Greeks," Yolanda said, her voice cracking. "Keep on track, here. The Greeks had nothing to do with the Maya."

"It's just an idea, I'm just thinking out loud."

"Let's not get negative," Manuel said, "the boy's trying."

"I just want us to keep focused," Yolanda said.

"Remember," I said, "not only do we have to think of what the riddle might mean, we have to figure out what my mother thought it meant."

"You're right," Yolanda said. "Did she ever talk to you about it?"

"Never."

"You, Manuel? Any theories?"

"No, dear, not at the moment. But I do wish you'd hurry and figure this one out, as it will be perfectly dark here soon."

But we couldn't hurry up and figure it out. We had no idea what to do.

For a long while we sat there in the forest, surrounded by the an-

cient rocks and the ghosts of old priests and gods, and the felled bleeding tree, and tried to think.

Did Juana write anything about it in that journal of hers?" Yolanda
asked, when no one had any ideas.

The trees darkened in the forest. The air, though still humid, was
less searing hot. Evening closed in.

"No," I said. "It was mostly about the Stelae. She only wrote one
comment about it, I remember, but it wasn't exactly . . . *well* . . ."

"What?" Erik said.

"Let's hear it," Manuel said.

I looked down at my pack and rummaged through until I found the
soiled, half-soaked, salmon-colored journal. I opened it up and saw
that the pages were tattered and clumped together; on some leaves the
ink had transformed from words into blue blossoms.

"Can you read that?"

"I think so," I said. "She did write one thing . . ."

I unfolded the diary. The leaves rode up, crinkled, and had to be
pulled out straight and reshaped again very gently. I sculpted the soft
book until I reached the page I wanted. I read to them the passage my
mother wrote out after she had transcribed her translation of the Stelae, and was making plans to head up here, north.

October 25. . . .

*My first task will be to use the Maze of Deceit as a map in the forest.
If I do come across the city, my second step will be to look around for
a dragon tree, according to the records.*

*As for the next riddle, the Maze of Virtue, I think that's fairly
straightforward.*

" 'As for the Maze of Virtue, I think that's fairly straightforward,' "
Yolanda repeated, slowly.

"It seems she figured it out quickly enough," Erik said. His face
turned purple with confusion. "It's not straightforward at all."

I began laughing, and so did Yolanda and Manuel.

"I am quite surprised that you are not demanding credit," Manuel crowed. "From what I understand it's quite unlike you, my boy, to miss out an opportunity for praise and glory."

"What? What are you talking about?"

Yolanda's scuffed face had transformed all at once; her mouth moved up, she began to smile. Then she started to pound Erik on the shoulder.

"Good God, what?" he said.

"Maybe you're not a clown after all," she said. "And you should know that is a very high compliment from me."

"It is," I agreed.

"And what did I do to deserve such praise?"

"Well, you solved it."

"You're losing me."

"You did!" I yelled. "The Greeks? The labyrinth made up of one continuous line?"

And then he got it, too. "Of course, I did! Yes! I'm a genius!"

"Let's not go that far," Yolanda said. "But good job, anyway—it's obvious now. The harshest road to take, and the hardest line to walk, is the *straight* line. Like you said."

"The straight and narrow," I chimed in.

"The Labyrinth of Virtue," Manuel said. "The virtuous man avoids 'crooked sin' and walks on the unswerving path. As will we. 'Toward the East.' "

Erik was so happy about his riddle-cracking that we congratulated him just a little bit more, and he received this abbreviated adulation with very good grace. Then we all stood up to get our gear and began to chase down this last, true course.

I had a harder time than the others, though.

By now my hip had stopped hurting so much, but this was not a good sign, as my leg proved only partially useful. I had to move my left thigh by aiding it with my hands as we pursued our direction through the forest, to where the Jade was said to be hidden.

Nevertheless, I kept up with my friends, and the four of us walked together for another mile until we came across the cave.

CHAPTER 59

Nrth of the river Sacluc, and east of the forest's infamous dragon tree, a few miles within the Maya Biosphere's core area, there is a small cave in the lee of a hill.

It is not easy to spot at first, particularly in the near pitch-dark, unless you are traveling with experts in the field of Maya architecture and topography. That is, unless you know what an ancient cave looks like.

Under the lee of this hill sat a tumulus, a primordial mound once hollowed out by hand. To the ancient Maya, caves, wells, and waterholes were sacred spaces; in-between zones where the living and the underworld communed.

Grass covered the sides of the hummock, as well as stonecrops and saxifrages with tiny white and yellow petals that were lit by pale fire when struck by our flashlights. Birds perched and pecked at the blossoms that strung across at the cave's gloomy mouth.

"We're here," Yolanda breathed. "We found it."

I didn't call out my mother's name; I was too afraid. I didn't say one word, and only gripped my Maglite.

I was the first one in.

The light flashed very harsh and pearly into a space that I couldn't gauge; the cave extended much deeper than it had appeared from the front, though the sides were close and narrow. The bottom of the cavern was filled with water up to my ankles, and as my torch moved over the area, I saw that it descended into some deep black place we'd have to plumb.

We moved down, and all three flashlights spangled across the stalactites and the dripping limestone halls like beacons. Red hieroglyphs blazed from the walls in the images of dragons and hunchbacks, which I didn't bother to read yet. Fool's gold glimmered from the crevices of the cave, as well as the flashing red eyes of lizards and bats. I heard a flapping; a flourish; water pouring. I ducked into a system of thin hot tunnels, which I had to maneuver through by touch, as there was insufficient room to cast my flashlight around. My hip was going numb, and I fell into the water before Erik grabbed me from behind.

But I walked on my own two feet most of the way. I breathed very heavily in the close air and heard my friends breathing too, and the sloshing of their feet through the water, and Manuel slipping, and Yolanda falling. We reached another very low, very black pass, which I squeezed through.

I found I could stand up. I was in some kind of room.

I moved my light back up through the air and saw I was in a large, carved-out space with half-faded markings on the wall. A long blue object sat on the raised and dry center of the floor. It was a massive piece of worked blue jade, rectangular in shape, and so pure that when I cast my torch on it, the stone burst into a dazzle of fiery cobalt light. The jade object's carvings threw sapphire and azure shapes onto the wall, stars and whorls and half-moons that flickered and revolved over the limestone like the lustral rays of a magic lantern. The surface of the stone, incised with the intricacy of the Flores Stelae in those hieroglyphs of gods and warriors, as delicate as Moorish calligraphy, reflected shades of turquoise and opal, peacock and dark veins of absolute indigo. Beneath the changeable surface of the stone's skin burned a constant, deep, dreamlike color: rich, on the edge of black, touched with gloss. A perfect blue.

But there was something else. This long angled jade didn't resemble the stone in de la Cueva's story. It was not a solid megalith at all but was instead—hollow. It was a box. An oblong box. There was something in it.

As I stepped forward again, unsure what I was looking at, I saw lying next to this box the prostrate figure of a woman. She was struggling to sit up and blinking in the light.

The woman pushed herself onto her elbows, and wet silver hair fell over her left cheek. My mother's black eyes shone out like an owl's in the flashlight's glare. The thinner curve of her cheekbones stood out against the blackness around her. I saw the fragile lines around her eyes and her mouth, which deepened into creases that fanned about her knifelike nose as she turned her head up to me. A large spreading bruise flushed around her left temple and eye, and a tracery of mud appeared on her neck. Her mouth moved, but she did not make a sound yet. Her white shirt and jeans were soaked and ripped into cotton shards; she had taken her shoes off, and her right leg was turned awkwardly around, as if it might be sprained or broken.

I ran. My heart rang and rang inside me like a church bell.

"Mom! Mom! Mom! Mom! Mom!"

I had my arms around her, and she put her face on my shoulder.

I continued to call her name, and now Manuel came up, crying terribly, and Erik and Yolanda crowded around us too.

"Yes, I'm here," my mother said. "We're together, my Monster."

"Mom," I said. "Oh, Mom." My face in her neck, I held her as tight as I could. I ran my hands down her shoulders and arms, I felt her legs, I looked for injuries. I wrapped my arms all around her and didn't stop hugging.

It was hard to loosen my grip so that the others could get to her and she could speak.

"I found it, Terrible Creature," she said in a weary voice. "Manuel?"

He bent toward her in the dark and crossed the pale beams of the flashlights. "Yes, Juana."

"I found it," she said, sighing.

"Yes."

She looked back to me. "I found what he was looking for."

I nodded. "What Tomas de la Rosa was looking for."

"Yes, darling."

Behind me I could hear Yolanda let out a noise.

"Where did you go? How did you get lost?"

"I couldn't get out," she said. "I had some . . . trouble with the weather. And I was hurt. There was rain for about five days—I couldn't see much—and I fell into this flood and made a mess of myself. As you can see, with this leg. Lost my backpack, too, in a marsh. And then I got here, but when I did, I didn't have anything but my flashlight, and nothing to drink but rainwater. So I just became tired, and I sat here, and—waited." She swallowed. "But now you've come."

"Mom, just sit up—I want to take a look at you."

"I found it, you see." As she pushed herself forward into a sitting position, I saw that her face, with the bruises, looked unwell. And I'd been right about her leg. It was twisted; she'd injured it in a fall days before, and the wound had probably become more severe since she had made it here. "I found that thing he wanted—and it was already excavated."

"I think this is enough talking," I said. "We have to get you out—"

But she wouldn't listen to me. "It was already—cleared. Opened. Someone was here before me. Not too long ago. And they didn't loot the site."

"Who could have been here?" Manuel asked.

"It could have been—no, that's impossible. I have no idea, and it doesn't *matter*. Because I still did find it. It's so funny, really, because it's not what we thought at all."

"What is it?" Yolanda asked.

"Is that—is that you, Yolanda? Come all this way?"

Yolanda stepped into the light shed by the Maglite, and her hat cast a large bird-shaped shadow on the wall. "Yes, it is, Juana."

"Well, you'll be interested in this, won't you?"

"I think that I will."

"And is that—that's not, you are not going to tell me that's *Gomara* standing behind you, is it, Lola?"

I laughed. "That's him."

"Oh, well, nothing would surprise me now."

"Hello, Dr. Sanchez," Erik said.

"Yes, hello, Gomara. Don't worry, I will thank you with as much effusion as I can muster—later."

"Can't wait, Professor."

Manuel crouched beside my mother and began looking at her leg.

"And I thought you were too frightened of the jungle," she said to him.

"There were other things that frightened me worse."

"Yes, well—coming here turned out to be a fairly bad idea. But really, it was that disgusting storm that ruined everything. And I didn't want to turn around, you know. Not when I was getting so close. So I slipped and hurt myself, and my leg's only become more of a nuisance since then. I made it to this place about three days ago." She paused. "You're not mad, are you?"

"I'm not mad."

"How did you *get* here?"

Manuel described how I'd found her journal in Antigua, and the transcription of the Stelae in it.

"Ah," my mother said. "My diary—that's—not something I expected." She looked at me. "Did you read everything in there?"

"It's so waterlogged now, the journal," Manuel said, half-lying. "You can barely read anything in it."

"But you already knew why I came here," she said to him, abruptly.

"I did." He hesitated. "It's because he died."

She touched her fingertips to his face. "I didn't know what else to do."

"It's all right."

"You know I love you, though?"

"Yes."

"And she knows, then? I can tell."

Manuel glanced up at me, then back at my mother. "I think so."

"Knows what?" Yolanda said.

Yolanda's face beamed at us through the torchlight; her eyes were glistening and dark beneath the brim of her hat.

"Knows what?" she asked again.

I looked at my mother, who bent her mouth down at the corners and nodded.

"That Tomas was my father too, Yolanda," I said.

"What do you mean?"

"Tomas was *my father*," I repeated.

Yolanda wouldn't understand at first. She stared at the ground, and then up at my mother, who confirmed it for her with her eyes. Then my sister took in a hard, ragged breath.

"In one way he was your father, Lola," Manuel said then. His voice sounded strange and raw and full of love.

I wondered how it had been for him to look at my face and see there features that—I now understood—resembled those of the broad-cheeked man that he had for so long hated.

But I just said: "You're my Dad."

"Of course he is," my mother growled. "There was never any question of that."

Yolanda glanced up at the blue shadows on the cave wall and tightened her jaw.

"Yolanda?"

"My father betrayed my mother," she said, after a second.

"Yes, that's so," my mother said. "And I played my part, too."

"And that's why you didn't want Lola to write me anymore, isn't it?" Yolanda asked. "Or see me. Because you didn't want to be reminded of your mistake."

My mother nodded. "Yes."

Manuel, Erik, and I had gone perfectly silent. Yolanda tried to clear her throat, but let out a small howl instead. Tears began streaming down one cheek.

She didn't speak for nearly a minute. We all watched her, waiting.

And then she said: "The truth is, we're all a disaster, aren't we?"

My mother closed her eyes. "I guess that's right."

Yolanda continued to stare at the wall with that furious face. But she looked as if she were deciding something.

"I don't want to be angry anymore," she said. "It doesn't help me."

"So *don't*," my mother said.

Yolanda turned to me. "I really wanted to make you pay before I helped you."

"Yolanda."

She touched her forehead, shielding her eyes with her fingers. "But I—I just should have remembered the good times."

I started to cry.

"I don't care about the rest of it," she said.

"Yolanda—Yolanda," I said, trying to get it out. "We're family, whether you like it or not."

She hesitated. The entire cave went silent again except for the sound of the water; the blue light from the jade flickered across our faces.

"I don't mind it," she said, when she was able; she worked very hard to get hold of herself.

I moved over closer to her and slipped my fingers inside her hand. And then she reached out and took hold of my other hand and my arm in a hot tight grip. She was quaking and trying to smile, though I was the less composed of us both.

While we held onto each other like this, Erik was not exactly sure what to do. Still standing a ways off, and clearing his throat, he raised his flashlight away from us. It flickered over to the thing in the room. He trained the torch on the blue jade object, shining the beam over the worked stone, the box shape, its strange contents.

"God," he said. "Will you look at that?"

"I told you, Gomara," she said. She looked away from Yolanda and me, and she sounded hoarse. "It's not what we thought. It's not what anyone has ever thought. But when you think about it, it does make sense."

"What makes sense?"

"The answer to our questions about the Stone."

"*What is it?*" we all cried.

"If you give me a second, I'll tell you."

Yolanda, Manuel, and I turned toward my mother. And now, with some relish despite her damaged leg, she began to explain to us the mystery of the Queen Jade.

CHAPTER 60

For the ancient Maya, as I've said already, caves were sacred places, where the living and the dead might communicate with the other world. Burial grounds were located often enough in these subterranean spaces, filled with mummies and relics and bones, so that the ghosts of the ancestors could travel with ease to Hades.

This cave had been similarly used.

Erik's flashlight, and then mine, and Yolanda's, passed up and over the blue jade object against which my mother rested. This huge jade rectangle was a coffin, fashioned out of one solid piece of blue jadeite that had been carved elaborately on all sides. Friezes of roses and geometric shapes, dwarves, warriors, the faces of priests, of witches, glistened in shades of cobalt and turquoise on its every inch. It stood approximately three feet high, had a width of about two feet, and was once covered by a solid slab of yet more jade that had been removed and placed to the side of the cave by some mysterious previous excavator. The sarcophagus was filled with the body of a thin ancient girl. She looked to me like a girl. She had been preserved and was the color of bog oak, and her bones had the texture of old amber. Her hands were a collection of fossilized twigs; her face, with its tint like wet teak, did not have a peaceful expression. Her legs had been long but now were aged into sepia branches and roots, like those of the thin young trees we passed by in the jungle. Her head was a delicate parchment dome. And her concave chest was room for a nest—but not of bird eggs, as we first thought.

Instead, this girl, upon her burial, had been draped and adorned and laden down with jades that were carved like diamonds and marked with gorgeous signs. She was heaped with jewels that glittered in blue flames all around her body. The gems were carved into the shapes of not just diamonds, we saw—but also roses, as the Aztecs had done with their emeralds, and tiny idols, and huge pearls, and raw large chunks chased with silver and gold. At the center of this treasure lay one large, flat pendant of the blue jade, which hung on a strand of small jade pearls. The pendant was carved with markings that I thought I recognized.

I picked it up and held it to the light; the hieroglyph turned red and gold inside the illuminated blue rock.

I knew this was the symbol for jade.

"But which one's the Jade?" Yolanda asked.

"You're not understanding yet," my mother said. "It's her. *She's* the Jade. The body's of a woman, in my judgment. And I know absolutely that the manner of burial is for a female."

"The Queen Jade," Erik said. "You're telling us the Queen Jade is this woman."

"Yes," my mother said. "Look on the wall—to the left, it's all there."

The flashlights all turned in tandem to illuminate that section of the cave where faded hieroglyphics had been painted in shades of blue, red, black, and green.

They said:

"What does that mean?"

"Well," Erik said, "if your mother's right, and I translate this liberally, I can make out—

My queen, my beauty
[]
[]
[]
world
[]
arms
[]
lost—

but nothing else. Not in this light."

"I know that," Yolanda said. "I know those words."

"They're famous, aren't they?" my mother said. "It's a very old poem."

"Are you sure?" I asked. "Can you be certain?"

"Yes, I'm sure," my mother said in a firm voice.

Yolanda approached the wall, reading the signs. Then, standing very straight in the dark and holding onto her torch, she began to half-sing, half-talk the poem to us while my mother murmured along:

My queen, my beauty
What have I done?
Why have you left me?
To live in this world
So cold and so empty

My treasure, my charm
Do you forgive me?
Stay safe in my arms
Where I can kiss you
Where you will stay warm

I lost you
I lost you
I'm lost, too
I'm lost, too
I'm lost
without you

My darling

"The Jade, as it turns out," my mother said when they had finished singing, "wasn't a stone, or a magnet, or a talisman. *Jade*—the word, the hieroglyph—was always a name. The name of this girl. That hieroglyph never signified a stone—we got that meaning from the translation of the Legend. But Balaj K'waill lied to de la Cueva. *There's a flaw in the translation.* The king was obsessed with his *wife*, not a jewel. And that song is the one he sings to her after her death. And we never knew."

"This is—outrageous!" Erik said. "It's even better than what they're finding in the Sierras."

She tilted her head. "What are they finding in the Sierras?"

"I'll tell you later, Dr. Sanchez."

My mother raised her eyebrows at Erik, decided not to pursue his hint quite yet, and then turned toward me again. She kissed me three times on the cheek.

"So, that's the answer, my Creature," she said. "And you came all the way here to find me."

"I found you," I said.

Then she turned up her gaunt face at Erik and tried a smile.

"Impressed, Gomara?"

"Very, Professor."

"I hope that you will hereafter regard me with nothing but absolute awe and total, devastated respect."

"Um—I'll work on it."

"Good. For now, maybe you could pick me up and help haul me out of this nasty cave. And then, if you will be so kind, perhaps you could take me to the hospital, as I'm not feeling so very well."

Erik walked toward her, brought his arms under hers, and lifted her up, which was no easy task. We left the cavern and burial site, dragging ourselves again through the narrow hot passageways and the standing water, and past the slithering chirping beasts. We found ourselves back in the warm black forest, where we'd have to spend another night before we would reach the city again.

CHAPTER 61

After we set up camp in a clearing off the mouth of the cave, Erik looked after my mother's wounds and gave her some painkillers while Yolanda and Manuel and I unpacked the gear from our bags. The three of us hunkered in a patch of turf, circled by the onyx trees, and by the light of our torches pulled out our tarps, our food, our water, fuel, and our nets. Yolanda and I shot knowing and nervous glances at each other, and I kissed Manuel several times all over his face. Then I turned back to Yolanda and took a good long look at her as she unfolded one of the hammocks. Her hat was still on, slanted to the side. The flashlight showed that her face was scratched, but not so badly. Her shirt was firmly buttoned up, and beneath her collar bulged a piece of jewelry. I bent over and kissed her, too.

"All right, all right," she said, keeping her cheek turned up so I could kiss it again. "We've got a lot to do before we can get any sleep, so it's no time to get all womanish and emotional."

"I thought I might have seen you getting a bit emotional back there in the cave."

"It's true, my dear," Manuel said.

"If I *were*, I can probably be excused, seeing as how I just discovered I had a sister. But considering all that we've been through, I actually would rather gloss over the painful parts concerning fathers and disillusionment and other family shockers for the moment, thank you."

She was in truth starting to look very pleased despite all that, even as she lowered her eyebrows and told me to concentrate on finding that magnesium stick for the fire.

"Maybe you can come and live with us," I said.

"*Live* with you?"

"Why not?"

"Well." She sighed, rummaging through Erik's pack, and then brought up the stick. "I'm sure there are a thousand reasons."

"Name one."

"That's easy. I'm not sure I remember you being the best roommate."

"I might be a little better at it now."

"I doubt it. But—now that you mention it, perhaps I could try it for a month or two, here and there. It will have to depend upon how long I can stand it."

"I'll let you dress up like the Cyclops and jump at me from the closet," I said.

"Oh, thanks—but I think I'll have to devise new forms of torture for you. *Still*—if—just thinking out loud—we really are going to spend more time together, there will have to be some changes."

"Changes?"

Manuel chuckled. "Here it comes."

"You obviously have no idea how to make your way around a jungle." She lifted up her chin, goading me. "You've spent far too much time in libraries."

"I don't think—"

"I'll have to whip you into shape. Teach you how to ford a river without nearly killing everyone around you, for one thing. And for another, I'll have to give you a lesson in how to write a decent letter."

"Yes, yes," I said. "Mea culpa. Mea maxima culpa. I'm good and afraid of you now."

"As you should be."

She looked at me with a long solemn face, until an involuntary smile began to ripple over her mouth, and mine too. Hiding her face with the brim of her hat, she grunted out a few more critiques about my character and my camping skills and then gathered together twigs and leaves and threw them into the center of the turf. Next she began to flick her magnesium until the flint sparked. I kept my eye on her—and once the flames began to strain against the shadows, I noticed that beneath the collar of her shirt glimmered a few blue stones.

"What is that?" Under her shirt I saw the jade pendant that only minutes before had been draped around the neck of the buried queen.

"This?" she asked. "Oh, just a little something I picked up. Relax. I'll give it back. I'm only safekeeping it for a while. My father would have wanted me to keep a very close eye on treasures like this."

"We'll discuss that—later," Manuel said, looking at her sideways.

"Exactly. Now, what was I talking about? Oh—right—the future. The *future*. As I was saying, there's going to be a lot of work to do if I'm ever going to make you into a proper sister, but if we're very lucky, and things don't go to hell like they usually do, maybe you *will* turn out all right. . . ."

As she continued to describe the tremendous moral makeover I would have to accomplish before I could even hope to be recognized as a de la Rosa sibling, I watched as within the heart of the campfire the flames began to catch on the leaves and the twigs and the flowers, shedding a greater circle of light that flickered over the cave and its ancient girl, and then the ferns, the large smashed trees, the marshes and monkeys, and the birds. Quetzals flashed their green wings among the gold-and-soot branches of the mahoganies, and we could see the ocher mists twirl up through the fens. Deer ran through the bush; we thought we could hear the snuffling and truffling of unseen wild pigs and the footfall of possible massive cats. Yolanda stood up and dodged the monsters while gathering more bromeliad petals and wood before sitting back down next to me and taking my hand. And then the rest of our party curled up around the flames, too, while the gold light rose through the forest like a spirit and showed us its behemoths and its red-eyed amazing beasts, not the least amazing of which was my still-living mother, who looked like a beneficent witch with her streaming silver hair and wrong-way leg, and who fixed her eyes on mine from across the campfire.

I stared right back at her, stunned by thankfulness.

Neither of us smiled; our love was too fierce and raging for that.

CHAPTER 62

Long Beach, present day

At The Red Lion (which I still own, here in Long Beach), I now have at least six shelves devoted to pure history. The freaks and the gamers and the bibliophiles wander by, plucking a volume, paging through it, and frowning at the claims about knights and monsters and Amazons that the authors have written there. I sit behind my counter wrapping octavos, repairing bindings, and watch them argue and role-play. Or, more equivocally, I observe them as they sit cross-legged in the aisles and read my books whole, certainly deriving much edification from that literature, although not really buying much of it.

Occasionally a silver-haired and grumpy woman will enter, clanging the bells hanging from the door and scattering the customers in her wake. My mother, who healed nicely from her fall in the jungle, is back to work and business as usual. She and Erik are lately engaged in the pitiless struggle to gain dominance over Harvard professors, who have been making several trips up to the Queen Jade site that we found in the Peten. Not only was the queen recovered there, but slowly the scientists are excavating a small nearby city, half buried, with magnificent carved palaces and domed courts, some of which have sculptured friezes made of blue jadeite. Moreover, the search for relics, particularly jade, has become much more energetic since the day in 2002 when we looked in the local paper and found there news of the jade strike that the Peabody scientists began working on after the storm. "A U.S. team says that it has now found the fabled jade supply," the article reads, "in a Rhode Island–sized area of central Guatemala centered on the Motagua River." I thought that poor Tomas de la Rosa—one of my fathers—was certain to be disturbed in his grave. The mine uncovered in the Sierra de las Minas by Mitch is said to be huge and unprecedented, and so Guatemala is rich today in foreign geologists and archaeologists who periodically get a little homicidal with each other over the terrain—though battles like those usually put my mother in a fairly good mood.

Still, it's on both her buoyant and surly days that she visits me here at The Red Lion to check out my books and stare at me in her crabby way until I give her a kiss. I like to watch her frowning at my inventory, and hassling the RuneQuest and Dracula aficionados as they dawdle, in costume, in the aisles. I love it when she leans against my counter and plays with my hair while we talk about books, gossip, films, archaeology, the recovery efforts that still continue in Central America, where the effects of Hurricane Mitch are still being felt—and, much more rarely, of how I came to be born. But we do not often get into other related subjects, such as the reasons why she dissuaded me from writing to Yolanda.

Some subjects can be too difficult to broach.

My heart still sings like a bell when I see Mom walking across the threshold of my Lion, though since I've learned the truth about our family story, and of the distance that I should not have kept from my sister, I have felt a small change pinching my life. Sometimes I have to listen more carefully to hear that clear high soft ring, and occasionally I worry that it might just be the chimes on my door. But then it comes. It almost always comes.

There *are* days when I'm happy to know the real reason that I do not look so much like Manuel Alvarez. And there are days, too, when I think it's heartening that I'm so much like him because it's his bookish spirit, and not something as ordinary and predictable as blood, that runs through me.

But on other days I'm not so glad.

I often wish that I'd never read those passages in my mother's journal.

I know now that some secrets are better kept.

Nevertheless. I continue to stock the Lion with books of fantasy and mystery, and the hair-raisers filled with scarabs and puzzles. And sometimes, tinkering about in the "Great Colonial Villains in History" aisle, I might find a younger woman with a black hat, a set expression, and eyes and cheekbones that I now see look like mine. My only sister. And probably the strangest and greatest person I know. She's got scars on her arms now, from our trek through the jungle, and she hugs me with a crushing force. On every occasion that I've seen her since our adventure in the jungle, she's been wearing a large blue necklace that bears a hieroglyphic carving. I think that it's probably very expensive.

Manuel keeps asking for it back for the museum, but Yolanda says she's going to hold on to that pendant until she's sure he'll take proper care of it.

Just like her father, he always replies.

When he brings *that* name up, though, I think he'd like to stuff it back into his head again, as if he'd never enunciated it in the first place. It lifts the corner on a whole host of other problems—such as the strange circumstances of de la Rosa's death, the mystery of what killed him, as well as the issue of his unknown burial site. What did that poor man go through at the end? we all wonder. Privately we ask ourselves the more difficult and disturbing question of what could have happened to his body. It does not seem natural that such a gigantic personality could have vanished from the forest without one trace, track, or sign.

We've heard certain theories, of course, about assassinations in Belize and kidnapings in Italy and Elvis-like sightings in Lima. But we do not torture ourselves with these delusions, instead trying to remember Tomas in better ways. Concerning his patrimony, the Sanchez, Alvarez, and de la Rosa clan is doing its best to pursue some other of his archaeological projects, which means that my passport has not gathered much dust as of late. There's the question of the location of King Mon tezuma's gold, for one, and then there's the story of Excalibur hidden in the pampas of South America, both being other historical enigmas that the old archaeologist thought he'd be able to solve. . . .

But I won't get into that now, as this is the story of the Queen Jade, and it's nearly finished.

So I'll describe instead how Manuel comes into The Red Lion too on his trips to Los Angeles. My father slips in through the door, comes over to the counter, and kisses my hand. Things are almost exactly the same between us. We haven't stopped looking at each other with big burning eyes. And sometimes he writes me a check.

I still never have any money.

At night, after my long day, I close up shop, and sit for a while, writing (and I sit more than I used to, as I still feel a stiffness and a twinge in my left hip from that old wound). While I wait for Erik to come around, I handwrite my drafts of the book that I'm working on for my Red Lion Press. Even though I found I have more of a talent for questing than I'd thought, I still love my cozy, cake-fed, book-bristling world. Though that's not to say a life in bookselling is so much more secure than one spent racing through the forest with its pumas and peeing monkeys. In a store that stocks Adventure books, a reader can never quite tell what will happen. Or what to believe. For example, I have one volume here—very rare, and in excellent condition, though reasonably priced—which purports to recount the tale of the Queen of all Jades, and it tells the old false story of some talismanic stone that will make men so powerful they can win any war.

But a person is so easily seduced by such fantasies.

I've now written my own modern translation of *The Legende of the Queen Jade*. It is full of the deceptions of Balaj K'waill, and the cunning of de la Cueva, and treachery, and romance. Which is to say, I've been seduced myself.

You've just read it, now.

In the dark night, by the light of my lamp, and in the company of my books, I write out my refinements to the tale. I polish a phrase here, an adjective there. The task often does baffle me, but lately I've become convinced that bafflement might be the most normal state of mind a person can have—particularly when she devotes herself to deciphering a piece of literature like *The Queen Jade.*

Still, I do know now that when de la Cueva writes that sentence

When the mask fell from her eyes and she gazed at her cage, the Witch saw she could never read all the labyrinth's dangers and escape.

the word *read* should be translated literally.

Moreover, should I ever take an interest in translating the governor's letters, I'll know that in the passage that she writes to her sister Agata in 1541, the one that reads:

I will admit that I find this curious Maze a difficult bugger to scan

that the word *scan* is not used in its Latin sense, to describe leaping and climbing, but rather is employed in old Samuel Johnson's mode, so as to mean "examining nicely."

So I sit in my store, thinking these things, scribbling them down, until it's Erik who comes through my door.

He enters the bookstore; I smile and turn off the light. And when he approaches me through the shadows I'm not always sure what to do—make love or read to each other? Kiss or tell stories?

All of these at once.

When he's very lucky, I show him a bit of what I'm writing myself. One or the other person will read it out loud. It's not really a translation at all, but an original piece. It's a faithful rendition of the story. It's a factual telling of what happened, and what that story really meant, and where the maps honestly lead. I'm trying to tell the truth.

"Impossible, my love," he says, grinning. "But go on—I like it."

So I give him another kiss, then pick up my looseleaf pages. They are filled with my large looped handwriting, dotted with ink blots and scratches, exclamation marks and blue pencil—slightly crumpled so the foolscap looks like an old treasure map, or a manuscript found at the bottom of an old sea chest, or the work of a lost poet.

And as to the tale itself, I believe it could be real. Real, just on the edge of false.

Perhaps some of the meaning we found was the meaning we made.

Here lies the true story of the Queen Jade.

CHAPTER 63

. . . *After the King had put away his jade knife, and his crime had been committed, his wife's dying curse fell on his head and the souls of his kin. Only then did he comprehend what he had lost. In his mad grief, he escaped with her through the jungle, past the high river and the marshes, and to the place where she might travel in peace to the land of the dead.*

Years before, when he first knew her as his father's ward, and then his brother's bride, he coveted her. He was sure that in her, his rival owned the highest prize in the country, worth more than oceans, fields, and all the world's blue jewels.

He had resolved to possess her.

And so he vanquished his brother and his brother's people and took the Queen Jade to live by him in his green and fertile country. But he could not yet be satisfied. The King remained so jealous of her beauty, he ordered his architects and servants to wrest the blue stone from the mountains and build for him a labyrinth out of which she could never escape.

And she was trapped: by words, by jade, by the winding forest. For years, she could not find her way out of that dark wood and flee back to the sea.

But such malign plans are always destined to fail. Like all lovers, he would have done better to woo her with gentle words, or better still, with freedom. For she had tricks and traps of her own.

His lieutenant, the Dwarf, discovered her treachery; she had lured the Priest to his corruption, and his doom.

After this, none of them could be saved.

The King buried the woman known as Jade; he dressed her in her queen's robes; he composed a lay and inscribed it on the walls as a last love letter.

And as the wind outside began to howl, and his kingdom was crushed and scattered to the clouds, he understood his error. He resolved then to walk one last time the path of the good man.

He left the cave and walked straight into the storm.

ACKNOWLEDGMENTS

This book was written with the aid, friendship, and love of many people. Thanks to my husband, Andrew Brown; my valiant editor, Rene Alegria; Virginia Barber, Andrea Montejo, Shana Kelly, Renée Vogel, Sarah Preisler, Fred MacMurray, Thelma Diaz Quinn, Maggie MacMurray, Maria and Walter Adastik, Elizabeth Baldwin, Ryan Botev, Mona Sedky Spivack, Erik Nemeth, Dr. Aila Skinner, Victoria Steele, Katy McCaffrey, Jorge Luis Borges, David Burcham, Katie Pratt, Victor Gold, Georgene Vairo, Allan Ides, David Tunick, and the rest of my colleagues at Loyola Law School in Los Angeles. I'd also like to thank the owners and employees of the Iliad Bookstore in Los Angeles, the Poisoned Pen in Phoenix, Cultura Latina in Long Beach, and Tia Chucha's in Los Angeles, for nourishing my imagination and giving me inspiration for The Red Lion.

AUTHOR'S NOTE

The legend of *The Queen Jade* is a work of fiction, but a few elements in the novel are based on modern and historical fact.

As most of us know, Guatemala suffered through a terrible civil war that raged from the 1960s until the 1996 signing of the Peace Accord between Marxist rebels and the army. According to the books and articles that I have studied, this conflict claimed the lives of 140,000 civilians, who suffered an unimaginable degree of pain and terror.

In the wake of this national trauma, Guatemala and the rest of Central America would weather another catastrophe when Hurricane Mitch tore through the region in the fall of 1998. The storm claimed the lives of upward of 100,000 people, and when I traveled to Guatemala in 2003, I learned that many people in the country are still feeling the effects of that disaster today. A significant number of Guatemalans lost their homes, infrastructure, access to potable water, and economic stability, which they have not regained.

The Queen Jade also touches on Guatemalan colonial history. Beatriz de la Cueva was the wife of Pedro de Alvarado, the sadistic Spanish conquistador and governor of Guatemala until his death in 1541. De la Cueva succeeded her husband to the seat of power, though her reign as governor only lasted for a brief period. Some historical accounts list her rulership as lasting for two days, others for several weeks, but in the end she died in La Ciudad Vieja, the sixteenth-century capital that sits a short distance from modern-day Antigua. In 1541 there was a tremendous rainstorm, and then a great earthquake hit the city; the earthquake caused a crack in the volcano Agua, which had been filled with water. De la Cueva died in that deluge.

Balaj K'waill comes from my imagination, but it bears mentioning that the Maya word for the god of "royal lineage bloodlines" is K'waill; through naming, then, I have indicated that Balaj K'waill is the deposed king of Guatemala when he meets the treacherous de la Cueva.

As for the codes in *The Queen Jade:* I have taken tremendous liberties with my ciphers. A much more scientific approach to the science of Maya writing will be found in Michael D. Coe, *Breaking the Maya Code.* The hieroglyphs that I reproduce in these pages, however, conform very closely with their given meanings. The sign

for example, means "lady," "woman," or "mother," according to the Maya iconography. I have employed it to designate the identity of the queen.

For my studies of the hieroglyphs, I have found John Montgomery's *Dictionary of Maya Hieroglyphs* invaluable. The images that illustrate my novel, and their meanings, are all taken from that glossary, with Mr. Montgomery's generous permission.